Praise for Q

"Looting, lying, and the letter of   a
rollicking ride through the crimina... .... of post-WWI London.
Gritty at times and tender at others, *Queens of London* unmasks the most
lawless—and likable—gang of women you've never heard of."

—Sarah Penner, *New York Times* bestselling
author of *The Lost Apothecary*

"Webb lures readers into a page-turning, high-stakes game of cat and
mouse in her latest historical novel, *Queens of London*. When Lilian
Wyles, one of the first female police officers at Scotland Yard, crosses
paths with Alice Diamond, queen of the all-female crime syndicate the
Forty Elephants, neither woman will stop until they achieve their own
forms of 'justice.' But what neither Lilian nor Alice realizes is that there's
more to justice than meets the eye, and in a world disinclined toward
women like them, they must redefine loyalty and fairness to prevail.
Compelling and suspenseful."

—Marie Benedict, *New York Times* bestselling author

"Heather Webb returns with this compelling glimpse into London's underworld in the 1920s. Readers will cheer for Lilian's straight-arrow ambi-
tion, Hira's innocent desperation, and Dorothy's generous spirit. Add in
Diamond Annie's criminal intrigue, and Webb is able to weave a rich tap-
estry of women's lives in the early twentieth century. Webb's storytelling
shines, culminating in a fast-paced chase and a deeply gratifying finale."

—Stephanie Dray, *New York Times* bestselling author

"Strong women, ripped-from-the-headlines history, and page-turning
suspense in a rich setting, *Queens of London* grabbed me and would not
let me go. From the opening salvo, Webb spins an atmospheric and heart-
thumping journey into the heart of 1920s London. In these pages, we meet
Diamond Annie, the head of an all-girl gang, and Lilian Wyles, one of
England's first female detectives, as they each try to outwit the other to survive. With a cast of vibrant and witty wisecracking women and an orphan
who might upend it all, this novel will keep you guessing (and holding your

breath) until the last satisfying page. Known for her immersive historical fiction, Heather Webb has done it again and better than ever!"

—Patti Callahan Henry, *New York Times* bestselling
author of *The Secret Book of Flora Lea*

"An action-packed story full of glamour and danger, *Queens of London* transports readers into London's criminal world where Diamond Annie rules as queen and Officer Lilian Wyles is the only woman cunning enough to stop her. A gritty, glittering addition to any reader's shelf."

—Julia Kelly, international bestselling author
of *The Last Garden in England*

"Three unique but disparate women and a young orphan are brought together by love, loyalty, and crime in 1920s London. With highly engaging characters and vivid peeks into the secret haunts of history, *Queens of London* is a fascinating and cleverly rendered story of resilience and determination that kept me reading long into the night."

—Shelley Noble, *New York Times* bestselling author of *The Tiffany Girls*

"Diamond Annie is a true original—a heroine who is tough, feisty, and handy with a blade yet also capable of compassion, even if it's against her better judgment. *Queens of London* captures the stench and squalor of Elephant and Castle in the 1920s, in contrast to the glitter and fragrance of the new department stores in the West End. The dialogue is as sharp as Annie's blade, and the plot as fast-paced as her 'Elephants' fleeing after a heist. It's an unforgettable story of vulnerable but resourceful women finding ways to survive and thrive in a world where the odds are heavily stacked against them."

—Gill Paul, *USA Today* bestselling author of *A Beautiful Rival*

"Four fascinating characters whose lives intertwine to create one page-turner of a novel, *Queens of London* is an absorbing tale of three women and a young girl who take charge of their lives and excel at their chosen professions. Still, when those lives collide, you'll never forget Alice, Lilian, Dorothy, or Hira and the choices they make. Set in 1920s London, the novel's action revolves around the infamous Forty Elephants, a gang of female thieves who robbed London's best high-end department stores—led by Diamond Annie, a.k.a. Alice. The tale of a lady detective, an honorable thief, a department store clerk, and an orphan in Webb's skilled hands will keep you reading until the wee hours. A must read."

—Denny S. Bryce, bestselling author of *Wild Women and the Blues*

Praise for *The Next Ship Home*

"*The Next Ship Home* is a wonderfully immersive novel that kept me engrossed from the first page to the last. Through a seamless tale of immigrants, corruption, resilience, and hope, Webb illuminates a dark side of America too often lost to history. An important, timely read featuring a cast I loved to root for."

—Kristina McMorris, *New York Times* bestselling author of *Sold on a Monday*

"With meticulous research and deft prose, Heather Webb crafts an unflinching look at the immigrant experience, an unlikely and unique friendship, and a resonant story of female empowerment. *The Next Ship Home* is truly a beautiful and powerful book."

—Pam Jenoff, *New York Times* bestselling author of *The Woman with the Blue Star*

"Powerful and poignant, *The Next Ship Home* shines a literary light on Ellis Island's dark history, where the prejudices of the past often sit uncomfortably close to the present. Writing with a clear passion for the subject matter, Webb captures the injustices, suffering, hope, and determination of a generation of immigrants. Francesca and Alma roar from the page and leave the reader caring for them deeply. A richly imagined novel and a must-read for fans of historical fiction. Brava!"

—Hazel Gaynor, *New York Times* bestselling author of *When We Were Young & Brave*

"A touching and intimate story of two very different young women who join forces in turn-of-the-century New York City to overcome the odds.

As a longtime fan of Heather Webb's novels, I found *The Next Ship Home* to be her most accomplished and emotionally compelling book to date. The insightful historical details delving into the Ellis Island immigrations process make this novel essential reading for anyone yearning to understand the roots of the American experience. Highly recommended."

—Kris Waldherr, author of *The Lost History of Dreams*

"Centered around Ellis Island—symbol of America's greatest hopes and scene of some of her greatest travesties—*The Next Ship Home* is the heart-wrenching story of two young women fighting for freedom and independence. In this timely and utterly immersive story, Webb unflinchingly exposes the prejudice, sexism, and corruption rampant within the immigration system of the times while still weaving in hope that we can do and be better."

—Kerry Anne King, bestselling author of
Whisper Me This and *Everything You Are*

"*The Next Ship Home* is one of the rare stories that will nestle itself in your soul and make a home there. Heather Webb creates two remarkable, endearing heroines that you will root for from beginning to end. Her depiction of Ellis Island and turn-of-the-century New York is lush with meticulously researched detail. But most striking, Webb tackles the thorny and complex issues of immigration and workers' rights with sensitivity and grace. Her message is compassionate and timely, and I was blown away by how deftly Webb weaves it through Alma and Francesca's stories. *The Next Ship Home* deserves a place as one of the great books of the American experience."

—Aimie K. Runyan, international bestselling author of
Across the Winding River and *Daughters of the Night Sky*

"Reading this story is like stepping back in time to the gut-churning experience of arriving at Ellis Island in 1902 and being willing to do anything for a shot at a fresh start in a new country. The vivid historical details, the fascinating setting, and the tenacity of this book's main characters kept me thoroughly engaged from start to finish. *The Next Ship Home* serves as a powerful and humbling reminder about the courage it takes to start over."

—Elise Hooper, author of *Fast Girls* and *Angels of the Pacific*

QUEENS of LONDON

A NOVEL

HEATHER WEBB

sourcebooks
landmark

Published by Sourcebooks Landmark, an imprint of Sourcebooks
P.O. Box 4410, Naperville, Illinois 60567-4410
(630) 961-3900
sourcebooks.com

Cataloging-in-Publication Data is on file with the Library of Congress.

Printed and bound in the United States of America.
VP 10 9 8 7 6 5 4 3 2 1

For the women in my life who always have my back:
life would be unimaginable without you.

For my grandmothers, Alberta Di Vittorio
and Shirley Webb, with love

1

Alice wiped her knife clean. Specks of blood dotted the snow-white handkerchief even after what she'd thought had been a good washing the previous night. The man who'd met the end of her blade was strong, but she'd nicked him well enough that he'd turned heel and run, the tosser. Another street brawl, another lout who thought he could disrespect one of her girls, and she'd shown him a lesson all right. She stowed her razor in the hidden pocket of her dress and headed to the kitchen for tea and a bite to start the day. Her mum was still in bed as usual, with her latest illness and weak lungs. Her brother loudly skulked around his bedroom and her sisters were God-knew-where, but Dad was bent over his plate at the table. The only wretched member of the wretched Diamonds that Alice loved to hate and hated to love. Still, he was family.

Family first, above all else.

Alice had recited those words at her dad's insistence her whole life. If the family didn't rely on each other, they'd all be on the street, he'd say as he collected the earnings they'd made from emptying pockets, clearing out shelves, and swindling the gullible. And they nearly had been on the streets year after year, as he frittered away their income and landed himself in jail for picking fights with the wrong people.

Despite it all, Alice had never questioned her dad's motto. The family's proclivity for crime meant they must stick together, like it or not, and mostly, she didn't like it. She vastly preferred the family she'd made for herself: a certain group of friends—certain *associates*—who followed orders and watched her back, rather than beat it with their fists the way her dad had most of her life. Her girls were the Forty Elephants, and she was their appointed queen. Commander. Woman in chief. Anyway, if they tried the malarkey that her dad got away with, she'd give them what for, and they knew it.

"What's the mark?" her dad asked, drowning his breakfast tea in milk. His hair was slicked back with almond oil, and a spray of salt-and-pepper whiskers swept over his jawline. His eyes were red-rimmed from too much gin the night before.

"You know I don't talk," Alice replied, taking a bit of buttered toast that had already started to go cold. She didn't share details with anyone but those involved in the scheme. It limited the chance for double-crossing.

She brushed the crumbs from her wool dress and set her dish in the sink.

"Watch it, girl," he replied. "You're getting a big 'ead. That's when mistakes 'appen."

She was glad the codger couldn't see her expression. These days, her jobs brought in far more quid than his did. More importantly, her jobs meant posh dance clubs, free-flowing gin and Irish whiskey, the fastest roadster on the streets, and beautiful clothes. For a short time, her winnings gave her freedom from the squalid life in which she was raised; elevated her above the muck and mire of London's darkest corners south of the Thames in the Elephant and Castle neighborhood. For every bolt of silk she cashed in, she transcended the grimy violence of her day-to-day and became someone different, someone with endless possibilities. At least until the money ran out—and the money always ran out. She wasn't the type who believed in saving just to take it to the grave.

Her brother pushed past her much faster than most could on a peg leg. He'd lost his leg in the Great War, shot clean off. Served him right, some would say. He'd been a bully his whole life and mostly a good-for-nothing stirring up trouble with the McDonald brothers, leaders of the Elephant and Castle gang. At war, his time came due. Tommy had always looked after her, though she was the eldest of eight and he, nearly three years younger. They'd been inseparable for a time. Wasn't much she wouldn't do for him or him for her.

Her brother placed a piece of bread in the turnover toaster, cranking the knob on the metal contraption that pushed the bread over a heating element until both sides were evenly cooked. When finished, he scraped a knife laden with butter across the surface and downed the nearly burned toast in a couple of bites. "You going out?"

"Nothing you need to concern yourself with," Alice replied. "But I'll see you later. At the pub."

"All right then."

All her brother needed to know right now was that she had a job. It was Friday, a day when the stores were swarmed with shoppers—and her girls' best day of the week to do their own *shopping*. Alice knew better than to hit a store in the early days of the week, when the shopgirls were bored and paired up with customers two-to-one.

Before she could leave, her dad grabbed her elbow. "You've had some wins, but you're headed for trouble with that attitude, you 'ear me?" He squeezed, his fingers digging into her flesh until she cried out. He may not be able to beat her senseless anymore—she was a grown woman, taller than most men with large fists and a mind three times as quick—but he still had the ability to wound her.

"You underestimate me." She wrenched from his grasp. "And people see through you. That's how you always get caught."

He lunged for her, but she sidestepped his outstretched hand and headed for the door. "Don't wait up," she called over her shoulder. She snatched a brolly on the way out in case of rain.

He shouted expletives as Alice slammed the front door behind her.

A big head, my ass, she thought. He didn't know the meaning of humility except to dish it out to others. He'd never shown her mercy, not even as a little girl; he hadn't shown it to any of them. She and her siblings had collected impressive bruises over the years to prove it. Even the Lord Mayor of London had permanent scars on his face after a meeting with her combustible dad.

Outside, the scent of rain lingered in the air and a bank of clouds hung low and so thick that not a single shard of sunlight pierced them. Good thing she'd come prepared. She walked purposefully to her car, not losing pace as a rat scurried across her path before disappearing beneath a stack of abandoned crates. She'd grown up with them scampering through her flat—the nasty creatures were practically her siblings. She'd suffered their sharp teeth far too many times. Truth be told, she was lucky she still had all her fingers.

She opened the door to her shiny black Chrysler and slid into the driver's seat. She smiled as the smell of new leather rushed her senses. Nothing beat the smell of money. She drove across the borough, parked her car in the street, and strode to a shuttered munitions factory. These days, the old factory served as a meeting place for the Forty Elephants. It was quiet, abandoned, and not a place the coppers spent much time patrolling, though she and the girls had fended off squatters a little too often. Still, it was a decent location, despite the grit and grime that blanketed every nook and cranny.

She wound through the musty dark around broken machinery that had begun to rust from the perpetual damp air that seeped through the building's cracks and shattered windows. When she reached the back office, the Forty Elephants were already gathering, seating themselves around the table.

They were waiting for her, as they should be.

Alice took her role as leader of the oldest and strongest all-women crime syndicate very seriously. The Forty Elephants had been around since before Queen Victoria's days, though they'd never been properly organized until Mary Carr had come along as the first queen. When Mary passed away, Alice had taken over; made the gang stronger, larger, and taught them both the art of the con and how to use a knife when the circumstances called for it. The circumstances almost always called for it.

Maggie, one of Alice's best girls and closest friends, gave a short wave as Alice entered the office. Baby-faced Maggie looked youthful with her round face and blond curls, and the fact that she barely reached five feet in height. Her appearance fooled people; Alice had never met another woman as good with a blade as Maggie was. Her friend also had the foulest temper in London. On occasion, her hot head got them into trouble, especially when she'd been drinking, and drinking was Maggie's favorite pastime.

"Hiya, girls," Alice said. "Are we ready for a big day?"

The Forties whistled and clapped.

"That's what I like to hear. Enthusiasm," she said. "If all goes well today, we should bring in enough for new frocks and a nice night out."

Her words were met with more cheering.

Before listing the jobs of who would do what that afternoon, Alice quickly scanned the room, making sure everyone was present. Maggie and Scully, June, Marie, and Lily Rose. Sherry and Bertha and the other fifteen girls were also present. One face was markedly absent: Ruth.

She'd been out a lot lately, either sick or with injuries. With Ruth in and out, Marie's recent flightiness, and Lily Rose's obsession with the new boyfriend who kept trying to lure her out of the gang, Alice thought it might be time to remind them all how lucky they were to be counted among her esteemed band of hoisters.

"It's time we had a little chat about loyalty."

All eyes were trained on her, expectant.

"Who helps you put food on the table?" Alice asked.

"The Forty Elephants," several said in unison.

"Who has your back when your sweetheart leaves you in the cold?"

"The Forty Elephants!" Their enthusiasm grew.

"When you're in trouble or you need someone to do your dirty work?"

"The Forty Elephants!"

"That's right, ladies," Alice said. "Loyalty. And if you don't know who you pledge your loyalty to, you don't belong here. You turn your back on us, we turn our back on you—and leave you with a lasting mark you'll never forget."

The women whistled and pounded on the table.

Alice silenced them with one wave of her hand. "Your loyalty to us, and to me, must be absolute, or we all go down. Your mistakes become ours. We work together as one, you hear me?"

More cheering.

She paused to let her words sink in. She didn't like doling out punishment to her own. In truth, it always left her a bit sick to the stomach, but it had to be done. Being a leader wasn't an easy thing, and the rules—and consequences—that she enforced were always for the good of their vetted cocoon of thieves. Gangland wasn't safe without a system, without rules. And her rules were simple. First, sell all items that were hoisted; showing up in last week's frock was the perfect way to get nicked by a copper. Second, wear their Sunday best to a job to throw the clerks off their scent. Looking like a washerwoman was a sure sign they didn't have the cash to buy posh clothes in posh stores. Third, never ever take up with a man outside their ring of co-associates without Alice's seal of approval. Finally, one of Alice's personal rules and a code she'd always lived by: help any woman in serious need, as long as it didn't put the other Forties at risk.

Still, loyalty mattered most of all.

The office door flew open and banged closed, and a flustered Ruth dashed inside. "Sorry I'm late." She slipped into a seat gingerly, as if it pained her to move.

"Look who's late again." Lily Rose rolled her eyes.

"What was it this time?" Alice asked, though she already knew the answer. Ruth was boarding with her wanker of a boyfriend these days and they were seeing a lot less of her. "Don't tell me it's bloody Mike again." Alice looked more closely at her then. "Jesus, that shiner from him?"

Ruth looked down at her hands in her lap. "Mike came home from the gin house pissed as usual, after God knows how many pours. Angry as a lion, too." She sniffed, wouldn't meet anyone's eye.

"Let's have a look." Alice bent over Ruth, gently lifting her chin to examine her left eye. It was swollen shut and big as an orange.

"I think he's broken a couple of ribs, too," Ruth said, wincing.

Alice shook her head. "He's going to keep at it, you know. When are you going to leave him?"

"My brother is single," June offered.

"Your brother looks like he was dragged behind the back of a wagon," Maggie piped up.

"Too true," June agreed.

The titter of laughter eased the tension.

Ruth shrugged. "I–I don't know. I love him."

"Well, he clearly loves you, too," Alice snapped. She'd like to say she didn't understand it, why Ruth stuck around while he beat her senseless, but she did. Her own father had taught her what a man's love looked like: all fists and words that cut twice as deeply.

"I don't know what to do," Ruth said, tears streaking from her healthy eye down her cheek. "If I try to leave him, he may try to kill me."

Alice's anger gathered like a storm cloud. Her girls deserved better than this, but she couldn't very well force Ruth to leave Mike. Alice could hire an Elephant and Castle man to protect Ruth for a little while. Problem was, Mike was one of the gang, too, so that wouldn't be the best option.

"I seem to do things wrong all the time, so he punishes me," Ruth continued. "I guess I'm too dense to learn how to please him."

"You aren't dense, Ruth, and for Christ's sake, you don't need to be punished," she said. "You've done nothing wrong."

"At least I yelled back," Ruth replied, sniffing.

"As was your right."

"What time is it? I can't stay long." Ruth's eyes filled with fear. "If he wakes and I'm not there, he'll be spitting mad." She looked like a small, frightened bird.

Alice bit her tongue. She didn't know when Ruth had become less herself, had shrunk so small that she'd become this shell of a person, especially since she had all the backup she needed with the Forty Elephants. But nothing Alice could say would dissuade Ruth, and with the woman's broken ribs and black eye, she was bloody useless for the shopping they were going to do in a few hours anyway.

"Fine," Alice said. "But you're on the next job."

Ruth nodded and shuffled carefully across the room to the door.

After she'd gone, Alice assigned the girls their posts for the day's shopping trip. When they'd all left, she stayed behind a moment, thinking, feeling some semblance of guilt, an emotion she scarcely recognized let alone experienced. Ruth was a grown woman. She made her own choices, and yet, Alice couldn't help feeling like she was somehow responsible for the woman's safety. She was the queen of the Forties, after all, and her girls' business was her business. They counted on her. She offered them a better life than the worst of the slums where they'd come from, a life of good times and finer things.

But for the first time Alice wondered if what she was offering them was enough, and more importantly, if she was doing her job as leader of England's most notorious female gang. As she walked to her car, unease slid over her skin like the encroaching fog.

2

There was nothing Lilian enjoyed more than righting a wrong. The satisfaction of helping some poor victim find justice, of bringing order to chaos with precision and expediency. It made her feel as if her efforts mattered. She only wished the chief would give her more opportunities for work that actually made a difference. She hadn't hit upon that kind of opportunity yet, and after seven years of working for the Met, the Metropolitan Police, she was beginning to wonder if she ever would. She was still only a woman after all, and a very petite, plain one at that.

When the car rolled to a stop, she climbed out and opened the rear door.

"Out," she said curtly, motioning to the cuffed man in the back seat.

He glared, took his time, and bumped into her as he walked past.

"Watch it, Flake."

Jerrod Flake had been picked up at least half a dozen times. He was a fence, or trying to be one at any rate. As far as Lilian could tell, he was about the worst fence in London. This time, he'd likely enjoy a nice long stint at Wormwood Prison. *Wormwood.* Lilian had always appreciated that the prison was named for the gray scrub that covered the surrounding wastelands and was once used to cure parasitic worms. "Parasitic" was an apt description for the men who ended up at Wormwood. They were parasites on society, sucking others dry rather than contributing in any sort of meaningful way. A concept Lilian found utterly despicable.

"This way," said Inspector Lewis, the policeman working with Lilian. He steered Flake inside the police station to a holding room.

They walked past a front desk and rather bleak waiting room fitted with uncomfortable seating, and down a corridor marked by several offices, most of which were empty at the moment. Lilian had rarely seen the station so sleepy. Better enjoy it. She'd come to learn that silence in her line of work was a gift.

Inside the holding room, Flake dropped into a chair next to an empty table. His eye was beginning to purple, something watery oozed from his nose, and his split lip leaked blood onto his chin.

Lilian's boss, Chief Inspector Wensley, filed into the room behind her.

"What's with the lady copper?" Flake said.

Lilian didn't so much as raise an eyebrow or twitch her lips. The fence knew her—she'd brought him in before—and was trying to get under her skin. She wouldn't give him the satisfaction. Instead, she sat stiffly in her hard-won police uniform with pride.

"That's Inspector Wyles to you," she said sharply. Inspector Lilian Wyles of Scotland Yard, one of the first policewomen in English history and the very first assigned to the Criminal Investigations Department, she wanted to add. She was, in fact, one of the only female police at this point, but at least she had the power of arrest. It had taken five years to convince the government that female police couldn't be effective without the same full rights as the male officers, which had meant five long years of no real recourse with criminals and enduring constant mocking on the streets. Only now had she begun to gain a little respect. The emphasis on *little*, she thought as she met Jerrod Flake's eye.

"Who are you working for?" Lewis demanded.

"Why would I tell you a bloody thing?" Flake spat out. "Besides, you've got it all wrong. I work for myself."

"He works for the Forty Elephants," the chief said.

"Never heard of 'em," Flake said, sliding his cuffed hands across the tabletop and letting them drop in his lap.

The Forty Elephants—referred to as the Forty Thieves in the past—was a nuisance of an all-female shoplifting ring. They'd grown in size and power in recent years under their latest queen, Alice Diamond, or as the Met called her, Diamond Annie. Lilian had never seen the woman or the gang members, but she'd heard plenty about them and their all-male partner gang, the Elephant and Castle, led by Bert McDonald.

Eager to prove herself to the chief, Lilian leaned close enough for Flake's pungent spice cologne to fill her nostrils. "Withholding information will only hurt you. You and I both know the gang will leave you to clean up the mess. Do you work with Diamond Annie?"

"I work for Saint Nick," he sneered.

The chief nodded at Lilian. "Book him."

"Yes, sir," she said. Flake needed to rot in a cell for a while. See if it loosened his tongue.

As Lewis hauled the thief to his feet and forced him through the door, Chief Inspector Wensley motioned to Lilian to follow him. "I need to talk to you."

Anxiety swept over her like a sudden fever. Was she in some sort of trouble? After so many of her female colleagues—already too few in number—were cut from the Met, she constantly feared she'd be next. Which was precisely why she needed to bring in a big score, something that would impress her supervisors. She'd always hoped doing her job efficiently would be enough and so far, it had been, barely. But she knew she'd mostly been lucky.

They walked to Wensley's office. As he sat behind his desk, he motioned to an empty chair opposite him. "Have a seat."

Lilian perched on the edge of a chair, trying to ignore the grease stain on Wensley's necktie. The man could never seem to keep his clothes clean. She, on the other hand, couldn't stand to wear a uniform that wasn't laundered and perfectly pressed. It helped her think better to have everything tidy and in its place.

"Good work, Miss Wyles," he said. "We'll keep bringing Flake in until we turn up something. We're close and he's stupid enough to keep getting caught."

Lilian's brow arched at the name he insisted on calling her. When would the man call her *Inspector* Wyles? She smothered a sigh of frustration. "Thank you, sir."

"I called you in because I have some news. We're moving you to a new beat. We need you in the West End and central London, working as a detective in the department stores. My men can't do the sort of frisking we need to without making the front page of the *Sunday Times*."

She cringed inwardly. The department store beat was tedious and took an extraordinary amount of patience and focus, as well as a sharp eye. Worse still, it required very little use of her brain. Frankly, someone else at the Met would be better suited for the task. She had more education than most of the other officers in her precinct. Her father, God love him, had made sure of it by sending her to a boarding school followed by finishing school in Paris. She'd even enrolled in law studies so she might become a barrister, until the Great War began and she found herself working at the front. She never went back. Lilian might value the law above all else, but she'd rather be on the streets trying to do good work than writing treatises and poring over textbooks and documents.

Though her father had always been supportive, he persisted in questioning why on earth she'd want to be a policewoman. Maybe one day she could show him, prove to him that she was good at it. Perhaps even exceptional. It would be a small token of gratitude for the loving support he'd given her through the years.

"You want me to stand guard in the department stores?"

"That's what I said." Wensley flicked open a notepad and began scribbling notes. "It's a good position for a woman. You know the ins and outs of the shops and what sorts of things female thieves might try to steal."

"But sir, I go as often to a department store as you do. I hate to shop."

She'd been lucky enough to avoid the beat in the past. Instead, she'd spent three years supervising a small squad of policewomen, but since female police had been deemed unnecessary, expensive, and the work too dangerous for them, she was more or less on her own these days—and more or less stuck working whatever beat the boss gave her.

"Look," he said, "if you do a good job there, we can talk about another beat and move one of the others to it instead. How's that?"

If Sergeant Miles hadn't recently settled a lawsuit with Margaret Phillips, one of London's social elite who had been erroneously accused of shoplifting a mink stole, Lilian wouldn't be in this position. Miles had frisked the socialite clumsily and hauled her into the station. Naturally, one of the most upstanding and wealthiest women in London was innocent. Miles had received a good talking-to from both the mayor and the city council shortly thereafter. He'd made the Met look like amateurs. Chief Inspector Wensley had fumed and blustered until his eyes bulged. Apparently now Lilian would have to pay the price for Miles's mistake.

"Sir, I—"

"You'll also add orphans to your duties," Wensley said. "The orphan catchers have been overloaded since the war. The state of the economy has only made things worse. I think a woman might be able to help lure them in. Get them to trust you first."

Lilian felt heat blooming across her cheeks. The Met underestimated her. Her logical mind, her persistence, her strength of character. She was more than her sex, much more, and they refused to see it. Even the chief still called her Miss Wyles. She held her tongue when all she wanted to do was lash out. But she was nothing if not calm and sensible. It was one of her greatest attributes as an inspector and otherwise.

"Sir, you can put me in the way of a little danger. I'm not afraid, and I'm fast and strong." She'd explained before that she'd seen as much blood and carnage as any soldier at the front while volunteering as a nurse during the Great War. Her sensible nature and stomach of steel were assets in her chosen career. "Sir, please. I'd like real work."

"This is real work," he said, scratching at a red blotch on his cheek. "We need you to keep an eye out for the Forty Elephants. And we also need you to assess how many children you see in the West End. Report back, and we can make a plan of how to go about bringing them in."

Her nostrils flared in agitation. She respected Chief Inspector Wensley; he was among the best, not to mention the most famous of detectives in Scotland Yard's history. He'd been on the Whitechapel beat during the Jack the Ripper murders, and plenty of others. He'd had profound success, with medals from the queen to prove it. That was all well and good, but he belittled her now, even if unintentionally. She was perfectly capable of taking matters into her own hands with children!

But...perhaps if she managed to catch one of the Forty Elephants, or even better, cornered their queen, Diamond Annie, she'd gain a little respect at the Met. Perhaps then she might be able to do more than "woman's work." If she had to chase children or stare vacantly at women trying on new shoes for a while so that she might pursue more important work, then so be it.

"Wyles?" he pressed.

"Yes, sir?" she said, startled from her thoughts.

"Best get to it."

"Yes, sir."

With a smothered sigh of resignation, she headed to her first destination, Marshall & Snelgrove department store.

⇉ 3 ⇇

The sun rose high over the roofs of London's most prestigious shopping district until it took place of prominence in the sky. It was midday. Lunchtime, when the number of shopgirls waned as they took turns to break. Alice gave the signal, and the Forty Elephants moved into position. She waited in her car for Wilson, who'd join her, any minute now. Meanwhile, she couldn't put Ruth's pained expression out of her mind, or the careful way she'd walked. She'd had so many bruises, so many broken ribs. There had to be a way to help her—the others, too, who were also at the mercy of their boyfriends and husbands and fathers, far too often. Alice's girls were her charges, like children in need of a mother hen to protect them and give them direction. That said, they could be difficult to rule at times. They were, after all, a pack of tough girls from humble beginnings who'd learned to take the law into their own hands to make things go their way. To be a Forty Elephant meant to be self-reliant and strong-willed, mostly.

A round man in a black suit appeared around the edge of the building that marked the pickup point and walked nonchalantly toward Alice's car.

Wilson was right on time. He crossed the narrow street and

clumsily slid into the driver's seat. Usually Alice drove, but today she wanted to be quick on her feet. If something went wrong, she could slip into the car and be off in a hurry.

"Big day, hey?" Wilson asked as he eased the roadster onto the street.

Ignoring his question, she scanned the streets, scouting for police and anyone else who might follow them. Her car was well known in certain parts of London.

"Drive on, Wilson."

He steered around a throng of pedestrians, a mangy dog, and an old man who had lived in a house made of crates, boxes, and errant pieces of wood as long as Alice could remember. The man was a strange sort of neighbor but then, all of her neighbors on the other side of town were a bit strange, too. Survivors in one way or another.

She absently twisted the diamond-crusted bands encircling each of her fingers, a useful tool in a knuckle fight. Today's score would be big—if her girls didn't get caught, and they'd better not. She had plans for the spoils. She tapped the edge of the leather handbag in her lap as she scrolled through the details in her mind for the twentieth time. She'd chosen five girls for the Marshall & Snelgrove job. She'd tipped off the barman at Quincy's Pub in the West End two nights before that she'd be hitting Harrods, knowing full well the news would reach the coppers who floated through the bar in the evenings after a long day's work. The policemen would set a trap for her—and play right into her hands. Sometimes it was too easy.

She smoothed the collar of her squirrel-fur coat and touched up her lipstick. She might be fierce, but she always dressed to the nines. Presentation was an important part of being queen.

"Pull up on the pavement." She motioned to Wilson. "At the front door."

"On the pavement?" he said, turning to squint at her from the front seat. "But there'll be shoppers in the way."

She scowled. "Did I ask for your opinion?"

"Alls I meant was it'll make a scene, won't it?" Wilson said, his cockney accent so thick it sounded like he had a mouth full of marbles.

"Course it will," she said crossly. "That's the point." She should have driven the roadster herself. Wilson was a lackey from the Elephant and Castle gang. Nobody special, nobody worth explaining a bloody thing to.

He pulled to a stop in the road, pausing the traffic of horses, motorcars, and bicyclists behind them. A few drivers honked furiously while pedestrians took advantage of the moment and strode across the road in front of the car, among them a boy of fifteen who carried a box attached to a strap around his neck advertising meat pasties for sale. No one seemed to pay mind to the impending rain. Clusters of women, their hats pulled low, were coming and going in a stream like a never-ending centipede inching ahead to their destination. There were new hats and stockings and furs to buy.

Or to steal.

Alice pulled back her sleeve and glanced at the time on her wristlet. Three minutes to go—and there she was. Scully's dark waves were brushed and tucked neatly under a cloche hat, the hem of her dropwaist dress fluttering from beneath the edges of a wool wrap coat. Three others trailed behind Scully, all dressed in kid gloves, with rouged cheeks and stones sparkling at their ears or their throats. Notably absent was Marie.

Alice swore under her breath. Marie was supposed to be Scully's point person that day. She had better have a bloody good excuse for showing at the meeting and then bailing on them. She might have blown the whole job.

One by one, the girls stepped inside Marshall & Snelgrove, chatting politely to one another as if it were any old regular day. Alice pictured in her mind what came next. Two were heading to the jewelry counter to try on rings and admire trinkets. The others were spreading out across the store.

Alice counted to ten and stepped from the car.

A woman in the street gasped and scooted quickly past. Another stared at Alice with curiosity.

A third grabbed her friend's arm. "It's Diamond Annie," she hissed.

The bobbies had given Alice the nickname after a tussle in the streets with an officer who'd had the nerve to lay his hands on her. She'd landed her ringed fist right in his gob like he'd deserved. Gave him a fat bloody lip.

She strode past the gawkers inside the store, the whispers following her as she walked the gallery floor. Store patrons backed away, scurrying to the far corners to hide among the furs or leaving the store entirely. She smiled at one clerk and waved at another. They inclined their heads toward each other, whispering, their eyes wide. She winked. It was too fun not to toy with them.

She sifted through the frocks on the nearest rack and glanced at a woman who looked as if she'd seen a ghost. "Catching flies, miss?" she asked. "You really should close your mouth. It isn't polite."

The woman promptly did as she was told and scurried away.

Alice wanted to laugh, but she'd worked hard on her reputation. They knew her—they feared her—and that brought respect. Commanding respect was the only way to survive in her world.

A young shopgirl approached, her ginger curls bouncing around her face. Her lips were brightly rouged like a film star's, same as Alice's. The shopgirl was beautiful, but Alice suspected there wasn't much between her ears. She would have put the girl on door detail, had she been one of hers. Someone to play lookout who couldn't be trusted to do one of the more complicated or risky maneuvers.

"Good afternoon, miss," the young woman said. Her name tag said Dorothy in block letters. "We have a new line of ladies' oxford heels that might interest you. Would you like to try a pair?"

Clearly Dorothy didn't recognize Alice, and that was just as well. Alice would likely get better service that way—and act as the decoy she'd intended to be.

"I would," Alice replied.

Dorothy smiled prettily and bounced on the balls of her feet like a cheerful pup as she directed Alice to a chair. Alice looked over the row of gorgeous new oxfords. One pair sported a two-tone strap with lacelike detailing carved into the leather. Another had a pair of straps rather than one, decorated with tiny red bows where a buckle should be. A third—the Hollywood oxford—was her favorite with its shiny black patten, laces that finished with a bow, and a swirl of blond reptile leather on either side of the shoe.

She slid her size-nine feet into a pair. They fit like a glove. "I'll take them."

"Wouldn't you like to try the others?" Dorothy asked.

"I've made up my mind," she replied firmly. She never second-guessed herself or her instincts—it was an occupational hazard.

"Right away, madam," Dorothy said, scooting away quickly in search of a shoebox.

Alice took the opportunity to check on the others. Scully and June leaned over the jewelry counter as a clerk pulled out a tray of rings for her customers. As Scully slipped a ring on her finger, Maggie strode swiftly past, smashing her wad of chewing gum beneath the counter ledge without so much as a pause and moved to another corner of the store. June slipped on several rings while Scully squished a sparkler or two into the sticky wad beneath the counter. Both women grabbed at the tray now like greedy children reaching for sweets, trying on multiple rings and confusing the clerk in the process.

In the far corner of the store, Maggie relieved Marshall & Snelgrove of a few pairs of silk stockings, stuffing them into her knickers. Next, she tried on a fur and slipped her coat over it. In moments, Geraldine appeared from the dressing room and circled back to the jewelry counter to collect the chewing gum.

As Dorothy returned with Alice's shoes, a ruckus came from the jewelry counter—Alice's cue.

She tucked the shoebox under her arm and walked to the register. She didn't need to turn to see the clerk demanding Scully and June return the missing rings. She could hear their outrage as they were first accused and then searched, only to be found empty-handed.

Soon, Alice felt the heat of many pairs of eyes on her at the register. Diamond Annie, they assumed, must have stolen something, though she'd been nowhere near the jewelry counter. Everyone began to whisper.

She paid for her shoes, hands steady, her manner calm and still as a frozen pond in winter, and headed to the door.

A woman stepped between her and the doorway to freedom. "Well, if it isn't Miss Diamond," the woman said. "I see you're shopping today. What did you purchase? Anything of note?"

Alice glared at the woman for a moment, an action that typically inspired anyone with sense to get lost. This woman didn't because apparently, she had a death wish.

Alice pulled herself up to her full height and stepped closer to the pipsqueak of a person, taking in her dowdy brown hat with a maroon ribbon around its base, a plain coat with a trail of buttons over a long, dark skirt that nearly reached her ankles, and suddenly realized what she was seeing. She'd heard of lady detectives but had yet to cross paths with one.

"I'm Inspector Wyles," the woman said, meeting Alice's gaze with steel-blue eyes.

Alice didn't show even a flicker of fear. She didn't have so much as a bauble on her that wasn't hers.

"Excuse me. I have places to be," she snapped as if the officer were nothing more than a nuisance.

"I'm afraid I'll have to search you first," Wyles said, stepping closer.

Briefly, Alice wondered at her accent. The lady detective didn't sound like the rough-and-tumble police she'd always known. She sounded as if she'd had some schooling, come from a proper home.

"Is that necessary?" Alice fronted, catching sight of June and Scully out of the corner of her eye. They were headed for the exit—only Alice and the detective blocked it.

Wyles cocked a dark eyebrow at Alice. "If you have nothing to hide, you'll let me search you."

"Have it your way," Alice pretended to huff and stepped to the side, giving her girls a wide berth so they could exit swiftly.

Wyles patted Alice down, groping for hidden items, and finally gave up. "It seems you weren't lying after all, but I'm sure we'll meet again, Miss Diamond."

"You'd like that, wouldn't you."

The copper looked surprised at the quip and, after an instant, reddened.

Alice smiled at Wyles's discomfort and pushed past her out of the store. She waved her driver over, and in seconds, she slid inside the car.

"Finished then?" Wilson asked. "Got everything you wanted?"

Alice didn't answer. Her eyes were tracing the backs of her girls, slipping through the crowd of pedestrians. Soon, Scully, Maggie, and

June had separated and disappeared from view. They were off to the drop points where their fence would collect the goods. There was no sign of Geraldine.

Just then, a commotion came from near the door.

Geraldine dashed outside and made to run—not fast enough. The detective caught her, gripped her arm, and yanked her to the side with the kind of force Alice wouldn't have expected from such a small woman.

Geraldine stumbled, her fear visible on her face.

"Bloody hell!" Alice threw up her hands. Geraldine shouldn't act guilty for Christ's sake. The girl had obviously done her own job and then taken up Marie's since Marie hadn't shown, and now Geraldine was busted.

"Go!" Alice shouted. "Let's get lost."

Wilson screeched away from the curb, narrowly missing a street vendor hawking chewing gum, tobacco, and newspapers.

She clenched her fists in her lap. Damn it, Geraldine was a good girl, one of Alice's best. It was too bad she'd be locked up for a while. There was no way she'd get off, what with that many gems in her knickers. And all because of Marie. Alice would give Marie what for later. For now, she had a bigger problem. A lady detective on her turf—and one who knew to look for Alice and her girls—was far more dangerous than a whole crew of men combined. The men were stupid enough to underestimate Alice at every turn, but this Inspector Wyles could be a real problem.

Alice twisted in her seat to peer out the rear window. Geraldine was being led across the street in cuffs to a motorcar that Alice hadn't noticed when she'd first arrived. She frowned. She wasn't losing her touch, was she? First having one of her girls not show, Ruth's mess, then missing a police car at a job... Police cars were rarely marked, but they were almost always obvious—plain, older models, parked or cruising in the worst parts of town at a snail's pace. Alice needed to do better, be smarter than them. She needed to keep her position on top—it was all she had.

Inspector Wyles looked up then and gazed at the tail of Alice's rapidly disappearing car.

Alice whipped around to face forward. It seemed, at last, someone was on to them—a posh lady detective of all things—and Alice would need to keep the nuisance of a woman firmly in her sights.

4

Hira wiggled in her chair as she turned to page twenty of *A Lady's Guide to Etiquette in Polite Society*. She didn't understand why Uncle Clyde insisted on silly books like these. At ten years old, why did she need to know about "Hosting a Lady's Luncheon?" She sighed loudly and slumped in her chair.

The clock on the fireplace mantel chimed three times.

"You'd better finish this section, or your uncle will be displeased," Miss Lightly said. The governess fingered the ruler on the table, making her threat clear. "And sit up straight. You're not a hunchback."

Hira perked up, pushed her shoulders back. Miss Lightly was given permission to use her ruler when she saw fit, and she saw fit as often as it rained in London. Hira rubbed the backs of her hands and forced her gaze back to the page. Though she feared the thwack of Miss Lightly's ruler, it was her uncle that sent her scurrying to her bedroom to lock the door and hide in the farthest reaches of her room, her eyes squeezed closed and fingers in her ears as he bellowed like the wind on a stormy night. He never hurt her, at least not with his fists, but at times his words felt like a thousand tiny knives. Uncle Clyde took out his life's disappointments on Hira—and it seemed he had a lot of disappointments. She wondered, as she had a thousand times, if Uncle Clyde was so angry because the woman he was supposed to marry had returned her engagement ring years ago. The maids gossiped about it every time he shouted at them for some indiscretion. The only good thing she could say about her uncle was that he'd always provided for her, ensured she had cake for her birthdays and a few small gifts at Christmas. Though he was a miserable man, he wasn't a monster.

As the clock on the far wall ticked, she counted along with it until she lost track. When another half hour had passed, she was, at last, permitted to use the water closet—almost too late. She held her breath as she forced herself not to run through the halls to reach her relief. She threw open the door and closed it as quickly, plopping down on the cold porcelain seat.

Hira stared at the yellow and pink floral wallpaper, and at the tin ceiling imprinted with an oval pattern. Miss Lightly had told her many times how lucky she was to be surrounded with the beautiful things that graced the enormous manor where she lived: the marble hall, the parlor decorated with eighteenth-century French furniture, bedrooms lavished in silks and velvet, and a study composed entirely of mahogany with a library fit for a king. Hira saw her home in a different light. A house with many places to hide, the traitorous floorboards that creaked when she tiptoed as silently as a mouse to avoid being seen, and the shadows cast by the coatrack as the sun faded and her uncle was due home from the office—the time of day when she must be on her very best behavior.

Uncle Clyde was one of the most influential barristers in London. He appeared to know everyone of influence, and their home was often busy with dinner parties or men retiring to his study for brandy and cigars. Many of them stared at her, seemed surprised she lived there with her uncle and his many fine things.

Hira returned to the dreaded parlor. After her piano lessons, her lady's maid scrubbed her light-brown skin clean until it bloomed with red blotches and styled her hair into perfect dark ringlets. Once dressed in a sunny yellow frock and silk gloves, Hira affixed an expression of contentment on her features, her coal-black eyes smiling even if she didn't feel the emotion she was expected to exude. She was a beautiful child who said nothing until spoken to, who performed what she'd learned on command, and above all, who tried not to remind Uncle Clyde where she'd come from.

Her uncle clomped across the hall to the walnut dining table and tucked his napkin into the collar of his pristine shirt without so much as a glance at her.

"Good evening, Uncle," she greeted him from her perch in a straight-backed chair.

He grunted and reached for his wine. "What did you learn today?"

"I read Longfellow and a book about etiquette, and I practiced Gershwin, Uncle."

"Gershwin?" he said. "Is that so?"

Gershwin was the only thing she'd liked about the day. She liked music, especially from the piano, and the elegant way it transported her on a dream, away from her home to another place. To the place where her parents lived, so very far from England and so very, very far from her.

The waitstaff whisked into the room carrying a soup tureen and fresh bread.

Hira's heart sank as she realized the odor wafting from the ceramic bowl was cream of celery soup. She hated the bitter soup, no matter how silky the broth. She wished she could pinch her nose to block out the odor. Instead, she dutifully dipped into her bowl.

She'd scarcely swallowed a bite when the footman interrupted, carrying a silver tray with a small cream-colored card.

"Who could it be at this hour?" Uncle Clyde said, frowning.

"A telegram, sir," the butler said.

As Uncle Clyde read the letter, his brow furrowed. His face turned a shade that resembled the strawberry jelly they'd eaten for pudding the night before.

Definitely not good news then.

Hira watched as her uncle downed the rest of his wine and signaled to the footman to pour more. He nursed half a glass before he brought his hand to his forehead. For a moment, she wondered if she should skip away from the table and ask for her supper to be sent to her room.

He tossed the telegram back on the butler's tray. "I shouldn't be surprised, given how filthy India must be."

Hira's spoon clattered against her dish. *India*. Her parents. All sense of propriety fled. "What's happened, sir?"

"Your parents have died," he said without pause. "I thought the cholera pandemic had finally cleared up, but it seems it's still affecting some parts of the world. The debased, unclean parts."

She gasped at the news, his callous words chafing against her heart. Her parents were dead? Her father was a foot soldier serving the king at the East India Trading Company in Surat, and he'd fallen in love with her mother, a local silk-weaver. When her mother had become pregnant, they'd waited until Hira was a healthy one-year-old and sent her with a lady's maid to London to live with her uncle. For her education and her safety, they'd said in their letters. They, meanwhile, had been forced to remain behind until her father received orders for a change in his post. Hira had received a few precious letters from her parents over the years. She'd cherished them, reread each a hundred times until their words were imprinted on her heart. Now, she'd never receive another letter again.

Hira looked down at her half-eaten meal, tears welling in her eyes until fat drops slid over the fleshy hump of her cheeks and splashed into her bowl. She'd always hoped her parents would come for her, rescue her from her loneliness. But the dream was snuffed out, and with it, the little shred of hope and happiness she'd clung to her entire life.

"What are you sniveling about?" her uncle said. "It's not as if you even knew your parents. They shipped you off from the start. I've been the one to provide for you. Everything you could possibly want or need. Besides he was my brother. It is I who should mourn."

The tears came harder now, and a hiccup escaped her lips.

"May I go to my room, sir?" she asked.

"You may not. You will finish your supper first. Now, wipe your face."

She wiped her eyes with her napkin and forced down bites of the next three courses. When at last she was dismissed, she slipped away to the safety of her bedroom and threw herself on the bed. Her tears turned to sobs until she'd soaked her pillowcase.

Sometime later, a light knock came at the door.

"Pet," the housekeeper's voice drifted through the door. "It's me, Mrs. Culpepper."

Mrs. Culpepper was the only person in the household who'd made Hira's life bearable. Slipping an extra biscuit to her in the evenings or at tea, tending to childish bruises and scrapes, assuring Hira that her mother and father loved her and would one day come for her. Mrs. Culpepper had always been kind.

Hira wiped her leaky nose on her sleeve and opened the door.

"I've heard about your parents," the housekeeper said, placing a hand on Hira's shoulder.

She allowed herself to be scooped into the woman's arms and burst into tears again, wetting her starched apron in the process.

"There, there, child. It's a good job that you're here instead of India, or you'd be sick, too."

"Mrs. Culpepper!" Uncle Clyde's voice drifted up the stairs.

Her contrite eyes met Hira's. "We'll talk more later. Why don't you try to get some rest? But remember, they loved you very much."

Hira nodded and wiped her nose.

The housekeeper cupped Hira's face an instant and then turned to go—and met Uncle Clyde in the stairwell.

"What's going on here?" he said, words slurring. His cheeks were once again an alarming shade of red. He'd had enough wine at dinner to drown a horse, and now Mrs. Culpepper and Hira were in his crosshairs.

"I was looking in on her to see if she needed anything," the housekeeper replied. "What can I do for you, sir?"

"Tell the maid to light a fire in my study."

"Right away," she said, throwing a last concerned glance at Hira.

"Good night, sir." Hira began to close her bedroom door when her uncle caught it with his meaty fist.

"Not so fast." He pushed inside her room, his lumpy shadow stretching over her like a great ogre. "Now that you don't have parents, I can do with you what I wish. I'm tired of fielding questions about the half-breed who pollutes my house. Besides, you're a perfectly reasonable age to go away to school."

Hira hated herself for the tears that sprang to her eyes again. She didn't like to show Uncle Clyde any weakness. She dashed her hand across her face, wiping at the steady stream.

"Pack your things. Tomorrow morning you're to go to the all-girls' school in Northumberland. When I learned your father was ill last week, I'd already put in a call to the headmistress. They're expecting you."

Her stomach tumbled as if from a great height. Northumberland, a desolate and cold place, and as far from London as possible without being in another country. She'd heard all about the horrible school from her governess. It was crowded with too many orphans and had scarcely enough money to provide its pupils with basic necessities. Most pupils that went on from there became maids and washerwomen, or worked on farms, barely getting by. She would be cast off, forgotten. How could he send her to such a place? She'd have no home, no one to look after her. She'd have no Mrs. Culpepper.

A sob stuck in her throat. "You'll s-send me away, sir?"

He'd already started for the door, his corpulent form forcing him to waddle more than stride. "Tomorrow morning, first thing."

She flung herself across her bed, clutching her teddy to her chest. It had been a gift from Mrs. Culpepper many years before. Teddy's fur was matted on one side and half of the red felt nose had already fallen off, but the stitched eyes and his smile were still firmly in place. Perhaps it was childish to sleep with Teddy every night still, but he was her only comfort. Now he served as a handkerchief, his plush middle absorbing the puddle of her salty tears.

Uncle Clyde didn't want her—never had—and now she would end up somewhere else where she would be unloved and unwanted. She didn't belong anywhere, it seemed. She cried harder, until her nose ran and her eyes swelled, her thin shoulders heaving with spasms.

What would the school be like? She couldn't imagine sleeping in a room with dozens of other children, or eating gruel like the orphans she'd read about in Dickens's novels. Her uncle couldn't send her there! She'd run away!

She sat up suddenly. If she ran away, where would she go? She didn't have any money, and she didn't know much about London. Uncle Clyde rarely took her into public. Her brown skin drew attention, and it embarrassed him. He'd never concealed that nasty little detail. Would she draw unwanted attention to herself if on her own, too? The thought made her quiver with fear. She'd have no protection.

Yet, as an image of rows of iron bed frames, sullen children, and indifferent mistresses flickered in her imagination, her resolve gelled. She was going to run away.

Her pace quickened at the thought.

What should she take with her? She'd need money. It was all Uncle Clyde talked about, and though she didn't have the first idea of how much things cost, she knew she'd need it. She pictured her uncle grumbling about the bills and the payments he'd made to the governess, the cost of food for the household, curling over his desk in the study, the shiny jar of coins at his side where he emptied his pockets.

The jar was half-full now; he'd never notice a couple of handfuls of missing coins. Her pulse thudded in her ears at the thought of putting her hand inside it, fishing out the largest silver coins. Even if he noticed them missing, she'd be long gone by the time he did.

Hira waited until the house was dark and quiet. When all had stilled, she padded gingerly through the corridor. The faint sound of her uncle's snores followed her down the stairs until she'd slipped inside his study. She tiptoed swiftly to the desk. The change jar sat on its outermost edge. It struck her then that she hadn't thought of bringing something to carry the coins, so she peered inside a teacup left on Uncle Clyde's desk. A brown ring of dried tea circled the bottom. It would have to do. She tried to lift the glass jar of coins, but its weight prevented her from holding it steady enough to pour. Carefully, she scooped out coins with her hands until the cup was filled.

Suddenly, the sound of a machine whirred to life.

She jumped, knocking into the teacup that wobbled dangerously. Her hand shot out to steady it. As a brassy clang rattled the night air, she relaxed. It was only the grandfather clock. Still, she'd better hop to it before she was seen.

She took the stairs to her bedroom by twos. When the clock

chimed its twelfth chime, she closed her door and leaned against the wall in relief. The first part of her mission was complete. Now she must pack. She glanced around her room, deciding. Teddy would definitely come with her, as would *The Tale of Peter Rabbit*. Uncle Clyde thought it absurd she should love the book so much when she could already read Henry James and Charles Dickens, but she loved the colorful illustrations, and the book still made her giggle. Laughs were hard to come by in the Wickham household.

She retrieved her leather satchel from the vanity and tipped it upside down. The vile etiquette book, two novels, and a writing tablet plunked against the wooden floor. She carefully poured the coins into the center of a clean handkerchief and tied the ends together, forming a pouch. Next, she retrieved the small bundle of her parents' letters from her dresser drawer and the colorful elephant-headed figurine covered in tiny diamond-shaped mirrors that her mother had sent to her years ago. Ganesha, she'd called it, the god of new beginnings and the remover of obstacles. She'd need Ganesha more than ever now.

Hira held the idol against her cheek and closed her eyes, summoning the image of her mother that had haunted her dreams—but only for a moment. There was no time to lose. She needed to escape under the cover of night.

She dropped the figurine in her satchel. Lastly, she tucked an umbrella inside the satchel, too, in case it rained, and it always rained in November. As she stepped into the hall once more, her nerves began to quiver like the flan she'd had for pudding. Could she really go through with it? What choice did she have?

With a deep breath, she padded downstairs to the kitchen for a bread loaf, a box of tea biscuits, and a couple of shiny red apples. Her wool overcoat and a blue knit hat were the last of her things. As she stood before the heavy oak door that marked the path to her freedom, she took a last look at the only home she'd known her whole if small life and whispered goodbye.

Heart pounding in her ears, she turned the key in the lock and squeezed the handle latch. Before she could change her mind, she ducked outdoors and began to run.

Hira ran as fast as her legs could carry her into the inky unknown of the London streets.

5

Dorothy McBride touched her red ringlets and leaned in to the looking glass to check her lipstick. It was California pink, as her mum had called it, though Lydia McBride had never been to California and neither did she wear lipstick. To her detriment, Dorothy thought, as she turned her head to the left to see her dangling earrings sparkle and then right to admire her better side. She pursed her lips, her dimples remaining hidden until she felt the urge to smile. Too bad there wasn't much to smile about at the moment. Those nasty Forty Elephants had made off with silk lingerie, jewelry, and furs and God knew what else, and Ugly Mildred had told the boss it was Dorothy's fault.

Dorothy had been too involved with customers to notice the store was being emptied of its treasures. She was doing her job! Busy with the queen of hoisters herself, Diamond Annie, and then with a gentleman buying a ring with stones so small, they were barely more than flecks of glitter. If her husband had given her such a thing, she'd tell him to take it back. Really, who would buy diamond chips? She hadn't hesitated to tell him he'd be better off buying a nice piece of costume jewelry or something from the pawnshop. He'd blushed but insisted on buying it anyway. His poor wife, she'd thought then, and again now.

Dorothy glanced around the main floor of Marshall & Snelgrove. It was a quiet morning, probably because bad news traveled fast. Legitimate customers didn't want to shop among the dangerous thieves of gangland. She sighed heavily and leaned on the countertop, resting her chin on her hand. It was going to be a long day.

Mildred walked past the display of handbags and change purses, artfully designed to show off the lustrous sheen of Moroccan leather. Leaning on the jewelry counter, she scrunched up her face into a faux smile, making her beak of a nose look like it belonged on a prehistoric bird. "Mr. Harrington wants to see you," she crowed.

Dorothy wouldn't give her the satisfaction of looking alarmed. The boss had already blustered and carried on about the missing items to the whole staff. What could he possibly have to say now? She walked around the jewelry counter, strolled past ladies' lingerie, wound through the shoe section where she'd helped that scoundrel hoister pick out a pair of oxfords, and threaded down the back hallway to the staff room.

Mr. Harrington poked his head out of his office when he saw her coming and waved her inside. He looked pristine as usual, his hair slicked with almond oil and combed into a smooth dip on his forehead. His gray suit and black necktie were pressed and expensive, if a little dull. She envisioned him in a pin-striped suit with a bright purple or green tie. It would jazz him up a little. Still, he was handsome in a classic, well-bred stallion kind of way, and Dorothy admired that. Most of the men she'd known wouldn't know a nice cravat or suit if they tripped over it, never mind own a successful department store. Come to think of it, her exes were more likely to frequent the local pub to keep it in business and less likely to be the kind of person that owned it. And that was why they were exes.

"You wanted to see me, sir," she said, feeling like a child waiting to be chastised.

"You look very pretty today, Miss McBride," he said, eyes flicking to her dress a moment and back to her face. "Is that a new dress?"

Taken aback, she didn't reply but smiled brightly. Her peach and petal pink dress was adorned with rose clusters, but her favorite thing about it was the hanky hem that brushed her calves as she walked. It was a little fancy for work, but recently Mr. Harrington had decided uniforms weren't necessary since their own colorful wardrobes provoked more customers to buy. But this frock was one of a kind. Dorothy had designed and sewn it herself.

"Do you like it? I made it myself," she said, folding her hands in front of her the way her mum taught her to do.

"How nice," he said. "Miss McBride, did you know you're one of my best workers?"

"I... Thank you, sir. I like working here."

"That's apparent, and you seem to like the merchandise."

"Oh yes, sir, I do," she said, her reserve falling away. "The silk stockings are among the best in London, and we have a terrific range of shoes and handbags. It's the jewelry I have trouble selling."

It was only a little white lie. While she liked some of the store's inventory, she found most of it dreadfully dull and uninspired. If she were in charge, she'd hire one of the new designers she'd seen in the fashion pages or, better still, she'd work with a dressmaker on her own designs. In fact, she wished she had the nerve to show them to Mr. Harrington. She couldn't seem to bring herself to do it. If he dismissed them, or worse, thought they were awful and looked at her like she was a silly girl with hopeless dreams... Well, she couldn't stomach the thought.

Maybe she was making too much of it. Mr. Harrington was an excellent boss. Supportive of his staff, he worked with them on their schedules, always awarded them a yearly raise in pay, and trusted them to sell merchandise in their own way. Perhaps he'd be open to her designs one day—if she ever worked up the nerve to ask.

He clucked his tongue. "I've noticed your trouble at the jewelry counter, actually, which is why I've assigned you to it for the rest of the week. Perhaps if you grow more familiar with the inventory, you'll gain more confidence with it."

She hesitated, deciding whether she should be honest. If he wanted more people to buy the jewelry, he should order better pieces. The only things worth having were the few items the gang had stolen. Now the case was left with diamond chips, bronze cuff bracelets, a few gold bands with various small flourishes and etchings, and a handful of topaz rings.

She bit her lip. If he wanted her to spend time trying to sell the god-awful jewelry that only Ugly Mildred would wear, well, then Dorothy should probably share her opinion with him.

"Sir," she began, pursing her lips while she decided how to say it.

"Go on."

"Well, it isn't confidence that I need. Not exactly."

His brow arched. "Oh, no? What is it then?"

"I need...better merchandise." She noticed his frown and rushed on. "Women are wearing brooches on their jackets, long strings of pearls, stacks of bauble bracelets, rubies and emeralds cut in the new Parisian art deco style, and full-sized diamonds. There's a new type of faux jewelry, too, that's made of colored glass. It gives women who can't afford the more expensive items a chance to keep up with the trends. Novelty jewelry, they're calling it, or—"

"Costume jewelry," he cut her off before she'd finished. "Yes, I know. I've noticed its sudden popularity. The Americans are selling quite a lot of it, but Americans are cheap, as are their goods. We, Miss McBride, are English, and we are not."

"Are they making money, sir?" Dorothy pressed. "The Americans?"

He reddened across the bridge of his nose, highlighting a light spray of freckles. He really was handsome, even if he was daft when it came to women's jewelry.

"I presume so, but the American market is different from ours. I'm not certain costume jewelry is the right fit for our store."

Most of the women on her block wore costume jewelry, and she owned some herself. She received compliments every time she wore her emerald and diamond necklace that resembled a stack of bricks in a chic geometric pattern. Geometric wasn't a word she thought she'd ever use to describe something as pretty but well, here she was. She wanted to look like a Parisian. Who didn't?

"Yes, sir. If not novelty jewelry, than maybe a few new pieces to spruce up the case?" She bit her lip. That was all she'd say on the subject, lest she irritate him and get herself sacked.

"Perhaps." He nodded thoughtfully.

She smiled. At least he was listening to her. "Thank you, sir."

"I wondered if you might join me for dinner tonight, Miss McBride. I'd like to talk more about your ideas," he said. "That is, if you don't have plans already? A young woman of your poise and beauty must have many offers for the weekend."

Poise and beauty? She felt her cheeks go pink. Wasn't he married? Or perhaps she'd just assumed he was, given his age. He must be at least forty. She searched her memory for gossip about his wife and none came to mind. She'd never seen a Mrs. Harrington in the shop either.

"Thank you, sir. I don't have plans. I... Bobby and I broke up." She looked down at her beautifully filed and polished nails. She had never been married, but men doted on her, at least at first. For some reason, things never seemed to last. Bobby was a particularly harsh breakup, although... Tim hadn't been easy either, or John or Lester. Lester had even stolen her favorite silk scarf. What he'd planned to do with a ladies' scarf she had no idea, but she'd been furious when she'd discovered it missing.

"Well, I'm sorry to hear it, but he's a fool. Anyone can see you're a woman worth holding on to." He smiled, showing his very white teeth. Bobby's teeth always looked like they could use an extra brushing. She was struck then with a thought she'd never had before: perhaps she'd been choosing the wrong kind of man all along.

She blushed again. "Thank you, sir."

"About dinner. What do you say? There's a place on Regent Street with a nice plate of risotto. Do you like Italian?"

"I've never had risotto before, but it sounds exotic." She flicked her hair over her shoulder. "I like to try new things."

Another smile played around the edges of his lips. "Well, Miss McBride, I do, too. It seems we have that in common."

She might not be the most accomplished woman or the brightest, but she knew what that look meant. He liked what he saw, and she didn't blame him. She was nearing thirty years old, but she was all curves, bouncy red curls, and flawless skin. She'd been a pretty child and had become a beautiful woman. It was what had made her worth knowing—at least, that was what the boys had always said. Her mum had told her to ignore them, told her men were trouble just like her absent father. Dorothy didn't know if she should be glad or offended when men made these comments to her, but she chose gladness whenever possible. Being sad or offended was boring. And besides, she was convinced that her cranky old mum was just lonely.

"Are you sure that's a good idea, Mr. Harrington? What will the other girls say?" Dorothy pressed. The only women in her life were those she worked with, beyond her mum of course. She'd never had a lot of girlfriends. They were always either mean to her, called her dumb, or they were jealous and accused her of trying to steal their boyfriends. As if she needed to do such a thing. The men came to her! And truth be told, she'd prefer to keep a friendship over a man because they were far rarer, but she was not afforded the chance very often.

"What other girls, Miss McBride?" he asked, moving around the desk to stand nearer to her. "Do you mean my shopgirls? You and I will be discussing business tonight. How could they have anything to say about that?" He smiled widely, his perfect teeth pearlescent.

To date her boss could be trouble. If they were to break up, would he fire her? She couldn't afford to be sacked. Her income along with her mum's kept them in a reasonably nice flat. Without it, they'd be reduced to living in the slums. On the other hand, should things go well, should she *marry him*, things could change drastically for the better. She'd be moving up in the world, living with him in Mayfair, one of the wealthiest neighborhoods in London. Mum could move in with them.

She smiled and batted her lashes at him. "I would love to try risotto with you."

"It's settled then. I'll pick you up at eight o'clock."

Dorothy beamed. "Sounds perfect."

6

London was eerie at night. The lights blinked out one by one, giving the shadows life as they grew and contorted and swallowed the landscape. Pedestrians disappeared inside their homes until only the occasional wanderer remained and the streets were haunted by those who had gone there before. Hira didn't give a thought to where she should go as she raced away from her uncle's home. She didn't consider the encroaching chill of a London winter, or anything at all beyond escape.

She ran.

She ran until her lungs tightened, her coat grew too warm, and her bag too heavy. She ran as if her life depended on it. All the while, her ears perked for the sound of footsteps behind her. They never came.

When she grew too tired to carry on, she found a park bench and curled up there as tightly as a caterpillar in a cocoon until the rest of the night passed. She lay there, shivering, clutching her teddy and staring at the sky though the stars hid their light. Her parents were dead. She'd longed for their arrival to London every single day for as long as she could remember. She'd always believed they'd come for her; believed they were loving and wonderful and would spoil her with sweets and toys and, most of all, hugs. Now they would never come. As tears streamed silently from her tired eyes, the moon slipped down the arc of cold, dark sky like a ball of ice.

Sometime later, Hira awoke to the cooing of pigeons and her rumbling stomach. She stretched, trying to shake off the stiffness from the cold. She rummaged through her satchel for the package of tea biscuits. She tried to eat them slowly to conserve her limited supply, but she was so hungry that she couldn't help herself. In moments, most of the biscuits were gone. She wrapped the remaining few and brushed the buttery crumbs from her lap, sending the birds into a frenzy of warbling and pecking at the ground near her feet.

Hira looked around her. The park looked so different in the morning light. The grass glistened with dew between patches of flaming orange and yellow trees, and a row of scarlet bushes formed a border on the southernmost edge. Fallen leaves littered the benches, collected in pockets along the iron fence and the stone path that twisted through the garden. Most striking of all was the silence. She was utterly and completely alone. No one tossed a ball or shared a picnic. No one strolled through the park on their way to somewhere—somewhere was the place she wanted to be, too.

She didn't know where to go from here, but she feared someone might recognize her, that she was still too close to home. There weren't many brown-skinned girls in fine dresses in this end of town, or perhaps in all of London. In fact, she'd never seen another girl who looked like her outside of the photograph of her mother. She fervently hoped she wasn't as alone in the world as she felt.

For now, Hira needed to leave, go far from here. She sorted through her satchel, pulled out the handkerchief of change, and palmed a few coins. She'd always wanted to ride the double-decker buses she'd seen from the window of her uncle's motorcar. He'd always denied her the chance, but now she could do as she wished! The thought gave her renewed vigor, and she set off for a new destination.

She walked until the sun was high in the sky and she'd warmed up a little. As the city woke from its slumber, the bustle of pedestrians and vendors, motorcars and the occasional carriage, grew louder and more frenetic with each passing hour. When her feet began to hurt, she stopped to buy a greasy sausage roll from a vendor, scarfing it down while it was still steaming hot.

After, she stood on the street corner, looking left and then right. Which way should she turn? Did it make a difference? After another few minutes of indecision, she asked a pretty lady with a bright-red hat that matched her lips to help her buy a bus ticket.

"Should you be traveling alone, young lady?" the woman asked.

"Yes, madam." Hira nodded vehemently. "My dad is waiting for me. I'm supposed be traveling with my nanny, but she left me alone. He'll be angry with her."

"I see. And where are you going?"

She recalled her uncle ranting about something happening in the Elephant and Castle neighborhood, though she couldn't remember what it was. She'd liked the name of the place. That same afternoon when she was supposed to be studying, she'd doodled a picture of an elephant living in a castle.

"Elephant and Castle," she blurted out.

"Elephant and Castle?" The woman's pencil-thin eyebrows arched, disappearing under the brim of her hat. "You sure, love? A little young lady like yourself? That isn't a nice neighborhood."

Hira shifted nervously from one foot to the other. She wondered what that meant. Reluctantly, she nodded. "Elephant and Castle. That's where my father is meeting me."

"All right then. You'll need to cross the street and take the next southbound bus. It's three blocks from here. Why don't I take you?"

"Thank you, madam. That's very kind."

"I'd ride with you, but it'd make me late for my lunch date."

Hira was both relieved and disappointed the woman wouldn't be riding along. She felt a little calmer having a nice, pretty lady looking out for her. But she needed to grow accustomed to traveling alone, eating alone—doing everything on her own. At the bus stop, she climbed aboard, avoiding eye contact with anyone, pressing herself against the interior wall. When the bus driver called out her stop, she tentatively left the safety of the bus.

The West End had always seemed alive and noisy, but the Elephant and Castle neighborhood was deafening. Throngs of people pushed up and down the streets. Vendors called to passersby, shoving pamphlets, newspapers, or flyers with special-offer items into the open palms of the unsuspecting. The clothes were different, too. Instead of the beautiful dresses with long strands of shimmering beads and silk gloves, fancy fur coats and polished leather, women wore dated overcoats and weathered shoes in dull colors. Their faces were drawn and thin. The buildings looked run-down and beaten by the weather and injustice.

As Hira passed a dingy alley, a man peered at her from atop a crate. His jaw moved back and forth like he was chewing on something.

"Hey, kid, you lost?" he said.

She didn't like the gravelly tone of his voice or the black smear on his left cheek. In fact, he looked like he hadn't bathed in a long time. She picked up her pace and quickly turned a corner. She threw a look over her shoulder and, when she saw he wasn't following her, exhaled in relief. Still, the incident made her ill at ease. She hadn't thought about the hours and days and nights she would spend on the streets. How scary it would be—how scary the people might be. She walked on, her heart rate slowing as her steps fell into a slow rhythm. Some minutes later, she crossed a major intersection. Ahead, a pack of boys laughed and jostled each other. One boy passed his cigarette to another, and they shared it between them.

Some instinct flared inside her. Once she neared them, she would cross the street if possible, hide among the pedestrians and the vendors, and the piles of garbage.

Soon, she was right behind the boys. Time to move. She looked left and right, but motorcars and bicycles packed the narrow street, and vendors jammed the pavement on either side. She sucked in a deep breath. She would have to go around them. It would be fine, she told herself. She didn't have a reason to be afraid. She'd go quietly and mind her own business. She ducked her head and walked swiftly past them.

At once, they noticed her and sped up to walk beside her.

"Look at the little girl, all by herself," one boy said.

"She looks scared," another said.

"Are you going to cry?"

Heart hammering against her ribs, Hira kept her eyes forward.

"She's a half-breed," one sneered.

"Hey, brownie, why don't you to back to where you came from?"

Where she came from? She was as English as they were, even if her skin was brown. Even if her mother was Indian.

"She's a Paki, can't you tell? The nose. The black eyes."

"Nah, she's from India."

"A darkie then."

"I think she's a witch."

Tears welled in her throat as fear collided with panic. They could call her names—her uncle had—just as long as they didn't try to hurt her. She walked as fast as she could without running.

"You know what they do to witches," the largest boy in the derby hat said. He sidestepped to stand in front of her, halting her in her tracks. His derby hat was cocked sideways; his blue eyes were bright with intent. He grinned a vicious smile.

She hesitated an instant—and bolted.

"Get her!" he shouted.

She ran as fast as her legs would take her, sliding twice on the wet cobbles, her satchel slamming against her side.

Their pounding feet behind her echoed the rhythm of her thunderous pulse.

What was she doing here? If she were home, she'd be starting her lessons with cranky old Miss Lightly, but she would be safe. Then the truth hit her like the thwack of a ruler on bared knuckles. She wouldn't be practicing her handwriting and reading the boring passages of Henry James. She'd be on her way to Northumberland, to a school for the poor and for orphans.

This was her life now.

She bit back a sob of panic and slipped around a corner.

They followed close behind, the bigger boy pushing ahead. For the first time in her life, she was thankful she was small and agile. She weaved through pedestrians and vendors, ducked between a couple with interlocked hands, looking ahead, trying to find an escape. Somewhere she might hide.

Panting, she tossed a glance over her shoulder.

Two of the boys had given up and were nearly a block behind her. Only the largest boy and a skinny kid who looked like he could use a hot supper continued their pursuit.

She streaked past pubs, pawnshops, and the odd food market; maybe she could enlist the help of a grown-up to warn the boys off. Throat dry, lungs burning, Hira leaped over a pile of garbage and dove inside the nearest shop. As the door closed behind her, she bent over, hands on her knees, gasping for air.

"What do you want, runt?" a man with corn-colored teeth asked. He was a tiny man, barely tall enough to see over the counter behind which he stood. He had a large voice despite his size, shaggy hair, and an eye patch. He looked like a pirate.

"I—" she rasped, trying to catch her breath, "Someone was chasing me. Please, sir—" She stopped, realizing where she was. She gaped at the glass counter showcasing slabs of raw, bloodied chops, steaks, and pink rumps labeled "ham hocks." The butcher's apron was smeared with blood.

He screwed up his face, making his already-sallow cheeks appear hollow as a skeleton's. "I don't harbor fugitives, you hear me? Now get on out of here!"

Just then, the two boys crashed through the front door.

"There she is!" the tall boy shouted.

"Oy! You there! What do you hooligans want with a little girl?" the butcher growled. "Leave her be, or I'll call the coppers on you!"

"We were just playing a game with her, mister," the older boy said.

"The hell you were! Do I look like an idiot? Be off with you."

The boys looked at each other, deciding whether the butcher was serious or not. The older boy shrugged, and reluctantly, they both left.

Relief rinsed through Hira's limbs. She leaned against the case, resting her forehead on her arm. "Thank you, sir."

"Any reason those thugs were chasing you?" he asked.

She shook her head. "They called me names, sir."

The butcher's brow arched at the sound of her voice, at what she was beginning to understand was a posh accent. She didn't sound like those on the streets around her, and this butcher had noticed it instantly. His frown softened a little.

"Can I call anyone for you?" he asked. "Seems like you're far from home."

"No, sir. I'm supposed to meet my father soon." She repeated the story she'd told the pretty lady. "We're going to the shops today."

He eyed her suspiciously, looked at her fine shoes, the silk hem that peeked from beneath the edge of her coat. And Hira understood something else: with her clothing and her accent, and the fact that she was a girl with brown skin, she was a target. She would need to change all of that, or at least change what she could, until she found her new home. Wherever that might be.

The butcher rummaged behind the counter and wrapped a thick slice of ham in paper. "Have a bite. When you're hungry."

"Thank you, sir." She took the ham eagerly and stowed it inside her satchel.

"Good luck, miss," he said, his single eye following her movements.

Reluctantly, Hira left the safety of the butcher shop. She paused outside the door, glancing both ways to make sure the boys weren't waiting for her. Throngs rushed down the street, women and men carrying their parcels and leading children by the hand or striding confidently toward their destinations. The boys were nowhere in sight. She joined the masses and walked like she knew where she was going.

And just where would she go from here? Panic rose in her throat once more, but she pushed on aimlessly. Hours passed and her legs ached, and as daylight seeped from the sky, her eyes pricked with tears. She couldn't walk forever. She would need a safe place to sleep very soon. And she was hungry. She walked two more blocks and came upon a narrow alley adjacent to a bakery. Tucked in the corner, a large empty flour drum lay on its side as if it had been tipped over. She paused, deciding. It looked big enough and it was out of the way of traffic. Most of all, it didn't look too dark or scary.

She headed toward it, deciding this was it, at least for the night. She climbed inside the drum and curled her limbs into a ball. As the city grew quieter, darker, she tried to ward off her fear. What would become of her? No one knew or cared where she was. No one would come looking for her. In one day, she'd been chased. Exhausted, she eventually fell into a restless sleep.

Sometime in the night Hira awoke to a low whine.

She opened her eyes to see a tiny dog with gold fur sniffing around her head. He licked her face before she had a chance to sit up. The tip of his left ear looked as if something bigger had taken a bite out of it, but his brown eyes were sweet, pleading, and chocolate brown.

"What's your name?" she whispered, lest someone unseen appear in the dark.

He sat on his hind end and peered at her a moment before he pawed at her knee, whining anew.

"What is it, boy?" she asked.

He yipped, and she jumped at the unexpected sound, knocking her head against the inside curve of the flour drum.

"Shh," she said. "We don't want anyone to find us. Are you hungry?"

The little dog whined again.

She withdrew the precious piece of ham from her satchel, tore it in half, and outstretched her hand.

He snapped it up, licked his chops, and waited for more. She couldn't part with the second half of the ham. She was saving it for the morning. When she tucked it away, the dog lay down beside the drum, resting his face on his paws.

She tentatively reached out a hand to pet the scruffy fur on his head. The dog flinched as she reached for him, and she quickly retracted her hand. He was shy. Better not push him too far lest he bite her.

The dog lay down again, curling himself into a small, furry lump, his eyes fixed on her. A smile tugged at the corners of Hira's lips. She might not know what to do next, but at least she had a new friend.

7

Hira passed three days on the streets and three nights in the flour drum, the little dog at her side, her eyes swollen from crying herself to sleep. By the fourth day, she grew so hungry she knew she had to do something she didn't want to do. She had to steal. She'd begged at markets and restaurants, begged shoppers and ladies and gentlemen to spare a morsel, but everyone shooed her away as they hurled their insults at her. Street urchin. Filthy orphan. Dirty Indian. But that day, she no longer had a choice. Her stomach ached, and her head felt light as air. She must eat. Something, anything. And she'd have to put all of the manners she'd learned aside—and what she knew to be right and wrong—to do it.

During the long daylight hours, she studied other street children. Sometimes they ran in packs, surrounding a shopper to outnumber them and strip them of their possessions. Others would sneak up on the unsuspecting on their own and, quick as a flash, slip their hand into a pocket or handbag and extract a wallet. This approach, she thought, would be terrifying but the only way for her. The problem was, those who lived in the Elephant and Castle borough had little to spare and likely very little in their wallets. They also held fast to their possessions, clutching their handbags or their shopping with guarded expressions, wary of others. This could only mean one thing: Elephant and Castle was home to scoundrels and criminals and, most of all, the poor. Hira would have to walk to the West End near her uncle's, where she knew the shops—and the wealthy—were plentiful.

She walked for over an hour, stopping now and again to ask a less-than-scary lady directions. When at last she made it to bustling Oxford Street, she leaned against a doorway to catch her breath. She was weak, hungry and thirsty. Her feet ached. Her dog was tired, too, and plunked down on the pavement at her feet. But they were here, in the right place, and it was now or never. She perched across the street from Selfridge's, watching as women came and went. Waiting, gathering her nerve. Should she go inside and follow a shopper or remain outside? She hesitated. It would be easier to be caught—and trapped—inside. She closed her eyes briefly, wishing she didn't have to do this. But as a hunger pang gripped her stomach, she lurched forward.

She darted across the street to the department store. As the door swept open, a group of people poured out into the street. She eyed a woman in a beautiful gray coat and fur-trimmed hat who appeared to be alone. She was the one.

The woman crossed the street, people rushing on either side of her, eager to get out of the chilly November air.

Hira followed her, pulse thudding in her ears. She wasn't a thief or a criminal. The thought made her feel icky and silly at the same time. But she had to eat, or... She put on a brave face. She tried to pretend she was a detective from one of the novels she'd read. Watching and waiting for the right moment to strike.

The crowd thickened up ahead and she picked up her pace. When she'd nearly closed the gap between them, unexpectedly, the woman paused to study the mannequins in a window of Marshall & Snelgrove.

Hira came abruptly to a halt, almost bumping into her. She inhaled sharply and walked in the other direction.

The little dog looked up at her, tilting his head to one side as if he was trying to make sense of what she was doing. He didn't bark.

"Good boy," she said, reaching down to pet him softly. He'd begun to trust her, allow her to pet him on the head, and he never left her side.

When she glanced up, the woman was on the move again.

Hands shaking, head light, Hira began to skip the way a child liked to do, until she was very close. Close enough to reach out and—

The woman looked over her shoulder. "What are you doing! Get away from me, you scoundrel!"

Hira's hands closed around the strap of the handbag.

The woman held it fast. "Stop it! Get away from me! Help!" she called out. "Thief!"

She yanked harder, pulling the woman forward.

The woman lost her grip and crashed to the pavement.

Hira tucked the bag under her arm and bolted in the other direction. She beat down Oxford toward Piccadilly Circus. Her dog yipped and raced beside her. So many people milled about on Piccadilly, she could hide in plain sight. She pushed ahead, not daring to look back. Her breath came fast, her tongue dry from lack of water. Just a little farther and she could rest. As she reached the busiest shopping area, she slowed, a graininess invaded her vision. She was so hungry.

When she caught her breath, she looked back. She'd run several blocks and so many people swarmed the pavement that she could no longer see Oxford Street or Selfridge's–and the woman was nowhere in sight.

She sighed in relief. "We did it."

Her little dog looked up at her expectantly and whined.

"I didn't like it either," she said.

She thought of the look on the poor woman's face; her outrage and her surprise as she fell. Hira closed her eyes briefly, her cheeks burning. This had to be temporary. She had to find a better way to keep her belly full. And for goodness' sake, should she need to steal again, she'd have to do a better job of it, without knocking someone over.

With a deep breath, she rifled through the handbag. Pushing aside a pocket mirror and some tubes of makeup, she found a soft change purse with a gold clasp. Inside it were three five-pound notes. She nearly wept in relief. Fifteen pounds! Now she could buy a pair of trousers and a hat. She could say goodbye to pretty little Hira Wickham in her lace dresses and polished shoes, made up to look like a doll and a lady that only invited trouble on the streets of London. She'd remake herself, become a survivor. She wiped her streaming eyes, took a deep breath, and marched toward the food stalls.

First, she would eat her fill. Her dog would eat his fill, too.

"Come on, boy," Hira said, part relief, part resigned sadness. "Let's buy something to eat."

8

Day after day, Lilian followed orders without question. She stood watch at her posts at various points in the city, or inside the doors of Harrods, Whiteley's, or Marshall & Snelgrove, waiting for the Forty Elephants to make another appearance. Other shifts, she patrolled the streets for orphans. Most street children who crossed her path were in such a pitiful state, they were relieved to go to an orphanage where they'd at least have a bed and daily meals. Still, that didn't keep them from fighting the whole way there.

The morning before, Lilian had managed to corral one boy who had loitered around the fishing docks for weeks. The occasional fisherman had taken pity on him and fed him or let him sleep in the hull of their boat. The day she'd caught him, Lilian had been approached by a concerned dockhand. A ship captain without a soul had slapped the boy around until the dockhand had intervened, but not before the poor child was beaten black and blue. Needless to say, the boy went with her willingly. She'd also arrested the captain, though he was released soon after. Lilian would never understand the monsters who saw fit to abuse children.

That day, she decided to comb vibrant, raucous Piccadilly Street for hungry children lost among the crowds. She tried to look nonchalant as she studied building fronts and alleys, her eyes roving over the faces of pedestrians. Assessing, searching, ready to make a move. She was always alert, always ready to aid someone in trouble. It was more difficult on the streets of Soho where pedestrians crowded the pavement and funneled in and out of shops. Colorful signage, sandwich boards, and posters caught the eye. Displays in shop windows beckoned people inside. There was so much to see that she had to work harder, pay closer attention.

After walking another hour, peering behind rubbish bins where children liked to hide, she continued north toward the shops in the West End. She shivered as the sun slipped between the clouds like a game of hide-and-seek and an angry wind blasted between buildings. The damp from last night's rain was receding far too slowly for her liking.

As she turned up her collar against the wind, she noticed a slip of a boy up ahead with too-short trousers and light-brown skin skimming along a cluster of women. He was lightning fast, carried a satchel across his body, and beside him trotted a mangy little dog, no doubt as feral as the boy.

At last, the first potential win of the day! Lilian picked up her pace.

The boy turned left onto the next street, following the crowd of women who were too busy chattering to notice him.

Lilian followed, but as she rounded the corner, she paused a moment, struck by the enormous line of women that ran the length of the street as far as the eye could see. A march, at this hour on a Tuesday morning? She glanced at their signs that read "Women's Right to Vote," "Votes for All," and "We Are Citizens Too." It was the Women's Social and Political Union and any other woman on the street who had been inclined to join the march. The WSPU had been active for years, and finally women had been granted the right to vote seven years before—but the right came only to those who were thirty or older, with husbands who owned property and voted in local elections, or those with other exceptions, like women with an earned degree from a British university. In other words, the vast majority of women still couldn't vote. The vast majority were angry as ever and picketing when they could gather a crowd.

Lilian watched them a moment, in awe of their sheer number, of the purpose in their stride and strength in their voices. Perhaps one day she would join them when she wasn't on duty. After all, she'd worked tirelessly to prove herself to the Met these last six years, and they still didn't seem to grasp that women could strengthen the police force rather than make it appear weak. Clearly there was still work to do.

In that moment, the little boy swept past a couple struggling to hold an enormous sign over their heads.

Lilian picked up her pace, trying to push through the crowd, but found it easier to stride alongside them as the orphan boy had done. Ahead, she spotted him again as he darted around three people holding hands. He scarcely missed a step, deftly avoided knocking into anyone. The women didn't notice the boy hovering near them. And there—Lilian saw the very thing she'd expected to see—the boy dipped his hand into their handbags, extracting a change purse here and there and shoving it into his satchel.

"You there!" Lilian shouted.

Several of the women nearby turned. The boy didn't. She fumbled with her air whistle, bringing it to her lips. She blew hard, and the shrill sound split the air. The marchers didn't miss a beat. After years of protesting, years of confrontations with the police—even gathering to a crowd of fifty thousand for a march to Hyde Park several years before—they didn't so much as pause in their mission, and their chants only grew louder.

Lilian broke into a run. Her skirts wrapped around her legs, restricting her movement, and she swore under her breath. She'd never understand why she couldn't wear trousers, but the chief had given her a firm no when she'd asked.

As she gained on the boy, he caught sight of her—and disappeared suddenly, little dog and all. Exasperated, Lilian pressed on. At last, she saw the top of his hat in the crowd bobbing along as if it moved on its own. She reached for her whistle again, paused, and let it drop to her chest where it dangled from a string. She'd have more luck catching him if he couldn't hear her coming. After several minutes of shoving through pedestrians, he broke free of the crowd. He dashed to the adjacent street jammed with motorcars. He'd have to cross the traffic to escape.

The boy threw a look over his shoulder and met her eye. He grinned and raised his hand, giving her a little wave.

You little rat, she thought but didn't lose pace.

The boy smiled at Lilian's expression—and darted into the traffic clogging the street. He slipped across the hood of a car. His dog leapt after him. The driver poked his head out of the window and shouted a string of obscenities.

Lilian made to follow, but traffic suddenly lurched forward.

She came to an abrupt stop, unable to make her way across quickly enough to catch the child. Frustrated, she watched as the boy ran ahead. When the cars and carriages finally stopped, she crossed the street and paused to look around her. Pedestrians swarmed the pavement, but there was no sign of the child.

She sighed. She didn't want to return to the station without a win, yet again. Be patted on the head and told it was all right, that they hadn't expected a woman to be able to do much anyway. Determined for a better outcome, she searched both sides of the street, ahead and behind her, too, lest the boy had tucked himself away somewhere nearby. But he was nowhere to be seen.

The boy, in fact, had fooled her. He was gone.

———

As the sun set, Lilian walked past office buildings, the occasional shop, or triangle of greenery, and restaurants coming alive for their dinner service. Ahead, the river came into view. She loved the Thames; the river twisted and curved through the city, a wise and ancient serpent, its waters dark under the night sky. Patches of light shifted over the surface like silver eels as the current tugged at all within it and all who dared to venture upon it. Something about the river gave her a sense of perspective. For an instant, she felt the timelessness of the world, and she, a part of it with her small but valiant life.

As the last remnants of the day's warmth dissipated, she picked up her pace. At the end of her shift, she usually checked in with her supervisor at the station, though lately she had been asked to report to Chief Inspector Wensley more and more often. A good sign, she'd hoped, but so far, any benefits were unclear, given the menial work he'd assigned her. And after a long, dull day of chasing orphans to no avail, she sank into an irritable mood. She hadn't been able to put Diamond Annie and the Forty Elephants out of her mind. Lilian knew in her bones that bringing in the leader of the gang—or at least a substantial number of the gang members—was the kind of score she needed.

She felt the weight of the task before her, of proving to her superiors, the government, and the rest of the squad that her work was valuable. She knew what she did or didn't accomplish very well might lead to the end of the women's unit entirely. She stayed up nights thinking about it, about the remaining twenty policewomen and their disappointment when they'd all been sacked. It seemed so pointless, so ludicrous to fire them all when the Met already faced staff shortages to amply cover the whole of London.

Suddenly, Lilian knew with certainty that if she was going to bring in the queen of thieves, she'd have to take matters into her own hands. And the first thing she needed was information. She abandoned her walk to the station and instead set out for Scotland Yard. Her pulse quickened as she walked faster and her determination grew. There had to be some files on the gang, or at least on Alice. Soon, the Met headquarters came into view. Only a handful of windows glowed with light. Almost everyone had headed home, so only those who worked the graveyard shift remained. She walked around to the staff entrance. Inside, she darted down a corridor, half-lit, as the smell of ink and dust and something vaguely metallic swirled around her. Without pause, she headed straight to the records room.

Excitement humming in her veins, she reached for the knob.

The door opened.

"Oh!" She jumped back in surprise.

Bert Stanley filled the doorway, his graying eyebrows forming an arc over a pair of eyes so dark, it looked as if he didn't have pupils. "I was on my way out," he said tiredly. "I hope you didn't need me for anything."

"Actually, I was hoping to catch you," she said, breathless.

He groaned. "I'm meeting my mates for a pint, and I'm already running late."

"If you'd point me in the right direction, I could take care of the rest myself."

He shook his head. "I'd need to lock up. Besides, do you have permission?"

She considered lying, but it wasn't in her nature and she found lying disgusting. "I need to look up something, or rather someone. It's important, or I wouldn't ask. It might mean a big win, Bert. For the Met," she added hastily, "if I can just spend a few minutes... Please."

He sighed. "I'm not staying long."

"You don't have to stay at all," she replied. "If you'll show me how the filing system works, I'll look around on my own. Take a few notes." She patted her handbag where her trusty notebook was stored. "I promise to put everything back exactly where it goes."

"I don't know..."

"I'll meet you at the pub after to give you the key. And should anything be out of place, you can report me to the chief."

His expression shifted and she knew she had him.

"Oh, all right. Follow me."

"Thank you," she said.

He explained how the files were organized, warned off any liquids in the room, and left her with the key. "I'll see you in one hour at the Lucky Hen."

She nodded. "I'll buy you a beer."

When he'd gone, she went directly to the cabinet marked C–D and sorted through the files. When she found "Diamond, Alice," her heart skipped a beat. Eagerly, Lilian pushed aside the files on either side of it. It was a relatively thin folder, but several newspaper clippings had been filed inside it, along with conviction reports and a few notes someone had added. Lilian spread it all out on the table and began to read. There was a two-sheet report of arrests and convictions. Alice Diamond had also operated under the aliases of Alice Black, Diana Black, Mary Blake, and Dolly Blake. And those were the names they knew of—who knew how many others she'd used?

By sixteen Alice had been caught stealing blouses and was given six weeks hard labor for it, and by eighteen, she'd spent a year in jail for entering the staff entrance of a warehouse and stealing a few items. She'd also been picked up for falsifying references and borrowing an employee's Labor Bureau card to a munitions factory, where she'd attempted to steal explosives for safe-blowing.

Lilian's eyes bulged at the continued list of arrests. Most were theft-related, though there were notes about blackmail. Alice hadn't been arrested for any sort of violent act.

Lilian sorted through the items and read a few notes that had been scrawled by hand:

Mary Carr organized Forty Thieves in the 1870s with help of the Elephant and Castle gang. As men were imprisoned or killed, their women were left behind to make ends meet. Copied the methods of their criminal men. Eventually the Forty Elephants separated from the Elephant and Castle. Women's rights, most likely. Grew tired of handing over a cut of their hard-earned wins. Carr died and charismatic upstart Alice Diamond claimed head of gang after Great War around age twenty-three. Far better at organization—far more dangerous than Carr. Alice and gang operate out of Elephant and Castle and nearby Lambeth and Southwark. Major department stores are prime targets in West End and central London.

Lilian glanced at the clock. She couldn't believe nearly an hour had passed. She'd be late meeting Bert if she didn't finish up here, and fast. She opened her notebook, hand flying over the page. The scrawl bothered her, but she would rewrite her notes later at home as neatly as she pleased. When she'd finished, she skimmed the police records a last time and then looked for a file on the gang itself. Surprisingly, there wasn't one. She'd have to remedy that, should she go further with her investigation. For now, she was satisfied, stored the file, and locked the records room.

As she headed to the Lucky Hen, her mind turned over all she'd learned. She'd have to spend more time in the Elephant and Castle neighborhood if she wanted to find Alice Diamond. Lilian shivered a little at the thought of once again coming face-to-face with the towering woman who knew how to use explosives, carried a knife, and dominated the underworld. Or perhaps the shiver was one of excitement. If Lilian managed to arrest the most notorious female thief in London's long history...

She smiled to herself in the dark.

9

Dorothy grumbled as she pushed around the women's march clogging the street. Though she supported their cause, she was running late for work. She'd been too busy taking extra care with her appearance that morning for Mr. Harrington—for Allen. She hadn't meant to sleep with him that night after a plate of creamy risotto with mushrooms, but he'd been so charming, and she'd been a little drunk on champagne. He was a complete gentleman in bed, more so than her previous lovers, even if she'd hadn't been quite as satisfied as she'd like. All in good time, she thought dreamily as she finally made her way inside the store. She hoped for a slow day at work because all she could think about were Allen's lips and the look in his eyes as he'd taken in her slinky red dress with drop waist. The fresh hotel sheets they'd left in heaps on the floor.

She'd asked him why he'd rented a room, and he'd told her that he was spontaneous and romantic. He'd also admitted that he had a flatmate who had a way of turning a great date into a disaster. His flatmate was annoying and persnickety about things, was the way Allen had put it. And anyway, how could she say no to a beautiful hotel? She'd only had one other boyfriend who had spoiled her, but he'd also suffocated her with his overly rehearsed declarations and his constant attention.

Allen was far more exciting, more mysterious and debonair. She smiled to herself as she walked to her post near the door.

She was proud to work in one of the largest and most popular stores on Oxford Street. Marshall & Snelgrove was a well-known and highbrow department store like Selfridge's and Harrods, selling women's practical clothing for everyday and more elegant items, too, from headdresses, hats, and furs to silk-lined dressing cases. They sold accessories and jewelry, stockings and shoes with each and every rack, display case, and themed section designed to be beautiful. The store's gleaming windows and mannequins dressed in the latest fashions enticed ladies from the street to buy, buy, buy. Working at the store also gave Dorothy time to study hundreds of women as they came and went, sparking new ideas for her own sketches.

At opening time, she unlocked the front doors.

"Miss McBride?"

She blushed at the sound of Allen's voice and turned to face him. "Yes, Mr. Harrington?"

His eyes swept over her, and a smile touched his lips. "Don't you look lovely today."

She did. She'd made sure of it, choosing a sleeveless purple dress with a scoop neck that showed off her creamy skin and made her red hair all the more striking.

"Thank you, sir." She couldn't keep the smile from her face.

He glanced over his shoulder to make sure no one else was nearby. Mildred, Judy, Evelyn, and Marcy were busy at their own posts, or pretending to be while Allen was on the showroom floor.

In a low voice he said, "How about we see a picture after work?"

Dorothy felt her face brighten. "That's a fine idea."

He cleared his throat and a bit louder replied, "Very well, Miss McBride. Now if you'll excuse me, I have some interviews to conduct."

"Yes, sir." She smiled, watching him go before returning her gaze to the front window.

A new sign had been propped against the glass. It said: *Hiring. Apply inside.* Lately, the store was swarmed with customers on the weekends, so they definitely needed another person or two. That had become quite clear when they were robbed. Even with the lady detective standing watch, they hadn't been able to protect the merchandise.

Dorothy watched a family hustle down the street fighting the same brisk wind she had that morning. She didn't like the autumn; everything was wilted, withering, and dying. Besides, she looked terrible in yellow and hated the color brown. She even preferred the gray and white of winter. At least then she could wear her beautiful coat with the fur collar that Lester had given her before he'd left her for a pretty brunette with a bigger bosom. It was just as well. Lester kissed like a fish, and it made her shudder every time she remembered his rubbery wet lips on hers. Mr. Harrington—Allen—was a perfect kisser.

Through the window, she spotted a little boy running at top speed, a satchel at his side, and a little dog racing after him. He didn't so much as falter as he approached the shop.

Dorothy's eyes went wide. Surely, he would veer right and head to the park? He would hit the glass if he didn't slow down soon.

He didn't.

She held her breath as the boy practically skipped the last few steps, threw open the door to the store, and barreled inside.

"Come on, Biscuit," he called to his dog.

"Oh, no you don't," Dorothy said, stepping in front of him. "There are no dogs allowed in here. This is a ladies' department store, not a pound."

"Please, madam, they're chasing me," the boy said. "I'll only stay a few minutes and be on my way, I promise. Biscuit won't make a fuss. He's a good boy."

The boy not only spoke the King's English with perfect diction like someone who had spent most of his years in school, but his voice was suspiciously feminine. In one swift motion, Dorothy whipped off his hat and a long, coiled braid of dark hair fell down the little girl's back.

"Aha! I thought so. You're a girl."

The girl reached for her hat, but Dorothy held it high above her head.

"Give me my hat, madam, please." The little girl hopped up and down, swinging her arms overhead in an attempt to rescue the stolen item.

"Who's chasing you?" she demanded.

The girl glanced worriedly at the window and pushed deeper inside the store to the shoe section.

"Where do you think you're going?" Dorothy shrieked. "You can't be in here!"

"I'm... I can't tell you," the child said, out of breath. She peeked out from behind a shelf laden with women's boots attractively arranged for the fall season. "Please, I'll only stay for a moment."

Dorothy turned to see the flash of a fleeting silhouette. "Looks like whoever that was just missed you."

The little girl heaved a sigh of relief, her shoulders curling forward. She was petite and fine-boned with dark eyes. One day she'd be quite pretty, though at the moment she desperately needed a good washing. In fact, it looked like she needed more than a good washing.

"Are you hungry?" Dorothy asked. "I've brought an extra piece of cold chicken for lunch. Would you like it?" She hadn't brought extra, but this wisp of a girl needed it far more than she did.

The girl nodded, suddenly shy. "Yes, please."

"You stay here," Dorothy said. "I'll be right back."

She walked to the staff room where she'd left her lunch and over-coat, passing Ugly Mildred on her way. "Leave the little girl to me," she said. "I'm giving her some food and sending her on her way."

"What little girl?" Mildred asked.

"Never mind." Dorothy went to the staff room, moving quickly. She never spent much time in the dingy room; the air smelled of must and a single lamp scarcely illuminated the sterile space. The exact opposite of the colorful showroom floor. She rummaged through her lunch sack for the wrapped chicken, hesitating only an instant before taking out her apple, too, and the tea biscuits.

When she returned to the shoe section, she realized she shouldn't have mentioned the girl to Mildred. The nasty woman held the child's arm. The dog, meanwhile, yapped uncontrollably, sending customers right out the front door. The other ladies working the floor gathered to watch the spectacle unfold.

"Let me go!" the girl said, twisting away.

"Unhand her!" Dorothy gave her coworker a slight shove. "I asked you to leave her be."

Ugly Mildred gasped in surprise. "How dare you! I was trying to keep this filthy creature from stealing anything." She crossed her arms over her chest and glared at Dorothy.

Dorothy reached for the girl and led her to the door. "Come on. I'll see you out." At the exit, she held out her lunch. "Here. Take this." The girl reached for the food, hunger shining in her eyes, but Dorothy pulled back her offer and held it to her chest. "On one condition."

The girl dropped her hand. "I'm not going to an orphanage."

So that was it. She'd been running from an orphan catcher or, per-haps, the police.

Dorothy shook her head. "That's not my condition. Tell me your name."

The girl sniffed, looked down at her worn boots. "Hira."

"Well, Hira, why don't you meet me here on Thursday? I'll bring more food for you. How does that sound?"

Her dark eyes lit up and she nodded eagerly. "That's very kind, madam. Thank you."

The child really did have impeccable manners and diction. Clearly she had once belonged to someone wealthy. Dorothy wondered what had happened. Perhaps the child was a war orphan. There were plenty of those wandering the streets still, even years later.

Hira tossed one of the biscuits to her dog, who caught the treat midair.

"Hey, that was for you," Dorothy said, frowning.

"He's hungry, too," she said, voice sad. "And he likes biscuits. That's why I named him Biscuit."

Dorothy couldn't help but smile. "That's a fine name for a little gold dog. Well then, Biscuit and Hira, I will see you Thursday."

With that, daring little Hira stepped out into the street and blended in with the shoppers who didn't even pause as she flitted past them.

Dorothy wondered what it was like to live on the street. It must be terrifying. She couldn't imagine how much courage the child must have. She'd never done a single thing in her life that her mum or her boyfriends hadn't told her to do, outside of her sketches and her sewing. It was better that way. It kept her out of trouble, as her mum always said, especially a girl who wasn't exceptionally bright. Her mum and plenty of others liked to remind her of that. She'd come to accept their judgment of her. Pretty but dumb and decent with a needle and thread. She'd never questioned their verdict of who she was. After years of hearing the same thing, she'd simply accepted it as true.

"Miss McBride." Mr. Harrington's voice. "We don't have time to stare out of the window, do we? I need you at the counter."

She blushed and hurried quickly to her station. She might have a date with Allen after work, but for now, she was on the clock, and she was his employee. She must do what was expected of her, as always, and she would do what she was told to do. For now.

— ≡ 10 ≡—

Morning dawned ice cold and dishwater gray, as if the last colorful days of autumn had shriveled overnight to make way for winter. Alice swore as she walked from St. James's Park to Victoria Station. It was a good job she'd worn her boots. Her toes were frozen, and her cheeks stung from the bitter wind. Cripes, it was only mid-November, but it felt like the arctic. Despite the weather, she needed the walk that morning. Sometimes walking helped her sort through her thoughts, helped her make sense and give order to problems she needed to work through. That morning her mind circled the Ruth problem first, followed by the lady detective and what to do about her, and then it shifted to Marie.

After the meeting, Alice had given Marie a good, hard crack on the face, threatened a visit from the blade next time, and warned the girl off leaving the Forties in the bloody lurch when she felt like it. The job at Marshall & Snelgrove became flawed the minute Marie didn't show, and now Geraldine was paying the price for it, locked up for six months with hard labor. Marie had seemed contrite, but Alice was beginning to question her trust in the woman, despite their longtime friendship. Marie hadn't acted like much of a friend lately. She hadn't acted like much of anything but a cowering ninny.

Still, the woman's tears had made Alice cringe inwardly, though she'd been all stoic business on the outside. It was the job. The role of the queen of thieves was to keep the group unified, looking out for one another, and to do that, she had to remind them who was boss, enforced by the occasional blow. No self-respecting leader would put up with nonsense. Refusing to do so kept the others safe. Besides, what choice did she have? Rule or be ruled, those were the only choices in London for a woman who had been born in a workhouse and raised by crooks from the slums. And if those were the only choices in life, well, she wouldn't be anything less than a leader.

Alice made haste when the train station came into view. The dusty old building had been there forever, boasting a redbrick and granite face, eleven chimneys, and a large Roman clock in the center of the roofline. The train station was good cover for business with the ever-shifting crowds and the ability to leave in a hurry if necessary. But it was the row of storage lockers that made the meeting place indispensable. When a shopping trip was complete, her girls transferred their items to storage lockers at Victoria Station, to a place on Bond Street, or at a location near Piccadilly Circus. Their fence collected the goods from the lockers, disposed of them in his careful way through a network of underground buyers, took his cut, and turned over the remaining funds to Alice. A masterful plan, if she did say so herself.

As she opened the door, a gust of warm air swooshed around her, lifting her hair from her neck. She stepped inside and rubbed her hands together. She'd had plans to send Lily Rose to meet with the fence that morning, but she didn't trust her these days to do the job without skimming off the top. In fact, she was growing to distrust Lily Rose more and more. Recently, the police had given Lily Rose the nickname she'd been craving, a sign she truly was making her path—and Alice didn't like it one bit. Soon, the Bob-Haired Bandit would want to flex her growing

power, or leave the gang entirely to do her own thing. Alice would make
that call as was the queen's right, push her out when it was time.

The Bob-Haired Bandit. What a stupid nickname, she thought.
Nearly half of her girls had bobs, herself included.

Another thought occurred to Alice, and she stopped in her tracks.
That made two she didn't trust: Marie and Lily Rose. Though it wasn't
unusual for Alice to need to watch her back, to assume no one was truly
trustworthy, this felt different. Her inside ring was changing and with
it, the demands of her leadership. The unease she was beginning to
recognize reared its head again and her stomach clenched. She needed
to do something to unite the gang again, give them a reason to come
together, and force those who no longer fit out, but what that something
should be, she didn't know. For now, she had a job to do.

She wove through the crowded station looking for a familiar face.
Finding her fence was harder than she expected. Every male in the station wore a long black or gray coat and a derby hat. It didn't help that
Freddy Grimes also had a medium build and was of average height with
average brown hair. A good thing for melting into the background, and
an irritating one when trying to find him. Freddy wasn't her favorite
fence, but she'd fired that wanker Jerrod Flake who got picked up by
the coppers nearly every job he pulled, and her best fence, Max Frank,
had recently died, poor sod, so she'd been forced to use the next best
thing. She'd found that in Freddy and a couple of others. Each fence
had their own beat, determined by the items they needed to move, but
all had one thing in common: they must be trustworthy and, no matter
what, wouldn't nark to the coppers. And if they tried to undercut her
or make off with any of the goods she'd collected, there'd be hell to pay.

Alice waited nonchalantly beneath the schedule board, pretending
to read the list of arriving and departing trains. The smell of morning
buns and coffee and stale cigarettes permeated the air. A voice echoed

over the loudspeaker announcing some change made to the schedule, though no one could understand a bloody word of it. She didn't know why they bothered. In a cavernous room with so many people, you couldn't hear the person bloody next to you let alone a muffled announcement.

The minutes ticked away, and she looked over her shoulder. Where was Grimes? Turning, she glanced at the large clock affixed to the back wall above the galley of platforms by the train tracks. It wasn't quite ten o'clock yet. She was early, but no sooner had she turned around than she spotted him. He met her eyes and veered left. They walked to the farthest bank of lockers, mostly out of sight of the crowds. She started toward him a moment—and stopped. He was being followed, by a little boy and a dog, of all things. A pickpocket, no doubt, who was likely after Freddy's padded wallet—his wallet filled with Alice's money.

In a flash, the pickpocket's little hand darted out and a glint of silver caught the light. The kid had a knife, or...no, a pair of scissors? Alice wanted to shout out a warning but drawing attention to herself and Freddy was the last thing they needed. Instead, she walked as swiftly as she could without breaking into a run. She was a few paces away when the thief slit the bottom of Freddy's satchel and snatched the jewelry and wallet hidden inside.

Freddy spun around, noticing that his bag had just become lighter. "What the devil?"

Alice beat him to the punch. She stepped into the boy's path and gripped him by the shoulders.

"Let me go!" The boy squirmed and tried to kick her. When he couldn't reach Alice, he attempted to bite her hand.

She slapped the kid hard across the cheek, stunning him long enough to drag him away from the crowd toward the lockers. The mutt yipped and clawed at Alice's leg until Freddy swatted him away.

"Grab his other arm," Alice said. "He's much stronger than he looks."

"Oy, this is the second time that little bastard has robbed me," Freddy said.

Alice took a good hard look at the child, whose hat had been knocked askew in the struggle. Ropes of plaited hair peeked out from beneath it. She ripped the hat off, pulling out two pins in the process.

"Ouch!" the child said, as several hair strands ripped. "Give me back my hat!"

"He's a girl," Freddy said.

"He most certainly is." Alice shook the child. "Who are you? Who are you working with?"

"Let me go!" the girl said, twisting and turning, desperate to get away.

The tiny dog lunged then, trying to take a bite out of Freddy's leg, but Freddy slapped the dog away for the second time. The mutt yelped and skittered backward.

"Please," the child said. "Do what you want with me, but don't hurt my dog. He is trying to protect me. Shh, Biscuit. Shh. Good boy. It's all right."

"Well, well," Freddy said. "Not only do we have a girl, but we have a posh one."

"Who do you belong to?" Alice asked, squinting at the girl as she took in her dark eyes and sharp cheekbones, the determined tilt of her chin. The skin under the kid's eyes looked bruised from lack of sleep and likely not enough to eat, given the sallow look about her.

"No one. I don't have any parents," the girl said, sniffing.

"What's your name?" Alice demanded.

"Let me go!" The child squirmed insistently against Alice's grip—to no avail.

"If you don't quit your squirming," she said, voice dripping with menace, "I'll take my blade to you."

The girl sagged in her grip.

"Now. I said, what's your name?"

The girl held her tongue.

"Fine. You can make up a name at the orphanage when I turn you over to the police."

"No!" she squeaked. "Please. I can take care of myself. I–I don't want to go to the orphanage."

"Your name then," Alice said, keeping her voice even.

"Hira. My name is Hira. My parents are dead. They died in India. Of cholera."

"And who are you working for now?" Alice said. She'd seen it before—hordes of little boys roaming the streets in a pack, pickpocketing as they went, and when they felt like it, terrorizing mothers and young children. They rarely had the gall to steal from a man who clearly didn't belong in the West End because he'd likely have no qualms about bruising them, or worse. But this little girl had stones.

"No one," Hira said. "I swear it. I've...I've run away from my uncle."

"An uncle with money, judging by your accent," Freddy said.

"He was going to send me to a boarding school so I ran away." Hira wiggled under Alice's clawlike vice. "You're hurting me."

She didn't release the kid but loosened her grip a fraction.

"What a sad tale," Freddy said. "But we don't give a horse's ass. We want the jewelry and my wallet back. All of it." He stuck out his hand expectantly.

Alice watched the girl thoughtfully. She was quick, furtive, and she'd managed to steal from her best fence—and one of the best in all of London—twice. The kid was small, and she had even smaller hands, but it was the edge of determination in her jaw that appealed to Alice most. With a few lessons in cons, she could be useful.

"You're coming with me." Alice dragged her toward the front of the train station.

"Where are you taking me?" Hira asked, her voice shaking.

"To meet some people and, if you're lucky and you come along quietly, to feed you, too."

"Can Biscuit come, too?" Now the girl sounded as if she were about to cry.

Alice glanced down at the mutt. He was cute, if a bit greasy, and she guessed he was the kid's only companion. She might be a tough woman, but she wasn't heartless. She nodded slightly. "Fine. But if he tries to bite me, I'll punt him into the river."

"Thank you, madam," Hira said, voice quivering.

"Alice. Call me Alice. Now let's go." She led the little girl away.

⫸ 11 ⫷

Biscuit yapped and scratched at Hira's leg. She scooped him up, holding him tightly in her arms, his steady heartbeat against her chest calming her. At least Alice let her take Biscuit. Hira tried to keep pace, but the woman's legs were too long, her strides enormous and hurried. Instead, Hira ended up trotting beside her. She'd contemplated running away, but twice she'd been yanked by the arm and warned not to even think about it or else. That had been enough to keep her in line. Something told her she didn't want to know what "or else" meant.

They hopped into a big, beautiful car the likes of which Hira had never seen and sped away, taking no heed of pedestrians and bicycles and sharp turns. She braced herself, gripping the dashboard to keep from sliding against the door as they whipped around corners. Within minutes they arrived at what looked like an abandoned factory and screeched to a stop.

"Right. We're here. Follow me," Alice barked the order, not leaving room for discussion.

Hira regarded the tall smokestack, the blackened brick around the edges of the column, and the dingy glass of neglected windowpanes. A film of coal hovered in the air in this part of town, turning the sky from simple gray to sinister. Fear trickled down her spine and over her skin. Where was Alice taking her? Not wanting to anger her, Hira bit back the question. Alice was as tall as a giant with broad forehead and large hands, intelligent eyes, and a defiant tilt to her chin. Despite her fancy dress and coat, her accent was the same as the boys who had chased Hira that first day on the streets. In all, the woman was terrifying.

As they entered the factory, damp air rushed Hira's senses. Many of the windows were shattered and a soaring ceiling arced over long tables set up with identical workstations for an assembly line. What was once some kind of factory now looked more like a graveyard of broken machinery. She glanced at Biscuit, who was unusually quiet. He was busy sniffing out small animals who had sheltered inside the old factory, out of sight.

Alice moved expertly through the near-dark around the workstations, stepping deftly over scattered piles of rat feces and a bird carcass or two. Hira would have cringed at the sight once upon a time before she'd been sleeping on the streets. Now she'd grown used to the filth. Briefly, she wondered what Miss Lightly would have to say about that. Would the old bat be worried about her disappearance? She doubted it, though perhaps Miss Lightly no longer had a job, now that Hira was gone. The thought made her happy, naughty as it was.

As they approached the edge of the factory floor, voices drifted through a doorway in the back corridor. They were women's voices.

Hira's nervous stomach eased. Somehow, this calmed her a little.

"Meet Hira," Alice said as they entered the office. "Say hello." She nudged Hira's shoulder.

"Hello," she said, voice soft. "How do you do?" She hadn't forgotten her manners. Miss Lightly's ruler had taught her not to forsake them, not ever.

A couple of the women smiled at her polite speech; another sneered.

"Take a seat," Alice said. "Lottie, move over."

The woman named Lottie scraped her chair across the floor as another in the group brought one to the table for Hira. The dozen or so women wore plain skirts and blouses and would be perfectly ordinary if not for the way they stared boldly and unabashedly at her, arms crossed, brows arched. The way a lady shouldn't—the very way Hira had been instructed never to do.

She fixed her gaze on a long scar carved into the tabletop, avoiding eye contact with anyone. They were all a little bit scary, though none as scary as Alice.

"You going to tell us where the girl came from?" Lottie asked.

Hira glanced at Lottie, who wore a glittering peacock brooch pinned in the curve between her collarbone and her right shoulder. Her lips were pert and bright pink, and she had fluffy brown hair like the fairies in Hira's books.

"This little runt managed to rob Freddy," Alice said with a grin. "She's fast and agile, and he didn't see it coming. She could be useful to us."

"She's also another mouth to feed," replied a woman wearing a shell-pink hat that cupped her head like a bottle cap.

"If she can help us on a job, she'll more than pay for her keep," Alice replied. "She nicked a gold watch, a ruby pendant, and all of Freddy's necklaces. And his wallet, with our money in it."

It dawned on Hira, then, exactly who the women were—they were a ring of thieves. She squinted as she thought about this. In the books she'd read, the men were always the bad guys, stealing or hurting other people. They were the ones who went to prison. But here, on the streets of south London, it seemed there were female criminals, too. She gawked at them, studying their hardened eyes, their overt gestures that would earn them a slap from Miss Lightly's ruler, and listened to their vulgar language as they mumbled among themselves, or dissolved into side conversations and brash laughter.

"Listen, up!" Alice leaned forward on her knuckles on the edge of the table. "If this kid is going to be one of us, we look after her. Who will take her in?"

"Why is she our responsibility?" asked the pretty one with the lipstick drawn in the shape of a heart in the middle of her lips. The woman looked like the kind of person who told you they liked you and then said mean things about you to your other friends. Like Emily Baker, Hira's nasty neighbor. Well, Emily wasn't her neighbor anymore, Hira thought with satisfaction. She'd never have to see Emily Baker again.

"Why are any of you our responsibility?" Alice demanded. "Because I say so and we take care of our own. Besides, she belongs with us. She's a natural."

"She's a kid," a woman named Scully said, doubt etching her features.

"Precisely," Alice replied. "No one thinks twice about a kid. They don't even see them."

"Hard to miss 'em in our neighborhood," Scully said. "They run in packs like wild dogs."

A woman with two black eyes spoke up next. Hira couldn't look away, though she knew it was rude to stare. She wondered what had happened to the poor woman.

"I have an extra room at Mike's, but—" she began.

Alice held up her hand. "I will absolutely not send her with you, Ruth. You can't even keep his hands off you. I won't have him beating this kid to a pulp. She'd be better off on the street."

Hira flinched. Ruth was being beaten up, and she still lived with that man when she didn't have to? Hira didn't understand. Why would she stay with someone so mean? Even Hira had run away and she was only a child.

"Kids snitch," another woman added. "Ever thought of that?"

"I can read and write," Hira heard herself say, and then wondered why she felt she needed to convince them to keep her. She could go back to her flour drum, have her freedom. She didn't want to steal for them, and neither did she need this group of criminals to keep her safe. But then she thought of last night's chill; the way frost had coated the cobbles in a slick sheen, the bite of raw air on her exposed skin, and it was only autumn. Winter would soon arrive and where would she be then?

"No one cares, kid," someone snarled.

"Might it be useful?" Hira asked, her heart thudding in her ears. What had possessed her to speak up?

"Your small hands and fast legs are more useful to us than reading and writing," Alice replied. "In fact..." She paused a moment, and a slow smile spread across her face. "I know what you'll do, kid. We've got a nuisance of a lady detective on our backs. Inspector Wyles, she's called. You're to follow her. Find out her beat and report back to me. We need to keep an eye on that one."

She was to follow a policewoman? She wondered if it was the same one who had chased her. The thought made her shiver with fear. If she made a wrong step, off to the orphanage she'd go. Still, she didn't know if she could tell the leader of the thieves that she wasn't going to do what was asked. Alice didn't seem like the kind of person one said no to, no matter what the cost.

A yap came from the direction of the door. Everyone turned to find the source of the sound.

Hira froze. Would they make her put Biscuit outside? If so, he might leave her... She tried not to panic. He was the only friend she had.

"Who's he?" someone asked.

"How did he get in here?"

"He's a cute little thing."

Hira jumped to her feet. "Biscuit," she said, moving toward him. He yapped and when she knelt beside him, he licked her hand. She tucked him into her arms. Though Hira felt eyes on her, she kept her gaze on the back wall. She didn't want to read their faces. Where she went, Biscuit went, and they'd have to get used to it or she'd run away the moment they weren't looking. That was it. That was what she'd do.

"He's mine," she said.

"Who's keeping the kid and her dog?" Alice demanded, bringing the conversation back on track. "It doesn't have to be for long. We can give her a trial run, see how she does."

Hira wondered what that meant. Should they decide she didn't belong with them, would they turn her over to the police or, worse, hurt her?

"I would offer, but there's no room, what with the children and Ralph's parents," one woman said.

"I'll not have a street dog in my house," Lottie said, disgust twisting her features.

"What about you, Scully?" Alice asked.

"You know it's best she don't come wif me," Scully replied, her eyes darkening.

Hira looked down, scratching Biscuit behind the ears, blinking to keep from crying. No one wanted her, not even a bunch of thieves. Well, she didn't want them either. She didn't want to be here at all, in fact. "I'm going to go now," she said, standing, Biscuit still wrapped tightly in her arms.

"You're not going anywhere," Alice said sharply. "You're coming home with me. And there'll be no more discussion about it. Now, same time tomorrow, ladies. We need to plan for the weekend shopping."

"Shopping," Hira was coming to realize, meant raiding stores for goods, stealing valuable items.

Everyone filtered through the factory in a stream, disappearing through the door and into the wan daylight. Everyone but Hira and Alice.

Hira shifted from one foot to the other, the scratchy wool trousers she'd bought two weeks ago rubbing against her skin. She looked shyly at Alice. Maybe staying with her would be a good thing. Hira wouldn't startle awake in the middle of the night every time Biscuit raised his head and peered into the darkness, a growl rumbling in his throat. In a real bed and under a roof where someone was looking out for her, she wouldn't wake up stiff with cold and hunger.

Alice reached for her handbag. "The first time that mutt chews anything or bites someone, he's out. Understand?"

Hira nodded. "His name is Biscuit," she added softly.

Alice smirked. "Let's go. And you can come too, Biscuit."

He barked at the sound of his name and, wonder of wonders, Alice laughed.

For the first time since Hira had left home, she felt an ounce of relief and perhaps even a tiny measure of happiness.

≡ 12 ≡

Alice drove across town to her flat. The girl sat quietly—barely squeaked out a word—and Alice realized the kid was either afraid or angry that she'd been kept against her will. Too bad for her. This was her best option; she was a lot safer under Alice's care and far warmer indoors than on the street this time of year.

Alice showed Hira up the stairs and inside the flat. She glanced around the parlor, seeing her home as if for the first time through the eyes of the girl at her side. The sofa had a boulder-sized divot in the middle cushion and the seams of the armchairs were slowly unraveling. Greasy black smudges ringed the doorknobs and window latches where one too many dirty fingers had left behind their prints. The odor of stale cigarettes and spoiled meat hung in the air. But it was the random patches of faded wallpaper that took the cake. At one time the wallpaper had been scarlet with a white floral print. Over time, the red had faded to a hideous muddy brown. And this was precisely why she'd been saving her pennies—for a proper flat on Milverton Road in Kennington Park that she'd been eyeing. She could hardly wait to escape this dump, or to have her own place.

"Why'd you bring that mutt in here?" her dad growled.

"He'll only be sleeping with us," she replied, motioning to Hira to sit down for tea. "Most days we won't even be home."

Hira did as she was told and put the dog on the floor beside her chair. He sat patiently without so much as a whine. At least the creature had the good sense not to be a nuisance.

Alice filled two plates with mushy peas and fried fish and a healthy portion of boiled potatoes. When she set a plate in front of Hira, the girl pounced on the food as if she were starving. In fact, the kid didn't look up from her plate even once. She was too busy eating as fast as she could while maintaining the best manners Alice had ever seen. Given the girl's manners and the posh way she spoke, Alice guessed she must have been beaten or worse to run away from a home that had provided for her. She clearly hadn't wanted for much.

Except maybe affection.

Much like Alice had wanted as a girl. Now Alice knew better. Men took what they wanted, saddled you with a child, and then had the nerve to boss you around. Total bullocks. She didn't fall for any of it.

She forked a bite of greasy fish in her mouth, her eyes never leaving Hira. As she pondered the girl's innocence, she was hit with a memory of her fifteenth birthday. Her mum had given her a couple of shillings to buy a small cake. She'd run around with friends after to celebrate, laughing, taunting the boys, proud of being another year closer to grown. On her way home, all of that joy drained away in an instant. She'd been cornered. She gritted her teeth as the man's face flashed through her mind, the greedy look in his eyes, his hands on her. Her brother, Tommy, had found him hours later, beat him into a coma, and the next day she'd started carrying a blade. She'd never again be that naive and vulnerable. She'd vowed to be the toughest, cleverest damn woman on the streets. And she was.

Alice's dad scraped his plate clean and pushed up from the table, roughly shoving his chair in, and sauntered off to the shelf where the spirits were stored. He refilled his glass and sat outside on the front stoop with his mates to complain about the king of England and to watch passersby. She would have to make sure Hira stayed out of his way. Once he'd had a few whiskeys, he was a real bastard. Even though she barely knew the kid, she wouldn't put her in harm's way if she could help it.

Alice got up from the table and Hira scurried after her without a word.

Good, Alice thought. She's learning to keep her mouth shut.

"Let's get you in the bath. This way."

Alice showed Hira to the communal bath. The water would be cold, but she'd be clean. While the girl bathed, Alice prepared her sister's empty bed. At least that was lucky; her sister, Louisa, lived with a boyfriend at the moment so Hira wouldn't have to sleep on the floor. Her other siblings wouldn't dream of sharing their beds. A family of ten made for a crowded flat.

When they were both in bed and Alice had turned out the lights, she lay on her back and stared at the ceiling.

"Alice?" the little girl's voice cut through the dark.

"Do you have enough blankets?"

"Yes, thank you. I just wondered…"

"Well, go on. I'm tired."

"Why does that man hit the lady with the two black eyes? The lady from the factory."

She glanced at the kid without answering. Hira's innocence was as clear and pure as ice. Alice had forgotten what that kind of naiveté looked like. "Because he's an ass," she replied at last. And then she realized this might be a good moment to teach the kid something. "Ruth thinks she deserves it. Mike tells her she does everything wrong and then he knocks her around, and she believes him. It's bollocks. Don't ever stay with a man who raises his fist to ya."

Confusion filled the kid's eyes. "But Ruth is a grown-up, so why can't she leave?"

Alice was once again struck by Hira's simple view of the world. If someone wasn't nice to you, you left, or so it seemed, and why not? It made perfect sense, but clearly the kid didn't understand that nothing was ever that simple.

"I don't know," she replied in the dark. "She doesn't know any better."

"But you do?"

"Yes," Alice said.

"Can she move in with you?"

Alice was silent a moment. Ruth had shit taste in men and always chose poorly. She'd likely find some other lout rather than move in with Alice.

"She could temporarily, while she got on her feet," Alice replied. "But I doubt she will."

"That's very sad," Hira whispered. "I wouldn't like to be hit by anyone. Not even mean old Uncle Clyde hit me."

Alice didn't answer. She had a feeling Hira didn't know the true definition of "mean."

"Could you move into a new flat and bring her with you?" Hira asked.

"It's expensive to pay rent, but you wouldn't know anything about that, would you," Alice said dryly. "You must be from Mayfair."

"Not anymore," Hira said, a note of defiance in her voice.

Silence stretched between them for a moment until curiosity got the better of Hira—again.

"What about your friends? The ladies in the factory. Could they live with you, too? Would it be expensive then?"

Alice stopped picking at the tiny knobs of fabric on her pilled blanket. "What made you think of that?"

"It seems like they need money, too, or they wouldn't steal necklaces."

"You're a little thief, too, you know," Alice replied, a note of sarcasm in her voice.

The girl was quiet for a long moment. Alice was sure the kid had fallen asleep when her voice drifted through the room again, this time heavy with sadness.

"I'm a thief because no one wants me. I have nowhere to go. You have a family and friends. If I had so many friends... You're lucky."

"I suppose, when you look at it that way."

Satisfied, the girl turned on her side.

Alice had always thought of herself as someone who made her own luck—and as someone who had often taken the hard end of the stick—since birth. She pulled the blanket up to her chin.

The seesaw sound of Hira's breathing filled the room as she drifted into a deep sleep.

Alice didn't know why the kid had suddenly entered her life, but there was something about her innocence that appealed to Alice. And maybe the kid was on to something. Perhaps the Forties would be interested in pooling their resources, beyond the regular weekly fees. Though they barely had enough to cover their expenses and enjoy a celebratory night out on the town as it was... And even if they did pool the resources, what would they do with them?

Alice turned on her back and stared at the slightly less hideous blue-and-cream-patterned wallpaper that appeared black and white in the dim light. Thinking, musing, coaxing to life the beginnings of a new plan.

13

The following evening, Alice held her hat to her head and pushed against the howling wind. Rain drove sideways from the sky, but she hadn't bothered with a brolly in this mess, not for the short distance from her flat to the pub. It would turn inside out and be a nuisance anyway. Braving the weather was worth it. She needed a drink before she settled in for the night. She'd been thinking all day about the conversation she'd had with Hira about Ruth. The girl's questions had been innocent, but more insightful than Alice had expected from a ten-year-old.

That's very sad.

Hira's simple words had cleaved Alice open to hear it put so plainly. It *was* sad—very sad living under a roof with a man who beat a woman senseless. Unlike Hira, Alice had accepted the brutality from her dad as a matter of course. A lot of women she knew had either been knocked about by their fathers or by their husbands and lovers. She'd barely known what to say to the kid.

Alice couldn't stop picturing Ruth, her swollen eye, the way she winced as she walked. She wasn't exactly defenseless against Mike's abuse—she knew how to use a knife as well as the rest of the Forties from their training—but with each kick to the ribs, Ruth let Mike treat her like she wasn't worth more than what he'd decided at any given moment. One day he'd kill her if she wasn't careful. One day, Alice might kill *him*.

She was relieved to see the welcome beacon of golden lamplight spilling through the windows of McGill's Pub. Hastily, she stepped inside, water dripping from her hat and from the hem of her raincoat. She hung her wet things on a rack near the door to dry, though they'd likely still be damp when it was time to go home. Not much she could do about that. Clothing always took an age to dry in a godforsaken city that was wet more often than not.

She plopped down on a barstool and ran a hand through her hair, slicking back clumps away from her face. She glanced around at her surroundings. The pub had opened a few weeks ago and she'd yet to try it. It was cozy, all dark wood and framed pictures of verdant Irish countryside. A panel of yellow-and-orange stained glass framed the top of the bar above the rows of liquor bottles, and modest lamps were scattered throughout, giving the whole place a cheery glow.

"Hiya, what can I get ya?" The barkeep's Irish brogue was as thick as clotted cream.

"Whiskey," she said.

"Irish or Scottish?" He wore suspenders and gray trousers, and his shirtsleeves were rolled to his elbows, revealing forearms covered in red-gold hair. If she was being honest with herself, she'd say he was attractive, but she wasn't, and she didn't have time for the distraction.

"Surprise me," she said.

"Suit yourself." He reached for a glass, and whistling as he went, he fetched a clean glass, held it up to the light to check for water spots, and reached for the bottle of Bushmills. He poured a finger of the amber liquid and set the glass before her with a smile. "There we are then. From the world's oldest whiskey distillery. That should warm you."

She downed the finger in one gulp.

He arched a brow at her. "A bad day, is it?"

She shrugged. "Not exactly."

"What exactly is it?"

"You're nosy, aren't you."

He grinned, revealing a mouth of white, crooked teeth that added to his charm. "I'm a barman. We're here for you to talk to."

"Last I knew, you were here to pour me a drink."

He refilled her glass, this time with a two-fingers' pour. "You don't have to tell me a thing. Enjoy your drink." He moved on to a slew of customers, some who'd just arrived from a long day's work, their cheeks ruddy from the damp cold, their clothes marked by grease or soot. Everyone had hair soaked through with rain.

She sipped her whiskey, feeling some semblance of calm as warmth threaded through her veins and made her limbs lighter. She had to do something to help Ruth. If there was one thing Alice hated, it was feeling helpless. Being helpless in one of the roughest neighborhoods in London wasn't just dangerous, it was a death sentence. She watched the barman do his job, moving from person to person, offering an ear to his customers. He seemed the relentlessly cheerful type. She wondered briefly if he had a family, or if he lived with his parents still as she did. It wasn't unusual for an entire family to share a flat or a house if they were lucky enough. It wasn't easy to make ends meet. That was about the only reason she still lived with a man who had taught her that violence was the only way to show love. Her dad might lecture her about the importance of family above all else—about blood being thicker than water—but his fists said otherwise.

When the barman finally returned his attention to her, she'd already drunk half her whiskey.

"Are you ready to tell me what happened today?" he said, a smile plumping the soft curve of his cheeks.

She rotated her glass on the bar top with her thumb and forefinger, round and round in circles. At last, she said, "A friend of mine lives with a man who practices his boxing moves on her."

He grimaced. "I see."

"I'm trying to decide what to do about it."

"What can you do?"

She looked up from her drink, eyes sharp. "More than you might think."

"Given that you're Diamond Annie, eh?"

It wasn't a question—he knew who she was.

"Yes, given that."

"So what's it to be? A good roughing up? A slashing? Maybe you set the dogs on him? Or perhaps I could have a few harsh words with him."

She laughed unexpectedly at his tone and the gleam in his eye. "Your boss should give you a raise."

He grinned. "I am the boss."

"You own this place? You're McGill?" She waved her hand around, vaguely aware that her vision was now a little fuzzy with drink.

"Aye. Simon McGill."

"And you're Irish."

"My father is Irish, and my mother from Manchester."

"And you ended up here, in the shit end of London?"

"The Great War sent us all in a hundred directions, didn't it now?"

She contemplated his words. Not much had changed for her since the war, save the fact that she'd become queen instantly. For a handful of years, there were fewer men in the streets and fewer men in general. Her girls had been lonely, and crime fell at first and then had become rampant until the women's patrol stepped in to help police the streets. But the patrol was gone now. The men had returned, and with them, the expectation that women should retreat. A bloody stupid expectation.

She threw back the rest of her whiskey. "I'll have a lager this time."

"Aye, slowing down. A good idea." He looked under the counter for a clean beer glass and came up empty-handed. "Back in a jiff." He emerged a moment later from the kitchen with a plate of steaming shepherd's pie. Behind him, a boy carried a tray of clean glasses.

The smell of meat with gravy and whipped potatoes made her stomach growl. Perhaps she should eat something, too. She'd been too busy to stop for tea that day.

"Eat, lass," Simon said, placing the food in front of her.

She quirked an eyebrow as she asked, "How did you know I wanted that plate?"

"Anyone who drinks three fingers of whiskey and a beer that fast needs something in their stomach."

"Thanks." She forked a bite into her mouth, relishing the thick brown gravy and the savory meat. "This is good."

He smiled. "My cook is the best."

Simon placed a pint of gold lager with a thick foamy head in front of her. "So, have you decided what you'll do? About your friend."

She remembered Hira's words.

Could you move into a new house and bring her with you? What about your friends? Could they live with you, too?

Perhaps Hira was on to something... Maybe some of the girls would want to live together or, at the very least, shelter together when they needed a place to hide. They could hold their meetings there as well, instead of at that dump of an old factory building. They'd been run off from the shuttered building by the police too many times anyway, not to mention the squatters that moved in from time to time. And there was always the risk that someone was listening in, hiding out in one of the dark corners waiting for them.

She set down her fork. "I'm considering moving out of my parents' flat. Bringing my friend with me. In fact..." Saying the words aloud gelled her thoughts and suddenly, she knew that was precisely what she wanted to do. She wanted a haven for her girls, a real headquarters. The Forty Elephants needed a place they could meet undisturbed—or shelter, or live for that matter, in their own building. A house perhaps, or a tenement that they owned.

Excitement bubbled inside her. It would be a fresh start for her and all her girls. Perhaps, too, it would bring them together again, settle some of the petty arguments between Marie and Bertha, and sway those who were starting to lose faith in the Forties.

"You look as if you've just struck gold," Simon said.

She returned his smile. "I believe I have, Simon. I believe I have."

⟫ 14 ⟪

Hira spent a week in a warm bed with a full belly. The last time her belly had been so full, she'd had the wretched dinner at Uncle Clyde's when she'd learned the news about her parents. Now her uncle's home felt as distant as India and twice as lonely. At least she was no longer alone. She was grateful Alice had taken her out of the cold and off the streets. Still, she didn't know what to think about becoming a part of a group of thieves. For now, she'd do as she was told. If she stayed with them through the winter, she'd be warm at least, and then she could decide what came next in the spring.

As soon as the sun rose and Alice left the flat, Hira gathered Biscuit and headed to Westminster. Outside, a taunting wind pulled at her hat and the edges of her coat and cooled the tip of her nose. At least the sun had appeared, and if she avoided patches of shade, she was able to stay relatively warm. When she neared the police station, she ducked into her hiding place behind a large waste bin until the inspector emerged. Though Hira didn't like the job Alice had given her—feared the police-woman might one day see her and drag her to the orphanage—she didn't want to disappoint Alice. Following the inspector was the least Hira could do to thank Alice for taking her into her home.

When the policewoman stepped outside, Hira followed her from a distance along the Victoria Embankment at the river's edge, past the Met to the Westminster Bridge. The inspector posted herself there at the corner of the bridge, the impressive column of Big Ben rising behind her in the distance, and stared out at the Thames lashing against the shore. Hira couldn't go any further, or she'd be seen. She was glad for the rest. Her toes had started to rub against the side of her boot, and it was a long walk back to Marshall & Snelgrove where she was to meet Alice in a few hours.

Hira tucked behind the edge of the Blackfriar Pub, shielding herself from view. The pub was a queer little building shaped like a triangle with ornamental tiles and balconies, and even at midday, people were milling around outside it, stopping for something to eat or a pint of beer. She knew the inspector would stand watch for quite some time, so she slid against the side of the building until she landed on her rump atop the stone curb. Biscuit plopped down beside her and rested his head on her leg. She relaxed there for a while, petting her dog, humming to herself, thinking about what a difference a hot plate of food made. The world seemed less bleak and she was happier, in a way.

After tossing loose stones and watching people come and go for some time, she poked her head around the edge of the building.

The inspector was gone!

Hira frantically scanned the horizon, searching for the brown uniform and ugly boots. When she looked to her far left, she gasped. The inspector was headed straight for her!

Hira leapt to her feet.

"You!" The bobby blew her whistle.

Seized by panic, she bolted. Biscuit bounded ahead of her. She zigzagged through the streets, dodging people, ducking in and out of stores, lungs burning, fear clawing at her throat. How had the inspector seen her? She'd been careful. She couldn't—she wouldn't—go to the orphanage or back to her uncle's.

She ran, ran, ran, the sound of her boots on pavement thundering in her ears. When she felt as if she couldn't go any farther, she dove inside a chemist shop to hide. Panting, she moved to the farthest edge of the window to shield herself from the street view and peered out. Her gaze picked carefully over the street, the buildings, and the faces of the pedestrians outside.

"Can I help you, miss?" a clerk asked. He had a kind face and Hira took advantage of it as she'd learned to do since she'd become homeless.

"I–I just need a quick moment. They were chasing me. Some mean boys bigger than me," she lied. "Just give me one moment, please, and I'll be on my way. I won't touch a thing, I promise."

"Better be quick about it. I don't want ruffians here, and I don't want your dog messing on my floor."

"Yes, sir," she said.

He eyed her, appreciating her manners, likely wondering what she was doing here.

And then she realized he'd called her "miss." He knew she was a girl. She felt for her cap; her fingers brushed thick, soft braids. She must have lost the cap in her flight. She wondered if the inspector knew she was a girl now, too. She scolded herself for the mistake. She didn't like that her disguise might be blown. More importantly, Alice wouldn't like it either.

As she waited, she steadied her breath until the clerk eyed her again. She had overstayed her welcome. If the bobby was there waiting for her... Well, she'd have to take her chances. With a deep breath, she left the shop. She darted down the street as if she were still being chased and found cover in a nearby garden.

To her relief, the inspector was nowhere to be seen.

Hira started toward Oxford Street to Marshall & Snelgrove. She wouldn't tell Alice about this mistake—she'd be disappointed in Hira.

Hira was disappointed in herself. The only good news was she hadn't been caught, and she'd lost the inspector in the end.

At least she thought she had.

Lilian waited for the child to leave the chemist shop and followed her to Oxford Street. She'd discovered she was being followed days before from the station to wherever her beat entailed and today, the girl—not a boy as Lilian had first thought—had been so close, so obviously in plain view, that she'd decided it was time to make it known to the child that she'd seen her. Her little dog was with her, too. Lilian smiled. That would make her easy to spot from now on. This time, however, Lilian wouldn't give chase. She'd make the child come to her.

The girl paused to stare inside the store. Lilian paused, too, considering the best way to approach. As the dog at her side yapped, a smile arced across Lilian's face. The dog was the ticket. She cut the line at a nearby vendor and bought a sausage roll. Grease oozed from the pastry and soaked into the paper and, no doubt, all over her gloves. She walked swiftly across the street and ducked behind a cluster of women heading into the department store.

The child hovered on the other side of the doorway, watching, waiting.

Lilian crouched to the ground, tore off a piece of the sausage roll and dangled it within the dog's line of sight. He perked up and attempted to go through the pack of ladies at first and thought better of it, deciding at last to go around them.

He approached cautiously, hesitating a moment.

She stretched a little farther, holding out the treat.

He inched closer, snatching the morsel from her fingers, and backed away to gulp it down in one bite. The girl, meanwhile, hadn't yet noticed her dog was gone. She was too busy watching the women, specifically their handbags.

Lilian tore off another hunk of meat, and this time the dog came closer. She tried to pet him—and to grab him—to no avail. The dog skittered away.

The poor rascal had probably been abused, given how cautious he was.

"Come on, boy. Here, boy." She whistled softly.

He managed to wrest the meat from her grip and back away, again too quickly.

"Damn," she muttered, tearing off another chunk of the sausage roll, leaving one remaining piece.

He didn't hesitate this time and headed straight for her. She prepared to leap at the dog—when a voice barked out an order.

"Biscuit! No! Come, Biscuit!" The girl now stood a few feet away. Should he come any closer, Lilian could grab her, too.

"Come here, boy," Lilian said, holding out the last two pieces of the sausage roll.

He looked back at his young mistress as if offering an apology and then trotted toward Lilian. In a flash the girl darted out, snatching the dog and pulling him into her arms.

Just within Lilian's reach.

"Got you! You're coming with me."

The girl twisted in her hands, and the dog began to bark.

"Hold still!" Lilian commanded. "You'll only make this harder on yourself."

"Let me go!" the child shouted, writhing in Lilian's grip.

The girl leaned forward and sank her teeth into Lilian's hand.

She screeched and pulled her hand away, giving the girl all the room she needed. The child pulled free and ran in the opposite direction—and smacked into a very tall woman in a luxurious peacock-blue coat.

"Whoa, there," the woman in the blue coat said. "It's all right."

Lilian's mouth dropped open a moment before snapping shut again. It was the one and only, the infamous Diamond Annie, ringleader of the Forty Elephants, and the very woman she'd been trying to find.

The little girl sagged against Diamond Annie in relief, as if she knew her.

Lilian frowned. "Hello, Annie."

"Alice," she said with an icy smile that didn't reach her dark-blue eyes. Her hat might be in the fashion catalogs and her coat might be fresh off the racks from Babbage's or Harrods, but Lilian knew she was a tigress of a woman. Her ringed fist was legendary, her skill with a blade as good as any man's. She'd read all about it, becoming an expert on the queen of thieves since her first interactions with her.

"This orphan belongs in a shelter," Lilian said, "so if you don't mind handing her over, we may both get on with our day." She wanted to take Diamond Annie to the station—a far bigger score than an orphan—but she had nothing on the gang leader. If she arrested Alice, she'd receive a reprimand. The chief didn't put up with nonsense, in particular if it involved a female. Much as she liked Chief Inspector Wensley and saw him as something of a mentor, his expectations were higher for her than her male counterparts. Besides, arresting Alice now would make Lilian an overt enemy of the queen of thieves, and she didn't need that animosity brewing. Yet.

"She's not an orphan," Alice snapped impatiently. "She's my cousin. Let's go, cousin."

"Your cousin?" Lilian looked from the girl to Alice and back again. "I don't think so."

The little girl slipped behind Alice to hide.

"Care to dispute it?" Alice growled. Her hand went to her waistband and Lilian wondered what the woman kept there. A knife? A firearm? Likely one or the other. Gang leaders never went without protection.

"You'd better watch your tone," Lilian said sharply. "I'm a detective. Speak to me with respect."

Alice laughed, a biting, angry sound. "I hardly call a woman standing guard in a department store and chasing orphans a detective. Really, you should look into another pursuit. One where you might actually have the respect you're clearly very desperate for."

A shock of anger rocked through Lilian. Alice's needling irked her... and that was precisely what Alice wanted. According to what Lilian had gleaned from others at the Met, Diamond Annie was known to rile up even the most stoic on the force. She was clever, and the clever ones were always the toughest to crack. And anyway here, at midday near the marketplace where women poured in and out of boutiques and department stores, Lilian didn't want this little talk to become bigger than it needed to be.

Hira peered out from around Alice, her eyes round with curiosity and fear.

"Tell your *cousin*"—Lilian paused for emphasis—"that I've watched her steal twice now, and if she's caught again, she'll be hauled to a Borstal where she belongs." She pointed at Hira. "Do you understand me?"

The little girl nodded, clearly terrified at the thought of a detention center for wayward children.

Alice stared coolly at Lilian. "We'll be on our way, copper, and you should be on yours." She led the little girl away.

As Lilian watched them walk away, she made a split-second decision about her shift. Forget the department store duty! She was going to follow them. Only after following them for two hours, Lilian had discerned nothing; they'd walked in circles through Soho and then Mayfair, and at last, she realized that Alice knew she was being followed and had led her on a merry dance through the West End and central London.

Resigned, Lilian melted into the crowds of Piccadilly Circus and headed home. She was better off starting her shift tomorrow and following the girl while she was on her own. Thankfully, Lilian was good at watching, good at waiting. She was patient, and she knew practicing patience was the very best way to catch a thief.

— 15 —

Alice was irritated the rest of the day. The lady copper—the very same who had collared Geraldine and led her to prison—had her sights on Hira. Worse, the woman had followed them around all bloody afternoon.

"Where did she see you?" she demanded, trying to keep her temper. Hira was just a kid, after all, and new at being a Forty Elephant.

Hira blushed. "In Westminster, across from Big Ben by the Blackfriar Pub."

Alice was glad of that anyway. Westminster was the coppers' turf and not the Forties'. At least Hira hadn't been seen near the factory. The last thing they needed was another copper sniffing around their turf. "You were supposed to be watching her, not the other way around."

"I'm sorry, madam. I've been following her all week, but she finally saw me, I guess."

Alice glared but said nothing. With a little sleuthing and a bit of help from her contacts, they'd tracked down the lady detective, and Hira had determined the copper's beats quite quickly. Wyles mostly stayed in the West End or central London, looking behind bins or alleys between buildings, combing the parks, and standing watch inside several of the larger department stores. On occasion, Hira hadn't seen

Wyles leave the Met or the police station nearby where she reported every morning, and Alice assumed they were either the copper's days off work or, perhaps more worrying, she might be working beats in other parts of the city.

They'd have to keep a closer eye on Wyles. She'd clearly taken an interest in Hira, and the child and her dog didn't exactly blend in with the other ruffians on the street. Something Alice might need to consider in the future. The copper now knew Hira was with the Forties, too, or at the very least in Alice's orbit. For now, they knew where to find the copper—but the copper didn't know where to find them.

Still, her nerves tingled with trepidation.

———

The following day, Alice drove her Chrysler to Cartwright Street near the Katharine Buildings and killed the engine. She studied the forty-year-old tenement neighborhood, situated near Tower Bridge and the old Tower of London. A few of the tenements were still in use as housing for the working class. *The working class.* She sneered. What a load of shit. The working class was code for the poor sods who carried the weight of the world on their backs and never really caught up in life. Not her. She was going places.

Alice checked the time on her wristlet. She was early, as usual. She didn't like to feel rushed. She'd spent the better part of the past week putting the word out that she was looking to buy property. When the name of Jimmy Church surfaced, she'd promptly set up a meeting. She wondered what the toff had to say about selling one of his buildings to a woman. It wasn't common—in fact, women still didn't have all the same rights as men when it came to property legislation, in spite of the WSPU and their marches—so she'd have to convince the bloke that dealing with her wasn't a waste of his time. Luckily, she had her *methods*. She'd only need to find a way to pay for the property. After scribbling down some basic math, she realized she'd need something much more substantial than the winnings from the Forties' shopping trips.

She watched as the first snow of the season floated from the sky like sprinkled sugar. It dusted the pavement and the rubbish bins, the roofs in need of repair, broken bicycles and bed frames left in the street, but its magic lasted for only an instant. The ground was still too warm for the snow to accumulate. It dissolved within seconds as if it hadn't fallen at all.

Alice perked up as a sleek new Ford turned onto the street. Church was here. He stopped in front of a row of buildings that had been abandoned since the war. His buildings. That son of a bitch owned most of the city block and his asking price was outrageous. She hoped to talk him down. She could be very persuasive when necessary.

She met him across the street.

"Well, let's have a look, shall we?" he said. She was taller than most men but not Church. He had a few inches on her. His limbs were spiderlike, his face long and lean like that of a horse.

"Let's," she replied.

"Do you want to tell me why you're looking?" he asked.

"No," she said.

He chuckled at her bluntness. "Very well. It's none of my business."

"No, it isn't." She smiled to soften her harsh words. "I need space, lots of rooms."

"You'll have plenty of that in any of these." He motioned to the row of redbrick buildings stretching to the edge of the block that looked to be four or five stories tall. "Let's start there."

They walked to the end of the block. Inside the first building, Alice could scarcely see in front of her. Many of the windows were boarded up, and those still intact were coated in dust and grime.

"Was this a tenement, too?" she asked.

"It was. It was closed down when the landlord was murdered. Sad story, really. He was on his way home from the pub one night. He was robbed and stabbed, poor bastard. He didn't have any relatives, so the buildings went up for auction and I bought them."

"Before the government stepped in and took the others."

"Something like that," he said with a sly grin.

So he played dirty, Alice thought. That was good to know.

"It's ain't pretty, is it," she said.

"Nothing a little hard work and polish couldn't fix."

"Show me the others."

"Right," he said. "This way. I have a couple that are larger."

They walked through two adjacent buildings that smelled as if something had died inside them. The floor had rotted in one, and in the other, the rooms were so small and dingy that it reminded her of Holloway Prison.

"This is it?" Alice said, crossing her arms. "You own more than this block, Church." She'd looked into him, knew he owned a posh building in the West End and two others in Pimlico that had promise.

"Not for what you're offering to pay," Jimmy said.

"You're never going to sell these as they are. They need too much work," she replied. "Come on, cut me a deal and we'll talk."

He shook his head. "I'll renovate them. Sell them for a profit easily. I always do." He gave her a pointed look. "If you're interested, you'll need to get me a deposit by the end of the year."

She couldn't imagine anyone buying these hovels, but then again, Jimmy Church was well known for his acumen. He seemed to always know the right person at the right time.

"And the buildings in Pimlico?"

"They're almost double what this lot is."

There was no way she could bring in double the cash. She'd have to settle for one of these dumps and fix it up as the money came in over the next several months. Besides, if all of her girls helped, they could at least set up the place and clean it.

"How about a deal," she said. "I get you a sizable deposit by the end of the year, and I'll pay the rest by the end of spring—but you'll cut me a twenty-thousand-pound discount."

"I'll make a profit on these. Why would I cut the price?"

"For one thing, if you think you're going to make a profit during this shit economy, you're mad. I'd be doing you a favor, taking one off your hands. The other reason? My good friend Bert McDonald of the Elephant and Castle would be happy to speak to you about that discount. I wouldn't want things to get…nasty. If you know what I mean." She didn't like to rely on Bert's men—frankly she rarely did—but she knew the gang inspired far more fear than if she'd threatened Church with her trusty razor, or even with the entire pack of Forties behind her.

He met her eyes.

"Well? Do we have a deal?" she pressed.

After a moment's hesitation, he said, "You have a deal. But I want a down payment by the end of the year or it's off the table."

"Done," she said. "Shake on it?"

They shook hands and he tipped his hat at her.

"It's been a pleasure, Miss Diamond."

"Entirely all yours," she replied, and he laughed as he walked back to his car.

As Alice watched him go, she let out an exasperated breath. Even with the discount, they weren't clearing enough to buy a single one of those dumps. She'd definitely have to think bigger. What they needed was a heist—a multipronged venture that would pull in a pile—and they had to move fast. Tension rippled over her shoulders and settled in her neck. It was only six weeks to the end of the year. Plus, Ruth needed the cover and so many others could use it, too, Hira included. In fact, Alice wasn't sure how much longer the kid could stay at her flat. Dad complained bitterly about their houseguest every day.

Alice chewed her lip as she walked back to her car. Perhaps she shouldn't have taken in Hira to begin with; it had been an unchar-acteristic move to bring in a street urchin. But the kid had been too good—too quick on her feet and very sharp, in spite of her upbringing in Mayfair. Alice considered the girl's fine manners and speech. Perhaps she'd dress her up and use her as a decoy. No one would think twice about a young girl in patten shoes with a posh accent. Her brown skin might cause a momentary lapse, a curiosity maybe, but if they nabbed her for stealing, so what? What did Alice care anyway? It wasn't as if she was the kid's mother or even her guardian, for Pete's sake. Hira was a squatter in the end. And Alice had gotten too close to the girl anyway, been a little too soft with her, and being soft never served Alice well.

She would do well to remember that.

⇌ 16 ⇌

The sun had not yet risen, but Hira left the Diamonds' flat in a hurry. She did her best to stay out of Alice's family's way. Mrs. Diamond seemed ill most of the time, or she was "out on a job" as Alice had put it, and the other siblings looked past Hira as if she didn't exist. Mr. Diamond, on the other hand, disliked her intensely and made no secret of it. He'd bluster and slam around the flat as if he might hurt her, and perhaps he'd try. She never stuck around to find out; she spent as little time there as possible.

She shivered outdoors while she waited in a recessed nook between two buildings. When, at last, the lights began to flicker to life and the city teemed with people rushing to work, she walked to Marshall & Snelgrove. Before taking the chance to dash inside, she peered through the window. She was there, Dorothy McBride. Hira looked down at Biscuit, deciding, and finally pulled open the door. The pretty lady had invited her back, after all, and Hira hadn't eaten much. She'd been too busy carefully tracking the inspector to make up for her blunder.

As she entered the store, a well-dressed woman with a crooked nose and a scowl took one look at Hira and moved in her direction. Hira darted left around a mannequin with spooky, unseeing eyes and arms posed in an awkward position. She scampered swiftly between racks of frocks and coats, following the beacon of Dorothy's red hair to the jewelry counter.

Biscuit yipped and followed at her heels.

The scowling woman shouted, "Stop! You there! Stop at once!"

"Shh, Biscuit," Hira scolded. "Be quiet!"

She skipped through the store, past a counter displaying gloves, winter hats, and scarves, and at last reached Dorothy. Her pretty face brightened at once.

"Catch her!" the mean woman said.

"It's all right, Mildred," Dorothy said. "This little girl is my friend. She's here to see me."

"You can't be serious." Mildred scowled. "How do you know this... this creature?"

"That wouldn't be any of your business, now would it," Dorothy replied and held out her hand to Hira. "I've brought something for you."

"You'd better get that mutt out of here before Mr. Harrington sees it!" Mildred called after them.

Hira took Dorothy's hand and cast a last glance over her shoulder at Mildred and did something completely out of character—she stuck out her tongue.

Mildred huffed and stomped off to the registers.

Hira blushed. What Miss Lightly would say about her manners! She'd probably go without dinner if she were at her uncle's. But she wasn't. She smiled as she followed Dorothy.

"Isn't she dreadful?" Dorothy whispered, leading them to a back room with a table and a row of overcoats hung neatly on the far wall. She dug into a bag and handed two packages wrapped in parchment paper to Hira.

"It's a ham sandwich and a slice of sponge cake. Eat up. It'll put some flesh on your bones."

"Thank you," Hira said, slipping them into her satchel. "That's very kind of you, Mrs. McBride."

"Heavens, child, I'm not an old maid, and I'm not married. Call me Dorothy."

Hira nodded sheepishly. She'd learned in *A Lady's Guide to Etiquette in Polite Society* how she should address women in a respectful way. She hadn't considered that some women would prefer less formal manners until she'd met Alice and the Forty Elephants, and now, Dorothy.

"Say, where do you sleep?" Dorothy asked. "I was thinking about you last night when it started to rain and wondered if you were soaked to the bone."

Hira hesitated. Perhaps she shouldn't tell Dorothy with whom she was living. "I've made some...friends. They're letting me sleep at their house, for now."

"Well, isn't that wonderful," Dorothy said. "Now I'm not your only friend."

Friend. Was that was Dorothy was? And Alice and the Forty Elephants? Hira didn't know, but she sure liked the sound of it. She smiled shyly and in return received a bright flash of perfect white teeth.

"Do you mind telling me what happened to your parents? Where is your mother?" Dorothy asked. Seeing Hira's fallen expression, she added quickly, "It's perfectly all right if you'd rather not say."

Hira looked down. "My mother died. Both of my parents died in India of cholera."

"Goodness, I'm so sorry," Dorothy said, her hand covering her mouth. "Why weren't you in India with them? I suppose it's a good thing you weren't."

"I've lived with my uncle in London all my life, but he..." Hira sniffed. "He doesn't care for me. He was going to send me to a school in the north for poor children and orphans, so I ran away." She met Dorothy's eye.

"Well, at least you have friends to look after you now." Dorothy smiled kindly.

Hira felt another rush of warmth. Alice and Dorothy were so different from each other, but it was nice to feel like she wasn't entirely alone anymore. She didn't know if she would call Alice a friend, but at least she was looking after Hira, however temporary. After that…Hira didn't know what would come next.

Biscuit began to whine.

"What is it, boy?" she asked, bending to pick him up. She fed him a chunk of the ham sandwich, and he licked her face. "Where do you live, Mrs.—Dorothy?"

"I live in the East End with my mum."

Hira couldn't imagine what that must be like, waking up to your mother every morning, and having her tuck you into bed each night before you went to sleep. She conjured the image of her own mother, sitting at her bedside reading aloud, running her fingers through Hira's long, dark hair. She didn't know what it was to be touched or embraced, truly cared for in that way. The closest thing to a mother she'd had was Mrs. Culpepper, and she'd been paid to be the housekeeper, not Hira's caregiver.

"Oh, I almost forgot," Dorothy said. "I've got something for Biscuit, too." She produced two digestive biscuits sprinkled with sugar.

Biscuit barked and greedily lapped up the treats.

Dorothy laughed and put her hand on Hira's shoulder. "I'm glad you've found a place to stay. If you need anything, you come and see me. In fact, why don't you stop in again next week, same time?"

Hira nodded, a shy smile lighting her dark eyes. "Same time."

After her visit with Dorothy, Hira did her usual duty of following the inspector. When it was time, she made her way back to the Elephant and Castle neighborhood for the meeting with the Forty Elephants. She surveyed the changing landscape thoughtfully as she walked. She was always struck by the contrasts between boroughs. Here, rubbish littered the gritty street, broken beer bottles lay scattered where they'd been dashed against the pavement the night before, and broken furniture was left to rot in the rain. Soot stained the facades of many buildings, but the worst of the dwellings could scarcely be called a building. The hovels were stacked atop each other and leaned upon one another, side by side in a haphazard way. Many didn't have so much as a front door, and their windows were covered by tattered scraps of linen.

At one time the sight would have surprised Hira, even frightened her perhaps, but she'd grown more accustomed to the way the poor lived. She'd become one of them. She'd never realized how much she had while living with her uncle: soft bedsheets and silk nightdresses, a library filled with as many books as she could read, roaring fires, hot baths, and beautiful silver spoons to scoop up her morning porridge. And the piano. She sighed. She missed the piano. It all seemed like a dream now.

A man stepped suddenly out of a shadowed doorway.

Hira jumped, startled by the unexpected movement.

He wore no hat so his blond hair fell over his brow, and he stood with his legs parted, his fists on his hips, as if he were trying to bar someone from pushing past him.

Her.

She gulped down her fear. She must stay calm. He thought she was a boy, for one, and she was probably faster than him.

"Want some sweets, little boy? You look hungry."

His oily smile sent a shiver over Hira's skin. He didn't want to give her sweets, and she didn't want find out what he really wanted.

She shrugged, eyeing the narrow space between him and the row of buildings.

He smiled again—and she took off like a shot. Catching him off guard, she raced past him.

He pounded after her, much faster than she'd expected. Soon, he'd be upon her.

Panic streaked through her as she leapt over garbage and a stack of bricks. She wasn't far from the factory now—

A hand clasped around her arm and wrenched her backward.

She stumbled, losing her footing, landing hard on her hind end.

"Where do you think you're going?" the man snarled. He yanked her to her feet.

Hira cried out as his fingers dug into her arm.

"Shut up, you! Now walk!" he commanded, half dragging her toward a dingy building. "Didn't your mum teach you that the street is no place for children?"

Biscuit lunged at him, sinking his teeth into his leg. The man howled and made to swat her dog away when a voice came from behind them.

"If you know what's good for you, you'll let the kid go."

A voice Hira knew. As she threw a look over her shoulder, her eyes welled with relieved tears. It was Alice, tall and strong—taller than the tyrant that held her fast—with two of the Forty Elephants standing like sentinels at her side. Their cheeks were pink with cold, the edges of their coats blowing open slightly with the wind. Menace darkened their eyes.

Alice took a step forward. "I suggest you hand the kid over, or we'll have a heyday carving you up."

He laughed. "A bunch of girls? Get lost or I'll have my way with you next."

"Apparently this fool has cotton in his ears, Maggie," Alice said. "Shall we have a go?" A clicking sound came next. Something silver flashed in her right hand. A knife.

"I think I'm going to enjoy this." Maggie brandished her own blade. Scully followed suit.

"Get him!" Alice shouted.

As the Forties lunged, Hira twisted and kicked, making contact with the man's knee.

He howled and threw her to the ground.

She scrambled to her feet, her trousers damp, her hands scraped from trying to catch her fall. Biscuit scampered after her as she moved out of the way.

The man eyed the women's knives and held up his hands. "I've let him go. Now leave me alone."

"Something tells me you haven't learned your lesson," Alice said. "That some other poor unsuspecting child could wander along minding their own business and you'd snatch him up just the same."

"I think he needs to learn a lesson, Alice," Scully said.

"A good one," Maggie added.

Like a strike of lightning, he was surrounded, and Alice pounced. She slashed once, twice, three times.

The man cried out and collapsed at her feet. He covered one cheek with his hand. On the other, a flap of flesh wept blood.

Hira gasped at the gruesome sight and hugged Biscuit more tightly. Alice had cut his face! With a knife!

The queen of thieves stepped back, putting distance between her and the man, her blade scarlet with blood. Maggie handed Alice a handkerchief to wipe it clean.

Alice made quick work of it and said, "Keep your mitts off the kids. You 'ear me? If I see you again, you won't get off with a little nick to the face."

He whimpered but didn't reply.

"Are we done already?" Maggie asked. "I wouldn't mind another go at him."

The man's eyes widened. He scrambled to his feet and ran.

Hira watched him flee, her eyes locked on his retreating form, unable to look away. The streaming blood, the knives, the terror in his eyes. The gaping wound. Her stomach heaved.

Alice took one look at Hira's expression, and said, "It looks like our charge has seen enough. Let's go, ladies. We have a meetin' to get to."

Hira stared, wide-eyed, at the Forties. Would Alice have killed him if given the chance? Would the others? Tears sprang to Hira's eyes and she willed herself to be brave. Her tears might anger Alice—and now she knew precisely what Alice's anger looked like. Hira didn't want to be on the other end of it.

She'd be better off pretending as if nothing had happened at all.

⇒ 17 ⇐

Morning dawned wearily, the sun struggling against the clouds for space in the sky. At least it wasn't raining. After yesterday's knifing incident, Alice needed to spend some time with the kid, teach her a few tricks of the trade. She kept forgetting that Hira wasn't really a creature of the streets like the other orphans that raced around in packs, taking anything that wasn't nailed down. She'd had a home. She'd had everything she could want and more, in fact, and she'd chosen to leave. She was a brave little thing, if too innocent to survive the street life, but Alice would help her with that—beginning with the first lesson about drawing blood from a no-good tosser who deserved it.

She shook Hira's shoulder, rousing her from sleep. "Wakey, wakey. We've got some work to do today."

Hira's dark eyes popped open instantly, as if she slept on high alert. When she saw it was Alice, she stretched and pushed back the covers. "What sort of work?"

"You'll see. Come with me."

Hira followed without question, she and her mutt winding through the neighborhood, walking single file on the packed roads near the ancient Borough Market in Southwark. The market was centuries old, something of a gem in London. Twelfth century? She couldn't remember exactly from one of the few school lessons she'd had as a girl, but that seemed right. Luckily, it was still relatively calm in the early morning. Soon the market would be swarmed with people picking up fresh fruit and veg or looking for a bite to eat and a quick pint. She could usually count on running into one of her girls there, or the Elephant and Castle men. It was a favorite haunt to carouse and lift a quick wallet or two.

When Alice reached a condemned building with an open courtyard not far from the market, she turned sharply, ushering Hira around to the back of the building.

"Where are we going?" Hira asked, peering up at the sky.

"Yes, it's probably going to rain. What else is new," Alice said. "It won't interfere with our lesson."

"Lesson, madam?" Hira asked.

"You're going to learn how to use a knife."

"I–I don't want to use a knife, madam," Hira replied.

Alice glared at her. "You want men like that swine tracking you down?"

"No," Hira said meekly, looking at the ground.

"Listen to me," Alice said. "There are bad people out there. Men who want to hurt you. I know what you saw yesterday scared you, but he deserved it. He would have done all sorts of nasty things to you, maybe even killed you and dumped you in a bin when he was finished."

Hira blanched as she considered Alice's words. "But I'm frightened," she squeaked.

Alice gave her a tight smile. "That's the thing about carrying a knife. You'll be a lot less frightened because you'll know you can defend yourself."

Hira didn't answer at first. "But I have Biscuit to protect me."

Her tone softened. "He won't always be with you. Besides, plenty of scoundrels could overpower your mutt, and where would you be then? With your knickers at your ankles and some brute between your legs."

Hira visibly cringed.

"All right then." Alice brandished a small knife with a leather handle. "There are a few ways to hold your knife. If you want to conceal it, you hold it like this." The blade peeked between her knuckles. "No one can see it, but you know it's there and if you get into a scrape, you can protect yourself, see. Take it."

Reluctantly, the kid took the blade.

"Good, that's right. Now, if you don't need to conceal it, palm it like this." Hira did as demonstrated. "Now swish your arm back and forth in a slashing motion, making a letter x. You start from above and slash down to either in the gut or the groin area, in your case. Got it?"

Hira did exactly as Alice had. Her tongue poked out from between her lips in concentration.

"Again," Alice said.

Hira continued for several minutes.

When she looked bored from practicing the same thing over and over again, Alice asked, "What happens if you come face-to-face with someone?" She spread her legs apart slightly and crouched, holding her blackjack in her right hand. "You need to be steady on your feet. See how my feet are planted? But I'm ready to spring. Go on then. Let's see it."

Hira replicated her stance.

"Your most important weapon isn't the blade. It's the element of surprise. No man expects a woman to carry a knife. And they never expect us to know how to use it." A knowing smile tugged at her lips. "The sods. Keep your weapon hidden until the last possible moment."

She demonstrated several more moves, including one that would target the vein in the neck. The kid may as well be prepared. She might eventually have to kill someone to keep them off her. Alice had certainly been close a few times.

"Am I doing it right, madam?" Hira asked, her arm moving quickly, as if slitting someone's throat.

Alice nodded, careful not to give too much praise. She didn't want the kid to think she could slack off or become too comfortable. There was nothing comfortable about being a Forty Elephant.

Hira practiced making a letter z in the air, doing the stab-and-turn and the x move. When she seemed tired, Alice demonstrated how to quickly retrieve the blade and conceal it in various ways, as well as how to deliver a fatal upthrust to the neck or the heart.

"Practice that a little each day for a while," Alice said. "Until you feel more comfortable holding your razor. Do you understand?"

Hira nodded. As she shifted to put the knife in her satchel, a trinket tumbled from her trouser pocket and hit the ground.

Alice picked up the wooden figure covered in tiny diamond-shaped mirrors. It had the head of an elephant and body of a human.

"Oh!" Hira reached for it.

Alice held it higher than the girl could reach, studying the colorful details and the mirrors that sparkled in the light. "What's this? I quite like it."

Hira blushed. "May I have it, please? My mother sent it to me. From India. It's Ganesha, a god."

Alice held it out, and the girl snatched it up, tucked it inside her satchel this time. It was rather fitting the kid should have an idol figurine with the head of an elephant. Seemed like an omen, of sorts, but she wouldn't tell Hira that.

"Now," Alice began, "Where to keep your razor... I keep mine in a hidden pocket in my skirt. We'll need to get you some knickers like the other Forties use for shopping. They have lots of hidden pockets. I'll have Lottie sew some into your new frocks."

"I'm to wear new clothes?" Hira asked.

"You can't very well go around looking like that much longer. Soon enough you'll have thrupenny bits. As it is, your face is already too pretty."

"Oh," Hira said, but it was clear she didn't have the foggiest idea what Alice was talking about.

"Thrupenny bits. Your breasts," she said.

Hira blushed deeply. "Oh. But can I still wear trousers?"

"No."

"I like wearing trousers."

"They're freeing, aren't they, but you can't wear them forever. I'll let it go a bit longer and then we'll see about some skirts and blouses."

"Thank you, madam. And thank you for the lesson."

Manners and perfect speech aside, Hira was fast on her feet and good with a knife. Most of all, she wanted to please Alice and that counted for a lot. It meant she'd follow instructions. It meant she'd be loyal when tough decisions had to be made, and that made a good hoister and a good Forty Elephant. Hira seemed to be sliding right into gangland, slick and smooth as butter.

Alice smiled approvingly at the girl. "You're a natural."

Hira smiled back.

Good girl, Alice thought. "Now, let's see about some lunch, shall we? I'm starving."

After the exertion with knife practice, Hira dug into her lunch with gusto. She knew her manners were starting to slide a little, and she didn't care. It made her happy to know she could take a large, lusty bite of a beef tongue sandwich without wiping her mouth between each mouthful. No one cared, least of all Alice, whose manners were dubious at best. As Hira watched the woman poke at the thick slice of meat between the slices of bread and lick her fingers with a smack of her lips, she grinned through her own mouthful.

"What are you smiling at?" Alice said.

Hira finished chewing and said, "The sandwich is good."

Alice arched an eyebrow but took another bite. When she'd nearly finished, she said, "So you're off to chase the lady copper? Have you any more information about her routines?"

Hira wiped her mouth with a serviette. "Mondays and Tuesdays she works at Selfridge's and Harrods. Fridays and Saturdays at Marshall & Snelgrove, but she's only at each for a few hours and then she's an orphan catcher. Sometimes she goes to one of the police stations, too, or to Scotland Yard. I haven't seen her the other days of the week yet."

Alice looked pensive as she wiped her mouth. "Brilliant. Now we know when to avoid certain stores."

"She wears regular clothes now when she's standing guard in the stores."

"Ah, yes. To work undercover," Alice replied, reaching for her glass. "Well, we know her face now, don't we? I want you to keep watching her for another few weeks."

Though it was boring, at least the task gave Hira something to do during the long, dull days. She didn't want to admit it, but she almost missed her lessons, and she definitely missed her piano. She didn't know if she really belonged with the Forty Elephants, or if she even liked Alice's praise. In fact, Hira was unsure of what she wanted. She'd never thought about what she wanted before, or who she was meant to be beyond a dutiful niece. For the first time, she turned the questions over in her mind. Would she remain a part of Alice's gang after the winter, or would she eventually leave, find a new place to live, and be a different kind of person? One who didn't steal or carry a knife to survive? She didn't have the slightest idea what that meant, living a different kind of life.

As they left the cafe and parted ways, Hira kicked a loose stone out of her path. It rolled ahead in the direction she gave it, with only the slightest push.

⇥ 18 ⇤

L ilian curled over her notebook, documenting details from last
night's patrol: every street and every neighborhood, every person
with whom she spoke. Fastidious, Inspector Lewis had once called
her, a word she rather liked. She was, in fact, very fastidious. She
insisted on unwrinkled clothing, neat hair, and clean nails and teeth.
She insisted on a tidy living space and, just as importantly, a tidy
notebook. Who knew when she might need her notes for an investigation, or perhaps as a reference for some future opportunity?

She'd begun recording her days seven years ago, during the two-
week training when she'd started at the Met, in a classroom at Beak
Street Section House. She'd also pored over the police manual and every
Act of Parliament that might require police attention, as well as every
rule for police behavior. She'd been just as fastidious while learning first
aid and a handful of drills. In short, she'd been an exemplary student.
That was likely why she'd once upon a time been promoted to inspector
with a squad of women working at her side. And she'd done her best to
uphold the most basic of maxims: prevent crime rather than seek ways
to punish.

Now she hoped her fastidiousness would pay off in a bigger way—
she hoped to bring in the ringleader of them all. She'd discovered more

about the Forty Elephants since her initial research, including a list of names and addresses of various girls picked up for shoplifting over the years. She still didn't know, however, where they met regularly, or if they did such a thing. They must. Every gang had a den.

Lilian wrapped up her thoughts and took the bus to Westminster. She walked the last few kilometers along the Victoria Embankment, and as the two redbrick buildings of New Scotland Yard came into view, she felt a surge of pride. Sometimes she still couldn't believe she worked here. The headquarters of the Met wasn't exactly an imposing sight, but it was hated more than nearly every other place in the country. The building and its surroundings—and nearby police stations—crawled with police officers and detectives, the offended and the offenders, barristers, and all manner of citizens in desperate need of aid. She loved it as much as others reviled it. It symbolized everything she believed in: service to others, strength, and above all, justice.

After she checked in with her supervisor, she spent the morning at Marshall & Snelgrove numbly watching shoppers come and go. She was biding her time. She'd known Alice's girl was following her, and that afternoon, Lilian would use it to her advantage. Perhaps the child would share some morsel of information. Anything that might be a reason to bring Alice Diamond in to the station.

When Lilian's shift ended, she pretended to head back to the station. Several times she caught sight of the girl's reflection in a shop window. The child was clever, but she was still only a child. In minutes, Lilian gave her the slip, only to catch up with her—unseen. This time, Lilian would do the spying. She followed her and the dog over Westminster Bridge through Lambeth until at last they arrived at a shuttered factory. When the child disappeared inside, Lilian waited several doors down across the street, crouched in the deep shadow between two shanties on the verge of collapse.

Moments later, women began to slowly filter inside the factory. When a sleek, dark Chrysler parked nearby, Lilian nearly stood and blew her cover. There she was. Diamond Annie.

Lilian's heart skipped a beat.

London's most notorious female criminal held a lot of power in the city, and the sight of her always sent Lilian's pulse into a frenzy. There was something special about Alice Diamond, beyond her height and strength, and steady-if-terrifying gaze. Something that couldn't be learned. A person was born with it or not, and Alice had enough of it for three people: charisma. That untouchable, intractable something that drew others to her everywhere she went. The head of every gang had it. Billy Kimber, Bert MacDonald, Darby Sabini. But Alice was something special, unique, and she knew it. Lilian knew it, too.

Alice emerged from the car, slamming the door behind her. She rushed toward the factory and disappeared inside.

Lilian shifted her weight but didn't move from her perch, watching as more women trickled inside the factory. And suddenly she realized what she was seeing: the meeting place of the Forty Elephants. She smiled as victory thrummed in her veins. Knowing where they met on a regular basis was the first step in tracking Alice Diamond's movements. And the first step toward booking her at Holloway Prison.

Lilian took out her notebook from her jacket pocket and scribbled down some notes, including the address and description of the old factory. For the first time, she felt like a real detective on the hunt to flush out a criminal. The only problem was, Alice Diamond wasn't easily caught. So far Lilian hadn't seen anything that signaled the woman should be arrested. Should she barge into their rendezvous, she'd have no valid reason to do so. Her nerves twitched as she watched, waited, wondering what would come next, what she should do next.

She didn't have to wait long.

Less than an hour later, the women began to leave, and soon Alice reappeared. Lilian held her breath as she watched her drive away. She couldn't go running after the car or blow her cover. Frustrated, she huffed. She'd have to come back, stake out the factory. For now, though, perhaps she could make contact with the child again.

As if summoned, the little girl exited through the factory door.

———

Hira joined the Forties in the back room for the meeting, careful to arrive early. It had been a long morning in the cold, waiting outside of Harrods. She knew the inspector's routine by now, but she didn't want to ask Alice for more work. Truthfully, she was afraid of what that might mean.

The factory office was scarcely warmer than outside, and she shivered as she listened to the order of business. Soon, she felt Alice's eyes rest upon her and then flick to Scully. They exchanged a meaningful look. Hira was beginning to realize that more passed between the women silently than what was ever spoken aloud. Perhaps it was a skill she should learn if she were to stay with the Forty Elephants.

"I have a job for you," Alice said.

Hira's belly dipped. She knew she'd have to participate in their plans eventually beyond chasing the lady detective, but she'd hoped it would be later. Much later. In truth, she'd hoped she'd be long gone, left the gang behind, before she was required to do more.

"Take this." Alice gave her a sealed envelope. "All you need to do is give the note to Bert McDonald. He'll be in the East End today at Cable Street. Meet him at the Tortoise and Hare Pub."

Hira suppressed a sigh of relief. Delivering a note wasn't too scary. "Yes, madam." She put the envelope inside her ever-present satchel.

"Don't read it."

"No, madam," she replied.

Alice grinned. "I'm still a madam, am I?"

She blushed but nodded. She could tell it pleased Alice to be treated like a lady, even if she poked fun at Hira's manners.

"Bert won't have anything for me, but I'll be seeing him later."

It dawned on Hira what was happening. This was a test. Perhaps just like spying on the inspector. This was the next step to becoming one of them. Alice wanted to see if she was trustworthy and if she could follow instructions. But it was more than a test, Hira realized. It was a warning of sorts, too. Alice might be kind to her by feeding her and lending her a bed at night, but the queen of thieves still expected complete obedience—and she expelled those who didn't serve their purpose to the Forties. Well, Hira was nothing if not obedient, and she'd prove it.

"If you get into trouble, use your razor," Alice said. "The way I showed you."

Hira gulped. She had planned to lose the knife. Drop it down a drain and let it be whisked out to the river, like any other lost treasure for which the mudlarkers hunted, eventually found embedded on the murky floor of the Thames.

"Yes, madam. I have it here with me." She tapped her bag at her side.

Alice nodded. "I'll meet you at two o'clock, next to Parson's. Got it?"

"Yes."

Alice's eyes were sharp but approving. "Good then. Off you go." She gave Hira train fare since the walk would be long, and she'd already walked half of London that day.

Hira accepted the money and left gladly. She didn't want to know more about the Forties' plan to hit three stores that day. She thought about Dorothy and the lady detective. The less Hira knew the better, at least for now.

She shepherded Biscuit along the street to the train station and on to Limehouse. The East End wasn't so different from Lambeth or the Borough with its run-down apartments, packs of roaming children, shops teeming with customers, and vendors promising hot chips or pasties. The further she walked, though, the more she realized she was wrong. The neighborhood began to change, and the people looked...more like her. Brown skin, dark hair and eyes, fine bones.

A strange feeling washed over her. Relief? Happiness? Confusion and discomfort? *Longing.* She paused outside of a restaurant named Patel's. After a moment, she pressed her face to the window and peered inside. Beyond the glass, a slip of purple silk embellished with gold thread hung on the wall between vivid portraits of men, women, and animals. Luxurious fabrics draped between the tables. At once, she perked up, recognizing similar drawings to those in the book Dorothy had given her. They were Hindu gods and goddesses.

The door was propped open, so she hovered on the doorstep, inhaling the scent of thick spices. Spices Hira had never smelled before. She wondered what they could be.

Biscuit seemed to like the smells, too, and in a flash, slipped past her inside.

"Biscuit! Biscuit, no!" she called after him.

He yapped to acknowledge her but continued to investigate, sniffing around the chair legs looking for scraps.

"Biscuit, come!" she scolded.

Any minute, someone would emerge from the back and tell her to take her dog and leave before they called the police. But Biscuit didn't come, and Hira found herself studying the cozy, beautiful restaurant.

It was modest from what she could tell from the very few she'd been allowed to enter. She counted six sets of tables and chairs. A curtain of beads separated the kitchen from the sitting area, and a large golden figurine sat on a shelf on the back wall.

"You have found Shiva," a woman wrapped in bright-green fabrics said as she pushed aside the curtain. Beads sparkled at her neck, her ears, and in her hair.

Hira stared at the woman's beautiful clothing, her dark hair pinned to her head, and the small red dot on her forehead. Would she be dressed as the woman was, had her mother come from India to fetch her? Would she know the spices in the air? The altar filled with brass figurines and flowers? She was certain she would have learned to weave as her mother had, and she would be accustomed to the vivid braid of colors; relish the scarlet, violet, and gold the likes of which she'd never seen in London until now.

The woman spoke again, but when she saw Hira's confusion, she paused. "Ahh, I see you do not speak Hindi. I was saying, we aren't yet open. Come back in one hour."

"Yes, madam. I wanted... I am leaving."

"Are your parents outside?" She looked past Hira to the window and the street beyond it.

"Yes," she lied. "She couldn't bear to tell the woman the truth. She couldn't say *they are dead* one more time."

The woman hesitated and then said, "Wait here one moment."

Hira watched her go, a cloud of lily-scented perfume whisking around her. Perhaps the woman could see through Hira's lie, that she didn't have parents waiting for her. Perhaps she would bring her husband to shoo Hira away.

Hira's heart skipped a beat in her chest, and she threw a glance at the front door. She should go.

As she began to inch toward the door, the woman returned. In her hand, she carried a small package of wax paper. "For you," she said. "It's just come off the skillet."

Relieved, Hira accepted the gift. "Thank you, madam."

"Now, I'm sure your parents are waiting for you. Run along."

"Yes, thank you. I just need my dog."

"Dog?" the woman asked, frowning.

"Biscuit!" she called.

The sound of his little feet and the click of his nails on wood grew closer as he ducked out from under a tablecloth and trotted to Hira's side.

The woman's smile tightened, but she waved Hira on as she closed the door softly behind her.

Hira stepped into the street and unwrapped the package to find two pieces of flat bread sprinkled with bright green herbs that glistened with some sort of oil or butter. The edges of the bread were crispy, and several large bubbles had formed in the dough. She'd never seen a bread like this. She poked her finger through one of the bubbles and took a bite, wondering what it was called. A waft of fresh yeast filled her nose. It was delicious. She gulped down most of the rest, giving the last of it to Biscuit.

After she slipped her hand inside her satchel and felt for Alice's note, a reminder of what she was doing here. An anchor to the world in which she now lived among the Forties: a life of knife fights and stolen silks and gin-soaked nights, at least on the part of the women who now ruled her life. It couldn't be more different from the life of the woman with the skin like her own, working at the restaurant with delicious odors and beautiful figurines, or from that of Dorothy, who worked for her earnings and lived with her mother.

A sensation stirred inside Hira that she couldn't place. She was no longer the little rich girl from Mayfair, not that she'd ever felt like one, but was she truly a street ruffian and thief, or did she belong in a different world entirely? The one thing she did know was that she wanted to return to the place of her birth, her mother's world and her father's adopted one. Someday. For now, she must simply survive.

She continued on her way toward the Tortoise and the Hare Pub. She was nearly there when she heard the sound of footsteps. She paused, her pulse thumping against her eardrum. She swiveled around quickly.

No one was there.

She began again, faster this time.

The sound of footsteps echoed her own. She turned swiftly, but once again, no one was there.

She was imaging things, surely. She scolded herself for being paranoid and started again, turning the corner onto the next street.

A person stepped out of the shadows, blocking her path.

———

"Don't run," Lilian said, throwing up her hands. "I'm not going to drag you off to the station. I simply want to ask you a question."

The little dog growled as if he were some sort of wolf breed rather than a pint-sized fleabag.

Lilian pulled out her truncheon, ready to whack the dog if necessary to keep him from biting her.

"Biscuit!" the girl hissed. "It's all right."

The dog recognized the panic in the girl's voice and stopped to look back at her.

"Come!" the girl called.

The little animal returned to her side and peered up at her. Whining, he wagged his tail.

"Good boy," she said, kneeling beside him a moment to soothe him.

Lilian immediately noticed the child's accent and paused. So she wasn't from the Borough or anywhere south of the Thames, that was for sure. After a moment's hesitation, Lilian said, "I wanted you to know that if you hear anything—anything that seems wrong or that makes you uncomfortable—you can come to me. At the police station or Scotland Yard, or at Marshall & Snelgrove if that's better. We both know you've been watching me, and you know where to find me."

The girl reddened but didn't reply.

"Your *cousin* is dangerous, and so are her friends," Lilian continued. "They may ask you to do things you don't want to do. Things that aren't legal. Do you understand?"

"Yes, madam."

"That's Inspector. Inspector Wyles."

"Yes, Inspector."

"Is there anything you want to tell me?"

Slowly, the girl shook her head. "No, Inspector."

Lilian knew the girl had plenty to share, but for now, she was keeping mum just as Alice wanted. But perhaps if Lilian offered her a deal, she'd be more willing to share in time. For now, Lilian would save that card until she needed it.

"You won't be in any trouble, should you decide you want to talk to me. Do you understand? Anything at all, about the gang, or Diamond Annie...or anything."

The girl's eyes widened a fraction, but she remained silent and with a lingering look, she inched away slowly at first and then broke into a run.

Lilian knew she must first present the offer and let the child go to build trust. *Next time, though,* she thought. She'd get something from the girl next time.

19

Alice glanced at the hexagon face of her Gruen wristlet. It was a beauty of a ladies' watch, designed in the art deco style with triangular panels crowned by a row of tiny diamonds, finished with a chain-link metal band that fit her perfectly. A job well done nicking that one, if she did say so herself. It was one of the only items she'd kept after hoisting it, but she didn't count the pawnshop owner as a threat. The greedy bastard would never rat her out. He was too busy scamming the unsuspecting. Besides, they had an agreement between them.

She frowned at the time. It was already ten o'clock and she hadn't given the girls their instructions. They'd need to get moving. They had shopping to do. She whistled to gain the Forties' attention.

"We're at Harrods today," she said. "Scully will choose the teams."

Scully was Alice's lieutenant, and not only was she obedient, she was also levelheaded and about the most loyal friend a woman could have. Alice knew she looked out for her at all times, and Alice returned the favor. Maggie was her other hand, but the woman's hellcat anger and heavy drinking were becoming more and more of a problem. As Alice glanced at Baby-Faced Maggie and her bloodshot eyes, she wondered how much longer she could count on her friend.

As Scully divided the girls into threes and fours, Alice laid out the plan. "Today we'll do the baby pram, the stones distraction, and the bag swap. I want the skunk stoles, sealskin jackets, suede coats...a tray of rings, too if we can manage." She grinned. "But as always, collect anything you lay your grubby hands on."

They would load into a series of taxis and ride to Harrods on Brompton Street near Hyde Park. Alice wanted to go unrecognized for this job, make off with her own stash of goods, so she left her car behind. Maggie, meanwhile, insisted on driving her shiny new Ford. She'd had it fitted with a periscope on the roof complete with a spyglass that dropped down into the driver's window. Alice had rolled her eyes the first time she'd seen it. She didn't know what her friend thought she'd do with the thing; the car wouldn't exactly go unnoticed. Since, the periscope had proved useful on multiple jobs for watching coppers from a distance. Alice had eaten crow on that one.

"Maggie, if you insist on bringing your car, don't drive like your knickers are on fire, 'ear me? We don't need to call attention to us."

"Me? Call attention to us?" She batted her eyelashes innocently while the others laughed.

Funny indeed.

As the taxis deposited them near the department store and Maggie parked the car, they moved into position to time their entrance. When June pushed the baby pram—fit with a baby doll in a blanket, the very top of its head the only thing showing—through the front door, they were off. Like a child's marbles, the teams scattered in different directions inside the store. Some orchestrated distractions with the shopgirls while the others slipped blouses into their knickers or jackets under their winter coats. The Forties were lithe and fluid, working in tandem like a school of eels slipping in and around the silt bottom of the river, too fast to catch. Alice was damned proud of her hoisters. They were the best London had to offer.

When a clerk stooped over the pram to coo at the sleeping baby, June explained the baby's sleeping habits, talked about pretty little gifts she'd received, and shared her hopes and dreams for her little darling. Worked like a charm every time. While June went on and on to the shopgirl like a leaky faucet, Alice slipped two silk negligees inside her handbag and moved on to the gloves. She plucked four pairs trimmed in fur made of kid leather from the display table and two pairs of satin evening gloves that would jazz up an evening frock. Certain no one had seen her, she pivoted swiftly and made her way to the front of the store where Marie browsed racks of blouses. The large handbag at her side was filled with a few innocent lipsticks, a hairbrush, and a compact mirror. An identical handbag to Alice's.

In a flash, they exchanged bags, and Marie turned toward the door.

Alice should have let Marie leave, get clear of the store as fast as she could with the loot, but she couldn't resist the opportunity to have a quick word while she was alone. Her friend had been too absent lately. This was the first job she'd pulled in a few weeks.

"Glad to see you're with us today," Alice said, voice low. "I'm going out with the girls tonight. Join us?" She wasn't going to say she missed having Marie around, but the truth was, she did. Marie wasn't just a top-of-the-line hoister, she'd been one of Alice's few real friends. At least she had been in the past. Things had changed of late. Redmond Sandys, Marie's cheating husband—who had shagged Bertha, one of their own, no less—had become more important than the Forties, and apparently more important than her livelihood.

Sherry walked by them, winnings stuffed inside her coat, and pushed through the front door as nonchalantly as if she were going for a stroll through the garden on a summer's day.

Alice watched her go. She'd nicked the tray of rings. Good on her. Alice would reward her handsomely for that score.

"I promised Redmond a nightcap tonight, when he's home tonight," Marie replied.

There was nothing Alice disliked more than a woman consistently choosing her man over her friends, especially when the man was a no-good tosser. Marie deserved better, but she'd already gone and stupidly committed herself. And now, Redmond was stirring up trouble with the gang. Something, or someone, would have to give.

"It's the man again, is it? Right. Better get lost then." Alice nodded slightly at the door.

Marie flushed and turned to go, scurrying out of the store as fast as she could without alerting the shopgirls.

Disappointed—and annoyed at the easy way Marie shirked her commitment to her friends and to the gang—Alice balled her hands into fists and watched her go. She'd do well to keep an eye on that one. She'd do well to get a handle on all of her girls.

⊨ 20 ⊨

After shopping at Harrods, Alice spent the rest of the afternoon at home. She liked to hide out after a job. Relax after the stress and excitement of robbing London's finest stores. Truthfully, though, she was waiting for Hira. The kid hadn't shown at the flat after allegedly delivering a note to Bert in the East End the day before. She worried that something had gone wrong, or maybe she'd been premature in trusting the kid. She'd find out one way or the other that night when she paid her brother a visit at the club. Bert and his boys of the Elephant and Castle would likely be nearby as well. She'd been stewing over how to bring in enough quid for Jimmy Church's down payment and hadn't yet had a spark of a real idea. She hoped Tommy might. On occasion, he could plot a brilliant scheme or two.

When evening arrived, she dressed for a night out in a gold beaded dress that shimmered to her calf. Nearly ready, she leaned closer to the mirror by the front door and dragged a tube of cherry-red lipstick across her lips. She fluffed her wavy bob for good measure and cocked her face sideways to peer at the diamond studs that winked in the light. Ready to hit the town.

As she pulled on her coat, the front door opened, and Hira knocked at the door and peeked inside, her eyes filled with fear, the lines of her face tight with caution. She was probably looking out for Alice's dad. Alice couldn't say she blamed the kid.

"So you're not dead after all," Alice said, straightening her slip beneath her frock. Hira's face registered alarm, and Alice laughed. "I'm only joking. Come in, shut the door."

"Where are you going?" Hira asked.

"Out."

"Can I come, too?"

She smirked. "The clubs are no place for a kid. Stay in my bedroom, and you'll be fine. Did you deliver the message?"

She nodded.

"Good girl. Where were you last night?"

"I was here, madam. Your mother let me in late, and I left before the sun came up."

Alice didn't ask Hira why, but she assumed it was to stay out of the way. She liked that about Hira. She could read cues.

"Alice?"

"What is it?"

"The lady detective saw me. She talked to me." A flash of guilt crossed her face.

Alice studied her expression. If there was one thing she knew how to do well, it was reading people, watching an emotion flicker in a person's eyes or pass over their features from the twitch of the lips to the crinkle of a brow or the tight lines around their mouth. An essential skill to manipulate a situation to go her way. "And? Out with it."

Hira looked down. "She said I could come to her if I ever wanted to tell her things about the gang. About you."

That wench was trying to get the kid to spill the beans. Alice would make sure that was never going to happen. Her tone shifted to ice, her eyes to daggers, and she leaned very close to Hira, until she was inches from her face. "My girls don't squeal. Is that clear?"

The brave little thing didn't even break eye contact. "Yes, madam."

She had to hand it to the kid. She was much tougher than she looked. And that was precisely why she belonged with the Forty Elephants. In time and with proper training, she might become one of their best.

"Good, then," Alice said. "I've left you some supper covered on the table. Wash your dish when you're finished and stay out of the way."

She reached for her mink stole and pinned a diamond pendant on the lapel of her coat shaped in the letter A that sparkled as brightly as her earrings. She only wore the pendant when she wanted to be recognized, or on party nights. And tonight definitely felt like a party night.

She and the girls started at a fine dining restaurant, had their fill of oysters and gin and tonic, and soon they were juiced enough to dance.

"Let's go to Kate's new one," Alice said, her eyes alight with mischief. Kate Meyrick owned several night clubs. She knew everyone, befriended anyone, was in good with the toffs, the starlets, and the gangsters alike. She'd served jail time for ignoring curfews and serving laws. She did her best to please her customers, and everyone wanted in at her clubs in Soho. As long as they paid the cover fee, they were golden, and she'd make them a new friend.

"We looking for anyone in particular?" Scully said, pushing up from the dining table.

"I need to have a word with Tommy."

"Your brother? He doesn't dance."

"Having one leg will do that to you."

Scully chuckled at Alice's joke.

Her brother poked fun at himself to make light of his accident, and she humored him in that way, too. Made his memories of the war a little easier to swallow, if there was such a thing. The Diamonds didn't believe there was any sense in dwelling on what was or could have been. Eyes forward and on to the next thing was Alice's life motto.

After Maggie dropped a wad of pound notes to pay for their dinner, they jumped into the roadster.

Alice took off at a screeching start.

"We're in for a ride, are we?" Maggie said, sitting back against her seat. "Nothing like a little gin to get the engine oiled."

"Hold on to your girdle!" Alice shouted over the engine.

She was feeling reckless, eager to blow off some steam after the week she'd had. Maybe she should be saving every penny for the building, but she worked too hard and risked too much not to have at least a little fun. She tore through the streets, narrowly missing a lamppost and racing over newspaper pages blowing across the road. Ahead, she took a corner without slowing—and missed the stack of crates on the side of the road. The nose of the car hit them with a crack. On impact, they catapulted into the air.

"Alice! Jesus Christ!" Scully shouted, wincing as one of the crates smacked the hood.

"Bloody hell," Alice said without stopping. "That will leave a mark."

Scully laughed. "I'll say, you maniac."

A black model Ford pulled out of a side street behind them.

"Shit! It's a copper," Scully shouted. Her makeup was smudged and her frock wrinkled. It had been a hell of a night already and they hadn't even made it to the dance floor.

Alice glanced over her shoulder and swore loudly. "Let's see if he can handle this!" She jerked the steering wheel wildly, taking an unexpected turn. She whooped with glee as they roared down the street, running over a curb.

If only it hadn't been a dead end.

"Shit, Alice!" Maggie said, laughing. "You've gone and made him mad, and now we're stuck here."

When the copper pulled up beside her, Alice cranked her window open but didn't bother to get out of the car.

"It's only Reggie," Scully said, sighing with relief.

Reggie Banks. Alice had grown up one block down from him. Sometimes he was in a charitable mood, and sometimes he liked to exercise his power. Depended on whether he had his knickers in a wad that day. She wondered which version she was going to get tonight.

"Hiya, Reggie," she said with a smile.

"Alice, what the hell do you think you're playing at? Running over crates, taking turns like you're on a racetrack. You're going to kill someone."

"Come on, Regs, we were just having a little fun. I'll slow down now, I promise," she said.

He ignored her lackluster attempt to appease him. "Where are you headed?"

"To the 43. To go dancing."

He looked at Scully and back at Alice. "You meeting anyone?"

She had to keep herself from rolling her eyes. He was fishing for information on gangland activity. Like she'd tell him a bloody thing.

"Hopefully a whole lot of people," she answered. When he frowned, she said, "No one, Reggie. It's just my friends here. We're going dancing for a while, ease some stress, and head home like good girls."

He snorted. "You haven't been good a day in your life."

She grinned. "That's not what David said."

David was a mutual friend of theirs from their neighborhood and a one-time lover of hers. That had been ages ago now.

Reggie laughed at her overt crudeness. "All right then. Run along, ladies but behave. And Alice?"

"Yeah?"

"Slow down, or you'll run over a granddad and end up in the nick."

"Yes, sir," she said with a mock salute.

He shook his head and walked back to his car. When he pulled out of view, Alice eased back onto the street, careful of the traffic.

"You got lucky," Scully said.

"Lucky is what we're going to be tonight," she said as they pulled up to the dance hall.

They laughed as they climbed out of the car.

Inside, the band had already begun to play, and people packed into every nook or would-be open space. The singer's voice was rich and sinuous, and the accompaniment of piano, horns, and saxophone had everyone hopping. A smoky haze drifted overhead, and a continuous stream of customers flowed from the bar on the back wall, carrying their coupe glasses, pints, or highballs of whiskey to a table that flanked the dance floor. Alice recognized lots of acquaintances, a few friends, and a couple of store managers she'd robbed last week. She smiled. The stupid nobs. Dancing shoulder to shoulder with the very people who set the dogs on her—only to fail—gave her a perverse sense of pleasure.

Across the dance floor, she caught sight of Lily Rose, the Bob-Haired Bandit. She was beautiful in a white silk dress with drop waist, feathers along the hem, and tiny straps that exposed much of her chest and shoulders. She hung on the arm of hoister and gangster Ruby Sparks, laughing and flirting as he leaned in her ear. Filling it with nonsense, no doubt. He was the wanker who encouraged their smash-and-grab style. At least he was with the Elephant and Castle men but seeing Lily Rose all over him was all the confirmation Alice needed to put her on grunt work. Nothing that required any confidence, or she might run entirely.

Alice continued her way around the edge of the dance floor to the bar. And there was her brother, lounging against the bar top.

He lifted his glass in a salute.

"Looks hot tonight," Alice said. "Everyone is here."

"What is it you couldn't wait to talk to me about?"

"I didn't want Dad to overhear us. I need some advice."

"Fair enough. What did you have in mind?"

She leaned to his ear. "I need a sizable payment for a building. And I need it fast."

He shrugged his thin shoulders. "You know Bert is your man, not me. Not for this."

She didn't want to bring Bert into things, but if he was the best option, she'd have to. She really wanted that building. And she needed to check in with Bert anyway about Hira. "Alright. Fine. Let's talk to Bert."

Tommy set his high ball on the bar. "Why don't we head to the back."

She threaded through the crowd behind her brother. She and Bert had had a fling a few years back. Hot, heavy, and brief. She didn't like being told what to do or to be followed. She also didn't like a man giving her girls direction. And that had been the end of that.

At the door, a large man dressed in a striped suit stood watch, but when he saw Tommy, he motioned them inside to a long corridor. Patrons could rent the rooms for private meetings, gambling, or other business. For the right price. They passed several small parties that were smoking and laughing among themselves. After a sharp turn, they entered a room that smelled of lavender cologne and cigar smoke. Alice recognized every face in the room.

"Alice," Bert MacDonald said. "What are you doing here? I thought we were meeting tomorrow."

"Don't worry, I'm not here to see you."

His mustache twitched into a smile. "That's too bad."

"For you, maybe," she said, eliciting laughter from several of the men.

"She's here for advice," Tommy said, pouring them both a finger of fine whiskey from the decanter in the middle of the table.

She accepted the glass and leaned to her left as one of the men lit her cigarette.

"What kind of advice are you looking for?" Bert asked.

She hesitated. Though she didn't want the head of the Elephant and Castle in her knickers, she knew her brother was right. Bert would know what to do. It was what made him the big man in charge. "I'm looking at a headquarters for my girls. A place we can meet without intrusions that doesn't smell like a dead animal. Make it a boarding-house of sorts, too."

Bert cocked an eyebrow at her. "That's ambitious."

"I've never been accused of being lazy."

"Or ugly for that matter." He winked.

"Gee, thanks." She puffed on her cigarette and blew the smoke at his face. A murky cloud surrounded him an instant before dissipating. He didn't need to flirt with her. His charms had stopped working on her ages ago.

He chuckled at her sarcasm. "How do you plan to go about this?"

"I could save enough cash over a year, but I need it fast. The build-ing I want is going on the market formally after Christmas."

"Doesn't leave you much time," Bert said, lighting a cigar. The flame glowed hot orange for an instant as he drew air through its tobacco filters. "Do you need muscle to pressure the owner?"

"Not this time." She didn't want to rely on them for help; noth-ing was for free, and she'd be beholden to him and to the gang. She wasn't interested in owing anyone a favor, not when it came to her headquarters. It was too important. Besides, every time Bert's henchmen got involved in one of her jobs, they cocked it up from start to finish. They overcomplicated things and left a big mess behind. Her jobs were clean, precise, and involved as little bloodletting as possible.

"She's all grown up, gents," Bert said, eliciting a laugh from the three others in the room.

"Fuck you, Bert." She turned to go. She wasn't in the mood to be patronized. All she'd wanted was a little advice from her brother and a few good hours of dancing. With Ruth's crisis and Marie's disappearing act, Lily Rose and her smart mouth, and the pressure to bring in enough money for her building, she'd been on edge and needed a real good time tonight. Not this, not him.

"Come on, don't be a hothead," Tommy said, placing a hand on her shoulder. "See what he has to say."

"You need to think bigger," Bert replied before she could leave. "Hitting a couple of stores isn't going to bring in enough. Where do all of those frocks come from, and the furs?"

Despite her irritation, she felt a smile grow on her face.

Warehouses. That was where.

Bert nodded, dragged on his cigar. "From the look on your face, you see what I'm getting at."

She could stage a multistore *and* warehouse hit. She'd have to make arrangements to dump the goods carefully, but there'd be at least enough for a down payment, even before all the frocks were sold. It was near Christmastime, too. The warehouse stock would be at an all-time high.

She nodded. "I do."

"You're welcome," Bert said, propping his wingtip-clad feet on a chair opposite him. "How are you going to repay me?"

"I'll let you continue to see Lottie," she said, making for the door.

He laughed again. Alice knew he was shagging Lottie, and though she thought Lottie could do better—take up with a man who didn't have a revolving retinue of women—she wouldn't tell her what to do. It was Lottie's choice and Alice wasn't her mother. "Oh, and did you receive a note? From the Indian girl. Hira."

He nodded. "She looked like she was about to piss herself, but she gave it to me."

"Good." Alice closed the door behind her on the way out. Hira had passed two of the tests: tracking the copper and delivering the blank note. Three, really, if Alice counted the kid coming clean about the copper approaching her. As she'd thought, Hira was a natural, and she liked the runt a little too much.

When Alice returned to the main floor of the club, Scully was in the middle of a Charleston with a partner. Alice, on the other hand, wanted a good think and another martini. She'd use the best team for the warehouse hit. They'd need a means to load up the merchandise, the right fence to distribute the goods. As the gin soaked in and the hour slipped by, the crowd grew louder, the dance floor more packed. When one of her favorite songs began, she decided it was time and headed to the edge of the dance floor. As she assessed her dwindling choice of dance partners, a familiar face came into focus. Was that...?

Simon McGill met her eye from across the room.

In moments, he was at her side, a smile as wide as the English Channel on his face. His sandy hair was shaggy, his shirt was unbuttoned at the neck, and his sleeves were rolled to his forearms. His jacket had been tossed over the back of a chair somewhere, and he smelled faintly of beef stew and stale beer. He must have come from work.

"Well, if it isn't Diamond Annie." He smiled broadly, showing his slightly crooked front tooth.

"Alice," she said through a big stupid grin on her own face. Why was she smiling at him like that? Seeing him had surprised her—and apparently had made her happier than she could have expected.

"Yes, I know." He winked. "Care to dance, Alice?"

"I do care to dance." She hiccupped and her hand flew to her mouth.

He laughed. "Had a few, I see."

"Many."

"Well then, best dance it off." He led her to the floor, sliding easily into the popular swing dance. He moved expertly, smoothly.

She wondered when he'd learned to dance that way, but then again, if he frequented a place like the 43 Club, it shouldn't come as a surprise. She moved with him and around him, laughing, perspiration dampening the back of her luxurious gold-beaded frock. As more people joined the crush on the dance floor, their bodies collided clumsily, but each time they laughed.

"Do you come here often?" she shouted.

"Only when I'm looking for someone. Usually I'm working late."

"Oh? And who were you looking for?"

"You," he said.

Stupidly, she felt herself blush with pleasure. What had gotten into her? She liked toying with a handsome man from time to time, but they didn't usually win her over easily. "You don't pull any punches, do you?" she asked.

"Only on special occasions." He grinned and spun her round and round until she dizzied. "Has anyone told you that you're beautiful?"

"Most people tell me I'm scary."

He threw back his head and laughed. The sound was delicious. "You don't scare me."

"Maybe you don't know me well enough."

"Maybe I should get to know you well enough." He planted a kiss on her cheek and hovered there, an inch from her face. His breath smelled faintly of gin, and she wanted those lips on hers for real this time.

"Would you, now?" she breathed.

He leaned into her neck, inhaled her perfume, then planted a kiss on her jawline. "I would," he murmured.

She sucked in a breath. Maybe she would let him in, just a little. She missed having a man in her bed, and what harm was there in keeping him around a while to amuse her?

When he dipped in a second time to kiss her chin, she tilted her face. Her lips met his.

He smiled against her mouth and then kissed her, sweetly but firmly.

Christ, he made her squidgy inside.

"Let's get out of here, yeah? To my place," he said.

"I can't stay," she warned.

"You can come and go as you please, my diamond."

At that, she smiled. Suddenly it was the best night she'd had in a long time. "Yes, I can."

21

The first night Alice spent with Simon—and the next five—had gone well. So well in fact that she'd had trouble tearing herself away from his bed. He was attentive, funny, and a damn good lover. And then there was last night. She'd given in and stayed over, and sometime in the middle of the night she'd regretted it as she knew she would. She'd awakened covered in sweat and shot out of bed after a nightmare that had haunted her for years. It was less a nightmare and more a replaying of the past, of the time she'd been at Nelson Square in Southwark with her brother not long after he'd come back from war. There was a crackle in the air then, as the men had returned home. All that anger and sorrow fused together like a wick on a stick of dynamite, poised to catch, burn, and explode.

A member of the Sabini gang had come home from the war touched in the head, shifty-eyed and unsettled after being a rifleman. He'd made a comment or other to Alice and she'd mouthed off. She'd stopped taking lip from men since the war. The Sabini man hadn't liked a woman in a position of power, or any position save on her back. He'd beaten her up pretty good for it, and Tommy had nearly killed the man in response, as if he'd channeled every ounce of fury and regret and fear into his fists that had nowhere to go without a battlefield.

He'd made London his battlefield—they all had. He'd been only eighteen years old, too. In that moment she'd understood how much he'd changed. How much had been lost on the battlefields in France. And she'd lost something, too. Another layer of youth and innocence, of trust. Men always tried to control her. This was what she had learned time and again, and they were never worth the pain.

"Shh, it's all right, darlin, it's all right," Simon had said. He'd smoothed back her hair. "It's just a nightmare."

She shook for some time, trying to dispel the memory, trying to get ahold of her emotions again. She might be a hoister, dole out a punishment or defend herself and her girls when needed, but she was no murderer. Tommy had come so close that night. And the wanker who had beaten her could have killed her, too. She'd been a mess of bruises for weeks.

Simon brought her water and rubbed her back until she fell asleep, and she'd let him. He was a good man, too good. Too straight. She knew the rules—had made them herself—and yet, she found herself agreeing to his every invitation and had met him most nights after he closed the pub. A dangerous gamble, but one she was willing to make. She'd just have to keep things quiet. She didn't tolerate her girls seeing anyone outside of their tightly knit circle, and she couldn't do it either. At least not long-term, she told herself. For now, she'd definitely see him again.

She knew the nightmare meant something more. It was a sign of her anxiety. She'd been tossing around the idea of the warehouse hit, and though it was a good one, if she were busted, she'd go right back to prison. She'd seen enough of the inside of a courthouse and Holloway Prison to last a lifetime already, and if she had one more slipup, she'd go away for a good long while. And what that would do to her gang... Well, this job would have to be pristine. No mistakes, no rock left unturned.

Alice drove to the fourth and final warehouse after a long day of scouting. Sutton's Textiles was the largest of the four; the main building processed raw cotton, silk, wool, and the new artificial manufactured ready-to-wear dresses in a range of fabrics from silk to wool to jersey, and their latest addition, an artificial silk that had recently become popular. The adjacent buildings were for assembling and finishing the garments. It was a gold mine. The problem was, J. R. Sutton was known to be a cranky—and cautious—businessman. According to Alice's sources, he paid a policeman to scout the premises and the rest of the block after hours. Only, her source didn't know precisely which days or what time the security's shift started. Apparently it rotated, on purpose. She'd have to watch the place while she looked into how much the copper was paid. Should things not go her way that night, well, she'd have cash on hand just in case.

She parked the car a safe distance from the factory. Within the hour, women streamed through the doors and rushed away from the building, doubtlessly eager to go home. Their faces were drawn, and beneath their dowdy, shabby overcoats, their shoulders curved forward in defeat. She felt for the poor wretches. They must have a beastly supervisor to look the way they did. Too bad they didn't have enough sense to find another way to pay the bills. If they worked for Alice, they wouldn't be blistered and bent and underpaid. Her shopping schemes might be dangerous, but they were also thrilling, and the payoff worth it. She always took care of her own. That was precisely why she was here. To make sure her girls were safe and looked after—and that they were never tempted to stray.

She waited, watching, until at last the interior lights went out and two bright lights shone on the front of the building. She'd avoid the front entrance anyway. She held her breath as the supervisors left and the boss's car drove away. She didn't know when the copper would show, but she needed to get a good look at the padlock on the back door before he did.

She bided her time for another hour, and at last, decided to take her chances. She slipped from her car and darted across the street. In moments, she'd circled around to the back of the warehouse. When she reached the rear entrance, it was as she expected. The door was secured with a standard iron padlock linked with iron chains. In other words, her wire cutters could snap it with relative ease. She'd send in one of her girls to take care of it.

The sound of approaching footsteps sent a bolt of fear through her.

She scanned the area around her frantically, searching for a place to hide. Several large waste bins formed a line on her right, and behind them, a fence separated the factory from a series of other buildings. As fast as she could, she tiptoed to the bins.

Moments later, a copper appeared around the edge of the building. He beamed a torch at the back door.

Alice's heart pounded in her ears. She watched him, praying he was sloppy, wouldn't think or care enough to comb the entire back lot and, with it, her hiding place.

The copper jiggled the padlock and the door handle. Didn't budge. Seemingly satisfied, he pivoted and scanned the back lot, swinging his torch this way and that, directing the ray of light at various dark corners. His expression was marked by boredom.

Alice held her breath as the light swept over the bins.

The copper squinted in the dark. A moment later, he turned and sauntered away.

She exhaled. He hadn't seen her. The only tricky part was knowing how long to wait him out. In the meantime, she checked her wristlet. Nine o'clock. She needed a pint and some kidney pie in a bad way, and she wasn't about to hang around the waste bins all night. She padded as quietly as possible across the back lot to the edge of the building and peeked around the corner.

The copper was halfway down the block. He must do circles, or perhaps he checked in now and again when he felt like it. She suspected Sutton wouldn't like that much. And she'd need to appoint someone to stake out the place for a few days, see if she could determine the copper's pattern.

When he turned the corner, she darted back to her car and headed home.

———

Alice didn't really want to go home, but she thought she'd look in on the kid. She hadn't seen much of Hira the last several days, and though she wasn't the kid's nanny, she did feel as though she were her guardian in some way.

"I'm off for the night to do some planning, but you stay here," she said to Hira, who sat on her bed. "I've left a meat pie for you. Eat up and I'll see you in the morning. Dad is out tonight with Mum, so it'll be quiet here for a few hours. Read your books. I'll see you in the morning."

"Can I help you? With the plans," Hira pleaded. "I could write them down for you. Read the notes at the meeting so you don't forget anything."

Alice stared at her. The kid had a point. It would be helpful to have her plans organized. She could scarcely read, and the same went for writing. Hira could act as her secretary at the meeting, should she need her. Alice shook her head. She didn't want a written record of her plans, something easy for the police to find. Unless...she could always destroy the notes after she announced to the girls who was doing what. Might be good to organize her thoughts, especially since there were multiple hits, multiple roles to dole out, and a lot was at stake. Her girls' protection, their new safe house, and most of all, Alice's continued freedom.

As she studied Hira's hopeful face, she realized just how lonely the girl was. Hira needed friends her age, but that wasn't something Alice could provide her with. The last thing she needed was more brats hanging around while she was trying to conduct business.

"Fine," Alice said at last. "You can help me on two conditions."

Hira smiled brightly. "Anything!"

"We destroy the notes immediately after the meeting, and you'll return here on your own tonight."

"Yes, madam," she agreed eagerly.

They walked to McGill's Pub and found an empty, secluded table in the back. Alice ordered a lemonade for the kid and a gin martini for herself and settled in for what would be a long night. She dictated her plans for the big heist to Hira and ordered them read back to her. She spent some time dividing the Forties into teams, moving names around until at last, she felt the women were matched well to their tasks. With a few more notes on location details and timing, she was satisfied with the operation.

Alice would tackle the dress warehouse with Maggie and June, perhaps Marie. See if she'd prove her dedication to the team.

Hira looked up from her paper. "And what will I do?"

"You'll come to the warehouse with me. Be our lookout."

Hira smiled and bounced in her seat, making Alice laugh in spite of herself.

"Busy, I see," Simon said, placing a plate of bangers and mash in front of each of them. "Been a long night. You need your strength."

"How did you know?" Alice asked, reaching for a fork. "I'm starved."

He tapped a finger to his forehead. "I have a mind for these things. And who might you be, miss?"

"My name's Hira, sir."

"Nice to meet you, Hira. Is Alice your friend?"

Alice felt the girl's eyes upon her but didn't look up from her plate. She wasn't the girl's friend. She was her mentor, and she hoped Hira didn't confuse the two.

"I think so," she said shyly.

"I didn't know she had any young friends like yourself."

"When are you finished here?" Alice interrupted, concerned by the hope in Hira's voice.

"I'll close the place in an hour. Are we meeting after?" His eyes drifted to where Hira bent over the notebook. She was drawing a picture of an elephant.

"Would I be here otherwise?"

He grinned. "Right then. I was hoping you'd say that." He winked.

"I'll just bring her home. Meet you at yours."

She walked Hira to the flat and hopped into her car to drive to Simon's. She'd scarcely made it through the front door when they pounced on each other like hungry tigers. He pulled her dress over her head, tugged at her corset, pausing to caress her until she moaned with pleasure. Moments later they were in his bed, laughing, kissing, satisfying each other's needs. The man could shag better than anyone else she'd ever been with, but his passion was tempered with a sweetness that frightened her. She must be careful around this one. He would want more from her eventually, and she had a sneaking suspicion that she'd want it, too.

An hour later, he brushed hair from her eyes and stared at her deeply, until something warm rushed through her.

"I've been thinking about you a lot, did you know," he said, his Irish burr soft in her ear.

"Have you," she replied, breaking their gaze. When he looked at her that way, she felt naked in a way she never had before. Like he saw the little girl that had been softhearted once upon a time. She'd long since abandoned that girl, sealed over the cracks in her heart and dipped it in iron. Yet, somehow Simon had begun to chip away at her shell.

"I have." He brushed his lips over hers. "I think you deserve a nice night on the town, or perhaps we go to the races before they close for the season? We've spent so much time together after hours, locked away in the bedroom." He grinned his perfect crooked smile. "Not that I'm complaining, mind you. You have a way of keeping a lad in raptures, Miss Diamond."

She laughed and swatted his shoulder playfully. "I'd love to go to the races."

He smiled and slid from bed, pulled on his trousers. "Tea? I could use a cuppa."

"Make it strong," she said, throwing back the covers.

As she pulled on her stockings, she thought of the look in his eyes as he took her in his arms, the earnest emotion in his voice. This was all moving so fast—and it was dangerous. She needed to end it, she knew, but as he returned with a tea tray, bare-chested, his sandy hair mussed, and a smile on his adorable face, she knew she wasn't quite ready to say goodbye.

22

Lilian angled her body away from people rushing through the hallways of the police headquarters. They were all men, some of whom still stared at her as if she were a circus animal even after seven years on the force. Others gave her openly hostile glares or insulted her. Much as she liked being a part of Scotland Yard and the Metropolitan Police, she didn't particularly enjoy the persisting derision. She couldn't avoid it that day; she'd been told to meet with the chief. He'd said there was an important case to which he wanted to assign her. She couldn't imagine what it was, but she was breathless with excitement at the thought. Anything was better than staring vacantly at shoppers.

She rapped decisively on his office door.

"Come in!" the chief barked.

"You wanted to see me, sir," she said, stepping inside.

Chief Inspector Wensley perched behind a table, a cigarette dangling from his lip, a steaming cup of tea at his left. Across from him, a well-groomed man with a bright-blue cravat and a head of curly hair carefully combed out of his eyes, sat in one of the guest seats. They both stood in greeting as was polite in feminine company—which irked Lilian entirely.

"There's no need to stand," she said, tone curt. "I am an inspector here, first and foremost. A woman second."

The chief harrumphed and plopped back into his chair. But to her annoyance, the other man, tall and lean, nodded and sat only when she did.

"Sir, what's this about?" she asked.

"This is John Lee," the chief began, "a barrister from Kensington. I'll let him tell you the rest."

"Hallo, Miss Wyles," he said.

"Inspector Wyles," she corrected him.

"I beg your pardon, Inspector." He opened his dossier, riffling through documents until he came upon the one he sought and slid it across the table in front of her. "I am representing my client, Captain Wickham. He was a foot soldier in the army."

"Was?" she asked, noticing the barrister's use of the past tense.

"Yes. I'm afraid he perished recently of cholera. Both he and his wife leave behind one child, a daughter by the name of Hira Wickham. She was entrusted to the care of Captain Wickham's brother, Clyde Wickham, who also happens to be one of the biggest criminal lawyers in the city of London."

"So she is cared for at least."

"One would assume, but that doesn't appear to be the case. She is missing, you see."

Lilian looked from the barrister to the chief and back again. "Do you suspect some foul play?"

"Yes, though not what you think," he began. "I am...a personal friend of the family. Of Captain Wickham specifically. We grew up together, but rather than attend Eton as his parents wished, he joined the militia to serve king and country. He was a bit of a rebel, you see. As for his elder brother, Clyde, I know the man, and forgive me for being direct, but his wealth does not make up for his lack of character. As children and young men, we all spent time together but lately...well,

I can't say I've heard a kind word from him or about him. I'm not sure why he has changed, but changed he has."

"He doesn't sound like a model parent, but I assume the girl has no other family," Lilian said. "Perhaps she is with a neighbor or a friend."

Lee shook his head. "If that were only the case."

"I think you'd better get to the point, Lee," the chief said.

The barrister waved his hand over his head in an absentminded gesture. "Right, yes, of course. The girl's father has left behind an inheritance. Captain Wickham's parents were wealthy, you see, and he and his brother, Clyde, split their estate when their father died several years ago. The money, the country home in Richmond, and what little the captain was able to save have been bequeathed to Hira. I've also been forwarded a few personal effects from him and Hira's mother."

"Here's the sticky part," he continued. "Clyde Wickham insists the child ran away a couple of weeks ago, after he informed her of her parents' passing. Naturally she would be upset, impulsive perhaps, but I've discovered something else."

The chief stubbed out his cigarette. "This is why barristers are richer than God. They can tell a story longer than Dickens and charge by the hour. Get to it, man."

Lilian would have laughed, if she hadn't already begun imagining the litany of terrible fates that could have befallen the girl. She'd seen the "cafés" in the East End that sold their girls to customers multiple times per night, and dozens of times over the course of the week. These girls were gaunt, hungry, twisted with disease, and burdened by too much knowledge of what a man desired from them in spite of their preposterously young age. These establishments, this existence, was far worse than the typical prostitute who haunted the pub doorways. It made Lilian ill and eager to help young girls find a better way. She glanced at the chief, suddenly struck with just how much she longed to do that sort of work, to help women and girls. She'd taken statements from some young women over the last few years, but she was consistently pulled to do other work less appealing. Perhaps after she landed a big win, she might talk to the chief about that very thing.

"What have you found?" She squinted, peering at the barrister who, like most in his profession, was unusually calm even under scrutiny. She supposed his sort was used to it.

"Papers for her transfer."

"What sort of transfer?"

"To a rural school in Northumberland," the barrister said. "It's one of the poorer, harsher boarding schools and is primarily reserved for the destitute or for orphans."

Lilian frowned. "The uncle was going to send her there? It sounds like he's wanting to banish the child."

Lee nodded. "It seems he was waiting for the opportunity to send the girl away. When Clyde's brother grew ill, he made arrangements to have her registered."

"But isn't he the child's legal guardian?"

"That's what has brought me to you today," Lee said. "Technically he would be her guardian, and especially since he has more or less raised her. Should she be found, she'd be returned to him. That said, Captain Wickham contacted me weeks before his death. Apparently, he had received a distressed message from the housekeeper, Mrs. Jane Culpepper, about how unkind Clyde was to the child, so Hira's father was in the process of changing custody rights when he died."

"Who is the child to go to?"

"That's what so terribly unfortunate," the barrister said. "His instructions were lost." He leaned forward. "Or they were destroyed. Unfortunately there is no aunt or grandparents, no cousins to speak of at least in London. Perhaps she has living relatives in India, which does us little good here. As of now, Hira truly has no one else. I honestly can't think who Captain Wickham was thinking of, and believe me, I've done my research there."

This Uncle Clyde sounded heartless. To send the girl away, or worse. The idea that one would abandon a child, leave them to their own devices in the streets, was unthinkable, and yet Lilian saw it every day. In fact, she'd become quite good at flushing out poor children's hiding places.

Her thoughts reeled to a halt.

Relatives in India? Lilian knew an Indian child on the streets. Could Hira Wickham be the girl living with Diamond Annie? She'd gone into the Indian restaurant in the East End, too...plus her accent. It had to be her!

Lilian sat taller in her chair, her attention sharper. She weighed whether she should tell them she'd seen Hira with Diamond Annie. Lilian didn't want the chief to put others on the case—other men—lest they manage to arrest Diamond Annie instead of her. This was Lilian's job, her case. The type of case that could change everything for her and for the female police squadron. If she could track Diamond Annie a bit longer, until she made a wrong move...

At least for a little while, the child would have to stay with the queen of thieves.

Appalled by her own selfish thinking, Lilian cleared her throat and said, "If Hira is alive and living on the streets, I'll find her."

"Seems absurd, but most children on the streets have living relatives," the chief said. "Their parents can't feed them or force them to work, and they run away."

"Yes, well, you see, if we don't find Hira Wickham, Clyde knows very well what he may do—sign for her property. If, however, she is returned home, he will likely send her to Northumberland and—here's the worst of it—I've been given a tip that there may be bribery at play with a magistrate that owes Clyde a favor. In other words, the paperwork could be "lost" if necessary, or potentially forged. Therefore, Clyde could still collect what is rightfully hers. He possesses the original deed to the Richmond house, you see. I'm sure Captain Wickham gave it to him for safekeeping while he was away."

"Have you spoken to Clyde about the inheritance?" the chief asked.

Mr. Lee shook his head. "No. I merely suggested there was a package of personal effects delivered from Surat. I thought it best to keep my cards close to my chest."

"And he has those effects now?" Lilian asked.

"No. I told him I would forward them on after Christmas, should the child not turn up."

"And does he know you have come to the police?" Lilian asked.

Mr. Lee shook his head again. "If he knew we were trying to intervene, I fear he might attempt to speed up the process of taking over Hira's inheritance. He has a reputation, you see. And I don't believe he is an honest man." He folded his hands in his lap and sighed heavily. "I'm sorry to say I have no record of the conversation I had with Captain Wickham, due to the captain's insistence on absolute secrecy. The housekeeper also refuses to speak up against her boss. Furthermore, Clyde Wickham stands everything to gain by losing the girl. He has no interest in finding her, or in bringing her home. This was clear when I spoke to him."

Lilian made eye contact with the chief. His lips stretched into a tight smile.

"You would like for me to find her, I presume," Lilian said.

"You have the best record with orphans to date," the Chief Inspector Wensley said. "For some reason, they come easily to you. That womanly presence I'm sure."

She reddened. Womanly presence? Why must he make that sound like an insult? Perhaps, instead, she was successful because she was good at her job, not because she was a woman. Surely lost children would come just as easily to male officers, should they be kind and cunning instead of brutes who forced a situation when it could be managed with care. She was too annoyed to be grateful for a compliment mixed with an insult.

"Mr. Lee, I am good at my job," Lilian replied at last. "If Hira Wickham is to be found, I'll bring her in. You can be certain of that. Once we have her in custody, perhaps then we can decide what's next. In the meantime, if you could find out anything more about this magistrate and his relationship with Clyde, that would be helpful, should we need to make a case against him."

"I am already in the process of it, Inspector."

"Good. If you'll indulge me with just one last question, Mr. Lee," Lilian said.

"Certainly."

"What do you stand to gain in this?" Lilian was no fool. She knew that most people, especially lawyers, didn't do things out of the kindness of their hearts.

John Lee looked taken aback. "It's my job, Inspector."

"And?"

"As I mentioned before, Captain Wickham—Henry—was a close friend. The closest, in fact. I've known him since we were boys, and we helped each other out of more than a few scrapes over the years. The least I could do is honor his memory by looking after his only child in any capacity I can."

She believed him, felt the sincerity in his words and in his manner. "And what of Clyde? If you knew Henry, I assume you also know Clyde well."

"To some degree, though I tried to steer clear of him. He was exacting, very intelligent but sharp with others, even as a young man. It's a wonder to me the brothers are related. They are nothing alike. Were, I suppose I should say."

She nodded. "Can you tell me what Hira looks like, or provide a photograph or a sketch? It would be useful."

The barrister opened his dossier and slid a photograph of the girl across the table.

Lilian smacked the desk with her hand. She was right! Hira was the girl she'd been chasing. Hira was older now, thinner—too thin, in fact—but it was definitely her. The dark eyes and hair, the pert nose. Her expression was different, however. She looked prim and unhappy. When Lilian had crossed paths with Hira, she hadn't been happy exactly, but she'd seemed lighter, freer than how this photograph portrayed her. Lilian studied Hira's uncle, his hand on the girl's shoulder. He was portly and stern.

Perhaps the child was simply running for a chance at life. Too bad she'd likely had no idea what street life was like. It was a wonder she'd survived this long.

"I know her," Lilian said carefully. "I've seen her, chased her even, but she got away."

Mr. Lee perked up. "You've seen her? Please do whatever it takes. My friend's child doesn't deserve such a fate."

"Maybe we should put some others on the case with you—" the chief began.

"That won't be necessary. I know precisely what to do, sir." For the first time in days, Lilian smiled.

23

The teakettle screamed, splitting the silence—and Dorothy's head that already throbbed from last night's multiple rounds of gin and tonic. She'd had far too much booze with Allen. They'd had another fantastic dinner, this time in the East End not terribly far from her flat, at a restaurant owned by an Indian family. She'd never had Indian food before, and she thought it strange at first with names she couldn't pronounce. After several mouthfuls of fragrant basmati rice and lentils and vegetables with a yellow curry sauce, she was hooked. She'd had curry at pubs before, but they tasted nothing like what she'd eaten at Patel's Palace. While there, she couldn't help but think of Hira Wickham. She'd wondered if the girl ate such dishes at home before she'd fled.

After the meal, Allen had taken Dorothy to a hotel room where they could spend time together in private. He was about the most eager lover she'd ever been with, if a little hurried. He'd left soon after to meet his flatmate for some errand or other.

"My flatmate is…a bit of a wanker, really," Allen had said. "A ladies' man, in truth. Every woman I've introduced him to falls for his looks and charm." He'd looked at her with pleading eyes. "I don't want him coming after my girl."

She'd warmed instantly to the new label. "Am I your girl?" she'd asked, straightening his collar.

"I should say so," he'd said with faux indignation.

She'd kissed him passionately until they were both out of breath.

"I suppose that means you will?"

She'd laughed.

He'd also pointed out that they'd just begun dating, and he didn't want to rush things and ruin them. She'd agreed that was best. This was too good, this thing growing between them.

She blushed again, just thinking about it. She didn't want to rush Allen, but they'd already gone to bed many times. What more was there to rush? She dropped two sugar cubes in her mug of tea, stirred the dark brew, and added milk until it was the color of salted caramel. Milky and sweet, what other way was there to drink tea? As she sipped the hot brew, she dreamed of what Allen's home looked like in Mayfair. She pictured a doorman and a vestibule with brass and marble and crystal that gleamed in the soft glow of candlelight. Fresh flowers on every surface. A sweep of plush Turkish rugs scattered throughout the flat, and gauzy curtains that fluttered when a breeze blew through the open window. And the master bedroom—fluffy duvet and bed skirts in navy with blue-and-white-striped pillows, a mahogany dresser, and the faint scent of sandalwood and spice in the air. She'd make the room more feminine in time, but equally as beautiful as the image in her mind.

"What are you smiling at?" her mum said, breaking the spell.

"Oh, nothing."

"It's another man, isn't it?" Her mum moved around the kitchen with ease. "You aren't getting mixed up with another hooligan, are you?"

Dorothy set down her steaming tea. "Not this time. He's rich, Mum. And handsome."

Her mum rolled her eyes. "That's what you always say."

"No it isn't," she said indignantly. Really, had she called Bobby rich and handsome? He'd been attractive, other than the chipped tooth and heavy pomade he always wore in his hair, but he'd turned out to be a swindler. And Eddy Smythe before him was certainly handsome, but he'd called her dumb almost every day, and then he'd kissed her once-upon-a-time friend Josie. Dorothy hadn't spoken to either of them since.

"How do you know he's rich, eh?" her mum pressed.

Dorothy watched her slather butter and Marmite on her bread, the knife scraping against the crisped edges of the toast. "He owns Marshall & Snelgrove for one thing. He's taken me to dinner several times and to a movie, and never asked me to pay for a thing." That was another of Eddy Smythe's problems. He'd never had enough money on him for various reasons, and Dorothy had paid for most of their dates. Allen was a gentleman. She only wished he would update his wardrobe. One would think that owning a store touting the latest fashions meant that he'd keep to the new trends: three-piece suits, pinstripes, derbies and fedoras rather than top hats, and the occasional herringbone or tweed jacket. Instead, Allen wore dark, plain suits and electro hats, and he wouldn't dream of wearing a pattern or bold colors.

Her mother raised one penciled eyebrow. She'd attempted to fill in her rapidly thinning brows with kohl, a color far too dark for her graying red hair and pale complexion. She looked like a clown. Dorothy wouldn't say anything though, because her mum had made it clear in the past that she didn't want advice on that front. She'd have to go on looking silly.

"Don't do anything foolish," her mum scolded. "Like going to bed with him. He'll have had his way with you and leave you behind, just like the others."

"I broke up with the others," Dorothy pointed out. Well, she had stopped seeing them. Perhaps it had been more of a mutual thing in the end.

"I'm running late. I have to get to work." Mum left her half-eaten toast, pulled on her overcoat, and left without even wrapping her scarf around her neck.

Lydia McBride worked as a secretary for a barrister in Covent Garden. She'd had the good fortune of learning to read and write as a child alongside her brothers. It meant she'd always been able to provide for Dorothy, and a good thing, too. Dorothy's scoundrel of a father had left them to fend for themselves when she was but five years old. Dorothy hadn't seen him since. Luckily, between her mum's wages and her own, they were able to afford a modest living in an apartment that was mostly warm enough in winter with only one window that leaked. They'd always had a stocked pantry and a gorgeous secondhand radio. Dorothy could also occasionally buy nice fabric, beads, ribbons, and feathers to bring her sketches to life. One day, she hoped she could sell them.

She dressed for the day, tucked two scones and two ham sandwiches into her bag—one of each for her, and the other for Hira—and headed to work. Dorothy knew she didn't have to help the child, but there was something about her. Something that reminded Dorothy of her little sister, Katie. Her mood dampened at the thought of her sister. No matter how many years it had been, she'd never forget her favorite person in the world, gone too soon from an infection of the throat at only age nine. They'd been inseparable, she and Katie. There wasn't much Dorothy wouldn't give to have her back. It would be a whole new world, facing life with her sister at her side.

She pushed aside the morose thoughts and continued through her neighborhood, noticing truly, for the first time, the many Indian immigrants and British Indians that lived near her. It was as if meeting Hira had opened her eyes to possibilities, to similarities rather than differences that had been engrained in her as a girl. She paused outside of a bookshop. Perhaps she would pick up a book for Hira. Since Dorothy's meal at Patel's Palace, she couldn't stop thinking about her, and how sad it must be to have never known her mother. Dorothy might not like her mum sometimes, but she knew her mum loved her and always made sure she was looked after. And for some reason, Dorothy felt compelled to look after Hira in any capacity that she could. She was, after all, a poor orphan on the street, but also a brave, wise little girl, and Dorothy liked the reminder of her sister.

As Dorothy opened the door to the bookshop, a bell above the door tinkled. Inside, a waft of dust and parchment swirled around her.

"Can I help you, miss?" An older gentleman walked toward her with a cane. His silver hair stretched from one ear to the other in a band around the back of his head, his brown skin sagged on his cheeks, but his smile was bright.

"Do you have any books with pictures? For a young girl."

"In Hindi or in English?"

"English? Well, both? Either!" She laughed nervously. She wasn't sure what Hira would prefer.

"This way." He led her past a towering bookshelf and through a doorway into another room. Books packed the small space from ceiling to floor. "Start here, in this section."

"Thank you," Dorothy said and began sifting through a cart on wheels filled with children's books. Smiling, she chose one with brightly painted illustrations. Hira seemed clever for her age, but what child could resist beautiful pictures?

She paid for her purchase and took the bus to Marshall & Snelgrove. Inside, she stowed her things in the staff room and waited for the meeting scheduled that morning before the store opened.

"Ladies, have a seat," Allen said as he strode into the room. He tucked a match inside the bowl of a pipe, puffed a few times, and the tobacco caught, sending ribbons of fragrant smoke into the air. When everyone appeared to be settled, he said, "We have some new apparel in, from America. I know we tend to purchase inventory made in England and France, but it was time to freshen up the stock. I'd like to feature the new designs in a showcase."

Dorothy noticed the immediate excitement in the room. Her co-workers chattered excitedly, like a bevy of birds in a garden on a warm spring morning. A showcase might mean attention in the newspapers and perhaps bring new customers to the store.

Dorothy was suddenly struck with an idea, one that might make the showcase even more successful. Maybe Mr. Harrington would host a party of sorts, or perhaps the increase in sales might even mean a raise.

"Sir?" she said, interrupting the excitement. "I wondered if I might say something."

"Of course, Miss McBride." His smile was perfunctory, his tone distant and polite, and though she knew he mustn't show her preference at work, she felt a stab of disappointment.

She brushed a loose tendril of hair from her cheek and sat taller. "Perhaps you could make the showcase an exclusive event," she began. "Limit the number of people who are allowed to view the new items?"

"Last time I checked, limiting the number of customers amounts to less money," Mildred said, her voice dripping with sarcasm. "What would be the point in that? Really, Dorothy, you have the stupidest ideas." She made eye contact with a couple of the other employees and rolled her eyes.

A few of the women snickered.

Dorothy ignored the sting of embarrassment. "The idea is that it will be like our oxfords, the new ones the Hollywood starlets wear? We only have a certain number of pairs so they sell quickly. If we limited who could attend the 'special showcase,' everyone would want to attend. People would talk. Every woman in Mayfair will want to be on the list. We could do refreshments, too, perhaps, and dim the lighting. Make it a real soiree."

"That's an intriguing idea, Miss McBride, but I have an idea in mind already," Allen replied. "It's good to see you're always thinking, though."

"Of course, Mr. Harrington." She blushed deeply, looking away. He didn't ask for her ideas, and why would he? She was making a fool of herself in front of him, and that was the last thing she wanted to do. What she wanted was for him to think her the most alluring woman he'd ever met, to fall in love with her.

Mildred and Marcy smiled at her discomfort, the hags, but Dorothy pretended not to notice.

Allen explained that the event would take place in December during the holiday rush to drum up excitement. They had a month to plan it all. When the meeting concluded, Dorothy beat the others to the door. She hadn't gotten far when she felt a hand on her arm. As she turned, she met the wolfish expression of Ugly Mildred.

"You should just do your job and shut up, or you're going to be sacked," Mildred sneered.

Hot emotion pushed up Dorothy's throat. Why must this woman always be horrible to her? "At least people like me," she snapped. "That makes me a better employee than you."

Mildred flushed red. "At least I'm not stupid!"

"Could have fooled me," Dorothy said. And with that, she headed to her station by the door. She held her head high, but she was trying not to cry. Maybe she *was* dumber than the others, but they didn't have to point it out all the time...or maybe they were jealous of her. And they simply couldn't stand the idea of a woman being pretty *and* smart. She blew out a frustrated breath. She didn't understand why she had to bear the brunt of everyone else's insecurities. She had to work as hard as they did, and frankly, they had more friends than her, too. That was the sad price she paid for her gifts.

The rest of the morning, Dorothy greeted patrons with a smile and helped them with various items in the store. After lunch, the postman arrived, whistling the tune of "Yes, Sir, That's My Baby" one of Gene Austin's hits. Dorothy had never seen this postman before, and he seemed far more cheerful than their last. Perhaps old Mr. Pritchard had retired at last. He'd hobbled between the shops in Mayfair, looking as if the weight of his letter bag might make him topple over at any moment. Or—she gasped—perhaps the old man had died.

"You're new," Dorothy said in greeting. "I hope Mr. Pritchard is well? Poor thing is having trouble getting from here to there these days."

"He's fine," the man said. "He moved in with his daughter and her husband in the country."

"Oh," she put her hand to her chest, "that's a relief. I was worried something had happened to him."

"I'm Dennis," the postman said, tipping his hat. "Dennis Sloane."

"How do you do, Mr. Sloane," Dorothy said, tossing her red waves over her shoulder. Her hair had been in the way all morning, and she wished she'd pinned it up instead.

He smiled. "I'm doing well, thank you. Beautiful day, isn't it?"

"I suppose so," she said, trying to be polite. She looked past him at the gathering clouds, crowding out every thread of sunshine. Really, must it always be overcast in the autumn? She sighed.

"Have you worked here long, miss?" the postman asked.

She glanced at his entirely too eager expression. He had brown eyes that shone with good humor, brown hair of a nondescript variety, and a small dark mole planted above his lips on the right side of his mouth.

A large smile split his face. He was pleasant enough she supposed, also younger than her—and standing far too close to her.

"Mr. Sloane, as you can see, we're busy today and I need to get back to work."

He glanced around at the meager customers idling over a pair of gloves or a gauzy hair scarf, and his eyebrows lifted in surprise. "If you say so, miss—?"

She knew he was asking her for her name, but she ignored him.

She was happy to see Hira bounding into the shop in her tattered trousers and derby hat. The child desperately needed new clothes, but her timing was impeccable. Now Dorothy could brush off Dennis Sloane.

"Good morning, Miss Dorothy," she said, her breath ragged, but still ever polite. She looked as if she'd just fled something or rather someone. Biscuit barked his hello, too.

"Ah, Dorothy, it is," Dennis said, grinning. "Well, then, I can see you have a visitor. I'll leave you to it. Until tomorrow." He lifted his hat, walked swiftly to the door.

Dorothy smarted at the way he'd snatched up her name like a gift. He seemed like those irritating types that fawned over her and bored her to death. No, thank you. Besides, she had Allen now.

"I think he likes you," Hira said, missing nothing. She was smart, this little squirt, and she'd one day be quite beautiful if she wore proper clothes and took care of her skin. Perhaps Dorothy could bring her some face cream and teach her how to run a brush through her hair. One hundred strokes each day to make it shiny, the way she used to brush her sister's. Dorothy imagined Hira's hair loose, falling nearly to her waist, a luxurious curtain of mahogany brown. It really was sad she didn't have a mother to look after her or, at the very least, a big sister.

Dorothy nodded. "I think you're right, but I don't like him."

"Why? He was nice. He smiled at you," Hira pointed out in her innocent way.

"He only wants to kiss me, Hira. And I don't want to kiss him. I have a boyfriend already."

Hira blushed. "You have a boyfriend?"

"Yes, and he wouldn't like it if I flirted with the new postman."

Confusion filled the girl's eyes. "Were you flirting?"

"No, but Dennis was. Now," Dorothy said, changing the subject, "enough about that. I've got something for you."

Hira's face lit up, and Dorothy smiled, glad to make her happy. "Come with me." She led her to the back room and produced the food wrapped in wax paper and the book she'd bought on her way to work.

"Thank you," Hira said, holding it as carefully as a treasure. "I do love to read."

"I remember," Dorothy said. "I found this in the bookshop in the East End. The owner helped me find it."

Hira gasped as she flipped open the cover to find a book filled with colorful illustrations; women or men with many arms, each of their hands holding swords or pearls or instruments. And then she saw an image she clearly recognized. "This is Ganesha."

"I thought you might like a book about India," Dorothy said shyly. "Well, I suppose it isn't about India exactly, but there are stories about the gods, and the pictures are beautiful." While the girl stood speechless, Dorothy rushed to add, "Or perhaps you have something like it already?"

Hira hugged the book to her chest. "No. It's perfect. Thank you. I–I..." She stopped, too emotional to speak.

Warmth coursed through Dorothy's limbs. She'd thought Hira might like the book, but she hadn't realized how much it would mean to her. She gently placed a hand on the girl's shoulder. "You'll have to read it and tell me all about it when you're finished. I don't know anything about India."

Hira nodded vigorously in agreement. "I will! Can I come back next week?"

Dorothy smiled. "Come anytime."

Hira smiled and her pretty face lit up, overshadowing the grime from going too long without a bath. "Thank you, Miss Dorothy."

"You should be going before they toss you out of the store."

"Yes, miss." With a small wave, she placed the book in her satchel and let the heavy front door close behind her.

Dorothy watched her go, noticing Hira join a figure standing in the window. Wasn't that...? The brown hair and wide-set eyes, the towering height. It was exactly who Dorothy thought it was, and Hira was talking to her!

Dorothy felt a shiver of fear.

Diamond Annie, in all her glamorous and dark, dangerous glory was Hira's friend and had watched their entire exchange.

⇉ 24 ⇇

Alice watched Hira accept a gift from the shopgirl and stepped back from the window, surprised at what she'd seen. How had the kid made a friend with the perky redhead who worked at one of the best department stores in the city? Alice wondered what else the little imp was up to when she wasn't around. She looked from Hira to the redhead. Perhaps this budding relationship would prove useful in the future.

A few minutes later, Hira struggled with the heavy door and joined Alice on the pavement outside.

"Who is that woman you were talking to?" Alice asked without bothering to greet her.

"Miss Dorothy," Hira replied. "She's my friend."

"How did you meet her?"

The girl hesitated a moment and then said, "I was running from the police. When I hid inside the store, Miss Dorothy gave me biscuits and chicken."

"What for?" she asked, amused. It seemed everyone was willing to hide the kid from the police.

Hira shrugged. "I was hungry, and she was nice to me. Now I visit her once a week."

"She gave you a book."

"Yes." Hira's hand went to her satchel where the book was stowed.

This Dorothy seemed kind—and a perfect way in. Alice filed the information away to examine a bit more closely later. For now, she needed to pay a visit to Ruth. Ruth hadn't shown up to a meeting in over a week, and after seeing her so busted up, shiners and all, Alice thought she'd better look in on her. She wanted to pay that cad Mike a visit, too. Make sure he knew he wasn't only messing with Ruth, but with one of Alice Diamond's girls, and that brought consequences.

"Where are we going?" Hira asked.

The kid was starting to smell bad. She'd need a bath again soon. Frankly, the mutt could use a bath as well. Alice didn't know how Hira could sleep with him and his filthy, greasy fur. In all, having a kid around was a bit of a nuisance. But when Hira curled up with her teddy at night, Alice was reminded just how young—and obedient—the girl was. She was a good kid but still needed someone to look out for her. And though she was learning the ways of London street life, she hadn't hardened around the edges yet. She seemed the tender-hearted sort. It would take some time for her to grow some calluses. At least she'd proved to be useful, and she never asked too many questions. When she did speak, somehow she always managed to make Alice think.

"To see about Ruth first," Alice said. "After that, to meet with the Forties. I have a big announcement."

"Is Ruth all right?" Hira asked.

"That's what we're going to find out."

Her mind raced with every terrible possibility as she steered them toward Larcom Street and parked the car near Mike's flat. Something was dodgy for sure. Ruth had been absent for over a week, and she wasn't one to shirk her responsibilities.

"Let's go," Alice said, slamming the car door.

Hira scurried after her as she bounded up the steps.

She knocked three times and waited...and waited. With a sinking feeling, she pounded on the door a fourth time.

"Ruth!" she shouted. "Open this door! It's Alice! Open up!"

At last, the door opened a crack.

Ruth stood in the doorway, her face a mass of peeling skin. An angry red patch spanned the middle of her cheek and looked raw and sore to the touch.

"Alice," Ruth said, her hand flying to her face.

"Yes, it's me," she replied, pushing past her inside. "Where in pigging hell have you been? And what's happened to your face!"

"I've been here, recovering," she replied meekly. Her shoulders were curved inward, as if she scarcely had the strength to hold her spine straight and her head up.

"What did you do wrong this time? Look at him funny?"

"He said I flirted with his friend, Steve. Of course I denied it—I don't even like Steve. He's mean as a snake and twice as ugly. Steve denied it, too, but that only seemed to set Mike off."

Alice seethed. "How did he do it? Your skin looks like it's been melted off."

"The range."

Alice's eyes bugged in their sockets. "He burned your face with the cooktop?"

Ruth shrugged and then relayed what happened. The son of a bitch had burned her, put first her hand directly over the gas burner and then had shoved her face close enough to make it bubble and blister on her left cheek. Where her shiner had been on her right eye, the black and purple had faded to a sickly green and yellow. She looked a fright, like she'd just returned home from the front, for Christ's sake.

"That was why I haven't been to the meetings. Everything hurt too much."

Alice choked on the rage that surged up her throat. She wanted to kill the bastard—and she wanted to shake Ruth for staying with someone who demeaned her, battered and bruised her, and made her small—so small that she was becoming someone Alice didn't recognize. Soon, Ruth would disappear completely.

"But he apologized, and he really means it this time, Alice," Ruth rushed to add. "He's brought me flowers every day the last week."

Now that Ruth mentioned the flowers, Alice was struck with the sweet odor that infused the air. Roses, lilies, and carnations were stuffed in every available vase, water glass, and food tin. She wondered where Mike had found the money to pay for them. He was low on the list with the Elephant and Castle gang, and the downturn in the economy meant jobs weren't easy to find.

"He scarred your face! Bloody flowers don't make up for it. Jesus Christ, next time he might kill you."

Ruth shrank away from Alice, withdrawing into the shell she'd created.

"Pack your things," Alice demanded. "Come home with me for a while."

Ruth shook her head. "I don't want to get in the way."

"You ain't in the way, for Christ's sake!"

Ruth didn't reply and peered down at her hands. "Not everyone is as strong as you, Alice. Mike says he loves how feminine and soft I am."

Alice went nearly blind with rage at Ruth's obtuseness. It wasn't Ruth's femininity the tyrant loved. It was her weakness. Her inability to stand up for herself. He was the variety of man that hated women, feared them and wanted to control them because it gave him someone to hate more than himself. But Alice knew she couldn't convince Ruth of this. The only thing she could do was encourage her to join the Forties at their future home. Let it be her place of refuge. There, they would have safety and strength in numbers. They could prevent Mike from ever touching Ruth again.

"Listen, I have a plan," Alice said. "I'm going to buy a building for us. Mike won't be able to hurt you there. We'll have some of the Elephants watching over the place when need be, too."

Ruth was slow to reply. When at last, she spoke, she couldn't meet Alice's eye. "That's a good plan. But I love him."

"I love Biscuit and I could never hurt him." Hira's childish voice came clear as a bell.

Alice had forgotten Hira was there. The girl held her dog close, watching the entire scene. And once again, she was struck by Hira's wise words. *I love Biscuit and I could never hurt him.* All those years their dad had beaten them up and raised them to be hardened thieves like him, he'd only kept them around to help pay the lease. He despised them. Mike despised Ruth. Both men despised themselves. They were disappointed in their lot, devastated by circumstance and rotten choices, and they wanted everyone else to pay for it. This was why Alice would never have a man in her life, not permanently. She didn't need to be held responsible for every lousy, stupid thing they'd ever done, or for their low of opinion of themselves.

She squeezed Ruth's shoulder. "Hira is right. You don't need a man who doesn't love you. You'll see. I'll help you see."

———

Alice couldn't put Ruth out of her mind. Her ruined face, watching her cower away from Alice, sealed Alice's determination to see her plan through. She'd get her building and then she'd take a bloody tire iron to Mike's fancy car to remind him that the Forties weren't a bunch of helpless women. That included Ruth.

Alice led Hira and the mutt toward the car and rode to the factory. Inside, she took her place at the head of the table and waited for the others. She always arrived early. That was expected of the queen, or maybe she expected it of herself. The queen wasn't late or sloppy or forgetful. The queen anticipated what was next and planned for potential problems so they could be avoided or, at the very least, handled. She made a damn fine queen, even if she was still younger than more than half the women there.

As the girls filed in, the room grew noisier with conversation and laughter. When it looked like most had arrived, she did a head count.

"Where's Marie?" she asked.

"Haven't seen her," Scully replied.

"Marie?" Lottie said. "She's probably with her husband."

"Redmond Sandys?" Alice asked.

"That's the one."

Alice watched Bertie's expression fall. Bertie was shagging Redmond, despite the fact that he was Marie's husband. Seemed he'd had the two women going at once for a while. Either way, Alice didn't like it. Redmond wasn't part of their extended "family," and he was coming between two of her girls. Given the amount of infighting the wanker had started, she'd assumed he was a real catch, but he wasn't even a looker. She didn't understand what all the fuss was about, but one thing was for sure, if things didn't clear up soon between the three of them, she'd step in and make a decision for them both. Besides, Redmond was straight—law-abiding, which simply wasn't their way of things—and straight had a way of bringing the police to their door.

"I'll look in on Marie later," Alice said.

The girls murmured among themselves, and soon, the room dissolved into side conversations.

"Oy!" Alice shouted to gain everyone's attention. The murmuring in the room died down. "I've been doing some scouting and I've come to some decisions."

"Scouting for what?" someone piped up.

"That's what I'm about to tell you," Alice snapped. "Don't interrupt."

The woman reddened, and Alice began again.

"I'd say it's time we had a real meeting place. One that doesn't smell like dead animals and piss, or leave us freezing because of broken windows. I'd like to buy us a proper place," Alice went on. "A refuge. Somewhere we could live, away from our families if we like. At the very least, it could be a place to meet without being disturbed, and if one of us needed a place to bunk, you could." Her eyes rested on Hira a moment.

"I'd love to get away from my family," someone said, causing a ripple of laughter.

"Think of it as a shelter. As a home base," Alice continued. "It's time we left this shit factory and had a real place of our own."

"Have something in mind?" Lottie said.

"I'm looking at a place near the Katharine Buildings. Jimmy Church owns it, but he's willing to sell it to us before it goes to market after Christmas. Once he puts it up for sale, he's going to double the asking price, so we need to move fast."

"You think anyone will buy it right now?" Scully asked. "Seems to me no one has that kind of cash."

"Rubbish. Plenty of people have cash—the right kinds of people."

"Not the likes of us," June said.

"We're going to change that," Alice cut in. "Here's the plan. We'll hit three stores in different boroughs on the same day. Use it as a distraction to keep the coppers busy. That same night, we'll pull a much bigger job. A warehouse. A small team will join me to clear out all of the stock."

The girls exchanged uneasy glances.

She ignored their concern. "It's a lot to coordinate I know, but I'll work it out. I'm going to finish mapping out the details in the next few days. And we'll pull the trigger in two weeks. That's a tight turnaround, but I know we can handle it. Clear your schedules for December ninth."

"Will we be able to unload all of the goods at once?" Bertha asked, lighting a cigarette.

"We'll be working with more than one fence," Alice replied.

"What if we get nicked?" Marie piped up.

"The warehouse would mean real time," June said. "And I can't go back to Holloway now. Ralph barely affords the rent as is. He's always losing our money at the races."

Though Alice secretly shared the same fear, she couldn't show it. What they needed from her was a leader, one who wasn't afraid to take risks for the good of them all. They needed someone who took charge and made things happen.

"In the meantime," Alice continued, "we need to expand our profits in creative ways and start saving. We'll have to pay the rest of the balance in the spring." A murmur rippled through the room as they debated her idea, and she grew impatient. She was setting this up for all of them. They would all win in a big way. Why were they poking holes in the plan?

She raised her voice to silence them. "We'll start by working from the inside. Lottie, Carla, and June, you'll apply for jobs at a shop. We'll discuss which ones," Alice said. "You'll learn the floor layout and the inventory. What's coming and going, who's coming and going. It'll make it easier to pull off a big job that way."

"Why can't someone else do it?" Lottie whined.

"Because you know how to keep your mouth shut, and besides, you're pretty." A smile appeared on Lottie's lips. Alice knew she always liked a compliment.

"But what does being pretty have to do with it?"

"It'll be easy to get hired."

Lottie shrugged. "All right then."

"We'll start there," Alice said. "See how things go. All of the extra profits will be put into a bigger pot to benefit all of us. We won't be dividing up the spoils."

"How do we know you aren't skimming off the top?" Lily Rose piped up. Her eyes, the tilt of her chin, were challenging.

The others glanced at each other, back to Lily Rose and then at Alice.

Anger flickered in Alice's belly as she glared at the goddamn Bob-Haired Bandit, but she remained cool. "I should think by now you know I have the gang's best interests in mind."

"If you say so," Lily Rose said, and a hush fell over the room.

Alice locked eyes with her, her gaze hard as iron. She might have to teach Lily Rose a lesson, if she didn't watch herself. "I say so, and that should be enough."

Suddenly Biscuit growled at some unseen animal on the other side of the office door. Hira jumped to her feet and let him out, and as he charged after an alley cat with matted fur that had found its way inside, a few of the girls laughed, breaking the tension.

Alice didn't laugh, and neither did her gaze wander from Lily Rose, who had already dismissed their confrontation and was looking into her hand mirror while applying more lipstick. This one just earned herself a demotion, Alice thought. The Queen of the Forty Elephants wouldn't take lip from anyone. Besides, she didn't have time for petty disagreements. She had much more important things to do—to pull off a score the likes of which they'd never seen. And if she failed, they all failed. The Forty Elephants would lose most of all.

⊨ 25 ⊨

Dorothy fished her sketch pad and lead pencils out of the drawer and sat at the kitchen table. With relish, she pored over her latest drawing. It was a flapper gown with a drop waist, sewn with a waterfall of gold and silver beads. Simple and beautiful, and definitely in fashion. When she'd finished, she flipped back to the more original idea she'd started the week before. Fitted bodice to the waist, with an iris-colored skirt that puffed out over bouncy crinoline that fell to the knee. Tiny vines dotted with flowers scrolled over the fabric. She turned the sketch pad this way and that, admiring the sketch from different angles.

"Let's have a look." Her mum padded into the kitchen in her bathrobe and looked over Dorothy's shoulder. "That's a pretty one."

"You think so?"

"It's a bit short, but you should show these to your boss. Maybe he'd give you a raise."

"He wouldn't give me a raise just for showing him my drawings."

"Worth a try, isn't it?"

Dorothy pondered her mum's idea. It was only worth a try if he didn't laugh at her and once again tell her she was out of her depth. Much as she was growing to care for Allen, she hadn't forgotten the slight.

Her mum put on the teakettle. "Better get on with the day. It'll be a busy one." She put a hand to her back, twisted a few times to work out the soreness in her muscles from sleeping.

Dorothy packed up her things and headed to work. As the train rattled over the tracks toward Mayfair, she thought about her drawings and what Mum had said. Would Allen like to see her dresses? She didn't want him to think her silly, or the drawings a woman's way to pass the time like sewing and gossip and tea parties.

At work, she'd scarcely entered the shop when Allen summoned her to the shoe section. He was talking animatedly to a woman she didn't recognize.

"Miss McBride," he said, "I'd like you to meet Miss Charlotte Taylor. You'll be training her."

"Me, Mr. Harrington?" Dorothy replied.

Charlotte had large, round brown eyes, a pert nose, and a light dusting of freckles across her cheeks. She was pretty, if a little elfin. Dorothy imagined her in a dress made of light-pink silk fitted with gossamer wings at her back.

Allen nodded. "You know the floor quite well at this point, and I think you're more than capable."

More than capable. She warmed to the praise, however slight. Allen depended on her. "I'm happy to help." She beamed at him, trying to catch his eye to exchange a private smile, but he was all business and distance and never once looked at her directly.

"Very good. Now, Miss Taylor, if you have any questions, direct them to Dorothy, or of course you may seek me out as well."

Charlotte fluttered her thick eyelashes at him. "Thank you, Mr. Harrington. I'm so lucky to have such a kind boss."

Dorothy felt a prickle of irritation. Was Charlotte flirting with him? Allen smiled pleasantly and headed back to his office.

"How hard can it be, pushing beautiful things on rich women?" Charlotte said. "The dimwits."

She laughed roughly and Dorothy stared at her. Charlotte was pretty and had dainty features, but the second Allen left and she opened her mouth, the illusion was shattered. Something about her didn't sit well with Dorothy. She had the distinct impression that she'd better keep an eye on Charlotte Taylor.

Suddenly Dorothy wondered if she, too, changed in Allen's presence. Did she put on an act to please "the boss"? Maybe a little, but she wasn't trying to please him, not really. She was trying to do a good job because she liked her work—because she had dreams.

"I'll show you around the store first," she said. Even if the new girl didn't take her job seriously, she would show Allen that she did, and that he'd chosen the right person to train his new employee.

She led Charlotte from shoes to jewelry counter, to women's hosiery and undergarments, and back to the main floor where their ready-to-wear section had been artfully arranged to show off the best of their collection. After she'd completed the tour, she ushered Charlotte to the entrance to greet customers. Given the way Charlotte had spoken of their customers, Dorothy thought it best to teach her a few manners about greetings and give the woman lots of practice.

Dorothy motioned to the policewoman beside the front window display. "The lady detective will arrive soon, and between the two of you, you'll watch out for thieves. Inspector Wyles is her name."

"Right, I'll be sure to keep an eye out," Charlotte said with a smile and a salute.

Satisfied, Dorothy headed back to her post, willing the hours to speed by. She could hardly wait for her date with Allen later that evening.

Dorothy fluffed the ends of her hair. Allen had met at her flat this time, which she found curious. His place must be much nicer and have more space given where he lived. But she knew he didn't care for his flatmate, and recently he'd mentioned moving out, buying a place of his own. She'd tried to hold her excitement in check. If Allen had his own place, they could spend more time together—and perhaps he was considering their future. In fact, she was dying to ask him the question that had preyed on her mind for days: did he love her? He acted as if he did and now with the talk of finding his own home...She grinned at her reflection in the mirror.

Leaning toward the glass, she checked her teeth a last time, running her tongue over their smooth, slick edges. Satisfied with her appearance, she joined Allen in the sitting room. Thankfully, her mum was out with a couple of friends at the pub, so the apartment was empty.

"Come here," Allen patted the sofa cushion next to him.

She scooted closer, enveloping them both in a cloud of lilac perfume.

"You wore the Debonair," Allen said, smelling the scented air approvingly.

She blushed. "For you."

He had gifted her the perfume on their third date. She'd been so happy, she'd nearly cried. No man had given her anything so expensive before. It could only mean one thing: he was well and truly smitten with her. The thought made her heart dance in her chest. She was smitten with him, too. In fact, she was pretty sure she was falling in love.

Allen tucked his hand beneath her chin and kissed her possessively until passion rose between them. When they gasped for air, he leaned his forehead against hers and said, "You're something else, Dorothy."

"What do you mean?" she asked coyly, hoping he'd elaborate.

"You're one of the best salesgirls I've ever had, for starters."

She cocked her head to the side, taken aback by the path the conversation had taken. His best salesgirls? That was what he liked about her? She sat back a little, pushing deeper into the sofa cushion to lean away from him. "Well…I suppose that's a good thing."

"Very good," he said, placing his hand on her knee. "In fact, I have something I'd like to give you."

She perked up. Another gift? Her hope jumped ahead to what came next. A necklace? A ring? She bit her bottom lip. "Oh?" she said. "You're so sweet, Allen."

He took her hand in his and placed a metal object in her palm. She closed her fingers around it, feeling its edges. It was a… What was it? She opened her hand and peered down at the heavy object.

"A key?" she asked, doing a poor job of keeping the disappointment from her voice. "To what?"

"The storage room," he said.

"The storage room? At your house?" she asked, hopeful once more. She clutched it to her bosom. "I'd love to have the key to your flat."

Confusion settled on his features, and he frowned. "To my flat? No, the key is to the storage room at the store. I've ordered some new expensive items that need to be kept under lock and key until we put them out on the showroom floor. As they sell, you can restock the inventory."

"Oh," she said, her gaze dropping to the key once more. It really did have to do with the store. All of it, his trust in her and the key. It wasn't a gift for her after all, but a gift to him—some way he could delegate responsibility to someone else. It was a good thing, she tried to tell herself. It just wasn't what she'd had in mind. At all.

He cupped her face in his hand and pulled her chin toward him until they were only inches apart. "Darling, I'm giving you this key because you're an excellent worker and because I trust you above everyone else. If you are looking for meaning in that, well, it's there, dear girl. I couldn't do this without you." He read her expression. "And I wouldn't want to," he added hastily. "You're my best girl."

She warmed to the earnest tone in his voice, his soft expression. "All right then, I'll take the key," she said at last.

"I was hoping you'd say that." He pulled her toward him, and as they kissed, his arm snaked around her lower back. In moments, he'd slipped her beneath him on the sofa cushions, removed his trousers and pushed up her skirt around her waist. "Dorothy, beautiful, beautiful Dorothy," he breathed in her ear.

She relished the feel of him on top of her, gave in to him, his needs and desires. They were her desires, too, as he moaned against her mouth. He was so good to her; he took her to nice places and, above all, had faith in her abilities. Wasn't that what so many women dreamed of?

When they'd finished and their passion had ebbed, she ran her fingers through Allen's thick blond hair and whispered the question that had burned in her mind all day. "Do you love me, Allen?"

He stood abruptly, pulling up his trousers and smoothing his shirt.

She frowned. "Where are you going?"

He cupped her face an instant. "How about some dinner? I'm famished."

"Sounds divine, but you didn't answer me." She adjusted her clothes, ran her hand over her hair. "If you don't love me, just say so—"

"Of course, dear Dorothy."

She smiled. "Really?"

He kissed her passionately. "How's that for an answer?"

She beamed. He loved her! He really, truly loved her. She couldn't wait to tell her mum. They kissed again for several long moments, sending her heart soaring.

"Ready to eat?" he asked.

She smiled at the thought of another lovely meal, another lovely evening with him. "Ready."

And as they walked to his car, she allowed herself a brief dream of what it would be like to become Mrs. Allen Harrington, wife of a wealthy store owner. All in good time. All in good time.

$\dashv 26 \vdash$

Nightfall always came too soon.

Though Hira was grateful she had a place to go, she prayed each night, as she climbed the rickety stairs to the flat, that Alice would be home and she wouldn't be left to join the Diamond family on her own. Since the announcement about the heist, Alice had been noticeably absent many nights, and when she did return, she never explained where she'd been. Hira feared a sharp rebuke should she ask, so she kept her questions to herself. It wasn't her business, and she knew it.

After one such night, Hira awoke and dressed in her ratty trousers hurriedly, grabbed her things and her pup, and made her way to the factory. It gave her consolation, at least, to know she'd see Alice at the meetings. She knew the queen would never miss one.

Hira arrived at the abandoned factory a little early and leaned against the brick wall in the alley to wait for the others, out of sight. Forever out of sight. Even in her uncle's home, she'd stayed out of the way. At least he wouldn't physically harm her; at least she had plenty of food and a warm bed and her books and piano. To her surprise, an errant tear slipped down her cheek. She wondered what it must be like to be wanted, what it would be like to have someone who didn't see her as a nuisance. Someone who loved her.

A beautiful face flickered in her mind: a woman with flaming-red hair and a soft, sultry voice. Hira did have one other friend. Dorothy McBride. She'd given her food and a kind word, and the beautiful book filled with gods and goddesses. With Dorothy, she wasn't afraid, and with Dorothy, she'd felt as if she was worth knowing somehow. The only trouble was, Dorothy had never so much as hinted at inviting Hira to her home for any reason, let alone to stay with her.

Biscuit sniffed around a pile of garbage, at last deciding something was edible and gulped it down. She'd tried to keep her furry friend fed, but she was having enough trouble keeping her own belly full when Alice decided not to show. Hira still had a little coin left that she'd saved from the last wallet she'd stolen. She hesitated to use it, wanting to wait until she was truly desperate. Since she'd eaten yesterday afternoon, things weren't too dire, yet. She'd have to go on being hungry for now.

Though it was an abnormally warm morning for late November, an occasional wicked wind still kicked up occasionally, whisking away the bubble of warmth she'd gained from her brisk walk. By the time the Forties finally started to trickle into the factory, Hira was bone cold and quickly pushed inside. She found a place to stand out of the way at the back of the room and waited for the meeting to begin.

Moments later, Alice burst into the room, her hair and clothing more rumpled than usual. She looked as if she hadn't slept much the night before.

Hira wondered at her appearance. Usually Alice couldn't stand to have one hair out of place; she was deliberate in the way she dressed and composed herself. Deliberate in her decisions, deliberate in her actions. Hira found Alice's exacting nature disconcerting, especially when she administered some kind of punishment, but it was what Hira had come to expect. Alice's sudden mussed appearance made Hira wonder if something had happened.

Alice caught Hira's eye. "Did you eat?"

"No," she said, looking down.

"I figured as much." Alice pushed a paper sack toward her. "Eat, child. You need to keep up your strength. I have a job for you."

Hira was too hungry to think about what Alice meant. She reached for the enormous raisin scones and gulped down both pastries, pausing only long enough to give Biscuit a hunk of each. He snapped it up and licked his lips, waiting for more. She gave him a pat on the head as a consolation.

For the rest of the meeting, Hira sat quietly, listening. When it wound down, Alice dismissed most of the others, calling for only a few of her closest Forty Elephants to remain.

"Hira, you stay. I want to talk to you," Alice said.

She willed her face to remain blank, but her heart thundered in her chest as most of the others left.

Lottie patted the seat beside her, and Hira slid in next to her, praying that whatever Alice wanted from her didn't involve a knife.

"Tell me about your friend," Alice said, closing the door.

"My friend?" she asked. "Biscuit, you mean?"

Biscuit wagged his tail and bumped his head against her hand.

Alice didn't smile. "The shopgirl at Marshall & Snelgrove."

Hira stilled. What did Alice want with Dorothy? "Do you mean Miss Dorothy?"

"The redhead," Alice said.

Lottie nodded. "That's her."

Alice leaned forward until Hira could see that Alice's blue eyes were flecked with brown and green. "She's been put in charge of a storage room, from what I hear."

Hira searched her memory, trying to remember if Dorothy had mentioned a storage room, or if she had seen her access one. Her gaze flicked to Lottie, who winked, and at once the truth dawned on her. It was Lottie who had seen something and reported it to Alice. Lottie, otherwise known as Charlotte, was the new "employee" at the store.

Hira reluctantly shrugged. "I'm not sure, but I can ask."

"She has a key," Lottie said, snapping her newly popular Wrigley's chewing gum.

"You're going to get the key for me, kid," Alice said.

Hira's heart sank. She would have to steal the key from her friend? Quick on her feet, she replied, "Can Lottie do it? She works at the store and sees Dorothy more often."

"Are you afraid, little mouse?" Lottie asked. "It's time to put your big girl knickers on."

Alice and Lottie chuckled. Hira, meanwhile, felt like she was going to be sick.

"Lottie will take care of clearing the storage room. But first, you'll lift the key and bring it to me."

Hira instinctively understood this job wasn't about helping with a job that Lottie could clearly do herself. Alice wanted Hira to prove herself to the Forties and, more importantly, prove her allegiance to Alice—again. If Hira was a true part of "the family," she had to show she was worthy and, above all else, loyal. Stealing from a friend outside the gang demonstrated that loyalty. It would also hurt Dorothy and it might potentially destroy their friendship, making Hira more reliant on the Forty Elephants than ever. Dependence on the gang was one of Alice's playing cards.

When Hira didn't reply, Alice continued. "You'll need to cozy up to your friend in the store. Find a way to get that key. How you do it is up to you. Since you can clean out pockets and handbags like the best of us, you'll figure something out."

"Dorothy is dumb as a post," Lottie cut in. "It'll be easy enough to get the key from her."

Hira didn't know if she could take advantage of her friend. What if Dorothy got into trouble with her boss or, worse, she was sacked? Hira's stomach turned over. What would happen if she said no to the demand? Would Alice hold a knife to her throat? Toss her on the street and set the bobbies on her?

"Hira?" Alice pressed. "Did you hear me? I want you to do it today or tomorrow."

She nodded, stomach roiling.

"This is your chance, kid," Lottie said. "Don't cock it up, or you'll learn a valuable lesson about what it means to be a Forty Elephant."

Hira felt Alice's steely gaze on her. What choice did she have?

With two pairs of eyes trained on her face, Hira stood. "I'll do it. I'll get the key."

⇛ 27 ⇚

Hira didn't sleep well that night, knowing what she must do. She racked her brain, trying to think of a clever way to take the key while Dorothy was at the store so the theft could be blamed on anyone at Marshall & Snelgrove. Nothing came to her, and it was out of the question that she traipse around the store without being noticed. There weren't exactly a lot of orphans roaming through racks of beautiful clothes, least of all a girl with a dog trotting at their side. Dorothy tolerated her for brief visits, but the others didn't and would throw her out instantly without Dorothy speaking up on her behalf.

At last, an idea surfaced as if bubbling up from the deep of a dark, glassy lake. Hira would play on Dorothy's sympathies. Appeal to the side of her that loved beautiful things and wanted to help make others be beautiful, too.

In the morning, as Hira caught sight of her face in the mirror by Alice's front door, she startled. Dirt smudged her cheek and her hair looked slick, heavy with dirt and grease. Alice hadn't offered Hira a bath since that first night, but if all went to plan, she hoped Dorothy would respond in exactly the opposite manner. She drew up her courage and headed to a park near the shop to waste time until Dorothy finished with work.

Nausea came with the nerves. What if Dorothy caught her in the act? Would she finally turn Hira over to the lady detective? She'd certainly never want to see her again. In the park, Hira chased pigeons with Biscuit, counted stones, paced around the park while counting her steps, willing the time to pass so she could finish the mission and forget about it.

At last, as the sun began to set and the crowd of shoppers thinned, Dorothy emerged through the front door of the department store. Hira watched from a safe distance across the street. She headed straight for Dorothy but pretended not to see her. With a swift but gentle bump, she knocked into her friend.

"Oh!" Hira said. "I–I'm sorry."

"Well, hello, Hira," Dorothy said, tucking her hands under her arms for warmth. "I've missed seeing you this week. Is everything all right?"

Hira nodded, then cast her eyes to the ground to appear sad. When she looked up again, concern filled Dorothy's bright eyes, and Hira realized she might not have to act after all. In fact, she yearned for someone to truly care for her. She always had. She yearned for her mother, a mother that would never come. As for Alice, she had been generous enough, but she made sure Hira didn't forget her generosity, and it felt as if something was owed in the end.

"I've been well enough," Hira began, "but I miss my dresses, my fine things. I miss being clean. I wondered if you could...if you could help me?"

Dorothy's face lit like a candle in a darkened window. "Come with me. We'll make you smell like roses and clean and brush your hair until it's shiny. You'll be pretty as a button."

"Can Biscuit come?"

He tilted his head when he heard his name, his large brown eyes glistening in the waning daylight. Hira could never resist that look, and she bent down to rub his ears and placed a kiss on his head.

"Well, we can't leave him here, can we?"

Hira smiled a genuine smile.

When they reached Dorothy's flat, they walked up four flights of stairs. Her flat was smaller than Alice's with only two bedrooms, but it was cleaner and smelled of lavender and vanilla. Yellow curtains patterned with apple clusters hung over the small kitchen window, and yellow-and-white-striped cushions padded the chairs at a worn dining table that had been scrubbed clean. In the parlor, there was a sofa with a wild red floral print, a rug with geometric design, and splashy curtains that completed the look. Hira loved it all—the colors, the patterns, the way nothing matched but all seemed to work in harmony to create a cheery home. It was just like Dorothy: pretty, vibrant, unique.

Hira glanced at the dining table where a bowl of apples was piled high. Next to it, a lead pencil lay atop a stack of drawings. By the looks of the drawing on top, they were sketches of women's dresses.

"May I look at them?" Hira asked.

Dorothy laughed softly. "You and your manners. It's quite cute, really. Be careful not to smudge them."

Hira flipped through the stack of drawings, marveling at the beautiful frocks and evening gowns, the trousers and jumpers for women, and scarves and hats for winter wear. Each sketch was outlined in lead pencil and shaded with bright pastels. She liked the evening gowns best with their sparkles and sashes and feathered headdresses to match. She longed to touch them, run the tip of her finger over the lines.

"This scarf looks like a butterfly," she said.

Dorothy laughed, her dimples showing her delight. "Why, yes. Do you like it?"

"Very much. I like them all." She gazed at a frock with stripes and a hem that turned to feathers. "I wish I could touch it. It looks very soft."

Dorothy smiled and stood behind Hira, peering over her shoulder.

"These stripes will also be white but made of satin instead of crepe, so they'll catch the light as she moves."

"They're all so pretty," she said, awestruck. She had never seen such beautiful drawings. Her own sketches she'd been forced to do with Miss Lightly had always been pitiful, and she'd been scolded every time she'd failed at the assignment.

"Thank you," Dorothy said.

She looked up from the pile. "Will you sell these to your store? Your boss would like these."

"You really think so?" Dorothy asked. A line crinkled between her eyebrows.

"Oh, yes," Hira replied enthusiastically.

"I've never shown them to anyone but my mum. She lives here with me, too, but she isn't home yet." Changing the subject, Dorothy said, "Why don't I take your coat?" She hung it on a rack near the front door. "Now come with me, young lady. It's time we made you pretty." She led Hira to her bedroom, tossed her handbag on the bed, and directed them to the bathtub. "First, you need to get cleaned up. We have running water, but it's cold. I'll just heat the kettle a bit to take the sting out of it." She ran water for the bath and gave Hira a bar of soap and a bottle of Watkins coconut shampoo.

Hira looked down at the bottle in her hands. She had never washed her own hair. She'd always had someone else do it for her. She'd attempted to use the bar soap Alice had given her on the one occasion she'd offered her a bath, but Hira wasn't certain she'd done a good job. She scratched her scalp, realizing then just how tangled her hair was.

"Would you like me to help you?" Dorothy asked gently.

Hira blushed deeply. She would have to strip down in front of her friend—the friend she was about to rob and put at real risk of being sacked. Hira didn't deserve such kindness. Her stomach heaved again, and she wished she'd never come, that she'd never agreed to do such a thing, but she couldn't go back on her word now. She'd promised Alice, and what was more, she was frightened of the outcome, should she not obey.

"Are you shy, child?" Dorothy asked. "Don't worry, I won't look. I'll just help you clean your hair. Why don't you wash your body first? Here's a cloth."

When Dorothy stepped into the corridor, Hira lathered the soap and washed her body like her maids used to do. As the steam rose and the scent of lavender soap filled the air, she relaxed, feeling happier than she had in a while. She'd underestimated how good it felt to be clean. When she'd finished, she wrapped tightly in a towel, let the water out of the tub, and Dorothy returned. Hira watched as her friend poured a small puddle of shampoo into the palm of her hand.

"This won't hurt, but I'm going to give it a good scrubbing, all right?" She leaned over the lip of the bathtub, sinking her fingers into Hira's scalp.

Hira squeezed her eyes closed.

As Dorothy worked, she clucked her tongue and made cajoling, comforting noises. Hira lay there, thinking about how much she liked Dorothy, how much she owed her—and how she could never repay her—and she tried not to cry. She didn't want to steal from her friend. Dorothy was a good person, a kind person. Hira blinked rapidly against the threatening tears.

Dorothy washed Hira's hair once, twice, and then picked through her tangles with a comb. Little by little, the snarls loosened until her hair fell in long, dark waves around her shoulders and down her back.

"There we are," Dorothy said. "I think we've scrubbed away all of the dirt. I washed your clothes while you were bathing, too, so they're drying on the radiator, but I have a dress I made some time ago that I think might be close to your size."

Dorothy produced a blue dress and smiled, but Hira didn't miss the flicker of sadness in her eyes.

"Are you sad?" Hira asked.

"Oh," Dorothy laughed dismissively, "No, well. It's just that you remind me of someone I once knew. My little sister. She had long dark hair and loved her books, too. And she was very brave, just like you are."

Hira warmed to the praise. "Where is she now?"

"She died when she was only nine years old. She had an infection of the throat. I've made some frocks for her. Well, for little girls in general, I suppose."

Hira didn't know what to say, so she watched Dorothy as she shook the wrinkles from the fabric and lovingly ran her fingers over the lace.

"Come, you can change in my bedroom," Dorothy said.

Hira followed her into a small bedroom that was largely consumed by a bed and an armoire. Atop her vanity, bottles of perfume were arranged in no particular order, and there was a hairbrush and hand mirror and a small wooden box carved with a floral design. There was a window, too, with a gold paisley cushion that looked inviting. The window opened to the street, but to the far right, she could see a small patch of garden. She knew at once that Dorothy spent much of her free time there, watching the pedestrians below and staring out at the garden dreaming, perhaps sketching her beautiful clothes, too.

"Now, I know this dress isn't what you're used to wearing," Dorothy began, "but it'll do for now."

Hira stared at the light but shiny fabric and the soft skirt that would flow around her calves.

"It's so very pretty," Hira replied.

"And you'll be pretty in it. I'll just let you change." Dorothy closed the door behind her.

Hira was happy, squeaky clean, and so grateful to Dorothy that she nearly forgot to look for the key! The entire reason she'd come. Her heart leapt into her throat. She had to do it, even if she didn't want to. As she pulled on Dorothy's dress, she glanced around the room until her eyes fell on the handbag on the bed. Dorothy would likely keep the key there, wouldn't she? Taking a deep breath, Hira reached for the handbag and snooped inside it. Beneath a change purse and a small brush, she found a key ring with what appeared to be a house key. She frowned, pushing around several other odds and ends. She slipped her finger inside a small pocket sewn into the soft blue fabric. To her immense relief, she felt another metal object. The storage room key was there, tied with a tiny silver tag that read M & S #4.

Hira's stomach clenched as she stared at the key. Could she go through with it?

"Everything all right in there?" Dorothy called through the door.

Hira jumped at her friend's voice. Then, without hesitating, she stashed the key inside her shoe. "One moment." She glanced at her reflection, surprised by the face she saw before her. She'd thinned considerably since she'd left home, and charcoal smudges appeared beneath her dark, haunted eyes. But her hair had begun to dry, the scent of coconuts still lingering in the air. She looked like a girl again.

She opened the door and found Dorothy on the other side of it. "Will you help me pin my hair?"

Her friend smiled. "I know exactly what we'll do with it."

Hira returned her smile, though her hands trembled. She was really going to go through with it, taking Dorothy for a fool. But she would make Alice very proud.

⇒ 28 ⇐

Lilian took the chief's directive to heart. She'd combed Lambeth and the Elephant and Castle neighborhood exhaustively, searching for any sign of Hira or Alice. Lilian's luck seemed to have evaporated. She hadn't seen either. In fact, there was no sign of the Forty Elephants at all, not even at the factory. Though she hadn't had success, she was relieved to at least have a reprieve from the mind-numbing department store beat for a few more shifts, even if they were mostly night shifts. She still had hope she'd flush them out.

As night fell, Lilian pulled her police whistle around her neck and put on a trench coat to block the wind. She'd be working with Inspector Lewis, her on-again, off-again partner for evening patrols. In years past, the female squadron had worked with each other in groups. Now, with the staff severely pruned, male and female police worked together. As it should be, really. Lilian thought the segregation of the sexes absurd.

"Hiya, Wyles," Lewis said.

"Nearly winter, isn't it?" she said, blowing on her hands.

"Cold as bloody hell," he agreed. The tip of his nose was red, and he was huddled as far as he could into his jacket, collar standing on end to shield his neck.

"Should we take a spin through the neighborhood, see what's on for tonight?"

"You lead the way," he replied.

They set out, passing pubs and chippies with their fragrant aroma of fried fish, winding past storefronts, through clusters of overcrowded and neglected buildings that housed some of London's poorest. As they walked, a slow, steady rain pattered against Lilian's hat and raincoat. She'd never minded the rain until she'd spent two years at the front in France. The regular downpours had filled the trenches, giving the soldiers all manner of diseases. Their feet rotted during cold months, and in the summer, standing water brought mosquito infestations. She'd never forget the screams of an unlucky soldier, whose trench foot had given way to multiple amputations. She shuttered the memory instantly. Packed it away along with the rest of the horror she'd seen. She could do that—compartmentalize and place things she'd rather forget behind a wall in her mind. It was how she didn't lose sleep at night, and how she returned to a job day after day that often showed the worst side of humanity.

"I'm already wet," Lewis complained. Always a rather funny thing to see from a man his size. He was of average height but broad-chested, muscular, and his hands were thick as ham hocks.

"It's not going to get any better, I'm afraid," Lilian said, glancing at a puddle that rippled as raindrops struck its surface.

"We'll stop in for something hot in a while," Lewis said.

They traversed a wide thoroughfare and snaked through more of the neighborhoods that sprawled in every direction. Sometimes Lilian's mind boggled at the number of people she saw each day, and the endless need that emanated from a city that often felt infinite, timeless. How could she do her job effectively in such a place? Perhaps it wasn't about doing it all but doing the best one could. Especially with the limitation of being female, she thought wryly, and therefore not being trusted to do things well. She'd wondered what it would be like to abandon her job. Her father had always been supportive of anything she wanted to do, though he believed her mind was wasted at the Met. But she was a policewoman through and through. Justice was essential to a civilized society, and she radiated with pride each time she helped someone obtain—or meet—that justice.

Lost in thought, she missed the step down from the edge of the pavement and stumbled, soaking her feet in a filthy pool of water.

Lewis laughed. "That's what you get for daydreaming."

She rolled her eyes playfully, and this time they both laughed.

They turned the corner, and at the end of the street, light spilled from an open doorway of someone's first-floor flat. A man's voice boomed, and even from a distance they could hear him calling someone a litany of less-than-flattering names.

"Sounds like a domestic," Lewis said.

"Let's have a look, shall we?" she said.

Lewis shrugged his enormous shoulders. "Best to keep out of those, usually, but if things are too rough, we can intervene."

As their shadow darkened the doorstep, a young woman raced outside and fell in the street.

"Are you all right?" Lilian asked, holding out her hand to help.

"I don't need help from the likes of you." The woman ignored Lilian's hand and pushed to her feet.

Lilian smarted at the angry reply. That would teach her for offering a kindness. Still, she had a job to do. "Can we help you with something or rather, someone?" she pressed.

The woman pushed a lock of hair out of her eyes, revealing a busted lip and a patch of yellow-green skin around her eye. Her cheeks were wan, and her collarbones protruded from her ghostly thin frame.

"What are you, some kind of bobby?" She crossed her arms over her chest and glared.

"I am," Lilian replied, preparing for the onslaught of mockery she'd endured almost constantly since she'd begun her police work.

The woman laughed. "You're in the wrong business, ain't ya? No one's scared of a lady detective. Not a runt like you."

Lilian kept her cool exterior firmly in place. If there was one thing she'd learned about those who broke the law, it was that they enjoyed heckling and taunting the police. For some reason, those who detested the Met thought the police to be brainless ninnies who blindly followed orders, as if they were completely incapable of understanding what life was like for those on the other side of the law. Lilian detested that part of her job—being seen as a villain. All she aimed to do was uphold the law and help others. She saw nothing but noble sacrifice in that.

"If I were you, I'd watch your mouth, young lady," Lilian snapped.

The woman laughed. "Oh no, I made the little copper angry. You want to come in and meet my Mike? He'd have a good laugh at a pint-sized lady copper."

"Watch it, miss," Lewis growled. "There's no need to be nasty."

A man stuck his head outside and glanced briefly at Lilian and Lewis. The sight of police at his door didn't seem to faze him. "Ruth," he barked, "get your ass in here."

Ruth shook her head. "I told the girls I'd stop in tonight."

"If you don't get inside, now, you'll have a hard time getting to sleep tonight, darlin," Mike replied.

Ruth already had a bruised eye and blood smeared on her cheek. If they left her there, she'd probably see a lot worse that night and wind up needing a doctor. Catching on quickly, Lilian reached for the handcuffs she kept locked on the belt loops of her skirt. The girl needed rescuing.

"Ruth is coming with me, down to the station," she said.

"Why does she need to do that?" the man demanded, his face going red.

"I stole a necklace," Ruth rushed to fill in and then glanced at Lilian, her eyes pleading.

Despite the woman's attitude, she clearly needed help. Being arrested—or at least pretending to be—would protect her from this brute, at least for the night.

"Let's go. You're coming with me." Lilian cuffed the young woman and directed her away. Ruth didn't put up even the smallest struggle.

Lewis grabbed her arm and leaned to her ear and whispered, "You sure you want to take her in, Miss Wyles?"

Lilian glanced at him, trying to read his expression, but the curved bill of his hat threw a shadow on his face, hiding his eyes. She hadn't missed the caution in his voice.. "Of course I'm sure."

"Well I'm not," he said. "I don't want to put my name on this. It'll be on you. Just remember that."

"Fine," she replied, steering the Ruth away from the flat and into the street.

"You'd better keep your bleeding mouth shut, you 'ear me, Ruth!" the man named Mike shouted as they walked away.

"Let's take a taxi," Lewis said. "I'm not hauling her across town on a bus or train in this weather. What do you think, Miss Wyles?"

As they rounded the corner to a busy thoroughfare to hail a taxicab, Lilian paused. "Lewis, if you call me Miss Wyles one more time—"

He held up a hand. "Sorry. I'm not used to—"

"I don't care what you're used to. I'm an inspector, same as you, and I'm tired of being referred to as a lady."

The girl snorted. "I never have that problem."

"Do you have a name?" Lilian asked.

HEATHER WEBB

"Ruth. Ruth Jenkins."

Lilian was certain Ruth Jenkins needed rescuing, and yet, Lewis's tone and his comments nagged at her. *It'll be on you, just remember that.* He seemed to know something she didn't, but he wouldn't say what in front of their captive. She glanced at the woman who stared out the window, an unspeakably sad expression on her face, and then back at Lewis. He shrugged.

Lilian did her best not to second-guess herself, and to ignore the unease swimming in her stomach.

———

Lilian held Ruth at the station for a couple of hours before they were forced to let her go. They didn't have the space for one thing, and for another, she wasn't being charged with a crime. And despite the fact that Ruth Jenkins obviously wanted to escape her situation, she wouldn't budge; she'd told them nothing.

"Fear is an excellent motivator," one of the other female police officers had explained. "If they nark, those women get beat to a pulp when they return home."

"Why don't they leave?" Lilian had asked.

"And have nowhere to go? No roof over their heads and no money?" Her colleague shook her head. "They believe they're better off, and sometimes they're conditioned to believe they deserve it and their abuse is normal. That they don't deserve more, or even know what 'more' looks like."

Lilian mulled her colleague's words as she set out for her morning shift in the West End. She had been naive as a young woman to the ways of the world because of her sheltered upbringing with loving and supportive parents. Years later, she realized she still had so much to learn. She wanted to understand these women and the cycle of abuse so she could help them, now more than ever.

A cold breeze lashed at her bare neck, and she flipped up her collar. Combing the streets during the winter months was always a challenge. Since it was only early December, they had a long way to go before sleet and freezing fogs retreated and made way for the warm, blue skies of spring. The good thing about winter was more time by the fire with a book and plenty of tea with brandy, a favorite after-work activity for her. She noticed the hour was getting on, and Lewis still hadn't shown at their meeting spot. They were supposed to patrol Soho that night, where the most popular gin palaces and dance halls already buzzed with activity. By eleven o'clock, they'd be vibrating with music and cheer—and trouble. She waited nearly forty-five minutes for Lewis before deciding to venture out on her own. He'd catch up with her; he knew the route. He'd probably been held up somewhere, and meanwhile, she was freezing and bored with waiting.

She walked toward the 43 on Gerrard Street, one of the most popular clubs in London. Nearly every Friday and Saturday night, the Met patrolled Soho, preparing for raids to crack down on prostitutes and clubs serving past legal hours. Kate Meyrick's many clubs served the aristocracy from all over Britain and Europe, movie stars and West End stage stars, and millionaires. What more could anyone want for entertainment on a Friday night?

A hot bath, Lilian thought as a wind ripped down Gerrard Street and sliced through her layers of protective clothing. She passed the alley tucked between the club and the building next to it, prepared to do a loop in hopes that Lewis might appear, when voices floated toward her.

A sharp cry split the air.

Lilian sucked in a deep breath. That sounded like distress.

Another scream followed it.

She strode quickly into the alley.

Two figures struggled in the dark.

Lilian's pulse hitched. At the end of the alley, a large man pinned a woman to the outer brick wall of the club. His knee was jammed between her legs and he bound her wrists with one hand. The woman's coat had been shoved aside and her torn dress revealed her breasts. Shiny beads that had once decorated her dress littered the ground around her feet.

"Please! Help me!" the woman cried.

Lilian catapulted toward them.

The man tossed a look over his shoulder, his shadowed face taking Lilian in a moment before his teeth gleamed in the fractures of light thrown from a nearby window. "Best be on your way, bobby. My girlfriend and I are just having a little fun."

"Fun, is it?" Lilian's voice was strangled by emotion. "Pinning a woman down and tearing off her clothes against her will?" She pulled herself up to her full height. "If you lay another hand on her, you're under arrest." This time, Lilian's voice was commanding, strong.

The woman began to sob, in fear and relief.

"And just how are you going to do that?" the man sneered. "If you haven't noticed, I'm bigger than you."

An understatement. She hadn't seen a man of his size in a while. He was a giant with a thick neck and wide chest. But a woman was in trouble. And Lilian had the authority to arrest him—and she would use it.

"I said, let her go." She stalked toward him, heart hammering against her ribs. She'd have to shove him to free the woman, club him over the head with her truncheon. She could do this, knock him out cold if she managed to hit him forcefully enough.

He ignored her demand and shoved his hand under the woman's right leg, lifting it upward. "Come on, baby," he said, putting his face in the woman's neck. "Tell her that we're just a couple of lovebirds being a little naughty in public."

The woman turned her face toward Lilian, her expression a mask of fear and disgust, and mouthed the word *help*.

That did it.

Lilian barreled into him like a rugby player after the ball.

Surprised by the force, he grunted on impact and stumbled sideways.

Momentum carried her forward, and she landed in a heap on top of the perpetrator.

The woman screeched and pulled her coat closed, hesitating a moment as she looked to Lilian for direction.

"Run!" Lilian shouted.

The woman didn't hesitate. She raced away, down the street and around the corner, before Lilian had gotten to her feet.

"You wench!" the man snarled.

She reached for her truncheon—too late.

He lunged at her, pinning her easily and wrapping his hand around her throat.

Fear rocketed through her, and in that instant, she wished she hadn't been so brazen and rash, so inordinately stupid as to rush a man his size alone. She could have blown her air whistle, alerting other officers in the vicinity. She could have gotten some backup.

"You aren't so bold now, are you, bobby?" He laughed and tightened his grip around her neck.

As Lilian stared into the black eyes of the would-be rapist, she began to shake violently, uncontrollably. But she didn't look away, even as his grip tightened. Even as she felt his hot breath on her cheek. She wasn't a coward, and if it was her time to go, saving a life was the most honorable way to go.

⩭ 29 ⩭

The club smelled of cigarette smoke and spilled whiskey. As the air swirled sluggishly in a thick cloud around Alice, she watched her friends laugh and dance in the steamy heat that arose from bodies in motion. They'd been dancing for over two hours, packed in among the crowd almost cheek to cheek. Alice's hair had clumped into sweat-soaked locks, and her dress stuck to her back. She could stand to cool off, take a breather in the night air.

"Want to smoke a ciggy outside?" she shouted over the music. Maggie and Lottie were polishing off a glass of water at the bar. They'd finally switched from gin to water, now that they were all thoroughly pissed. Had they kept going, they'd be horizontal already.

They followed her outside, the cool damp air washing over them.

Alice inhaled a deep breath. The girls moved out of the entrance to avoid the flow of people coming and going from the club.

"A light?" She passed her silver lighter as they each lit a cigarette. The initials SD were carefully etched on the lighter's surface. She wondered who SD was each time she used it. She'd picked it from a pawnshop a few months ago, so it was anyone's guess.

She leaned against the brick wall and looked across the street at a block of shops, their windows dark, hiding the promise of beautiful things inside. Much as she liked the thrill of her work, she lived for nights out with the girls and the lazy mornings that followed...particularly those after romping in bed with Simon. She smiled to herself as she tapped her cigarette.

"Who's making you smile like that?" Lottie asked, blowing a stream of smoke between the gap in her two front teeth. "He your boyfriend?"

Christ, it was as if she'd been thinking out loud. "Who?" she asked, playing dumb.

"The Irishman," Maggie replied. Her blond hair was matted with sweat and her cheeks were rosy. "Aww, come on, you know who I mean. Cute smile. Blond. You meet him at the pub."

Had Maggie been watching her? Alice had been entirely too messy, more than she'd realized. In fact, she'd have flinched in surprise at Maggie's comment had she not had so much practice in keeping her cool.

"Simon," Alice said but offered nothing else.

Maggie nudged her. "Ain't you going to give us details?"

"Nothing to tell," Alice said, the lie tasting of ash on her tongue. She was good at lying, but something about Simon made her feel ashamed to lie, especially about him. "He's a distraction, that's all."

"I'd like a distraction that looks like that," Lottie said, dropping her cigarette butt to the pavement and stamping it out with her red T-strap heel.

Alice enjoyed her time with Simon entirely too much. Scared the hell out of her, so she knew it couldn't go on like this much longer. He was getting a little too attached as well, showing up with flowers and pastries the mornings after. Making her laugh. Flattering her just the right amount and meaning every single word of it. He was a good, honest man—and that was a shame.

A cry rang out in the night, interrupting her thoughts.

"You hear that?" Lottie said, rubbing her bare arms.

"Probably came from the club," Maggie said, her words slurring. She'd had twice as many gin martinis as the rest of them. Alice was beginning to think she had a real problem.

Another cry sliced the air. The sounds of struggle came from the alley on the left side of the building.

"Better see what that's about," Alice said, dropping her cigarette butt and producing her razor from the silk pocket in her handbag. Maggie and Lottie followed suit, their blades flashing bright silver in the lamplight.

They crept to the edge of the building and paused. Alice peered into the murky dark, catching sight of the outline of a woman.

"Please! Let me go!"

Alice nodded at her girls and stepped into the shadow of the building, inching closer to the struggling pair. Upon closer inspection, she could see there were three people. Two petite women and one large man.

In the next instant, the smallest woman lunged at the man, knocking him off his feet, falling face-forward herself in the process. The second woman screamed and darted away, racing past Alice and her friends without so much as a glance.

A brisk female voice called out in the dark, "You'd better unhand me, or you'll find yourself in the clink."

The man laughed. "I'm not afraid, lady. Go ahead, see if you can arrest me."

It was a policewoman? Alice paused. Surely a copper could hold her own. Didn't she at least have a truncheon she could beat the bastard with?

Alice squinted in the dark, attempting to make out the copper's face and paused—it was Inspector Wyles. And she was alone and in trouble.

The man's hands closed around the inspector's neck.

Her muffled cry sent a shiver over Alice's skin. She might not like the lady copper, but she wasn't about to let some brute murder her. She was still a woman, after all, and though Alice wasn't in the habit of playing Robin Hood or savior, she also wasn't heartless.

She motioned to her girls and they inched closer, their heels clicking audibly now on the concrete. Given his size, they'd have to surround him quickly, strike fast. Surprise him, as she'd taught little Hira.

"Who's there?" the man demanded. "Show yourself!"

Alice stepped into a small shaft of light streaming from the club window. Lottie flanked Alice's right and Maggie, her left. She knew the girls wondered why she was protecting a copper, but they wouldn't dare question her. They were to obey, not doubt. Not question. And Alice knew a good turn for the right person was like money in the bank.

"This isn't the dance floor, chickens," he said. "Go inside. This is none of your concern."

"Do you know the time you'd get for killing a copper?" Alice said. "If I were you, I'd let her go."

"You really think they care about a lady copper?" He squeezed Lilian's neck, and she gasped for air.

"Girls, it looks like we've got a stupid one on our hands. Guess he'll have to learn the hard way." Alice flashed her blackjack, and her friends did the same.

The idiotic man laughed. "What are you going to do with that? Wave it in my face?"

"I thought I'd make a puzzle of your face instead."

"Hey, asshole, we're the Forty Elephants," Maggie said, her blond hair a torch in the dark alley. "The last time some dolt second-guessed us, he wound up blind with a few broken bones."

He grunted. "Never heard of you, and don't give a damn either way."

"Well, now, you didn't have to go and insult us. In fact"—Alice's voice dripped with menace—"that was a really bad idea."

"Bugger off!" he growled.

Inspector Wyles squirmed in the man's grip. Her eyes bulged and her hands pawed at his fingers without making purchase.

"I'm going to tell you one more time," Alice said. "Let her go."

"Piss off!" he growled.

A rush of adrenaline surged through her veins. She signaled to the girls, and they pounced, surrounding him in an instant.

"I'm really scared." He laughed gruffly and straightened, letting go of the copper to confront them—too late.

They each took aim. Lottie slashed the back of his neck, Maggie his right arm, and Alice, his left.

The man cried out, staggering back, his hands shielding his face.

"Don't ever lay a finger on a woman again, you bastard!" Lottie shouted after him as he raced from the alley, swearing at them as he fled.

"When will they learn?" Maggie slurred. In spite of the gallon of liquor that she'd consumed, her hand had been steady, her strike decisive.

Alice wiped her blade with the handkerchief in her handbag, as usual, and tucked it back inside the pocket.

Wyles stared at her, rubbing her neck where the man had tried to strangle her, bewilderment and gratitude etched in the contours of her plain, round face. "You helped me. Why?"

Alice shrugged. "Sometimes a woman looks out for her own. Even if they're not from the same…school of thought."

"Thank you," the woman rasped, holding out her hand.

"The lout had it coming."

"I'll say," Lottie said, fishing out another cigarette from her purse.

Alice eyed the woman who'd been trying to track her, had become something of a nuisance from her overeager interest in Hira, and suddenly felt a chill. Some premonition, as if she knew she'd come face-to-face with the copper again, perhaps not under the best of circumstances. At least for now, though, she had money in the bank. She'd saved the copper's life and that meant something.

Inspector Wyles touched her neck gingerly. "Thank you." Her voice was raspy from the strain. "I won't forget this."

Alice nodded. "See that you don't."

Yet despite the reassurance, the chill gripped Alice again. She rubbed her bare arms—the hair standing on end—as Inspector Wyles walked toward the light.

⇌ 30 ⇋

Lilian didn't sleep well the night after the attack. She wasn't usually one to ruminate on the day's events, no matter how gruesome a sight she saw while on duty, no matter how shocking or sad, or threatening to her person. It wasn't in her nature. This was what had made her a good nurse at the front, and it was what made her a good inspector. She was logical, calm, and steady, and not easily spooked. But the assailant with his large hands, and her near-strangulation, had given her a good scare. Her throat throbbed all night and into the next day. Still, she didn't take off work, and when Chief Wensley saw the haunted look in her eyes and the bruise blooming across her skin, he asked her if she needed time off.

"No, sir," she said. "Time off isn't necessary. The bruises will heal. I'm perfectly all right."

It wasn't just the perpetrator she'd been thinking about, it was Alice Diamond and her gang. Women who belonged behind bars, not only for their regular theft and lawlessness, but for the assault she was certain they administered on a regular basis. And yet, Alice had come to her rescue. She could have left Lilian there to fend for herself. She could have let Lilian die. Instead, Alice acted without hesitation, as if she saved random women all the time. And perhaps she did, In her way?

Lilian blushed. She'd been following the notorious thief for days. She would have booked Alice at first chance... And would she still? Lilian shook her head. What was right was right. What was just... Well, she had always instinctively lived by the principles of fairness and justice. They gave order to the chaos of human nature, brought light when all appeared dark or hopeless. But for the first time, she questioned what justice really meant. She was also beginning to see a sort of twisted symbiotic relationship between criminal and police. The line that divided them was far thinner than she'd ever realized. This truth was uncomfortable, irritating like a kernel of corn stuck in her teeth.

Did she owe Alice a favor at the very least? A favor for a life? Lilian's fingertips lightly stroked the sore spot on her neck.

Alice had helped her to her feet while the others circled her. She'd been badly shaken—and grateful—but she was pleased to report she hadn't lost her wits. Even in the face of danger, she'd managed to keep her sense intact though her authority had been completely overridden.

Lilian recalled the exchange between them after the assault.

"Is the girl still running with you?" Lilian had asked as she stood at the opening to the alley.

"You'll have to be more specific," Alice had replied.

"The young Indian girl."

"What's it to you?" Alice flipped her blade closed.

Lilian brushed off her skirt and her hand went to her neck, probing the soft flesh to assess the damage. "Her uncle is looking for her," she said, voice rough. "She has a home."

"Why would I turn her over to a man she's run away from?" Alice said, signaling to the others that they could return inside. The other women hesitated and then followed Alice's order.

"I can't share the confidential details now," Lilian said, "but suffice it to say, it's in the girl's best interest that I find her."

Alice stepped closer. "Her uncle, you say?"

"Yes." Lilian decided against telling Alice the truth: the girl stood to inherit property, perhaps some money, if the lawyer was careful to keep her under watch so the uncle couldn't ship her off to a miserable boarding school in the north and take her inheritance along with it. Should Alice discover the girl's worth, she might try to do the same and take what didn't belong to her. That was the queen of thieves' way, after all.

"I don't see how it's in her best interest to turn her over to people who don't want her," Alice insisted.

"She has a guardian—"

"Come now, Inspector. Things are rarely so clear cut. Surely you've worked at the Met long enough to know that. Now, don't worry yourself about Hira. I look out for her, and like my other girls, I won't make her surrender if she doesn't want to."

Surrender, as if she were a prisoner? Perhaps Hira Wickham was a prisoner of sorts, living with the gang.

At that moment, the chief waved his hand in front of her face, bringing her back to the present.

"Are you sure you're all right?" he said.

She focused again on the disorderly office around her. "I'm fine, sir. Ready to get to work."

"Better get to it then."

"Right." She was turning to leave when he barked out her name again.

"Wyles. About the woman you arrested."

"Which?"

"Ruth Jenkins."

Ruth Jenkins, the woman who looked battle-worn and was chased down by that bloke named Mike who had wanted to beat the poor woman into next Tuesday.

"Of course I remember her."

"She's dead."

Lilian's heart leapt into her throat. "Dead, sir? How? What happened?"

He held up his hand. "It's been ruled a suicide. She jumped into the Thames, got swept away with the tide, and ended up on the bank about a mile downstream. She looked battered, too, but that's not unusual for women of her ilk."

Lilian frowned at the chief's easy dismissal of a dead woman from the wrong part of town. Suicide didn't seem likely for Ruth, especially given the bruises. Especially given what Lilian had seen that night outside the pub. As she remembered Lewis's words of warning, a wave of nausea rolled over her. He'd understood something she hadn't. He'd known that meddling would only make things worse. But how had he known, and how had she been so naive?

The chief read Lilian's expression and closed the folder he held in his hands. "Look, Wyles, there's nothing you or any of us could have done to save her."

Words she knew well—had practiced herself so often in France on the battlefield that they'd become second nature, but they were a hollow consolation this time. This time, Lilian felt responsible for the girl. She'd arrested her to get her away from that place, keep her safe. She'd wanted to help. Instead, she'd endangered Ruth Jenkins—could, in fact, do nothing to help her—and defied Ruth's boyfriend in a way that had sent him over the edge. He'd taken it out on Ruth to punish her, to signal that she shouldn't reach out for help. And now she was dead.

Lilian swallowed the unexpected rush of tears and strode out of the office, eager to work, to distract herself. Perhaps she had no business moving on from department stores and orphans after all. A woman had died, because of her. Heart in her mouth, eyes blurred with tears, she started out for her post that day. She didn't believe for a moment that Ruth's death was a suicide. She'd been beaten to death and dumped in the river by that scoundrel.

She gritted her teeth against the wet wind. Perhaps she could redeem herself a little by persuading Hira Wickham to come into the station. But redeeming herself to whom, exactly?

Lilian shivered as a freezing fog enveloped her, stealing her breath and obscuring the path before her.

⟫ 31 ⟪

A veil of icy fog coated the car windscreen and, beyond it, thickened into a cloud so dense, Alice could scarcely see the road in front of her. She'd met with Jimmy Church again to do another tour of the building she planned to buy. After, they visited his properties in the West End. She especially liked the idea of hosting her girls in the West End, a part of town where the only criminals in town would be themselves. The Forties could live on the posh, watch the toffs come and go as their neighbors. The thought made her downright gleeful. But the truth was, it would cost three times as much for a deposit, and therefore, it would take them too long to secure it. The more practical decision was to stick to the original plan, and Alice was nothing if not practical.

She headed to the factory to meet with the Forties. With the weather and the traffic jam, the drive across town took much longer than expected, and by the time the factory came into sight, she was in a foul mood. Her friends—the inner circle of the Forties—were waiting for news, and she was waiting on a good clean whiskey. Soon. For now, she parked and grabbed her handbag and headed for the entrance of the building. She was starting up the walk when Bertie, Scully, and Maggie came bounding outside to greet her.

"The traffic was rotten with the fog," Alice said. "A horse was hit by a motorcar and everyone in bloody London stopped to see what was what. I was ready to run them over, the tossers."

"Alice," Maggie said, putting her hand on her shoulder. "We've just heard some news. Bert sent over Tommy to tell you, but you weren't here yet and he had to run. It's on account of Ruth."

"No!" Alice said, shaking her head. "Tell me she's all right. Tell me that son of a—"

"She's gone, Alice," Bertie said. "Jumped off the Waterloo Bridge. The coppers fished her out of the river."

Alice wore a mask of careful restraint but inside crumpled like a used handkerchief. It was her fault. It was her job to protect her girls, her job to ensure their safety. Though deep down, Alice knew Ruth had made her choice and that she couldn't protect the woman from herself, Alice still felt responsible. She'd failed at being the gangland boss she needed to be. With one of her girls mouthing off, one skipping out on jobs when she felt like it, and now one dead... Pain and panic collided inside her. She was losing her grip. And now, because of her, they'd all lost Ruth. A wail of frustration, of devastation, tore from her lips. Ruth had not only been one of the Forties Alice most trusted but also one of Alice's closest friends, and friends were hard to come by in this business.

The others watched her, and for once in their lives, they were silent.

Alice paced the short spit of pavement in front of the factory, trying to get ahold of her emotions, wishing she could clear them away like a smudge of dirt on a windowpane. Had she done something faster, sooner... Had she been able to reach Ruth, maybe she could have saved her from that bastard. A cry caught in her throat, and she stopped, put her hand across her mouth. She knew she was supposed to be the one in charge, the calm one who was nonplussed by violence and loss—it was all a part of the job—but the truth was, the job ate her alive sometimes.

"They said she was pretty beat up," Bertie said quietly.

"Black and blue. Breastbone crushed," Scully added. "I'm no expert but I think she was—"

"Murdered," Alice cut in. "Tossed in the river."

"And the police won't open an investigation for the likes of her," Maggie said, lighting a cigarette. "If we want justice, we'll have to take matters into our own hands."

Alice's mind chased her thoughts in dizzying circles. *Justice?* She could spit. Justice was something she hadn't seen much of in her life. She'd always had to create her own. Her cheeks heated as rage swept over her like a factory fire. She'd dish out some justice all right. It was time she taught Mike to keep his bloody hands to himself, once and for all. And she knew just where to find him.

———

Later that night, Alice ushered Hira into the car. Alice hadn't wanted to take the kid with her, but Hira had pleaded and worn her down. With the news of Ruth's death, she had felt too raw to say no. Still, she'd warned the kid about the night's activities. They had business to take care of, and it wouldn't be pleasant. Hira had been brave, Alice was glad to see, and she'd wanted to come anyway. The girl seemed eager to grow into her role, and so far, everything she'd been asked to do she had done—and done well.

They picked up Maggie and stopped at the pub they knew Mike frequented. They ordered a few pints to pass the time and waited. All the while, Alice watched Mike like a lioness watching her prey. The wanker downed one whiskey after another and threw games of darts, his aim becoming progressively worse as he grew more and more pissed. She watched his every move, his every expression, hate boiling inside her. What was it with men who used women like they weren't people? What gave them the bloody right to treat women like they didn't have a mind and heart of their own, like they ought to lie down or give over all of themselves? It was bollocks, all of it, and she was goddamn sick of it.

At last, Mike met Alice's eye. He glanced from her to Maggie and back at Alice again—and winked. The bloody nerve of him. He thought he was pulling one over on them, but the tosser was about to find out what she and Maggie thought of him and his terrible manners.

After an hour had gone, Hira wiggled in her chair, but she never complained. She was a good girl, knew when to keep her mouth shut. Finally, the barman yelled for last call. Mike ordered a final whiskey and started a game of darts. A shit example of a game, really, and Alice rolled her eyes as he missed the board not once but three times. When the lights flickered to send everyone on their way, Alice exchanged a look with Maggie.

"All right then," Maggie said, downing the last of her pint.

Alice laid a hand on the crown of Hira's head. "Are you ready?"

Confusion crossed her features. "Are we done?"

"Almost. Let's go."

"Do you think Biscuit is safe?" Hira asked as they walked to the car.

They'd left the dog in the car, and Alice knew the kid had worried about him ever since. "He's fine. And you can wait with him while we finish up here."

"Mike's about to leave," Maggie hissed.

They beat him to it, walking Hira swiftly to the car. They circled back through the small car park and positioned themselves outside the door. Right on time. Mike exited the pub, missing the last step and stumbling to regain his footing. He was pissed as hell. Likely trying to drown his guilt in whiskey for murdering his girlfriend, Alice thought, throat burning and muscles taut.

Stealthily, silently, they crept behind him as he strode across the lot. After a moment's hesitation, he ambled around to the back of the building and relieved himself against the wall.

When he turned, they sprang on him.

Alice punched him hard on the jaw, her row of diamond rings cutting his flesh. He grunted from the impact, and she smiled. "You liked that, did you?" She punched him again, this time knocking him off his feet.

"What the hell did I do to you?" He scrambled backward and once a safe distance, rose again to his feet.

"Is this about Ruth? I didn't do anything, I swear. She was mooning for ages about wanting to end her life. Nothing I could do about it."

"Nothing you could do, eh? So why was her sternum crushed? Her face a mess? I suppose she did that to herself," Alice said, voice edged with ice.

He shook his head. "I didn't touch her, I swear."

Rage poured over her like hot honey, sweet and sickening. "You won't touch anyone ever again, the way I see it," she said, waving at Maggie.

Maggie charged him from the side like a bull, knocking him to the ground. He swore and struggled blindly, the consequence of all the whiskey making his limbs heavy, his vision blurred. In seconds, Maggie had him pinned. She held him down as Alice punched him in his smug, stupid face, again and again. She lost count as her knuckles connected with flesh and bone, heart pounding in her ears, sweat stinging her eyes, or perhaps it was tears, she didn't know. All she knew was blind fury. Why did he have to hurt a woman who loved him? Why did he have to make her feel worthless? Did it make him feel more like a man? Her fist pounded his flesh, his face, his neck and shoulders again and again, her eyes blurring, her breath the only sound, ragged in her ears. He'd hurt her girl, made her feel like nothing. He'd killed Ruth. No man ruled her girls. No man ruled her.

He deserved this. He deserved this. He deserved this.

Fist after fist after fist, and the roaring of blood in her ears.

"Alice!" Maggie's voice pierced the haze.

Yet she couldn't stop. Her hands couldn't stop. Something arose from the deepest well inside her. How could her dad make her feel worthless, beating her senseless, hurting Louisa and Tommy and the others? But violence was the only way, wasn't it? It was what she knew; it was what had kept her safe, in the end. It was how justice was served. Perhaps she should thank her dad for making her tough and strong.

She whaled on Mike, unrelenting, not seeing. Kicking him until he went limp. His head went back, his eyes rolled in his head, his face a pool of blood, and still she hit him.

"Alice! He's out cold!" Maggie shouted. "Alice! You're going to kill him!" She shoved Alice hard. "You'll be arrested if you kill him. He's not worth it."

Alice stopped abruptly. Her shoulders rose and fell as she sucked in air, trying to slow her breathing. Her right hand throbbed, was a mess of blood and cuts and had already begun to swell. That would hurt in the morning, but she didn't care. This man would never hurt her or her girls again.

Maggie stared at Alice, not speaking. Not moving.

"Well," Alice said at last.

"Well," Maggie breathed. She bent over Mike and felt for a pulse at his neck. "He's alive, thank Christ. You could have killed him."

But she hadn't. She exhaled a breath of relief. Maggie was right. The wanker wasn't worth it, but one thing was for sure. He would remember her, and he would remember Maggie. Most of all, he'd never forget what he'd done to Ruth.

"Alice, did you kill him?"

Alice swiveled around at the sound of the small, distinctive voice. Hira stood behind the rubbish bins, her shadow stretching across the ground in the moonlight. She looked as if she might cry.

"He's not dead," Alice said, wincing as she flexed her hand. "But now he knows he can't hurt the Forty Elephants. Do you understand?"

Hira didn't answer a moment, but at last she nodded.

"Good girl," she said. "Let's get in the car. We're going home."

Alice sped away from the pub, her hand throbbing like the devil. Hira sat in back silent as a ghost, her face a mask of fear. After they dropped Maggie at her flat, they drove home in silence.

Alice stared hard at the black pavement ahead. Was this what was next, beating a man to death? She'd been a hoister nearly her whole life, and a bully when necessary, but it was always for her own protection and for the protection of her people. She was no murderer. But she'd been unable to stop herself. She could have finished him off, had Maggie not been there. He'd deserved it, hadn't he? She gripped the wheel tighter, trying to control her shaking hands.

She was no murderer.

When at last she put the car in park at the flat and killed the engine, she turned to Hira.

"Go inside."

"Are you coming?"

"Go!"

Hira slipped quickly out of the car, Biscuit trailing behind her, and paused momentarily at the door to peer back at the car—at Alice. When she closed the door to the flat, the final thread holding Alice together snapped.

Chest heaving, she began to cry.

⇛ 32 ⇚

Morning dawned, bringing a clear, frosty morning and a jewel-blue sky. Sunlight bathed the rooftops and the communal gardens and exposed the grime of the city that was normally hidden by banks of fog or clouds of coal dust. Seeing the city aglow was always something of a surprise; sunlight made it appear less sinister and dreary somehow, and far more alive. And yet, Alice resented the cheer of the day. It had been a few days since Ruth's death and the incident with Mike, and still she couldn't shake the thick malaise that had swallowed her like a pea-souper fog.

She was hit with the image of Mike's bloodied face, his limp body, and her unrelenting fist smeared in blood. She could have killed a man—with her own hands. An anger she hadn't known existed had bubbled up from inside her. Though she'd always considered herself tough and capable of violence when it served a purpose, she'd never gone that far. She'd never lost control.

It scared the hell out of her.

Subdued, she dressed and headed to Waterloo Station where she was to meet Simon.

Simon.

What would he think of her, if he knew what she was capable of?

He'd think her mad. He'd want nothing to do with her, that was what. And he'd be right to stay away. She was a villain and a leader of villains. What else was she to say about it? She'd never apologized for who she was and never felt the need before, and yet, she couldn't seem to look in the mirror that morning. She couldn't banish the image from her mind of the unconscious man who would likely be scarred for the rest of his life. Even if he'd deserved a lesson. Some line had been crossed, she knew, but she didn't know how to go back to the person from before that night—from before Ruth had been murdered.

As Alice walked the remaining blocks, she thought of Hira, her expression that night by the waste bins. She'd been so stunned, so sad and so...afraid of Alice, and not the kind of fear Alice had commanded on a daily basis from her crew, but a real, raw fear. She'd felt the kid's eyes on her in the dark, all night in the shared bedroom. And for the first time, Alice wondered if Hira might choose to leave the Forties for good, perhaps go to the inspector after all.

Alice would be faced with a choice then: let the kid go or make her pay for her narking the way any of the others would have to do. Neither option felt right.

As she arrived at Waterloo Station, she immediately caught sight of Simon. The moment he saw her, he lit up like the brightest star on a moonless night, and she felt herself go warm all over. *Damn him.* He was handsome in a cravat and coat, with his hair combed and oiled neatly for the races. A cigarette hung from his bottom lip. She'd dressed well herself in a hunter-green coat and cream cloche hat, kid gloves, and a pair of sparkling rubies at her ears to match the red of her lips. Mustn't go to the races dressed like a rag from south London.

"Miss Diamond, aren't you a sight for sore eyes," he said, leaning in to plant a kiss on her cheek.

"Ain't I though?"

He laughed. "I never can predict what you'll say."

"I'd like to keep it that way."

"I suspect you will," he replied with a wink.

She followed him to the train platform and landed in a seat at the end of the train car. Sitting next to him, she felt for a moment as if she could breathe again. As if he were a life raft and he would keep her from drowning. Handsome, good, cheerful Simon McGill. He was more than she deserved.

They traveled the hour outside the city to the Ascot racetrack in a tiny town near Windsor. When they arrived, an excited crowd was already streaming through the main gates. The track wasn't sophisticated with its dirt lanes, but the lawn beyond it was a deep, lush green and trimmed in perfect, even swathes of grass. At the starting line, horses were held behind a series of gates that looked like miniature stables, and a colorful row of flags stretched overhead. From a distance, the audience resembled busy ants milling about the tiered seats that arced toward the sky.

Simon led them to their seats beneath a large private box that hovered above them. Alice knew who watched the races from the highest, most exclusive point. The royals, at least during high season in the summer months. Well, la-tee-da, she thought, as she saw cousin someone or other kissing the Duchess of Who-Gave-a-Shit on the cheek. She didn't usually ride out to the Ascot track, and neither did the Elephant and Castle boys. But that day they were scoping out new turf to set up a bookie racket. The Hurst Park races were crowded with the Sabini gang who already "managed" the books. She wondered if Bert of the Elephant and Castle had something to say about her incident with Mike. The tosser was one of Bert's after all. Alice didn't know if she gave a damn. Bert must know that brute had it coming.

She glanced around at the men in their three-piece suits and fine coats fit for Sundays, and the dames trussed up in their winter finery.

When she'd been to the races in July, women wore silk stockings, elaborate fasteners with mesh netting in vivid colors, oxfords, and silk dresses in stripes, florals, or soft pastels that tapered and fluttered below the hem of their coats. Though a sunny day, the chill in the air that December day meant instead, beautiful furs and scarves, wool hats and gorgeous lined gloves. Alice knew she looked as good as any of them, even if she didn't walk or talk like the wealthy who floated through the crowd as if they were above it all. Above her. She grinned at the imagined conversation she'd like to have with them.

"Maybe we should have a look at the boards before we settle in," Alice said.

"You going to place a bet?" Simon asked, brow raised.

She shrugged. "Maybe. We'll see if any of the horses strike my fancy."

They threaded through the crowd to the statistic boards.

"Alice? What are you doing here?"

A voice she knew as well as her own. Her brother strode toward her, a couple of Elephant and Castle men at his side. Tommy had a cigar in his hand, and he smelled as if he'd already had a few pints.

"I'm here to do my blooming laundry," Alice replied.

The others laughed at her barb and then turned to the boards to study the statistics.

"Who's your friend?" Tommy stared at Simon, taking him in from head to toe.

Simon cleared his throat. "I'm Simon McGill."

"The fellow who runs the pub?" her brother asked.

"That's the one."

Tommy shook his hand. "Who are you betting on?"

"I'm not a betting man. I'm just here to watch, maybe buy Alice a gin and tonic."

Tommy pointed at Alice with the two fingers that held his cigarette. "What's your bid?"

She peered out at the race track, back at the list of names, and studied the poster with the sketches of each jockey and their horse. Jelly Roll, Orpheus, Dynamite, Oscar, Soleil.

"Stupid names," she said. "Who names their horse Orpheus?"

"Don't you know the story?" Simon asked. "Orpheus can't look back as he is walking out of the land of Hades, or he'll lose his lover. I think it's a clever name. The horse had better run and not look back."

"You would." She smiled to soften her sarcasm. Soleil was the only name that appealed to her. "Should we see what the others are saying?"

Tommy shrugged. "Suit yourself."

She stepped up to the betting booth and watched as a half-dozen men haggled over who they believed it would be.

"Five pounds on Orpheus," one of Tommy's friends said.

Another said, "Twenty quid on Oscar."

His friends beside him whistled. "Better hope you win, mate."

The bookie worked quickly, recording bids, taking money.

Alice noticed a man beside the bookie, working on his sheets. It was one of the Elephant and Castle gang, planning to pinch off the top of the bookie's winnings. A clever way to make easy money, as long as they had the muscle behind them to make good on any threats.

Simon seemed to know to keep quiet and even stepped back a few feet, distancing himself from the bookie and those placing their bets. Or perhaps it was to distance himself from what he knew to be trouble: the gang members, Alice's brother, and perhaps even her. Her stomach clenched at the thought of disappointing him, of not being the woman he wanted her to be—and she immediately became angry with herself for thinking such a thing. She didn't care about pleasing a man, least of all one who would never understand her world. She thought again of

Mike, of how disgusted Simon would be to know the truth. But when she glanced at Simon, now several paces away, there was no sign of disgust. Instead, he gave her a goddamn adorable smile. She didn't like what he was doing to her, melting her defenses, causing her to question her choices, her lifestyle. It made her uneasy, made her think about being someone else beyond queen of the underworld.

"He isn't one of us, is he?" Her brother's voice came in her ear. "Your boy Simon." When Alice didn't make eye contact with her brother, he pinched her elbow between his thumb and forefinger. "You know that's a bad idea, especially here at the races where he could learn too much."

She pulled out of his grasp. "I know. I'm just having a little fun, that's all. It isn't serious."

"Don't let it go on too long." Her brother's blue eyes were hard as cut glass. "He seems like a nice bloke. You might find yourself falling in love before too long. And that would mean trouble. Big trouble."

Her face heated at his words. "When's the last time I fell in love, you ass?" she snapped.

He held up his hands. "No need to be mardy. I'm just looking out for you. Giving you a little brotherly advice."

She *was* mardy, and she had a right to be angry. Her brother always put his nose where it didn't belong and he'd also insulted her. She'd never been a silly woman. She knew what she was doing. "I'll see you at home." She pushed through the small crowd of men to join Simon. "Ready to find our seats?"

"Aye," he said.

Their seats were a few rows up from the track, elevated just enough to see the race in its entirety, start to finish. They ordered drinks and peanuts from the service lad and huddled next to each other. At least they had clear skies and not even a whisper of a breeze. Coupled with bright sunshine, the day felt like early autumn rather than almost winter at Christmastime.

Alice wanted to forget her brother's warning—tried to push it to the back of her mind—but she knew he was right. She put them all at risk by being with Simon. And deep down, though Simon was trustworthy, she knew she could still never trust him. When things got...sticky, he could always turn on them. That was the problem; she couldn't trust anyone not to turn on her, except her family.

Alice sipped her drink and scanned the crowd. On their left, Darby Sabini sat in a box with a woman in a large violet lace-trimmed hat on his right, and on his left and behind him, he was flanked by an army of his men. She frowned. She'd thought the Elephant and Castle had staked their claim at this track. She wondered how it would play out in the end. The body count would likely be high.

Her mind drifted to the big job next week. She'd been working diligently on the details, gathering more information about the textile warehouse. When it opened and closed, who worked there, the locks, and how often the security patrolled the premises. She'd already alerted her fence to the potential cash bomb coming his way. All that was left was telling the girls the final details and dividing them into teams. It would be an enormous operation, staging a multipronged hit on three major department stores on the same day as the warehouse. Her nerves jittered each time she thought of it. It would go well—it had to. This was their best shot at buying that building—and their freedom. A home, a place of refuge. A place she'd wished she'd managed to claim before Ruth had gotten herself murdered. Her heart clenched and she downed the rest of her gin and tonic. Better to focus now on what was next. What she could do to help the others.

"What are you thinking about?" Simon asked. "You look right pleased with yourself."

She smiled. "Oh I am."

"And?" he said, eyes teasing.

"And I can't tell you."

"Ah, I see."

She noted the color of disappointment in his voice. "Look, it's about business. I'm going to buy a property. You don't need to know more, or it'll put you in the line of fire should things go south."

"You know, there is another way to do things," Simon said, casting her a sideways glance as he chewed on a handful of peanuts.

"What do you mean?" She dipped her left hand into the bucket of peanuts and cracked one of the shells in half. Her right hand still ached from Mike's ugly face.

"You deserve more than having to fight your way out of scrapes and bad situations." He glanced down at her right hand. He'd attempted to hold it in his on the train. She'd winced and pulled away, told him she'd bruised it badly. When he'd continued with his questions, she'd snapped at him. That had shut him up quickly.

"So I should sit there and take it, when someone attacks me or one of my friends? I may be a woman, Simon, but I take care of myself and my own."

He cleared his throat. "Of course. That's not what I meant. What I meant is, you don't have to…take things that aren't yours to make a living."

She realized then what he was trying to say. She didn't have to be a thief. She could get an honest job making horrid wages, wearing horrid clothes, and scrape by for the rest of her miserable life. It was as if he didn't know her at all. She realized then that the very idea of pretending to be someone other than Diamond Annie was foolish. He didn't know her, not really. He saw the soft side of her in the bedroom, the woman who loved to dance and party and enjoy life where she could get it.

The woman with nightmares and a soft underbelly that she showed to a very rare few. He'd been one of them and now she regretted it. He thought she could be someone different. But she couldn't. He didn't know the woman who beat a man within an inch of his life, who could have finished him off and walked away.

"What would you have me do instead?" she demanded. "Be a washerwoman? A cook perhaps, or a chimney sweep? Do you have any idea how many hours per day and how many jobs I'd need to put a roof over my head, never mind my family's?" She dropped the remaining peanuts on the ground. "If you can't handle a woman who makes her own living in her own way, then this little show between us is over. In fact, I knew this was a bad idea."

She stood hastily.

He grabbed her hand, and once again she winced and jerked it away.

"I'm sorry, darlin'. Please. Stay. I know who you truly are. Your talents and charisma. You are more than this. You're intelligent, capable. You deserve better—"

"Collect my winnings if Soleil wins," she interrupted him. "Treat yourself to something nice. Don't come around again, Simon. This is finished."

She walked quickly toward the exit. Eyes stinging, an ache opening in her chest. She cursed herself for being so foolish. She'd known better—usually avoided the heartbreak and the stupidity of being blinded by emotion. Now here she was, swallowing tears over Simon McGill. She was suddenly glad she hadn't told him enough to rat her or her girls out. Thankfully, she'd had the good sense to leave before they'd become too entwined.

Before they'd fallen too in love.

As she walked swiftly to the gate, she told herself she was relieved she'd ended things. Now she'd be able to focus on what mattered: the Forty Elephants and her headquarters.

Throat tight, eyes stinging, she hailed a taxicab to the train station.

⫤ 33 ⊫

Despite the shiny, sunny day, Hira was ill at ease. She'd replayed the image of Alice beating the man, nearly to death, in her mind over and over again until she'd become sick. Alice could have killed him—she nearly had. Hira shivered as she saw the woman in her mind's eye, covered in blood, her eyes wild like she didn't know where she was. More than ever, Hira understood she could never disappoint Alice or let her down, or she'd end up like one of Alice's targets. The terrible truth was beginning to sink in: no matter how kind Alice could be toward her, she was still the boss, and she still believed she must rule by violence. And Hira was under her care, temporarily.

As night encroached, the unusually warm day turned cold and once again, Hira was grateful she had a place to sleep, even if she felt like a burden. Even if she felt like she couldn't relax. Alice hadn't come home after the incident with the barman, and Hira hadn't seen her that night either. Worse still, Mr. Diamond seemed particularly angry and was crashing around the flat.

Hira slipped as soundlessly as she could through the kitchen to the bedroom. After shooing Biscuit in behind her, she closed the door and sat on the bed. The flimsy mattress sank instantly beneath her weight. She wondered where Alice had been going all those nights she didn't come home. She didn't like staying in Alice's room without her there. She felt like a stowaway that could be tossed out on her ear at any moment. Worse, she jumped at every sound in the night. She was beginning to wonder if she and Biscuit would be better off on the street after all.

A loud thud came at the door.

Biscuit's head cocked to the side and he began to growl.

"Shh, Biscuit," she said, pushing her index finger against her lips. She hastily shoved her things into her satchel: her books, the Ganesha, and the dress Dorothy had given her. Luckily, she hadn't yet removed her coat and scarf. If she needed to make a run for it, she could.

Another loud thud came at the door. "Open up!"

Hira's eyes went wide with fear. It was Mr. Diamond. He'd been threatening her for days, looking at her as if she disgusted him. The same way her uncle had looked at her. She didn't understand why some people noticed only that she looked different from them and that was enough to make them hate her.

She waited, limbs tense, praying Mr. Diamond would leave if she ignored him.

The pounding grew louder. "Open up!"

Hira began to shake. Biscuit crouched into position like he was ready to pounce, another growl rumbling in his throat.

The next moment, the door flew open.

Mr. Diamond stood on the other side, face red as an apple. Sweat dripped down his temples. "What are you still doing here?"

She didn't dare reply. She got the feeling he didn't care for an answer. He only wanted to be hateful, violent. She could see it in his jaw, the way he clenched his fists at his side. Slowly, she stood, prepared to make a run for it.

"I think it's time you paid your way, wench."

She darted toward the door—too late. He yanked her arm and

grabbed her by the hair, pulling until her head tilted back enough to see his face. Pain rippled over her scalp and down her neck. Tears sprang to her eyes. She bit down on her lip to keep from screaming.

"You don't live 'ere. I don't care what Alice 'as told you." He shoved her and she stumbled forward.

Biscuit began to bark, baring his teeth.

"Shut up!" he shouted. "Or I'll kick you across the room."

Biscuit ignored the warning, barking loudly, insistently.

Mr. Diamond lunged for him, his limbs clumsy from too much drink. Biscuit dodged him easily.

Hira screamed. "Leave him be!"

The man whirled around to face her. "Fine, have it your way." He started toward her.

Heart pounding, her hand found its way to the flap of her satchel. She lifted it quickly and closed her fist around a small leather hilt. Her knife. She stabbed the air in front of her, making the slashing movement Alice had taught her.

"You want to play dirty, do ya?" Disgust and rage twisted his features until he resembled a gargoyle.

She made the slashing motion again, holding the man off a few safe paces away. For the first time, she was glad she had the weapon. "I will leave, if you stand back and let me go." Her voice was strong, firm.

"What's going on in here!" One-legged Tommy staggered into the room, rubbing his belly, his hair standing straight on end. He looked as if he'd been asleep.

Hira took her chance. She dashed for the door. Biscuit followed at her heels, and in an instant, she'd darted out of the bedroom and the flat, leaving the door hanging open.

Mr. Diamond filled the doorway, waving a fist in the air. "Don't come back!"

She pumped her legs faster. Where would she go? She couldn't go to Dorothy's, not after what she'd done. Guilt had gnawed at Hira ever since, and worse, regret. If she'd only told Alice no, that she wouldn't betray her friend that way, she'd have another place to go.

A gale wrapped around her, stealing the last vestiges of warmth and carrying them away on the wind. It was nearly winter now, only a couple of weeks from Christmas—and she had absolutely no one and nowhere to go. Tears pricked her eyes, and soon she gasped for breath as sobs shook her lean little body. As another wind roared around her, she rested against the brick wall of a shuttered store. She couldn't stay outside overnight; she'd freeze or catch her death. She had to find shelter. But where?

Biscuit whined and wagged his tail. He wanted shelter, too.

Another answer pushed its way to the front of her mind: she could always go home, to Mayfair. To Uncle Clyde's. At the very least she'd be warm and fed. Even if she had to live in Northumberland in the end, she'd have a place to stay where she wouldn't have to steal to survive, or threaten people with knives. But they would take Biscuit from her. The tears began, and she wiped her eyes on her sleeve. The cold seemed to intensify every second, her wet cheeks freezing, and violent shivers racking her body. That was what she'd have to do—go home, if she couldn't think of something else very soon.

Her only consolation was that the Forties were to have a meeting tomorrow at the factory; Alice was going to lay out the rest of the plans for the weekend—the big heist—and Hira could tell her what had happened. Maybe she'd insist another of the girls take her in. And if not, maybe Alice could help her think of something.

An idea struck Hira suddenly, like a clap of thunder. The factory! She could sleep in the factory, at least for the night. Though not particularly warm, it would be dry in the office, and she'd be out of the wind.

She could curl up beside Biscuit for warmth. Perhaps find some cloth or a blanket or jacket left behind by one of the ladies.

She bent to pet Biscuit, to console herself more than him. His warm brown eyes stared back at her. He licked her hand and the faintest smile tugged at the corners of her mouth. At least she had her little furry friend with her. He always made her feel less alone.

"Let's go, Biscuit. Let's get out of the cold."

= 34 =

Dorothy checked her handbag and lunch tote for the hundredth time and let out a frustrated huff. She'd spent the better part of two days searching her flat from top to bottom without luck. It was time to face facts. The key to the storage room was gone. She must have left it at the store by accident, or dropped it on her way home. It wasn't like her to lose things or to be forgetful. She'd been so flustered by Allen's lovely gift of a long string of costume pearls that she'd forgotten all about the key until he'd mentioned it again the night before. When she'd returned to work the next day, she'd made a promise to scour the store on her lunch break, and if she still couldn't find it, to tell Alan the key was missing. She'd no sooner moved to her post when Allen's angry voice boomed from the office. The shopgirls scattered like marbles.

"Dorothy!" he shouted from the back of the store. "Come here at once!"

She froze, her heart dropping from what felt like a forty-foot cliff. The key. Had he found it? Now he would know she'd lost it, that she wasn't responsible or trustworthy.

"Dorothy McBride!" he shouted her name a second time.

She bit her lip and rushed through the store, ignoring the curious glances from the others.

The office door stood ajar, and inside, Allen was pacing back and forth like a tiger, telephone receiver gripped in his hand. He tripped over his words as he shouted into the telephone, his Adam's apple bobbing in tune with his anger. "Entirely empty. No, of course not." He huffed. "I'll come down to the station this afternoon." He slammed down the phone, eyes bulging.

She felt as if she was going to be sick. "What's happened?" Her voice was barely more than a whisper.

"It's gone!" he said, the vein in his neck throbbing. "All of it! Everything. The storage room is empty!" He pointed at her. "I thought you, of all of my employees, could be trusted."

She gasped. "All of it?" Tears pricked at the back of her eyes. He was right; he had entrusted her with the key, and she'd failed him, but she would not dissolve into a mess of tears.

"The earrings and brooches. The necklaces. The diamond-studded watch. All of it. What in hell happened? Did you leave the key somewhere, or did you play me for a fool?"

Though she fought the tears, they came anyway. He thought she may have stolen the items? How could he think such a thing? She'd never steal from her employer and most of all, she'd never steal from her boyfriend! "I must have dropped it. I've looked everywhere for it, but it hasn't turned up and now this. I swear it, Allen, I'd never do such a thing intentionally. You know that. I'm so sorry." She moved toward him and wrapped her arms around his middle to comfort them both. "If there's anything I can do..."

He recoiled as if bitten by a snake. "Are you mad? You are my employee."

Her arms dropped at her sides. "Oh, right, of course. I'm sorry, Allen. I—"

"Sir. You meant sir, or Mr. Harrington," he said, blowing out an anxious stream of smoke.

She stared at him in surprise before hurt stole over her. When he noticed her expression, his tone softened.

"We're at work, remember?" he said, squeezing her hand gently for an instant before letting it drop. "And I'm trying very hard to find a reason not to fire you."

"Oh. Yes, of course, I understand, Al—sir," she quickly amended. "I swear, I've looked everywhere and planned to tell you today. I really don't know what happened."

"Someone will have to replace the stolen items."

She stilled. If he wanted her to replace them, she could say goodbye to the little extras she purchased for her designs. She could say goodbye to her home. She and mum would have to move. Her eyes filled again. "You'll have me pay for them, sir? I couldn't possibly afford them—"

"Just get back to work! Until I decide what to do with you," he blustered.

She rushed out of the room, wiping her eyes, trying to collect herself. On the showroom floor, the others stared at her, wanting to ask what had happened but too polite to do so.. Except Mildred.

"You in trouble?" she asked.

"Aren't you a nosy parker," Dorothy snapped.

Mildred smirked, making her beak of a nose uglier than ever. "Everyone else will know soon enough."

Dorothy gave Mildred her back. It took every ounce of her focus not to cry. She forced herself to think about her mother's lemon tea cakes, her new scarf, and the design she'd begun last night. Anything to get her mind off the fact that Allen was angry with her. It would pass, she told herself. He'd forgive her. She'd work her very hardest, sell more than anyone else. Besides, he loved her!

Soon, the police were crawling all over the store, asking questions, poking through the storage room, the office, and the back room. They interviewed Dorothy and the rest of the shopgirls.

When the police left, Allen gave Mildred instructions for locking up later that evening and didn't so much as say goodbye to Dorothy. Despondent, sick to her stomach, she watched him go. He'd chosen Mildred this time and of course he had. He was still furious with Dorothy. And she felt horrid, wanting nothing more than to hide in her little flat with a large glass of gin.

A moment later, the front door to the shop swung open and in walked Dennis, the postman. He'd come every day with a smile and a kind word.

"Good afternoon, Miss McBride," he said. "You look beautiful today. Is that a new dress?"

It was and she didn't care, especially if Allen didn't care, and given the day, all she really wanted to do was put on her nightgown.

"Thank you, Dennis, but I'm really not in the mood."

He looked taken aback and she instantly regretted snapping at him. He clearly liked her, as Hira had once pointed out, but she wasn't interested. He would probably bore her and then she'd be unkind to him, as she just had been. Never mind that she was in a relationship with someone else. Maybe—she hoped. Her throat ached with unshed tears at the thought of Allen ending things between them, all for a mistake. A terrible mistake but a mistake nonetheless.

Dennis shuffled through a packet of letters in his hands, set some on the countertop, stuffed others back into his satchel, and sorted through a series of small packages. When he found what he was looking for, he frowned.

"I thought this was for Mr. Harrington, but it's for the Mrs.," he said. "My mistake. Too bad I've already been to their residence earlier today. Guess I'll have to leave it for tomorrow."

"The Mrs.?" she said. "Allen—Mr. Harrington isn't married. He lives with a male flatmate."

His eyebrows shot up, nearly reaching his hairline. "He lives with his wife."

The air left Dorothy's lungs. There had to be some mistake. Allen had mentioned a flatmate several times—said it was a "he" in fact, and a real lout of a man, but never a wife. She squeezed her eyes closed. How could this day have gotten worse?

"Are you all right?" Dennis asked, concern etched on his face. "Do you need to sit down?"

She shook her head. "I just remembered something I forgot to do is all."

"If you're sure?" Dennis's concerned brown eyes watched her carefully. His polite attention shouldn't irritate her, but it did. She just wanted to think about this new horrible news alone.

"Go on about your day, Dennis," she insisted.

"If you needed anything, you'd ask, wouldn't you?" he said.

"You're far too nice, and it's not necessary. Really, I'm fine."

He reached for the mistaken letter with the aim of putting it back inside his bag when Dorothy stilled his hand. "I'll see that Mr. Harrington gets this. I'm sure he'll be back any moment."

"Are you sure?" he asked.

"No problem at all," she said, forcing some levity into her voice.

"Cheers." Dennis tipped his hat and stepped out into the blustery day.

When he'd gone, Dorothy snatched up the letter and read the address printed carefully on the front. Her eyes blurred with tears as she saw the words "Mr. and Mrs. Allen Harrington" in a sterile type on the envelope. The return address was from Manchester. Dorothy knew there were textile mills in the north, so perhaps this was about business. Someone who didn't know Allen personally—someone who didn't know he wasn't married. A desperate supposition, but it was all she had. As soon as work ended, she'd go to Allen's home to deliver the letter. Find out the truth.

She twitched with nerves the remainder of her shift, watching the clock. When at last it was time, she pulled on her felted red hat and red leather gloves that had cost three months' savings. She hastily threw on her wool coat, paying no heed to the large lapel that flapped as she walked and ignoring the button that would have fastened the coat closed. She couldn't take it, the not knowing. She shoved through the front door, not bothering to say good night to the lady detective who had inconveniently arrived after Allen had left.

Dorothy huffed as she walked, gaining momentum and speed as the December wind howled around her. After several minutes, her fear and sadness gave way to anger. Was Allen really married? How could he have treated her this way, taking her out on the town, making love to her—telling her he loved her! The gifts, too. How dare he lie to her! Did he think she was dumb, as the others did? She didn't know what everyone saw that made them think her dumb. Her perfect makeup? Her porcelain-doll skin and cornflower blue eyes? She couldn't help that she was beautiful, if her taste was impeccable, and why should she apologize for it? She shouldn't and she wouldn't.

She didn't want to be that girl—the one whom everyone called dumb. She wasn't dumb! She'd sold three times the number of frocks as every other shopgirl that week. She had the highest number of repeat customers who sought her out when they returned to the store searching for a fresh look or a gift for a friend. She was good at her job! And she was clever *and* beautiful! She was tired of people making her feel otherwise. She stalked through Mayfair unseeing, passing the painted latticework frames of the sixteenth-century buildings, the artful brickwork of others, and dozens of windows framed by dormant flower boxes. She wound through impeccably clean streets, with luxury shops and private courtyards or patches of garden. Normally she relished a walk through the West End. That day she kept her eyes forward, her fists clenched, her anger red hot.

When she came upon Allen's building, at last, she stopped to study the entrance. There wasn't a doorman as she had once pictured, but the building was as charming and well-maintained as the many others she'd passed. She found a spot out of the way of the entrance, behind a statuette and two large conical bushes to shade her from view and settled in to wait a while. She'd wait until she saw him, and if he didn't show, she'd call at his door. She imagined the surprise on his face—his handsome face, she thought begrudgingly—and the hurried way he would send her off to speak to her later. But what if Mrs. Harrington was with him? Dorothy couldn't ask to speak to Allen without explaining who she was, or at least admitting she was a shopgirl who seemed deranged enough to follow her boss home.

Her eyes pricked with tears for the second time that day. Allen had been sleeping with her while he had a wife. What would Mum say? Dorothy could hear it now, her mum lecturing her for the dozenth time about how she needed to keep men at arm's length. She squeezed her eyes closed. It wasn't only Allen she was losing; they hadn't spent all that much time together yet. It was the dream of something more, something better than the quiet, dull life she shared with her mum. She'd grown fond of the dinners out, the shows, and the hotels. The attention and the gifts. But it was all a ruse that meant nothing. Again.

An hour later, her legs grew tired, her hands cold, and soon the anger drained away. What was she doing here? Had she really planned to confront him—while he was with his wife? She'd probably get herself fired, if she hadn't already after the incident with the key. As the sky deepened from blue to purple to silver and night fell, she shivered with cold. Maybe she wouldn't confront Allen, or she'd decline his next invitation—purposefully and loudly. His wife could have him. The thought of denying him felt powerful, and she liked the sound of that.

Lifting her chin proudly, she climbed out from behind the bushes and walked to the train station to head home.

⊐ 35 ⊏

Dorothy went straight home, poured a large gin, and picked at a plate of chicken and boiled potatoes before going to bed. After hours of tossing in the covers, her thoughts swinging between the missing key and the potential of a Mrs. Allen Harrington, she finally threw back the covers. Her hot-water bottle had cooled anyway and the night chill had begun to creep in. Perhaps she'd put the kettle on, have an herbal tea, and refill the bottle. She slid her feet into her pink slippers and padded into the kitchen. She opened the door to the stove and peered inside. The hot coals were smoldering now and needed a refresh. She added a briquette to the fire, lit the stove top, and filled the kettle with water. When she'd finished, she sat with her tea at the dining table. She retraced her steps for the hundredth time, thinking back to when Allen had given her the key. From the pocket in her handbag where she kept it while at the store, to the perfume tray on her vanity in her bedroom—

She stopped.

There had been one other person in her bedroom besides her mother. One other person who had spent time both in her home and at the store that could have taken the key. Hira.

Dorothy's mind raced ahead to the day when Hira had come in tears, filthy and lonely and in need of care. The day Dorothy had washed her hair, given her fresh clothes, and fed her. She'd cared for the girl without expecting a single thing in return. That was the way of things with children: they took and adults gave to them. But Hira wasn't just a child. She lived in the streets, spent her time with Diamond Annie and the Forty Elephants. Dorothy had seen Hira talking to Diamond Annie with her own eyes. If Hira wasn't a member of the Forty Elephants, she wouldn't have met the infamous queen of the Forties outside of the store—would she?

Heat rose up Dorothy's neck and blushed across her cheeks. What a fool she had been! To trust the child she'd seen with Diamond Annie. Of course Hira had taken the key! The little girl had duped her, played on her trust. When no one was looking, one of the Forty Elephants must have slipped inside and emptied the storage room. The only problem was, someone was always looking. How could they have unlocked and cleared the storage room without inviting suspicion? And they couldn't have broken into the store at night. Other items would have gone missing for one thing, and Allen was fanatical about locking up at night. There were twice as many locks on the doors as any other store. And his store was one of the few that left lights on inside all night long. It must be someone who could slip into the storage room unnoticed, who wouldn't arouse suspicion. Someone, perhaps, who already worked at Marshall & Snelgrove. A someone with a lot of nerve who didn't care about losing their job.

Only one name came to mind that fit the bill: Charlotte Taylor.

Dorothy's heart pounded in her chest. Charlotte was rougher around the edges than the other girls. She was mouthy and sarcastic, didn't do a great job working with customers. In fact, Dorothy hadn't seen her sell anything. That had to be it! Hira was working with Charlotte.

The tea turned bitter in Dorothy's mouth. She'd really liked Hira. She'd seemed innocent and refined somehow, her manners and her expressions. Despite her clothes, she was a pretty little thing and seemed remarkably sweet and naive. What a fool Dorothy had been! She'd been used and it was unforgivable. Well, she was done being kind and accommodating and done doing Allen's bidding, too.

Tomorrow was Thursday, Hira's visiting day. The day, Dorothy would turn the child over to the lady detective. And she'd tell Allen where he could stick it.

Dorothy had been unable to go back to sleep after her realization the night before. She was disgusted with Allen and furious with Hira and Charlotte. Now there was only one thing left to do: she must confront them all. She'd show them she wasn't the dumb, gullible woman they thought her to be. She deserved their respect. If nothing else, she wanted to respect herself. Look back on all of this and be proud of standing up for herself.

When Dorothy arrived at the store, she did her best to act normally as she watched Allen stride through the store giving instructions to each of the shopgirls. Charlotte skipped in fifteen minutes late and quickly disappeared to the frocks section.

Impatiently, she waited for Hira to arrive and for the right moment to approach Allen. But hours slipped by and she began to wonder if Hira might skip her usual visit to the store. They'd made it a habit to meet the last weeks. Dorothy fed Hira, and in turn, she'd ask to see Dorothy's drawings. She'd always been a dear, fawning over them, and Dorothy believed she'd been genuinely impressed. Now she wasn't so sure what to believe and yet, somehow, she couldn't reconcile the child she knew with the kind of person who would steal from her. All Dorothy could surmise was that Hira didn't have a choice. That she'd been threatened to do what the gang demanded of her.

As if she'd conjured the child with her thoughts, at last, hours late, Hira pushed through the front door of the department store.

———

Hira paused outside of Marshall & Snelgrove, her back to the brick between it and the neighboring boutique. Biscuit sat at her feet and looked up at her, confused as to why they were waiting.

"I don't want to do this," she whispered. Biscuit tilted his head sideways as if he understood her. "But I know it's the right thing to do. I like Dorothy very much."

He barked a reply.

"I'm glad we agree."

She took a deep breath and reached for the heavy brass handle.

Dorothy caught sight of her immediately and waved her toward the shoe section. Hira guessed she had a few choice words she wanted to say, and more dread trickled through her limbs.

"Hello," Hira said shyly. "I wanted to talk to you. To tell you something."

"You have some nerve showing your face here," Dorothy hissed. She crossed her arms over her chest. "After all I did to help you, and you repay me by stealing from me!"

Hira's large brown eyes filled with tears. "I didn't have a choice. I–I had to, for the Forty Elephants." She looked at Dorothy, her expression imploring. "I'm sorry. Please forgive me." The tears leaked from the corner of her eyes. "I didn't want to do it. I feel terrible, and that's why I'm here. I wanted to apologize and tell you the truth."

"I'm in a heap of trouble because of you." Dorothy waved an angry finger at her.

Hira nodded, sending a cascade of tears down her cheeks. "I know. I'm s-sorry. I came to make it up to you."

Dorothy glared. "And how do you plan to do that?"

"I know who took all of those things in the storage room."

"Your gang. Diamond Annie," she cut in.

"Yes," Hira said. "It was Lottie."

"Lottie?" she asked.

"Charlotte Taylor," Hira said. "She's one of the Forty Elephants. I took the key and Lottie emptied the storage room."

Some of Dorothy's anger seemed to drain away. "I thought as much. So she's one of the Forties?"

"Yes. She took a job here to be closer to the merchandise. Make it easier for their operations."

"You have to go to the police," Dorothy insisted. "I can tell Allen—Mr. Harrington, owner of the store, but you'll need to tell the police everything you know about Diamond Annie and the Forties, and Charlotte, of course. You could tell the lady detective. That's why she works here."

Hira shook her head. She would help Dorothy redeem herself at work because she liked her, and Hira owed it to her after what she'd done. But she wouldn't turn Alice and the Forties in. For one, they would know it was her and come after her. Secondly, the police would drag her to the orphanage. At least this way, she could redeem Dorothy but protect herself and Alice.

"I will help you, but I won't endanger Alice. She has looked after me. Been kind to me in her way."

Hira felt the weight of Dorothy's gaze, and she looked down. "I'm really sorry. I was sad to do it. You're my only friend." What she didn't say was how she'd been unable to sleep for a few days after the incident and how her tummy had ached too much to eat the next day.

Hira felt a hand on her shoulder and looked up.

"It's all right, Hira. Thank you for telling me the truth. That was very brave of you."

She met Dorothy's clear blue eyes. "Are you my friend again?"

Dorothy smiled. "I'm your friend."

She returned her friend's pretty smile and wrapped her arms around Dorothy in a quick hug. Biscuit licked Dorothy's leg, despite her stockings, and they both began to laugh.

"You're my friend too, Biscuit," Dorothy said. "Now, run along. I need to speak to my boss. I'll see you again soon."

Hira nodded, reluctantly leaving the store. She hoped Dorothy meant what she said, that they'd see other again soon. Very soon.

Feeling a little lighter, Hira joined the well-dressed crowds of Oxford Street.

———

Dorothy watched Hira flit through the crowd outside until she disappeared. Relief flooded through her. She really enjoyed the little girl, had even come to look forward to their visits, and now that she'd apologized, Dorothy felt like she could forgive her. In the end, Hira was a child and had been trying to survive like the rest of them. She'd done what she'd had to do while in the care of a gang. Hopefully she'd learned her lesson and would rethink the company she was keeping. A feat easier said than done, Dorothy realized. Hira had very few places to go.

The *ca-ching* of the cash register jolted her from her thoughts. She glanced at the clock. Twelve thirty. Allen would be having his lunch now. She left her post in the shoe section and hurriedly walked to his office, clasping her hands to keep them from shaking. Oddly, Allen's door was closed. She frowned. He never kept his door closed, not even when on business calls. Perhaps he'd stepped out and she hadn't seen him go? She hoped not. She had to get this off her chest now or she might burst. She'd just take a quick peek inside his office, perhaps leave a note on his desk telling him she'd like to talk to him. She turned the doorknob and pushed the door open quietly, tentatively in case he was on an important call. Not that she owed him the courtesy after her discovery of a Mrs. Harrington, but he was still her boss and thousands of dollars worth of jewelry had gone missing while she held the key. As angry and as hurt as she was, she still couldn't afford to get sacked until she found another job.

She peeked inside and gasped.

There, sitting on Allen's desk, was Charlotte, her legs parted. Allen stood between them, his hands moving up and down her back. Her arms were wrapped around his neck, and they were locked in a passionate kiss.

"Allen!" Dorothy snapped. "You're disgusting!" The words escaped before she could monitor herself. How many women did he have on the side? The anger she'd felt the day before lit again inside her, this time spreading over her like a raging fire. How dare he!

Allen looked up, his face a mask of confusion for an instant. "You know not to barge in here. My office is off-limits. You're already in trouble, Miss McBride."

She rolled her eyes and crossed her arms over her chest. All of the salesgirls had heard—and obeyed—his strict demands about his office, the showroom, the staff room. But here he was, breaking his own rules.

"Off-limits to everyone but Charlotte and her lingerie, you mean?" Dorothy said curtly. "So much for being inappropriate with the boss at work."

"Oh, shut up, you tramp," Charlotte shot back. "As if you haven't already been ass over tits for this man for months."

"You knew I was dating him and you still did this?" Dorothy's voice was shrill now.

Charlotte shrugged. "What do I care if he's got more than one woman?" She grinned. "I have more than one man at the moment myself."

Bile surged up Dorothy's throat. She didn't want to be this girl—wasn't this girl—the kind of woman who fought over a man. A man who lied to get women into bed and had no qualms about dumping them as soon as he tired of them. How had she not seen this before in Allen?

"You can have him. He's married, by the way," Dorothy said, her resolve strengthening. She didn't need this, and she certainly didn't need him.

"I know he's married," Charlotte said with a shrug. "Doesn't bother me a wit." She jumped off the desk and straightened her clothes. "See you after work, boss?" She winked at Allen, and he turned the cherry shade of Charlotte's lipstick.

By this time, several of the other shopgirls had gathered behind Dorothy to see what all of the commotion was about. Ugly Mildred, Chantelle, Beatrice, Lorelei. Clearly they wanted a show, and she would give it to them.

"Dorothy, I—" he began.

"Save it, Allen. I quit."

"There's no need to—"

Dorothy held up her hand. "Before I go…" She pointed at Charlotte who was gathering her handbag. "You should know your latest fling is one of the Forty Elephants. She stole the key from me, and everything inside the storage room. I'm sure it's all been sold. Isn't that right, Charlotte?"

Charlotte didn't answer. She was too busy pushing past Dorothy, picking up speed until she'd broken into a run. Within seconds, she'd already gone.

"I'd say that was all the evidence you needed," Dorothy said, turning to her coworkers, who stared in amused surprise. "If you were hoping to make nice with Mr. Harrington and become his next girl, just keep in mind that you'll have to share him with his wife." Chantelle giggled while shock imprinted on the faces of the others. "He's not much of a lover anyway," Dorothy added. "He's selfish, if you can believe it. Bye now. Have a nice life."

As she strode purposefully out of the office, Allen called out after her. "How dare you!"

She held her hand over her head, giving him the two-finger salute. And God did it feel good.

The others burst into laughter.

As Dorothy passed Ugly Mildred, the hag opened her mouth to say something but Dorothy interjected. "Oh, shut up, Mildred!"

Mildred looked taken aback at the rebuke for an instant and then called after Dorothy's retreating back, "That's what you get for sleeping with the boss. I always knew you were dumb as rocks."

Dorothy turned momentarily to give her second vulgar salute of the morning. "If you'd stopped being such a hag, you might make a few friends."

Mildred gasped and Dorothy kept walking. In spite of the fact that she'd lost a boyfriend and the dream of a wealthy husband—and her job—she was proud of herself. She deserved so much better, so much more. And she would make her way somehow, on her own. She pulled on her coat and hat, snatched up her handbag and lunch, and stormed to the door. As she moved farther away from the store, she was struck with exactly what she wanted—and it wasn't a man looking after her or selling merchandise for some other department store. The next morning, she'd call on Jasmine Miller—the wealthy American fashion icon who had stopped into the store—and bring her drawings with her. That was precisely what she'd do.

Dorothy smiled for the first time in days.

═ 36 ═

Alice forced herself from bed, dressed, and headed to the coffee shop where she was meeting her fence. Freddy Grimes wanted to go over a few last-minute details with her about the big heist. That morning, she'd have to put on a show. She'd didn't feel like talking to anyone, much less leading the charge today, but it was time. The heist was only a week away, and Jimmy Church planned to put the building on the market only a few weeks after that.

Simon flickered through her mind again. She'd hardly slept, kept picturing his face as she'd left the races. If she'd stayed with him much longer, she'd have been in real trouble. As it was, she missed him: his humor, his bright view of things. She hated every part of her that needed someone else—it made her feel weak. Besides, she didn't need some man giving her a morality lesson when she was trying to do her work. If Simon didn't like who she was, he could stick it. She wouldn't change for anyone. She didn't even know if she was capable of change.

But he made her feel alive. Like she was someone worth sticking around for.

She shook her head. This was the best thing, distancing herself. She was proud of the empire she'd built. Even if she wasn't proud of what had happened to Ruth.

Alice opened the door to Brewer's Paradise. Freddy sat near the back with a pot of tea, two cups with saucers, a pile of scones, and tubs of cream and currant jam. It was a good thing she'd missed breakfast.

She took the chair opposite him and pulled off her gloves and hat. They didn't often spend congenial time together—for a fence, it was best not to be seen with a known thief—but the café he'd chosen was off the beaten path, tucked in a quiet corner of north London where no one knew them.

"Everything set?" Freddy asked through a mouthful of raisin scone. Crumbs stuck to his bottom lip.

"Yes, are the pickup points the same?"

He nodded. Freddy was a man of few words.

"I'll pick up the cargo and feed the frocks into the marketplace a dozen at a time," he said. "I might have to go to some of the outer boroughs, or even to Birmingham if we're talking about an excessive number."

She smeared cream on a plain scone and then added a dollop of jam. "If all goes well, there will be."

He nodded, wiped his mouth with a napkin. "It'll take a few weeks to unload everything, but that should still mean a decent paycheck before Christmas."

She smiled. "Perfect."

"Alice?"

"Yeah." She stirred a cube of sugar into her tea.

"Be careful. They've beefed up security in the area. Lots of bobbies. A night patrol as well. You'll need a lookout and a backup plan."

"Good to know. Thanks."

"Your profit is my profit."

"Cheers to that." They clinked their teacups against each other and finished their meal in silence.

=======

After her meeting with Freddy, Alice finalized her plans for the heist. Next, she drove each route between department store and drop point, warehouse and storage locker, accounting for time and distance and any possible interference. She was nothing if not thorough, and she didn't like being caught showing her knickers.

When at last the day began to fade, she headed to the factory for a meeting. It was time to fill the Forties in on the remaining details. By the time she'd crossed the Waterloo Bridge, lavender and silver painted the sky in dainty ribbons. Soon they would widen and deepen to periwinkle and indigo, bleeding into one another until they disappeared in a sea of darkness. Twilight at this time of year, as they approached the shortest day and the longest night, felt delicate, a whisper between the bold colors of day and their absence after the sun set. Twilight might be beautiful, but Alice had learned long ago that it could be dangerous and to avoid walking alone. The police changed shifts as the light diminished and the streetlamps had yet to flicker to life. Most crimes took place then—and she would know. The innocent assumed that crime was born at night under the cloak of black sky, but the pros knew better.

She parked the car and walked inside, shivering with cold, or was it nerves? She'd been anxious, not sleeping, and on edge. Worst of all, she'd had trouble controlling her emotions. Her mood swung from confident to worried to angry in a snap. So much was at stake; should the heist fail, she might lose another of her girls, just as she'd lost Ruth. She might lose the Forties' confidence. They trusted her to do a job and do it well. Worst of all, she might find herself in the clink, should she be caught. The heist had to go exactly to plan.

Inside, the office light was already on. Someone must be inside. It was likely one of her girls, but she crept in quietly to be on the safe side.

Curled up on top of the table lay Hira and her dog.

"Tired, are we?" Alice demanded.

Hira woke with a start. Groggy, she rubbed her eyes. "Yes."

"You didn't sleep here, did you?"

"Yes," she replied sheepishly. "Mr. Diamond chased me out of the flat."

Alice shook her head. "I thought that might happen. He's a real crank, and when he's in a mood, you don't want to be near him. By the sounds of it, I've held him off for the last time. You shouldn't go back there."

Hira's face fell and she looked as if she might cry. "Can I... Can I stay here?"

"It's not very warm, but it's a roof over your head so I don't see why not. We'll get you some blankets and a wool jumper."

Hira nodded though she didn't look relieved.

Alice got the feeling the kid had assumed she would find her a better situation. That Alice was a friend or perhaps even a mothering figure. A dangerous assumption on the kid's part. Like the separation from Simon, this separation would be good for Alice, too. She didn't need Hira relying on her, and besides, she'd grown to like the kid too much anyway. It was one thing to make friends among the Forties but another entirely to have someone rely upon her for food and shelter and to expect special treatment.

"If my plan works—and it will—very soon the Forties, including you, will have a real place to live. You won't have to stay here for long."

Hira looked down at her dog and began rubbing him. The mutt promptly rolled over so she would pat his belly. "Will I be safe here?"

"Were you safe on the streets?" Hira shook her head. "And weren't you perfectly fine anyway?"

"I suppose so," the kid said, but she didn't sound convinced.

Voices drifted through the factory and one by one, the other girls filed inside.

Alice was glad for the interruption. This conversation was closed. She had nothing more to say about it, and she sure as hell didn't want to think about it anymore. The kid needed to look after herself.

As everyone settled around the table, Alice shushed them. She pulled out the sheet of paper where Hira had written down the teams and other details of the plan. Following the meeting, she would destroy the paper immediately.

"Listen up. I've your teams for the stores and the warehouse, and the drop-off points. Memorize it, because this paper isn't leaving this room. Hira is going to read it for us. Hira." She waved the girl over.

"Well, now you can show us how you read, you cute little thing," June said.

The others laughed, but Alice knew they were jealous. She was jealous, too, though she'd never cared a lick about reading and writing before. They all had minimal skills from a handful of years of schooling when they were young. Most girls she knew weren't allowed to go to school past age eleven, despite the law that enabled them. They had to work to help the family instead. Take care of more important things.

After Hira read the details aloud, murmuring rippled through the room. To bring in the kind of score they needed, they'd all have to do their job and do it well.

"Once we have the booty, each carload will need to be deposited at different sites," Alice continued. "There's a storage locker on Bond Street. We'll deposit the largest load there. The rest will be dropped at Walworth, Kennington, and Rodney. I have three cars on standby. Once they're full, they'll each go to their destination. This way, if one car is caught, we won't lose everything."

"As for the break-in itself, Scully and Maggie are going to switch the padlock. The one potential problem is that there's a police patrol at the warehouse."

A few of the girls groaned.

"On-site?" Sherry asked. "Risky, ain't it?"

"Can't we hit another warehouse without security?" June added, blowing a stream of cigarette smoke over her pretty blond head.

Alice shook her head. "No. Sutton's is the largest warehouse with the best merchandise outside of the fur factory, and I know for a fact they have security 'round the clock. We'd be pushing our luck," Alice replied. "Trust me, this is our best option. And I'm confident the security at Sutton's won't be a problem."

She wasn't going to tell them that she and Scully had staked out the copper for two weeks and hadn't yet detected a pattern in his patrol. He showed up whenever he felt like it, sometimes spending a good amount of time on the property and others, walking around back, checking windows and doors quickly and continuing on his way. He was likely working the job for extra cash and didn't take it too seriously. In some ways this helped them. In others, it caused a real problem. If he showed up while they were in the middle of loading up the cars, they'd be nicked. It was bad enough there was a police station a block away. Should the patrolman sound the alarm with his air whistle or rattler, he'd have backup almost instantly.

Knowing the truth, Scully and Maggie exchanged a look that didn't go unnoticed. Several of the others nudged each other.

"Sounds to me like it could be a problem," Lily Rose said.

"Sounds to me like you should shut your mouth," Alice snapped. At the expression on the others' faces, she softened her tone. "There's no sense in making everyone uneasy. We're professionals. Most of you will be pulling a regular job at a regular department store. Besides, because of the way I've set this up, the multiple hits won't appear to be linked in any way."

The murmuring began again as the girls shifted in their seats.

"Sherry's right. The police patrol is risky," Lottie said. "Ain't there a police station in that borough, too?"

"And the locker on Bond Street always has a guard," Bertha said. "How we supposed to get around him?"

The room split into a dozen conversations as they picked apart the details of the plan.

Panic prickled over Alice's skin. They doubted her—may not be fully on board—and for a job like this, there could be no room for doubt. No room for second-guessing. It had always been a challenge to corral and lead a gang of the daring and unruly, but suddenly it felt as if things were coming apart at the seams. As if a shift was at hand and she was powerless to stop it. Her head began to pound, from lack of sleep and nerves. She needed a bloody drink.

At that moment, the door opened, and Marie plopped down into a chair.

Alice glared at her. "Haven't seen you in a while and then you show up late. You're trying my patience, Marie."

The woman looked down at her hands. "Do all of us need to be involved in this one?"

Alice peered at her, studying her blank expression, her drooping shoulders. Marie wanted out. It left Alice no choice. She'd have to make Marie indispensable to the operation. Involve her directly to prevent her from feeling as if she could go to the police. She knew too much to let her go that easily.

"Yes," Alice said curtly. "In fact, your role is important. I want you to work with me at the warehouse."

"You want me as your right hand? But I—What about Scully or Maggie?"

"We need you," Alice said firmly. "They will have their own jobs.

We all have a job to do." She wanted to grab the chit by the shoulders and shake her. If Marie didn't do what she was told this time, she'd suffer a real consequence—but she was not, under any circumstance, to leave the Forties. Not until the heist was finished and she'd gotten her hands dirty helping with it.

"Right," Marie said. "I'll be ready."

"See to it that you are."

They would all be ready—or else.

After the meeting, Alice gave Hira a little money to buy something to eat and then rushed off to other business. Grateful for the change, Hira bought a newspaper cone filled with a greasy helping of fish and chips. After, she wandered from Shaftesbury Avenue to Oxford Street toward Mayfair, where beautiful boutiques nestled among expensive restaurants and clubs. A place where the rich spent their money. Garlands and wreaths were strewn decoratively over banisters or framed doorways. Strings of decorative lights brightened window displays. Hira stared wistfully at them, sadness rushing over her. She wouldn't have a holiday this year. She'd been sorely disappointed when Alice didn't offer a solution outside of more blankets for her to continue to sleep in the factory. A reminder that Hira wasn't family, and she wasn't Alice's problem. It appeared, Alice wasn't even a friend.

Hira wondered what Uncle Clyde had planned for Christmas. Though he'd never liked her, he'd at least sent Mrs. Culpepper to town to purchase a few gifts for her each year. They also ate roast goose with all of the trimmings, and Christmas pudding, and had a party to celebrate the new year with a string quartet and guests. She'd been allowed to attend those parties, on the periphery. Perhaps it was her uncle's way of apologizing for his negligent treatment of her, or perhaps it was a gesture to appease her father and mother, but whatever the reason, Hira always had a nice holiday.

Light snow fell from the sky, glittering as it transformed gray pavement into magical walkways, and evergreen shrubs to sugar-dusted biscuits. She loved the dazzling white, how it felt as if everything was made new again. Catching sight of London's most famous toy store, she crossed the street to peer into the window of Hamley's. Toy soldiers formed a battle scene: some were positioned behind a cannon or holding a gun, some lay prostrate on their bellies with a pair of binoculars in hand. Behind them, a beautiful train whirred over a tiny pair of tracks that bent and wound around a colorful drum and through piles of white cotton teased to look like snow. A shelf on the left side of the window was packed with plush toys—dogs, bears, teddies—and on the bottom shelf, two dolls with porcelain faces and shiny satin dresses stared, unseeing, out of the front window.

Hira was too old for dolls and plush animals, she told herself, especially now that she was part of a gang. They would mock her if they saw her brushing the shiny gold strands of a doll's hair. Still, she longed to touch the beautiful hair, the lace trim on her dress.

"Can we look at the toys, Mummy?" a girl's voice came from behind Hira. A voice that sounded vaguely familiar.

Curious, Hira turned to peer at the girl. Her breath caught. It was Emily Baker, her former next-door neighbor. The girl who had tortured Hira with mean looks and meaner comments almost as bad as her uncle's, though they lived in the same neighborhood with the same expensive clothes. None of that seemed to matter to Emily Baker. She needed someone to be hateful to, and a girl without parents proved to be her favorite target.

And then it struck Hira. Should Emily recognize her, she would point Hira out to her mum and they would probably call the police. Word had surely gotten around that Hira was missing. She ducked her head, pulling her hat down over her eyes—too late. Emily was staring at her, at Hira's filthy trousers, her worn boots, and once-expensive overcoat now dirty from sleeping on the ground. After a moment, Emily looked past Hira as if she didn't exist. She was, after all, nothing but a street child who wanted a toy from Hamley's, and judging by Emily's expression, she found the "boy" disgusting. Not sad. Not an unfortunate soul drifting through the city along the avenue all alone at Christmastime. Most disturbing of all, Emily hadn't recognized Hira.

"Not today, love," Mrs. Baker said as she tugged at Emily's arm. "We've got a few more errands to run, and you've already written your Christmas list."

Emily's face clouded with disappointment and then anger. She looked as if she were about to stamp her foot and insist on going inside but thought better of it as another little girl about her age passed them on the street.

They disappeared around the corner, off to finish their shopping elsewhere.

Hira wilted in relief—or in disappointment. She wasn't certain which. Had she really changed so much that her neighbors didn't recognize her face? It had only been a little over a month since she'd gone, after all. Perhaps it was the boys' clothes. Or maybe…Hira was invisible, and no amount of proving herself to the Forties would make her different, better, more accepted. Perhaps, trying to prove herself to them, to Alice, actually made things worse.

Hira started down the increasingly slippery pavement, pondering what it all meant. Where she was going, who she was supposed to be, and most of all, whether she wanted to be a part of Alice Diamond's world anymore.

===

Hira didn't know why she'd come all the way back to the East End. After seeing Emily Baker—the way the girl had looked right through her—Hira had taken the train away from the beautiful shops and Christmas decorations of Mayfair, her legs carrying her through the city streets to a familiar restaurant. She stopped outside of Patel's Palace. This time, the door was closed and locked. She stood for some time, studying the gilded sign and peering into the window. She didn't know what she hoped to see, but it was growing too cold to stay much longer. She needed to go back to the factory and try to warm her hands.

As she turned to go, she heard the click of a lock, and the front door opened.

"I see you are alone again." It was the kind Indian woman Hira had met last time.

Hira nodded, struck again by the woman's beauty, her dark eyes and brown skin so similar to her own. A little of the loneliness eased inside her.

"Come in, child. Let's get out of the cold. You may bring your dog, too," the woman said. She led them to a table away from the window where it was warmer. "What is your name?"

"Hira," she replied and the woman smiled.

"Ah, I thought you were a girl. I see I was right. And I am Amba. Amba Patel. My husband and I own this restaurant along with two others. You may call me Amba Ben."

Three restaurants? Hira thought that was wonderful. She'd never known anyone like Amba Ben before. All she'd known was lawyers and thieves. Now there were Amba Ben and Dorothy.

"Are you hungry?" Amba Ben asked. "How about some tea and lentils and rice to warm the blood?"

"Thank you, madam," Hira replied. And remembering a line from her etiquette book, she added, "That would be most pleasant."

Amba Ben laughed lightly at her formal manners, and Hira relaxed a little more. As Amba Ben disappeared into the kitchen, Hira glanced around the restaurant, eyes feasting on the bright colors. The thick perfume of spice hung in the air, and a curious sweetness emanated from a long thin stick that was lit at the end, like a cigarette might be. Hira liked it here. Very much.

When Amba Ben returned with the soup and a fragrant tea, and bread for Biscuit, Hira ate and drank, at first surprised by the spices and the slow fire they built on her tongue. By the end of her bowl, she realized she enjoyed the taste.

"Do you have a place to live?" Amba Ben asked gently.

Hira thought about this question and decided lying was the best answer. She didn't know the woman well enough to discern if she would turn Hira over to the police. "I do, madam. It isn't a nice place, but I do have a place."

"I see. And do you have a mother and father?"

Hira looked down at the yellow streaks of liquid left from the lentils in the bottom of her bowl. "No, madam. She died in India. Of cholera. My dad died, too."

"Oh my goodness, well, how sad. I'm sorry, child." Amba Ben laid a hand over Hira's.

Hira felt a lump form in her throat. She didn't want to cry in front of this nice, beautiful lady, and she didn't want to ruin this moment. "Thank you. I hadn't seen them since I was a baby."

"I see. And the people you live with, are they kind to you?"

Hira looked down again. "Kind enough, yes, but I am often alone."

Amba Ben leaned forward to meet Hira's eyes and said, "You may visit me whenever you like, but I warn you, I will put you to work. I will show you how to make paratha and curry and chai."

Hira smiled. "I would like that, very much."

"Well then, I hope you will return soon." Amba Ben stood, rustling the shiny fabric of her bright-pink skirt. "For now, I must get to work."

"Yes, madam."

"Amba Ben."

"Amba Ben." Hira smiled sheepishly. "Thank you."

Amba Ben placed a hand atop Hira's head. "You are my new friend."

Hira's heart ballooned. She was invisible to Emily Baker, a dirty orphan to those on the streets, and to Alice and the Forty Elephants, a useful tool, but here, at this place, she saw a reflection of herself she'd never known. She saw her mother. And now, she had a new friend.

Pushing her worries about Alice and the Forties to the back of her mind for now, she stepped out into the winter cold a bit lighter and happier, her little dog at her heels.

⟹ 38 ⟸

Lilian paced, didn't sleep, and picked at her meals for the week following Ruth Jenkins's death. Lilian couldn't help but feel as if it was at least partly her fault. Perhaps if she'd checked on Ruth again, offered her help or direction, she would still be alive. Alice Diamond's words floated back to Lilian: *Nothing is clear cut.* Her pride had led her to arrest the girl; her pride and her insistence on following the law to the letter. Lilian winced. She needed to use reason rather than to be reactionary, to follow her instincts and heed a warning when it was given. Frustrated, she wrapped her neck in a gray scarf, pulled on a woolly hat and gloves, and headed to her post in the West End, trying to shake the cloud of melancholy that held her in its grip.

To make matters worse, Lilian hadn't been able to accomplish even the simple task of finding Hira Wickham. The city might be vast and crowded, but Lilian knew it well—and she knew the places most orphans liked to hide. Staking out Alice Diamond's flat and the factory hadn't turned up anything either. What sort of policewoman was she, if she put people in harm's way? If she couldn't even find a child? Not a very effective one. Angrily, she pushed against the cold, snow flurries racing around her in a white cyclone. The department store was just ahead, thankfully. She didn't have the temper that day to spend an entire shift outdoors in the cold, and she held out hope that Dorothy McBride might know where to find the child.

"Good morning, Inspector Wyles," said the woman with dark hair and a long nose.

Mildred, she was called, and apparently not many liked her, least of all Dorothy. Lilian could see why. Mildred frowned every day, and when she wasn't frowning, she looked as if she had eaten something disgusting. At least she was polite.

"Good morning," Lilian replied, walking to her post without removing her outerwear until she'd warmed a bit.

The day passed slowly. After a while, Lilian grew tired of watching a bunch of silly women preen and peddle expensive undergarments and hosiery or the latest handbags. Things that were completely inconsequential in life. No one seemed to care, or even notice that she was there, except the owner, and frankly, she didn't like talking to Allen Harrington much. She guessed that one day, she'd walk in on him canoodling with an employee in the back office. He seemed the sort. Three new employees had been hired in the last two weeks at Marshall & Snelgrove, and they'd all been inordinately attractive. He clearly had a type—beautiful, petite, and prone to flirtation.

The moment Harrington entered the room, the ladies fawned over him and hovered around him like hummingbirds to a bloom. She was beginning to wonder if he'd slept with them all. She was certain he was sleeping with Dorothy. The overeager woman jumped at his every command and fluttered her lashes so much, she always looked as if she had dirt in her eye. Lilian had offered Dorothy a handkerchief one day when she'd been particularly obsequious. Another of the salesgirls, Charlotte, had laughed. Apparently Lilian wasn't the only one who'd noticed Dorothy's constant attention to a man who was average in looks and stature, and also of average intelligence.

After another hour passed, Lilian felt as if she'd die from the tedium. Perhaps she should ask about Dorothy. She hadn't seen Dorothy in days, and she'd like to question her about Hira Wickham. She'd seen them talk briefly one afternoon before she'd started after the orphan.

"Mildred," Lilian said, "I need to speak to Dorothy. Would you happen to know when she'll be in next?"

Mildred's lips twisted into a less-than-attractive smile. "She doesn't work here anymore. She quit. I think she may be in today, though. It's payday, and she'll want the last of her wages."

"I see. And have you seen the girl lately? The little Indian girl and her dog?"

"She doesn't come around when Dorothy isn't here. I guess they're friends or something."

Lilian's hopes plummeted. Perhaps she wouldn't find the child now without a full search team. But was the child better off under the care of the Forty Elephants? Hira clearly didn't want to be at home, and even now with the inheritance she stood to gain, her lot wouldn't be much improved until she was of age—if the uncle didn't sell the property from underneath her or conveniently lose the deed.

Lilian turned these thoughts over in her mind, trying to decide the right thing to do. Why did everything suddenly seem so complex? She'd never had trouble understanding the law or seeing it for what it was, much less making decisions. She'd believed what was right was right. But it was beginning to seem that what was right was negotiable—and that nearly anything was justifiable under the right circumstances. The question that had circled her mind all morning returned: what kind of policewoman did that make her?

One concerned for her fellow man and woman. And what was wrong with that?

Frustrated, Lilian remained at the store well past her shift, hoping

Dorothy would come, just as Mildred had said, for her paycheck. When at last the doorbell jingled and Dorothy breezed inside, Lilian breathed a sigh of relief. The woman looked smart in a beautiful bright-blue coat and matching hat, her handbag tucked under her arm. She also appeared as if she were on a mission, strutting purposefully through the store.

"Miss McBride!" Lilian exclaimed. "How glad I am to see you. I need to talk to you."

Dorothy's footsteps faltered. "Inspector Wyles, hello. I don't work here anymore." She stuck out her chin. "In fact,"—she raised her voice to ensure others heard her—"I've been commissioned to design a themed series of dresses for Mrs. Jasmine Miller. We'll be opening a boutique together, along with another designer." Her aloof expression dissolved, and an eager grin spread across her face. "Can you believe it? I'll be a partner of my own store!"

Lilian smiled. "Well, isn't that wonderful? There aren't many stores owned by women in this city."

"I know!" Dorothy's beautiful face was alight with joy.

Having overheard Dorothy's declaration, Mildred's mouth fell open in surprise. Several of the other salesgirls gathered around Dorothy, praising her and congratulating her. Their enthusiasm was contagious.

"I am truly happy for you, Miss McBride," Lilian said. "Now, about that other thing I wanted to discuss—"

"Thank you," Dorothy said to the others, basking in the attention. "Now I need to pick up my wages."

"Before you do, might I have a quick word?" Lilian cast a look at an all-too eager gaggle of women and said, "Let's step into the street a moment."

Puzzled, Dorothy frowned but followed her outside. "What is this about?"

A blast of frosty air hit Lilian in the face, and she curled into her coat for warmth. "I'll be brief. It's about Hira Wickham. Did you know she has a living relative?"

"No," Dorothy said, taken aback. "I knew her parents passed away in India. Is this relative looking for her?"

Lilian hesitated a moment. Dorothy seemed to truly like the girl and she was no criminal. Perhaps sharing a bit more with her might be all right, and might help Lilian's case. "Not exactly," she said. "Her uncle seems to be something of a lout. He's a powerful barrister, though, and he aims to keep Hira's inheritance for himself. He has no interest in finding her, and should he, he plans to ship her off to a distant and quite dreary boarding school. In either case, Hira will likely lose her inheritance."

Dorothy wrinkled her perfect nose. "Vile man. No wonder Hira ran away."

"The good news is, Hira's father's closest friend also happens to be a barrister and is the executor of the Wickhams' will. He is insistent on helping the child. Unfortunately she is too young, you see, to be able to collect and live on her own, so here we are. In a quandary."

"And what can I do to help?"

"She believes you are her friend, yes?"

"Yes, we are friends, poor little thing. She needs someone to look after her, but she's been running with that gang. I've tried to warn her, but she has nowhere else to go."

"Precisely. Do you know how to get in touch with her?"

Dorothy shook her head. "Sadly, I don't. And if I'm honest, I don't want to snoop around Southwark and Lambeth looking for her neither."

Lilian chewed her lip, contemplating the best course of action, when Dorothy piped up again.

"She knows where I live, though, so the next time she comes by, I'll tell her to meet with you. Will you have to take her to her uncle's?"

"I'm afraid so, or at least to the station."

Dorothy shook her head. "She'll never agree. She'll run away again."

"Then we must think of something."

If there was one thing Lilian would get right, it would be to find a way to help this child who was in danger of becoming a beggar, a common criminal, or a whore for the rest of her life. And she'd need to do it soon, before the harsh winter days took hold. "If you see her, try to persuade her to speak with me and I'll do the same. If she won't talk with me, perhaps we can arrange a meeting with the barrister." Lilian gave her a piece of paper with the barrister's name and address on it.

"Of course," Dorothy replied. "She's a sweet little thing. She doesn't belong with that gang. She's only trying to survive."

"Aren't we all, Miss McBride?"

She nodded. "Why yes, Inspector, I suppose we are."

⟰ 39 ⟱

The day of the heist dawned clear and bright. For the first time in ages, Alice was truly nervous. She was also hopeful things were about to change for the better; she and her girls were going to the next level. Alice would get her building, too, and put a roof over her girls' heads. She'd likely have enough funds to pay for her own flat as well. She'd been saving and she was nearly there. In truth, she needed this win. Things had felt beyond her control of late. The restlessness, the insomnia, the guilt. Most of all, she felt raw with emotion, exposed.

At midday, the Forties met at the factory and split up by team before setting off, one by one, to their designated department store. Alice and the warehouse team remained behind at the factory. All was going to plan so far—even Marie had shown.

Alice, meanwhile, could hardly sit still. She paced in the dank office, cursing the odor of rotting wood and urine. A squatter must have wandered inside and relieved himself. Another reason to walk away from this dump of a factory for good. She went over the plans again and again, obsessing about the details, gritting her teeth, biding her time. The hours flowed like glue on a cold day. She felt as if she'd go mad.

When the girls at last began to arrive with good news about the store hits, she breathed a little easier.

"My knickers were so full, I waddled out of the store," Sherry said. "The stupid cow standing near the door didn't even notice."

Alice cracked a smile, relieving a little of the tension.

Others returned, reporting success after success. Not a one was caught. Alice grinned when the last of the teams arrived with good reports. So far, all had gone to plan. She dismissed those who were done for the day and waited with the warehouse crew, watching the clock, waiting until it was time.

"Scully, did you remind Maggie about the roadster?" Alice asked.

Her friend nodded. "I did." Maggie had parked Alice's Chrysler outside one of her favorite clubs to throw the police off the scent.

The night before, the borrowed cars were delivered to the factory. Alice had no other choice but to ask Bert for help securing a few extras. She didn't have the funds or connections otherwise. It had pained her to reach out to him, but she'd promised a future favor in return.

Alice shifted her weight to her left foot. She kept seeing the patrolman in her mind's eye—and in her dreams from the night before. He'd grinned as he'd taken her to Holloway. She shook her head to dispel the image and looked around the room at her team. They were calm, talking among themselves. All but Hira. She sat quietly in the corner as she was wont to do. Alice would have been annoyed with anyone else's reticence, but Hira was a mouse; quietly taking it all in, developing her own ideas, and growing increasingly stealthy. She was quickly becoming Alice's secret weapon.

At thirty minutes to midnight, Alice checked her bag one last time. It was all there: her lockpick set, a torch, smoke bombs, and her knife. On the table sat a bag of caltrops. Usually she kept the tire-wrecking iron spikes in her car, but since the Chrysler was being used as a decoy, she'd had to remove them. She never worked a job without them.

"Girls, it's time!" she said. "Are we ready?"

All were dressed in plain gray and black clothes to blend with the dark. Their hair was pinned tightly to their heads to keep it out of their eyes.

"Yes!"

"Ready or not."

"Let's do this!"

Alice ushered them to their cars. One by one, they drove away in pairs to the site, ahead of her in timed intervals. When they arrived, they were instructed to park along the street in a staggered line near the warehouse. At last, when it was Alice's turn to leave, Hira jumped in the back seat.

The night was clear and crisp, but the moon was tucked in for the night. City block after city block lay dormant; windows were shuttered and streets dark except the intermittent puddles of light cast by the odd streetlamp. As the warehouse came into view, Alice's anxiety flared. She gripped the steering wheel and blew out a slow breath. It would be fine. Everything else had gone off without a hitch all day, and this would, too.

She parked the car and killed the engine. Looking over her shoulder, she nodded at Hira. "You remember what to do?"

"Yes."

"If you see someone coming, blow this whistle." Alice placed a whistle hanging on a string into Hira's palm. "If you see a copper, do the same and then try to draw him away from the building."

"How?" Hira asked.

"You'll think of something."

"And what if I am caught?"

"You're a resourceful little mouse. You'll figure it out. Now, hop out. Go to your position."

Hira trotted to the corner of the building facing the street, her dog ever at her side.

She'd be fine. This was a good lesson, to learn to rely only upon herself and so far, Hira seemed fairly good at it for such a young child. When she disappeared around the corner, Alice smiled to herself as an electric current of excitement zipped through her.

Time to move.

She grabbed her bag and slung the strap across her chest. In seconds, she'd crossed the drive that snaked around to the back of the warehouse. The girls were already waiting for her. They'd have to move quickly. There was no telling if—or when—the copper would show, and she didn't want to be the one left holding the baby.

Scully had already removed the padlock and now stood by expectantly.

Alice flipped open her lockpick kit, took out a tiny set of pliers and a skeleton key. She jiggled the door lock and adjusted the key to fit in the hole, and in less than a minute, the lock clicked open. All of that practice as a kid had paid off.

Like ants to a picnic, the others scurried toward the door in their dark clothes. Everyone but Marie. Again.

"Where the bloody hell is Marie?" Alice hissed. "She was with us at the factory."

June shrugged. "She made me drop her off. Got cold feet."

Alice ground her teeth in rage. Marie had abandoned them in their hour of need. Again. That wench would pay the price all right, but that would have to wait. Tonight, they'd have one less pair of hands, and they had piles of dresses to collect and store.

Alice changed gears quickly to cover their loss.

"Scully, you'll bring the cars around when you see one of us at the corner of the building." Alice pointed. "The rest of you follow my lead, one at a time. Make sure no one is coming. We have Hira acting as lookout, but she's still a kid. It's on us."

They crept inside the building, into a corridor with several doors that were closed and locked. They were likely the offices. Alice paused a moment, deciding whether it would be worth it to peek inside them. Perhaps someone had stored wages in a safe. But blowing a safe was noisy and took time. Besides, she didn't have any dynamite with her, and safes were usually far too heavy to carry. Perhaps there were checks? How much would they collect then? She imagined writing checks for hundreds of pounds that would likely bankrupt the factory owners, if stealing their entire inventory wouldn't already. Her stomach tightened at the thought of all that money.

She shook her head. She was being greedy, and being greedy always meant you got caught. She couldn't write and cash a large check anyway as a woman, without a man present. If she sent her brother to do it, or another of the Elephant gang, they'd take a cut. No, it wasn't worth it.

"Move along," she whispered to the others.

They weaved quickly through the factory between long tables fitted with enormous spools of thread and industrial-sized sewing machines, and past individual sewing stations where hand-stitching was done. Trays of buttons and zippers and beads reflected the wan lamplight from the street filtering through the windows.

"The garment rooms must be back here," Alice said, leading her crew past the main floor to a cavernous room. She smiled. The room was filled with racks of finished frocks.

"There's our treasure," June said, and they all chuckled softly.

"Better get to it," Alice whispered. "June and I will take them off the hangers and toss them into piles. Sherry and Lily Rose, you carry them outside. Be quick about it. The longer we're here, the more we're at risk."

They got to work, pulling clothing from hangers, carrying piles of dresses to the pickup point where Scully loaded them into the cars.

As she worked, sweat beaded on Alice's brow. She and June gained speed as they emptied rack after rack. Soon only one remained.

"This is it," Alice said, out of breath. They yanked the last two rows off the hangers. "You go first, June. I'll close the door behind me."

They each lifted a pile and headed to the door. June went ahead. When Alice heard the sound of a distant engine roar to life, she used the outside wall to steady herself and pulled the door closed. As she began the short walk around the building toward the final waiting car, a shrill whistle split the air.

Alice froze. Hira. Someone was here.

Alice's already racing heart kicked in her chest. Hopefully the others had gotten away. They were too close to sewing up the whole plan. She was too close to the kind of money that meant freedom. Hira would come through. She'd done everything right all along. Alice could count on her. She'd divert the person's attention.

But panic gripped her as a voice of doubt crept in—*maybe*. Hira would divert them *maybe*.

———

Hira perched at the edge of the warehouse wall, doing her job, watching for pedestrians and for the police. The Forties came and went, dumping armloads of dresses in the cars as planned. Still, her heart fluttered in her throat, quick as a bird's, as she surveyed the scene. She tried to put the fear of being caught out of her mind. She'd pickpocketed plenty, after all, but she'd never liked that either, and this was far worse. Should she be caught, she wouldn't have the luxury of going to an orphanage or a boarding school in the north. She'd end up at a reformatory school for troubled adolescents.

Hira threw a look over her shoulder as Sherry and then Scully hopped into their cars with the last of their loads. Both women roared down the drive of the warehouse and away, into the night, on to the next phase of the plan. A sense of relief flooded through her as she watched them drive away. Only one car to go.

Hira's eyes drifted to Alice's car. She and June were still inside.

The next moment, Biscuit froze, his eyes locking onto something moving beyond the warehouse. A growl rumbled in his throat.

Hira's head snapped up. There was a figure up ahead. A man. He ambled down the street, bundled against the cold. After another growl, Hira tensed, catching sight of why Biscuit stood stalk still, his muscles tensed. There was a second man, fifty yards behind the first pedestrian. A policeman.

He slowed as he neared the factory, pausing out front. When he turned down the drive as if to walk around back, Hira darted out from behind the cover of the warehouse. She streaked across the narrow lawn in front of the building, across the pavement toward the pedestrian, her pulse thumping wildly as she neared the unsuspecting man.

In seconds she was upon him, confronting him, pushing past him, her small hands slipping inside his jacket, her legs straining as she raced off at top speed.

"Stop! You there!"

She threw a look over her shoulder. The bobby and the pedestrian were giving chase! She reached for her whistle and blew into it as hard as she could, hoping Alice would hear it.

Hira pushed faster, fear carrying her. She knew whatever fate befell her was all her own. Alice couldn't save her—wouldn't save her.

The bobby's whistle screamed this time from somewhere behind her.

Hira panted, her lungs burning with exertion. Shuttered buildings streaked by in the periphery of her vision. Cold blasted her face until her cheeks were taut, her lips numb, her fingers tingling. Still, she ran.

He couldn't catch her. She couldn't let him catch her!

She thought again of Alice, of the Forty Elephants. Would they appreciate her sacrifice? Of risking capture, of being sent away for good? Alice's brutal attack on the bartender flashed behind Hira's eyes, and she ran harder still. Despite her fear of the police, a new darker truth settled over her skin like a heavy, cold blanket. She'd rather risk reformatory school than Alice's disappointment, and worse, her anger.

She ran and ran and ran.

Alice left the pile of dresses on the ground and slid along the outer wall to the edge of the building. She peeked around the corner. Hira pickpocketed a man walking swiftly down the street in plain sight. A few paces behind her, the patrolman followed.

Alice didn't move. She couldn't help the girl. She could do nothing but watch the scene unfold.

The copper saw Hira's theft instantly, as she'd intended. He blew his own shrill whistle. "Hey! You there!" he shouted.

The unsuspecting pedestrian looked back at the copper, bewildered. When he saw the little beggar race past him, he felt for his wallet and began to run, too. Hira, meanwhile, tore down the street, taking the copper farther and farther from the scene of the real crime.

The girl had come through—and she was a genius.

Alice raced back to the clothes she'd left behind, scooped them up hastily, and headed for her car. In minutes, she'd tossed all in the trunk, slammed it shut, and slid behind the wheel. She circled the block twice, looking for Hira, keeping her eye out for the policeman, but neither were in sight. She shouldn't stay in the neighborhood with a trunk full of stolen items, but at least she wasn't in her own recognizable car. Still, she'd chastise her girls for doing something so stupid. She did it anyway. She couldn't leave the kid behind.

After another loop, she began to worry. Where could they have gone? Maybe Hira had already been picked up. Alice suppressed a wave of regret. That was the breaks of being a Forty Elephant. Living on the edge meant real consequences.

After a final turn around the block, she gave up. The kid was on her own. She was fast and she was clever. She'd get away, and Alice couldn't do a bloody thing about it either way. She had goods that needed to be unloaded immediately and she'd already risked her neck by circling several times.

She passed the warehouse a final time—when the lights of two cars flicked on, putting her car directly in their sights.

A couple of bloody coppers.

"Goddammit!" Alice shouted, slamming her foot on the gas. She screeched away, catapulting down the street at far too fast a pace.

They gunned their engines and shot after her.

Why had she gone back? She knew better. She'd have given her girls an earful for doing something so stupid. She drove fast, wildly, over the curb, through a waste bin, turning corners in a mad dash to get away.

The coppers gained speed, and she cried out in frustration. Had they bought new cars? They were always slower than her, in their beat-up older models. But she wasn't in her eight-cylinder Chrysler now, was she? She ground her teeth as her heart crashed in her chest. She was so close to getting away, so close.

One car pulled ahead, edged closer, until their windows were neck and neck.

Panicked, she reached blindly for her bag, her hand rooting around until it closed around a smoke bomb.

"Pull over!" The copper shouted through his open window. "You're under—"

Alice launched the smoke bomb. It sailed through the open window.

The police car veered wildly as smoke filled the air. As the sound of a crash ripped through the night, Alice shouted in victory.

"That's what you get!" she screamed with a wicked laugh, adrenaline rushing through her.

But she still had one copper on her tail—and they were closing the gap between them fast. Too fast.

This time, she reached for the other bag on her front seat. She jerked the steering wheel with one hand as she loosened the drawstring with the other and barely missed a letter box on the side of the road. She cursed and straightened the wheel. Eyes on the turn ahead, she stepped on the gas, and just as she turned the corner, she dumped the open bag outside the car window. Caltrops littered the street.

In the next instant, the police car hit the spikes going top speed. Sharp metal tore through tires like a hot knife through butter. The copper jerked the wheel hard—and the car rolled.

Alice watched in the rearview mirror as the car rolled like a kid down a grassy hill once, twice, and slammed against a block of shops. On impact, the glass of the shop windows shattered.

She let out another screech of glee—and relief. She was glad she'd been smart enough to pin her hair against her head and wear plain clothes. The coppers couldn't have seen who she was, especially with the bomb, especially under the cover of night. She was certain of it. She laughed again. What a rush! This was the lifeblood of the job. The danger, the thrill of not being caught.

And that was something she was very, very good at, she thought with a big grin. She was good at not being caught.

⸻

A dark street stretched between a long row of houses, and Hira darted left. The policeman gasped for air but the beat of his boots on pavement never faltered, never slowed.

She couldn't seem to shake him.

Biscuit darted ahead of her and ducked inside what looked like a safe alcove. Her little friend had showed her the way! She followed him, racing after him, pausing only an instant to see the bobby round the corner.

The alcove opened to a narrow passage between a house and a shanty that looked abandoned. She dove inside. The odor of feces and something dead hit her with force, and she covered her mouth to keep from gagging.

Still, the sound of footsteps grew louder.

She tucked herself into a ball in a corner of the main room, beneath an opening where a window should be. The next instant, the bobby's footfall stopped. He huffed, his breath ragged as he looked for some sign of Hira.

She held her breath, squeezed her eyes closed, prayed he wouldn't see the small white puffs of her breath rising around her head. Biscuit instinctively followed her lead and curled in her lap, not making a sound.

At once, the footsteps began again, but this time, they seemed to change direction. They were moving farther away.

Hira sagged in relief against the filthy wall at her back. He was leaving. She should wait him out, make certain he'd gone and wasn't waiting for her.

She absently stroked Biscuit's back. "Good boy," she whispered. "I'll give you a biscuit just as soon as I can buy one."

He licked her hand.

As Hira's breathing slowed and the cold crept over her skin, she thought again of Alice. Alice always harped on loyalty, and yet Hira had never been paid for anything she'd done for the Forties like the others had been. She'd also been forced to steal from her only friend and put herself in the path of a policeman. But the most confusing part of all was that Alice seemed to like Hira at times, and at others, she seemed not to care that Hira did everything she was asked to do—or to care that she was there at all.

Hira didn't like doing the scary things demanded of her. She didn't like breaking the law or feeling as if she was hurting someone. And she didn't like that Alice had left her here to face the bobby alone. Chin quivering, she squeezed her eyes closed against the threatening tears. She thought of Emily Baker, her neighbor in the pretty coat and shoes, tugging her mum's hand and asking for a toy she'd likely receive under the tree on Christmas morning. There had to be more than drafty factories, cold stone floors, and being chased in the dark by scary men. More than beating a man until he was unrecognizable. More than the fear of being locked up every single day. She'd simply have to gather her nerve and tell Alice she didn't like being a part of this. Perhaps there was more, another way.

The sound of light scratching alarmed Hira again, until a moment later, a small gray mouse scampered across the dirt floor and disappeared inside a hole. She shivered and nestled into her coat, her neck disappearing inside it. All the while watching and waiting, until light peeked through the openings in the shanty, and the day began again.

─≡ 40 ≡─

Alice slept like the dead for the first time in ages. When she finally woke, she spent the rest of the afternoon at home relaxing. She knew she should lay low until her meeting with the Forties later that night. There were bound to be coppers crawling all over the city after the chase, never mind all of their robberies. But the goods were safely stowed, and Freddy Grimes and his crew knew just what to do with the large load. The car Alice had borrowed had new plates and was being repainted that very moment. She was goddamn proud of herself! She'd pulled it off! And even had a little fun in the process. Last night's success was a story for the books.

As the day wore on, she found herself pushing aside the curtains on the front window. Hira hadn't shown yet. Perhaps she'd done her job too well, and now she was paying the price for it. Alice pushed aside the twinge of guilt. Nothing she could do about it. The Forty Elephants took their chances, lived on the edge, and planned on having a whole lot of luck. Often that was the case.

Sometimes, it was not.

Alice had to stop favoring the girl anyway. If Hira had been nicked, she'd been nicked and that was all there was to it. Eventually the kid would make a mistake and have to face the police anyway, like the rest of them.

As the sun set, Alice ventured out, ready to head to the factory meeting. On the way, she picked up a couple of newspapers, in search of anything mentioned about the heist or the police. And there it was, an article announcing her triumph.

STAPLETON WAREHOUSE ROBBERY, MULTISTORE HIT, LEAVE CITY WONDERING IF THE MET IS DOING ITS JOB

She shot her fist into the air. "That's right, coppers! Better do your job!" She walked to her car, all smiles. She couldn't wait to show the article to the girls. She'd done it! She'd really done it. She'd put together a solid plan, and not only was it successful, but she'd be able to buy her building! Pride and hope flooded her limbs, and for the first time in weeks, she felt like she was on top again. The squabbles and infighting, the backtalk, the no-shows...none of it mattered because it was crystal clear that Alice Diamond deserved her crown as queen of the Forty Elephants. And they would know it and celebrate it, too—and maybe stop kicking up so many fits.

She drove to the factory on a high and had scarcely entered the office when she was greeted with applause.

"We've made the paper, girls," Alice said triumphantly. They whistled and catcalled, all smiles. "Listen to this." Alice read the article aloud:

"'December 9, 1925. Sunday night, the Stapleton warehouse was emptied of its entire dress collection set to be distributed to department stores for the Christmas season. At the scene, the police gave chase to a suspect. One police sergeant suffered minor injuries, while two vehicles were severely damaged. Stapleton's owner J. R. Sutton commented, "Must have been a master thief to pick a lock like ours.

One of the gangs, maybe. This has the markings of a gang, but of course there's no evidence. Rest assured, we'll be increasing security from now on. The same afternoon, three department stores were hit in Chelsea, Westminster, and Mayfair, keeping the Met busy. Scotland Yard was unavailable for comment.'"

Alice looked up from the paper, a grin stretching across her face. "Well done, ladies. Well bloody done!"

More cheering erupted.

"How's about a celebration tonight?" Maggie shouted.

"Pub first, and if we're up for it, dancing!" Alice shouted to whistles and clapping.

She concluded the rest of their business quickly to make way for the night's festivities, though in spite of the excitement, most of the women begged off and went home to their men. Only the inner circle joined Alice at Joe's Tavern. They ordered steak-and-ale pies and started in on their first pint, then their second. After a while, a third was followed by a fourth.

Alice's alcohol-fueled thoughts shifted with her fourth drink, latching on to the only thing besides Hira that was eating away at her good mood. Marie. Where the piggin' hell had she been last night? She'd stood them up during the biggest heist they'd ever pulled. Left them in the lurch without so much as a word. This was the second time in two months—and it would be her last. They were a family, and one didn't leave the family, or else they'd be cut from the brood and heavily *encouraged* to keep their mouths shut for good.

"I'm pissed. Stone-cold drunk off my ass," Maggie said.

Alice laughed. "You're not the only one. Let's have another round!"

As the barman set down their bottles, he looked past Alice. "Hey, you!" he said. "No dogs allowed. Get him out of here."

That could only be one person.

Alice turned swiftly, relief slicing through her. The clever little girl with dirt-smudged cheeks and mangy dog stood at her elbow. "I thought you got picked up!" Alice exclaimed. "Had me worried, kid."

Hira shook her head. "I climbed through a broken window in a shanty. Stayed there until I was sure the policeman had gone."

"We have a Houdini in the Forties!" Alice said a bit too loudly as she clinked her glass against Scully's. Scully laughed and Hira looked bewildered. Alice laid a hand on the girl's shoulder. "I'm glad you made it out, kid. I thought you'd been shipped off to reformatory school or something worse."

Hira shrugged. "He wasn't very fast. He had a big belly."

Alice laughed, but then her tone turned serious. "You did well. I'm proud of you."

Hira looked down at her hands. "I'm glad it's over."

"You all right?" she asked.

Hira shrugged again.

Alice began to lose her patience. Whatever was going on with Hira wasn't Alice's problem. The job was finished, and now the child would have somewhere to sleep. What else did she want from Alice? She took a large gulp of her beer. She didn't have anything else to give Hira and that was that. If the kid wanted to be morose, she'd have to do that somewhere else. Tonight was for celebrations.

"Where the hell was Marie, do you think?" Scully asked.

Alice scowled. "June said she asked to be dropped off somewhere. That little bitch left us high and dry. We could have gone down because of her. We still could, if she decides to tell anyone about our scheme."

"She's a menace," Maggie said. "She stirred up all that trouble with Bertha, too."

"Bertha stirred up the trouble with her, you mean," Scully said, finishing the last swallow of beer. "Bertha's got a husband and she decides to set her sights on someone else's. No wonder Marie cut her face."

"Bit her finger, too," Maggie said.

Alice's laugh turned into a guffaw. All the beer had gone to her head. Didn't help that she hadn't eaten much the last few days. She'd been too nervous. "Marie bit Bertha's finger? What are they, three years old? For crying out loud."

"I saw Marie go to the police." Hira's face flushed with the omission.

"What?" Alice turned to face her again abruptly, anger prickling over her skin. "When did you see her?"

"After I left the shanty, I slept at the factory for a while and then I went to my post to follow the inspector. The inspector stopped at the police station at Charing Cross, and while I was waiting for her to come out, I saw Marie go inside."

Alice felt herself flush, her blood go hot. "What in hell was Marie doing talking to the police?"

"Think she told them about our heist?" Scully asked, her brown eyes watery and red-rimmed from too much drink.

"I bet it was that straight boyfriend of hers. Told her to do it. If she narked on us, we'd be arrested, and she could—"

"Leave the Forties," Maggie cut in.

"Or make a play for queen," Scully replied.

Alice's anger went from zero to a hundred in a second. She pushed up from the barstool, knocking it to the floor. Whatever happened to loyalty? Whatever happened to looking out for each other?

"I think it's time we expel Marie from the Forties. What do you say, ladies?"

"Let's pay Marie and that Raymond Whatever-His-Name-Is a visit," Scully said with a grin. "She lives a few blocks away, on Johanna Street."

"Do I need to go, too?" Hira asked, clearly hoping to scurry away and hide under a rock somewhere. But she was one of them now.

Alice grabbed Hira's arm and dragged her toward the entrance. "You need to see how this is done. Maybe one day you'll be in charge."

When they were all outside, Alice slammed her bottle against the frame of the door to break off the bottom. The others followed her lead. Now, they had weapons.

"Let's go!" Alice exclaimed.

It was late, she was furious, drunk, and she was done letting some lackey betray the gang. She had a job to do as their leader. She had to hold everyone accountable, including herself. She'd given up Simon, hadn't she? She'd always taken only a fair share of their profits. She'd sacrificed, and she risked her own neck time and again to make ensure all of her girls were both looked after and kept in line to protect each other. Marie was a traitor. And she was about to learn what it meant to turn her back on the queen of the Forty Elephants.

Alice stomped down the lane, shouting, waving her broken beer bottle, blind rage propelling her forward. Hira stumbled alongside her at first, but as their number increased, grew more hostile—more fun—the child disappeared somewhere in the crowd. It was fine; Alice would pull her into the melee at the flat. Show her what it was to leave the gang without permission.

As they turned the corner, Alice's steps faltered. She'd forgotten they'd be passing Simon's pub. The way they'd laughed together, the softness of his lips—the disappointment on his face—flashed behind her eyes, and her stomach clenched. Why did he have to go expecting her to be someone she wasn't? He'd ruined everything.

The door to the pub swung open, and Simon stepped outside, hands on his hips, as he peered out at who was making all the noise.

At the sight of him, her heart skipped a beat. She watched him as he scanned the street, a frown on his face. She wondered what he thought of the angry crowd, with her at its head. Did it matter? It didn't. The sooner she stopped thinking about him, the better.

She gritted her teeth and raised her arm above her head. "To Johanna Street!"

At the sound of her voice, Simon caught sight of her.

Their eyes locked.

She'd have paid a hundred quid to know his thoughts, not that they'd do her any good. As worry tugged the corners of his mouth down and concern shone in his eyes, she looked away. She couldn't bear it. She couldn't bear the way he made her doubt herself. She didn't need that from anyone, least of all some man.

As she passed him, she trained her eyes ahead, as if she didn't know him.

"Alice!" he called after her. "This won't end well! Alice, stop! Talk to me, Alice! Come inside!"

Her heart lurched and she winced at the sound of his pleading. This was precisely why she'd left him. He'd never understand her, not truly, and she had a job to do, a living to be made.

Alice picked up her pace as more people in the streets joined the fray. She glanced to her right when a man stepped up beside her. He carried a crowbar, and his face was red from too much drink, but Alice recognized him. He was one of Bert's men, from the Elephant and Castle. Others gathered behind them, and soon their mass grew larger, louder. The crowd became a mob as they picked up chunks of concrete, carried broom handles and broken bottles.

Energy surged through Alice's veins. Because of Marie, every single one of Alice's girls was at risk. But Alice would end this woman and her betrayal, and it would send a clear message to the other Forties. Alice was queen, goddamn it, and she would take care of her flock. She'd also never surrender her position. Someone would have to drag her kicking and screaming all the way to prison for that to happen. Maybe not even then.

Glass shattered. One terrible scream followed another, slicing through the roar of voices. Lights went out on either side of the street, doors slammed, windows locked, and people shrank inside their homes. The cowards knew what was best for them. To stay out of Alice's way.

As she turned onto Johanna Street, the mob at her back, at her sides, she faltered for a single instant. A barrage of images flitted through her mind. Mike lying in a heap. The blood. Her uncontrolled rage. Hira's shock and fear.

What had Alice gained by the deed? Disgust with herself, if she was honest. Loneliness. An echoing darkness that had no end. And here she was, carrying weapons, after one of her own girls—one of her former girls—looking for blood.

She fought her impulses, wrestled with her instincts to stop this— stop the sloping path before her. To do and be someone different, but why should she? How could she deny who she really was? It wouldn't make her happier to live a life of poverty and obscurity, a life of regret, no matter the risks. She was Diamond Annie, queen of the Forty Elephants, and she planned to see her legacy through.

When they reached Marie's house at the end of the block, she turned to face the mob. All quieted an instant.

"You're with us, or against us!"

The crowd cheered.

Next, Alice gave the signal to charge.

―――

Hira kept pace with Alice as they charged from the tavern into the street and pushed up the lane like a band of misfit soldiers out for blood. At her side, Biscuit barked at the noise and the destruction. He barked at every scary person that barreled past carrying their knives and bricks and lead pipes. When he'd run ahead, Hira's panic mounted. What if she lost him in the melee?

"Biscuit, come!" Hira shouted, her voice straining against the noise.

Somehow, he heard her shrill voice through the noise and returned to her side. Her little mighty dog became her guard, snapping at the heels of those who ventured too close to her.

"Oy, watch your mutt," a man called as Biscuit lunged.

More and more people joined Alice and the Forties, and soon they packed the street, forming a cork that blocked cars and bicycles from passing.

Hira wanted to leave, run far from here. Far from the violence she knew was sure to come. But how could she leave, and more important, where could she go where Alice wouldn't find her?

Alice led the crowd, her red wool hat visible even in the gloomy night. Hira imagined what Alice planned to do with the broken bottle in her hand and shuddered. All of the blood, the barman's moans, haunted Hira's dreams. Alice was a match, always poised to burst into flame if struck at an unsuspecting moment. Would this be all Hira had to look forward to? Would she become the same? Hardened by time and circumstance, pushed to do things of which she was ashamed? Hira might never be the Emily Baker in silk stockings and lace-trimmed dresses again, but she would also never be Alice. Never truly be a Forty Elephant. What came after that, she didn't know, but this... She had to tell Alice the truth. That she was leaving and she promised to go to the grave with all she knew about the Forties, but she didn't want to do this anymore. And if Alice turned on her... Hira would have to take that chance.

She broke into a run, weaving around people until Alice was only a few yards away.

"Alice!" she called. "Wait! I need to talk to you! Alice!"

In that moment, a stone hurtled toward Hira. She ducked.

It whizzed past—and struck the person behind her. The man staggered a moment, surprised by the blow and the impact before he began to shout.

"You filthy ingrate, that bloody hurt!" He reached for Hira blindly. He clutched the back of her coat and dragged her backward.

Hira screamed. "Let me go! It wasn't me! Let me go!"

Biscuit lunged and sank his teeth into the man's flesh.

He swore and cried out in pain.

With the distraction, Hira broke free—but Biscuit crouched, prepared to lunge again. Not fast enough. The man kicked her dog so hard, Biscuit yelped and flew backward, slamming into the side of a building. He fell to the ground in a sickening, slack heap. The man went at Biscuit again, kicking him a second time.

"No! Biscuit!" Hira screamed, emotion strangling her throat.

She charged at the man and, with all her might, shoved him aside. He stumbled sideways, tripping over his own feet.

In seconds, Alice was at her side. "I heard you scream. What's wrong?"

"It's Biscuit. That man kicked him. He's hurt."

Biscuit whimpered but didn't move. Blood seeped into the tufts of white fur in his ears.

"Leave him and come with us. He's just a mutt. I'm sure we can find you another one. The dog was a real pain anyway." Alice pulled Hira to her feet.

"No," Hira cried. "I can't leave him. He's my friend." She cried harder until the world around her blurred, turning liquid.

"I said, leave the mutt!" Alice commanded.

Hira dashed her hand across her eyes and peered up at the

terrifying queen of the Forty Elephants. Alice's eyes were bloodshot, her words slurred. There was nothing Hira could say or do to stop this woman, and she knew she didn't want to be here, didn't belong here. She wasn't like Alice and didn't want to be.

"I'm going home," she said. "Go on without me. You don't need me."

"Home?" Alice demanded. "You can't go back to my parents' flat—"

"I'll find another home, away from here. From this."

A brief flicker of emotion flashed across Alice's face. It was gone so quickly, Hira wondered if she'd dreamed it.

"We'll talk about this later," Alice growled.

In an instant, Alice, in all of her dark glory, was swallowed by the crowd and slamming through the front door of Marie's home.

Hira leaned over Biscuit, who whimpered but still didn't move. Her tears turned to sobs. "It's all right, boy," she whispered as she scooped him into her arms. "I'll keep you safe. You're going to be all right."

She prayed it was true.

And without looking back, she left the crowd, left Alice, and walked toward what was next, all alone.

⊰ 41 ⊱

Lilian couldn't believe her luck. She'd come in to the station for her final shift of the week, planning to join Lewis on his beat in Lambeth, when she'd met Marie Bitten. Lilian wondered what Alice had done to the woman to make her sing like that, giving up every last detail of the heist. They may not have enough evidence to bring Alice in, what with no leads on the stolen items and the missing motorcar from the chase, and no clear identification of who was driving it that night, but they had an insider and that counted for something. Now they just had to find some way to make the accusation stick. In the meantime, thanks to Lilian's investigation the last few weeks, she had a pretty good idea where she might find Alice. And tonight, they'd have a little chat.

Lewis directed the car past the Victoria Embankment and the Whitehall Gardens, illuminated in swathes of light from nearby lamps though most was in shadow at that time of night. He turned left over the Westminster Bridge, the dark water moving as ever below them.

They'd scarcely crossed the bridge when Lewis slowed the car. "Do you hear that?" he said.

Lilian strained her ears and cranked open the window. In the distance, there was a low roar. Voices. Some sort of gathering or march. "Do you think it's a march?" she asked.

Lewis's eyes met hers. "Or a riot."

"Let's go." They'd circle back and drive through Lambeth to Alice's meeting place and the old factory later. This might be a real problem.

Lewis stepped on the gas pedal, and they hurtled through the narrow neighborhood streets.

Lilian kept the window down as they followed the distinct sound of voices, the tread of boots on pavement, shattering glass, laughter and screaming, and every sign that nothing good could be happening. When they turned onto Johanna Street, the crowd came into view. Most were carrying some sort of weapon.

"They're definitely looking for trouble," Lewis said, slowing and pulling the car to a stop.

"We're going to have to go on foot," Lilian said.

"I'll take the left side. You go right."

"We need to call for backup, too."

He nodded. "I'm guessing others heard the racket, but we'll raise the alarm."

Lilian reached for the rattler tucked in her belt. They'd need any men nearby to help tame the drunken, rowdy crowd. Looked to be fifty people or more. She whirled the rattler with all her strength. Some from the crowd turned at the alarm they knew only came from a bobby, but most pushed on, smashing, colliding with each other, kicking over rubbish bins and throwing stones. A true mob.

Lilian broke into a run alongside the crowd despite her skirts. "Where's everyone headed?" she called out.

The man on her left shrugged. "What's it to you?"

A loud crash split the air and more angry voices followed.

Lilian's heart leapt into her throat as she neared a mass crashing through the front door of flat number thirty-five. She swiveled to find Lewis and caught sight of him with a couple of policemen she didn't recognize. They fought through the melee, receiving blows of their own as they pushed inside.

Immediately Lilian took a hit to her left side. She gasped and bent at the waist a moment, before shoving the woman aside who had dealt the blow.

"Police! Out of the way!" she shouted.

No one paid heed to her cry. They didn't care if the police were among them. They were too busy following the lead, too absorbed in a fit of passion as they destroyed all in sight.

Beyond the threshold, a policeman tried to break up a fight. So there were several other policemen already on the scene. She felt a small rush of relief as she elbowed her way through the throng that clogged the stairwell, looking for the leader of the pack. The source of the mayhem. The screams grew louder and the sound of splitting furniture rent the air. At last, she reached the top of the stairs and weaved around a pair fighting in the hallway. Both bedroom doors were open. Lilian fought her way inside the closest.

And there she was—the leader of the pack, the very woman Lilian had wanted to meet with that night, throwing blow after blow.

The leader of the mob was Diamond Annie.

———

Lilian froze. She should have known a gang would be responsible for the violence. And here, at Marie's house where Alice, no doubt, felt the need to mete out justice. Still, Lilian hadn't expected this, a pack of women leading a drunken crowd brutalizing one woman and a couple of men. *Brutalizing a family.* Alice's face was red, her features twisted in fury. She was mad as a bull and three times as drunk. Completely out of her head. She held a woman by the hair, shook her violently, and slapped her before shoving her to the floor. Alice's friends dove atop the badly bruised woman, kicking her and punching her.

Lilian closed her mouth around her whistle and blew with every ounce of air in her lungs. Some paused in their fighting. Most ignored her. The next moment, a hard thump on her head made her stumble forward. The sharp point of a boot slammed into her leg. Someone had struck her! She whirled around to beat off the offender, only to find them gone—already fighting with someone else.

She blew her whistle again. "Stop! Police!"

As Alice picked up the woman from the floor, Lilian realized who it was. They were punishing Marie Bitten.

In that moment, five other policemen crashed into the room. They spread out, each tackling the worst of the offenders—Alice's friends— but Alice herself moved out of reach. She loomed over Marie, now curled into a ball to protect herself.

Alice met Lilian's gaze. Her eyes were hooded, and blood trickled from her lip. "Hiya, lady detective. What are you doing here? Shouldn't you be in some department store somewhere, waiting for thieves? I hear there's been quite the robbery. You coppers need to do your job. Seems as if the mayor ain't too pleased."

"What's going on here?" Lilian demanded.

"Taking care of a little business is all. None of it is yours."

"Starting a riot and trying to kill someone is my business."

"Well, let's say this is payback, and it had to be done. You wouldn't understand. This is the rule of the streets."

Lilian had worked up a sweat and now wiped her brow with her sleeve. "You've gone too far, Alice."

Alice's eyes narrowed to slits. "I'll do what I bloody see fit to do. This is my town! Now be on your way and leave me be!" When

Lilian didn't move, Alice stepped closer. "You owe me one, don't forget that."

Lilian froze, torn between the need to do what was right and the need to repay a debt. Despite the scene, despite Alice's crimes, there was a woman with a heart in there somewhere, a woman who looked out for others and believed everyone should have a fair chance at life. A woman beneath the hardened person who'd always done what she must do to survive. There was something to be said for that, Lilian believed. But this—brutalizing a woman nearly to death, for what? To teach her a lesson? What kind of lesson would Marie learn, other than to stay fast and far away from Diamond Annie and her thugs? This lesson was more about Alice, about her need to assert her power.

Lilian stared at the towering, powerful, furious woman who had earned every inch of her reputation—the very same woman who had helped Lilian in the alley that night, and rescued another woman as well. But now, in this moment, Alice Diamond teetered on the edge of a dark chasm from which she could never return. And there was only one way to save Diamond Annie from herself.

Lilian launched herself at Alice, taking her by surprise. Aided by the confusion, she pinned the thief against the wall and snapped handcuffs on her.

"You had it wrong. This is our town," Lilian said. "Those who respect it and those who respect others. Not people like you who manipulate and punish and take what isn't yours."

Alice struggled against the handcuffs, but at that moment, Lewis joined Lilian, holding Alice fast.

"This is the thanks I get for saving your life, is it?" Alice sneered. "I won't forget this, copper. I don't forget anything."

Lilian flinched at Alice's cold, hard tone. In spite of it all, the woman frightened Lilian a little, but she'd done the right thing. Justice might not be simple, but there was no guessing in this case. Alice had made sure of that.

"Neither do I," Lilian said at last. "You, Alice Diamond, are under arrest."

⇥ 42 ⇤

Hira cradled Biscuit in her arms. Her nose was numb and her feet ached, but she kept moving forward. At least it wasn't raining— something to be grateful for, given the circumstances. Biscuit didn't so much as squirm in her arms. Tears cascaded down Hira's cheeks, leaving tracks where the grime was washed away. She cried for her little friend in her arms. She cried for the nights she'd spent shivering in the alleyways while trying to sleep, or hidden in Alice's bedroom filled with terror at the sound of Mr. Diamond's heavy footsteps. She cried for the loss of Alice's friendship, flimsy as it appeared to be now. And for one terrible moment, Hira thought she'd go to Mayfair, knock on the servants' entrance at her uncle's house, imploring them to help her with Biscuit. But as the bundle in her arms grew heavier, her feet didn't steer her toward Mayfair. They took her somewhere else entirely. To the only place she'd ever felt safe.

Dorothy's doorstep.

"Oh my goodness, what's happened!" Dorothy exclaimed. Her hair was plaited in two long, red braids, her face scrubbed free of makeup. She'd clearly been asleep.

She led Hira to the living room sofa. "Is Biscuit hurt? Are you?"

Hira's tears came faster.

"Oh no, love, don't cry. Here, let me. It's all right." Dorothy mopped her face with a handkerchief stitched with happy bluebirds. "Shh, it's all right now. You're safe here. Biscuit is safe, too."

Hira could do nothing but stare at the kind woman who gave freely without expecting anything in return, and her tears turned to sobs.

Dorothy sat quietly, waiting for the tears to subside. When sobs turned to hiccups, at last she said, "Can you tell me what happened?"

Hira sniffed. "There was a riot with Alice and all of these people. They wanted to kill Marie...and a man kicked Biscuit a couple of times. Alice told me to leave him." She gulped in a breath, trying to calm the spasms, her sorrow. "I think his bones are broken."

"What's all the commotion!" Dorothy's mum trundled into the kitchen, squinting in the lamplight. She peered at Hira an instant, shock registering on her features. "Is that...is that our Katie?"

Dorothy stiffened. Her sister, Katie? Was her mum completely mad? "Mum? What are you talking about—"

As Hira turned, Lydia stepped back, her mouth formed into a letter O. The spell appeared to be broken.

Dorothy's mum ran a hand over her face. "Goodness me, of course it isn't Katie. But for a moment, her long, dark hair and petite frame..." She shook her head.

"Mum, this is Hira, remember? And her dog, Biscuit. He's hurt, and she needs a place to stay. She can sleep in my room."

"As long as the dog doesn't bite, that's fine by me," her mum went on. "I'm going back to bed." She waddled to her bedroom and closed the door.

"Can I take a look at him?" Dorothy asked gently.

Hira nodded, relieved to have help at last.

Dorothy prodded him gently. When she tried to move his hind leg, he whined. "I think it's his back leg. We can probably wrap it up tightly to see if it will help stabilize him. I'm no doctor, but I've seen it a few times on the street." She probed his middle, and Biscuit cried out. "Oh my goodness, I'm sorry, little fella," she said, and to Hira, "It must be his ribs. We'll take him to a doctor tomorrow. See if he'll help us."

Hira smiled weakly. "Thank you."

"Of course. Now, let's get you both some water and get you cleaned up. Have you eaten?"

Hira shook her head.

"We'll heat up some soup, too. I can take the soup bone out of the rubbish bin for Biscuit. He'd probably like that."

In moments, Hira's belly was full, and her limbs had warmed. Biscuit licked the soup bone while Dorothy sponged him down gently.

Hira didn't know what she'd do without Dorothy.

"You're next, into the bath," Dorothy said.

"After what I did, I don't deserve—"

"Nonsense. You're a child. You deserve to have someone care for you and look after you. Speaking of which..." Dorothy's smile faded, and her tone turned serious. "I have something to talk to you about. The lady detective spoke to me today when I went to collect my wages at the shop. She said a barrister is handling the paperwork for your father's estate. You probably knew this, but your grandparents were wealthy and divided their estate between your uncle Clyde and your father. Your father, luckily, set up a will before he died. You are to inherit a house in Richmond as well as a yearly sum when you turn eighteen."

Hira's pulse began to thud in her ears. "A house? I have a house?"

"Yes, but the problem is, your uncle is withholding the deed to the house so that he might sign for the property on your behalf should you not go home. And if you do, he may try to forge the document, or so the barrister believes. The way I see it, you have two choices."

Hira's head raced with the new information. Her parents had left her a home that she would own when she was old enough? But who would live with her? She supposed she'd have money for servants… Maybe she would have enough money to visit India someday, too. Meet her cousins or the grandparents she'd never known. Her throat tightened with hope.

"What are my choices?" Hira managed at last.

"You can move back with your uncle and take your chances there. But I'm afraid it's too easy to dispose of a young Indian girl."

"But I am English."

"Yes, love, you are. And you are both. People aren't always kind to girls who stand to inherit something valuable, never mind those with brown skin. Do you understand?"

"Yes." She'd grown to understand this since leaving her uncle's. She didn't know why people didn't like her immediately, or why they were so mean about how she looked. But one thing was certain: she was learning not to listen to everything people said about her. She liked herself just as she was. Alice had taught her that, to accept who she was, even if she'd had an odd way of teaching.

"What is my other choice?" she asked at last.

"You can live here with me and my mum. We can help you with the barrister. We don't have much, but you won't go hungry. And soon, we will have plenty to spare." Dorothy's face lit with happiness. She filled Hira in on her new job, working at Jasmine Miller's brand-new boutique featuring Dorothy's designs. "What do you say?"

The tears began again, and rather than answer Dorothy, Hira launched into her arms, looping her arms around the lovely woman's neck.

Dorothy laughed. "It will be just fine, my little friend. We'll speak to the barrister and to the detective. Everything is going to work out. You'll see." She smiled one of her blinding smiles.

"I could...could pay you for helping me and letting me live with you—"

Dorothy gently put her hand over Hira's mouth. "Don't concern yourself with paying me. I won't be paid for such a thing. You will be part of our family. You're like—" Dorothy paused. "Like a little sister, you hear me? Not another word about it."

Hira sighed heavily as the weight of a thousand burdens lifted from her shoulders. She didn't have to be a part of the Forty Elephants. She didn't have to hurt people and steal to stay alive, or grovel for people to accept her. She'd have a new life, one where she was wanted, at last, with friends. Maybe, just maybe, things could work out in the end after all.

⊣ 43 ⊨

A wet wind sneaked beneath Alice's collar. She swore under her breath and allowed herself to be maneuvered down the front walk to a waiting police car. She smirked at the older Ford model. This was precisely why she could always get away—they didn't invest in their trade. Only this time, she'd been caught on foot. This time, she'd made one of the dumbest mistakes of her career.

She'd let her emotions get the best of her.

There had been some awareness, some instant in the midst of the riot that night when she'd realized she couldn't take one more step without going over a cliff. She'd known it, and she'd done it anyway. Now here she was, headed to court, fighting to keep her freedom. As they pulled up to the Old Bailey courthouse, traffic thickened and the car slowed. Alice stared at the crowd standing three deep and winding down the sidewalk. Word had gotten around town apparently. She was a spectacle. Some small part of her was pleased.

And then she saw him, wedged in amid the others. Simon McGill's unruly hair peeked out from beneath his derby hat, and his eyes were bright. She couldn't believe he'd come. She'd found out after the fact that he was the one who had called the police, and she hadn't known what to make of it. Knowing Simon, she suspected it was his last attempt to save her. She'd been enraged at first, felt betrayed, but as the truth settled over her, she understood why and she understood him.

Alice looked back at him, over her shoulder, and he waved. Here he was, stubborn as a mule. She couldn't help but smile a little as she walked the icy pavement to the door.

Thankfully, the courtroom was warm. She opened her fist as the blood coursed through her fingers again. Prison was cold, dreary, and dull. The only amusements came from manipulating the guards for forbidden items or watching the other prisoners marvel at her prowess.

Newspapermen clogged the entrance and the vestibule of the courtroom. Alice pushed through them, catching sight of her girls. Scully, Maggie, and Bertha had been arrested alongside her. They exchanged glances. At least one, if not all of them, would be booked. Things had gotten too out of hand. People had been severely hurt, but that backstabber Marie wouldn't ever come crawling back, and she'd never breathe a word of what she knew about the Forty Elephants' operations to anyone, ever again. She'd learned her lesson once and for all.

Alice was led to a holding box with the others. Once seated, she scanned the crowd of onlookers. Would she be here? She searched for the petite brown face, a pair of dark eyes filled with trust and a flicker of admiration, and an angular jaw set with determination. But no, her youngest charge wasn't there. Perhaps Hira needed an escort to be allowed inside the courtroom, or, perhaps she didn't want to see Alice again. Not after all that had happened. She didn't blame the kid. Still, a sudden ache sat uncomfortably inside her and she found herself searching the room again, one last time. Hira seemed to care for her, and she was loyal as loyal could be. She'd be there, wouldn't she?

As the minutes ticked by and Alice felt the prosecutor's case gaining ground and heard the snickering from the morbid curiosity of onlookers, she understood the truth. Hira wasn't coming. She'd left the girl and her dog in the middle of the chaos, and Hira had been wounded, heartbroken. And if Alice was honest, the kid had never liked carrying a knife or doing Alice's bidding anyway. She'd been frightened into it and desperate. In the moment that Alice had left her with her broken dog, Hira had seen exactly who Alice was, down to the bottom of her soul. She'd seen Alice's great gaping need that would never be filled. Alice had seen it, too, reflected in the girl's eyes. She'd felt its reverberation to her very core.

She was surprised by the pain that rippled through her, the regret. She didn't do that—she didn't regret. It was a fool's game to look back or to ruminate on what was done. But in the courtroom, she'd be forced to look back, retrace her steps count by count, and tell everyone what had happened. Explain how foolish she'd been.

This time, Alice was wanted for attempted murder. This time, she knew she'd lost it all.

44

It wasn't until the following morning, after dragging Diamond Annie to the police station, that what Lilian had done sank in. She'd arrested and booked one of London's most notorious criminals! She'd done what she'd set out to do—make a name for herself and score a win so big, the Met couldn't ignore it, or her. Now she hoped against hope that her position—as well as those of the other nineteen women—was safe.

"Close the door behind you," the chief said as she followed him into his office. He sat down at his desk and fished in the top drawer for a cigarette. "We've had some news about Clyde and Hira Wickham. The barrister, John Lee, has found a connection between Clyde and that dirty judge. He's in the process of working out a way to expose him. That could take a while, however, and in the meantime, Hira has been found. She's living with a young woman named Dorothy McBride. Ring any bells?"

Lilian was glad to hear both pieces of news. The uncle sounded like a real scoundrel and deserved what he had coming to him, should Mr. Lee be able to prove malfeasance. And she was truly delighted the child had found a kind young woman who would take her in—someone other than Diamond Annie.

"She's living with the shopgirl then?" Lilian said. "I'm happy to hear it."

He lit his cigarette. "We'll need to make some difficult decisions. *You* will need to make some difficult decisions," he said. "I'm going to leave this one to you."

Lilian nodded. "Thank you sir." She knew precisely what she'd do. She'd talk to the girl and see what she wanted, rather than dragging her back to her uncle. Hira was resourceful, and if she was no longer running around with the likes of the Forty Elephants, and she had an inheritance to collect, she had choices.

"Also," Wensley continued, "I think it's time we took you off babysitting duty and put you on more crucial cases. You wanted to work with prostitutes and troubled women, and now is your chance."

"You mean it, sir?"

"Of course I mean it. You'll start tomorrow."

Her heart soared. "Thank you, sir! Thank you so much."

"I believe the thanks should be mine—ours, here at the Met." Wensley smiled. "I'm damned proud of you, Inspector Wyles. You and Lewis and the others. I've already spoken to them about the job well done, but I wanted to speak to you privately. I can't believe you managed to collar Diamond Annie and two of her top girls. We've been after her for ages. Great job, Wyles."

A rush of pride flooded through her. "Thank you, sir. I've been tracking Alice for weeks and finally got lucky. She found her way into trouble and that was that."

"She usually does," he said, sucking the end of his cigarette. "She's not the type that can change, except maybe to get in deeper. Most of them can't. And this time, I think we've got her cornered, at least for a while. She's being charged with attempted murder."

Lilian nodded. "Sounds appropriate."

"Inspector, I want you to know something," Wensley began. "Everyone has had their doubts about you, and about the women's squadron."

She felt her face fall, her mood dampen slightly. "Yes, sir, I know. It's been frustrating, watching the program grow only to see it cut down decisively and its importance dismissed. I've been trying to show how valuable we can be to Scotland Yard."

He smiled. "Well, the good news is, you have. I'm going to commend you at the next meeting with the superintendent."

She gasped. "You mean it, sir?"

"Of course I mean it. I'm going to commend the women's squadron as well."

A knot of emotion began to form in her chest, and her face grew flushed.

"Thank you, sir. I don't know what to say. I'm so grateful."

"If you keep this up, you may find yourself in my seat one day. I'd like to see a female chief inspector one day. One day soon."

The knot in her chest grew. "I–I don't know what to say. Thank you, sir." She gave him a wobbly smile.

"We'd be lucky to have you. Now, I suppose you should get to work."

"I suppose I should."

She said a strangled goodbye and quickly left Wensley's office. She raced to the water closet, slamming and locking the door behind her. And for the first time since the Great War had ended, Lilian's calm, sensible demeanor melted. She burst into tears. Wensley really believed in her. He saw how capable and competent she was, how much she could bring to the Met. He would fight for her and the women's squadron! The tears rushed down her cheeks and turned into quiet sobs. She leaned against the stall door for support. She couldn't believe it—her, chief inspector! She had scarcely let herself dream it could happen one day, but now, with this... She'd done the right thing, arresting Alice Diamond and her friends, and in taking a chance at this unsettling, dangerous profession. Every day her small squadron of policewomen could make a difference for other women. And perhaps the superintendent and the government would come around to that belief, too. All of her hard work had been worth it—she, Lilian Wyles, was the beginning of it all.

Alice Diamond's face flickered in her mind's eye and she smiled. Who was the queen of the London streets now? She wiped at the flow of tears and began to laugh. She couldn't wait to tell her dad everything.

When the tears ebbed, she adjusted her uniform and strutted into the corridor, through the station, and out into the early winter sunshine, bursting with pride.

———

With a skip in her step, Lilian bounded up the steps to Dorothy McBride's flat, a package tucked under her arm. She hadn't really thought she'd pay the woman a visit, but she was glad to do it for Hira Wickham's sake.

As the door swept open, Lilian pasted a smile on her face so as not to alarm anyone. "Good afternoon, Miss McBride."

Dorothy's brow arched in surprise. "Hello, Inspector. What can I do for you?"

"I'd like to speak to Hira Wickham."

Hira's face peeked out from behind Dorothy.

"Hi there," Lilian said.

"Come in. Would you like a cup of tea?" Dorothy asked.

"That would be lovely, thank you."

Dorothy opened the door wide. "Hira, show the inspector inside?"

"Hello, Inspector," Hira paled but did as she was asked. "This way."

While Dorothy busied herself in the kitchen with the stove and kettle, Hira led Lilian to a small but cozy parlor. The dog who'd always followed the child had a bandaged leg and lay sprawled on a chair opposite the sofa.

"Your little friend was hurt, I see," Lilian said.

"He was trampled. In the riot," Hira said, her voice edged with sadness. She fidgeted nervously, picking at a loose thread on the armrest of the sofa. "But the doctor said he'll be fine. He has a broken leg and some bruising, but that's all. You were lucky, Biscuit, weren't you, boy?" She scrubbed behind his ears and along his neck with her fingers. Biscuit licked her hand in thanks.

"Well, I'm happy to hear it." Lilian said. "Now, I've come to talk about your Uncle Clyde and your inheritance."

Hira's eyes widened. "You know my Uncle Clyde?"

"I know of him, yes. But given that you're safe and cared for here with Miss McBride, I don't see any reason to make you go where you aren't wanted. Or rather," she added hastily, "make you go where you don't want to be."

Hira brightened. "I thought you would make me go home again."

Lilian looked down at her hands a moment. "That was my original plan as it is what the law requires, but it seems sending you away will put you at a greater risk. You might possibly lose what is rightfully yours. And from what I understand, your uncle isn't a kind or just man."

Hira nodded shyly.

"Do you have plans to join Alice Diamond again?" Lilian wanted to ask her more but thought it best not to lead the child. She'd allow her to speak her own mind. If Hira had any interest in going back to the Forty Elephants, their paths would undoubtedly cross again anyway.

Hira shook her head. "No, Inspector. I don't…I didn't like the things Alice wanted me to do."

"I'm glad to hear it," she said. "It seems that Dorothy has allowed you to live with her—"

"I have," Dorothy said firmly as she whisked into the room carrying a tea tray. She set it on the table and poured them each a cup before offering a plate of simple digestive biscuits.

Lilian smiled. "Well then, I was told as much, but I wanted to see it for myself. Very good."

"It'll be like having a little sister around again," Dorothy replied, a warmth filling her eyes.

"Inspector, what's in the package?" Hira pointed at the small carton beside Lilian on the sofa.

"Ah, yes." She set down her teacup and held out the carton. "These are things your parents sent for you from India."

Hira's eyes widened.

She took the box onto her lap and made to open it, but then stopped. "I'll open it later."

The child showed remarkable restraint for one so young. Lilian didn't blame her for wanting to open her parents' things when she was alone. She dunked a biscuit in her tea as the others enjoyed their own refreshments. When they'd finished, she broached the stickier topic on her mind. "There's just one more thing, Hira. Has Dorothy told you about the other things your parents have left you?"

"Yes, Inspector. A house and a stipend."

"Good." Lilian leaned forward. "Your father's barrister has maintained the will, but unfortunately, your uncle has possession of the deed to the house. Therefore, you will have to work with him in order to claim your full inheritance. He is still your legal guardian, after all. But I'm afraid he hasn't been easy to work with, at least this is what the barrister said. Given that Mr. Lee knew your father and the Wickham family well, I rather believe him."

"My uncle won't work with me," Hira said. "He'll try to send me away."

"All we need is the deed to the house?" Dorothy asked. "We have the will already?"

"That's right," Lilian replied.

"Hira, do you have any idea where he might keep the document?" Dorothy asked.

Hira bit her lip and her eyes became unfocused as she pondered the question. At last, the girl said, "I think I know where he might keep it. Locked in his desk drawer. The bottom right one." A light filled her eyes. "And I know how to get the key."

Hira leaned toward Lilian, filling her in on her idea, her tone animated. When she'd finished, she rested her hand on Biscuit's back, waiting for their reply. "What do you think, Inspector?"

"What do I think?" Lilian said. "I think we have all underestimated you, Hira Wickham."

"I believe you have," Hira said with a smile.

Biscuit barked in agreement.

⇥ 45 ⇤

The frost-covered lawn and ice-tipped leaves glistened in the meek light of an early winter morning. Hira didn't need to worry about the cold anymore. She had a warm and comfortable place to sleep, enough food in her belly, and the friendship of not one but three women who cared for her. Dorothy, Amba Ben, and Lilian. She also had the beautiful sari her mother had made for her, her father's pocket watch, several photographs of both of her parents together, and a set of beautiful, shiny bangles. Treasures left to her that she would cherish.

And if she managed to pull off her plan, she'd have the deed to her house soon, too.

She rode the bus to Mayfair on edge and walked through the familiar streets to her former home, replaying her plan over and over again in her mind. What if it didn't work? What if she was caught? She would have to take that chance. Uncle Clyde couldn't make her do something she didn't want to do, not now. She'd tasted freedom, no matter how harsh it could be, and she had friends on her side. Grown-ups who understood who Uncle Clyde was and who cared about her.

As she neared the house, she was glad she'd arrived early, before her former neighbors scurried off to their jobs and shopping and appointments. She could easily hide. Two houses down from Uncle Clyde's, she took cover behind a pair of towering bushes to wait. And wait. At last, as the cold began to creep in and her toes were going numb, the front door opened.

At the sight of him, Hira gripped her hands tightly. This was it. Time to put her fears aside. Time to take what was rightfully hers.

Her uncle barreled down the front steps, checking his pocket watch as he went. He swore aloud and picked up his pace. He hated to be late. He was always prompt and exacting, something Hira had always found irritating, but now she was grateful for that dependability. She knew he would walk to his office nearby, only a few blocks away.

She followed closely, blending in with the scenery, ducking behind rubbish bins and shrubbery when necessary. She'd worn her boy's beggar clothes, her derby hat pulled low on her forehead, her hair pinned beneath it in coils as usual. He shouldn't recognize her if he didn't look directly into her face.

Her uncle stopped suddenly to cough and catch his breath.

Quickly, she darted behind a bush.

A passerby stopped to ask if he was well. Her uncle waved the gentleman on with an irritated huff. He cleared his throat and continued on his way.

As did she.

At the next block, the streets would widen and become busier, the pedestrians thickening to a crowd. A good place to be lost or go unseen when small and agile in beggars' clothes.

Hira toyed with the idea of making herself known to him. To knock his briefcase from his hands and tell him what she thought of him. In the end, she decided it would only put her more at risk of being caught. Instead, she waited for her friends. As she crossed the street, she darted to the right, around her uncle to join a group of people who walked in the opposite direction. Now she had a full view of his face.

Inspector Wyles appeared then at the corner, and Dorothy emerged from the drugstore opposite her uncle. She sauntered toward him in her bright blue coat the color of a spring sky and fluffed her red hair with her hand.

Hira watched as her uncle's eyes locked on Dorothy. She was nearly impossible not to look at in all of her colorful beauty on an otherwise cold, gray day.

At just the right moment, Hira darted behind her friend, using her for cover.

"Well, hello, sir." Dorothy used her most flirtatious voice.

"H-hello, miss," he stuttered.

The next instant, Dorothy bumped into him clumsily—to make way for Hira.

Hira swung around her friend, her hand darting rapidly inside her uncle's coat, into the hidden pocket, and felt for his keys.

"Why, you rat!" he shouted, realizing a pickpocket was upon him.

Hira dropped his wallet on the ground to distract him—and fled.

"Are you all right, sir?"

And that was the last thing Hira heard before the wind filled her ears. She ran as fast as she could, back toward her childhood home. It was a Friday, and she knew precisely what the staff would be doing. The cook would be at market to prepare for a large supper for her uncle's friends who dined and played cards with him; Mrs. Culpepper would be working on the ledgers to balance the kitchen budget; the butler had Friday mornings off to visit the barber, and the footman would be seeing to her uncle's wardrobe. That left only Miss Lightly, Hira's governess. But she shouldn't have a job any longer. Hira was betting on it.

She raced up the front steps, slipped the key into the lock, and heard it click as it slid open. Gingerly, she pushed the door and peeked inside. Instantly she was struck with the smell of furniture polish and tobacco, and fresh brioche baked that very morning. Memories flooded her senses, and for a moment, she couldn't move. How strange to feel she had changed so utterly, when the world she'd left behind had remained the same.

The clock in the next room chimed a brassy sound, startling her from her reverie. She must be quick! No one was about on the first floor, as she'd hoped. Without hesitation, she raced to the study in the back of the house. In moments, she was at her uncle's desk. Under her breath, she prayed the document would be in the bottom drawer. It seemed he'd kept everything important locked away inside it over the years. At least, everything he didn't want her to see.

She flipped the key ring around, sliding the keys over the grooves. At last, she clasped the small silver key between her fingers. It fit easily in the lock. She pulled open the drawer.

To her surprise, the drawer was nearly full. She rifled through folders and books and reached the bottom of the drawer at last. Hira gasped. On the very bottom lay a stack of photographs of her mother and father, and a small bundle of letters tied with ribbon. They were addressed to her! Her heart squeezed as she gathered them all and stuffed them into her satchel. When her uncle went looking for the deed and didn't find it, he would know it was her, or at least suspect that she'd been the one to take the things with her. But she didn't care. Her name was on the letters, and the photographs were of her parents. They belonged to her, just as the deed to the house did.

She rifled through his papers, scanning each quickly, searching for the only one that mattered. When only two folders remained, she found it. Hastily, she slipped it inside her bag.

A rustle of fabric came near the door.

Hira froze.

"Hira!" It was Mrs. Culpepper, her thin hand at her throat. "Hira, is that you? What on earth are you wearing? What are you doing here? We thought you were lost."

"Mrs. Culpepper, hello," Hira said, willing herself to remain calm. "I am. I was. I came for the letters from my parents." She flashed the bundle at Mrs. Culpepper and returned them to her bag.

"Yes," she said softly, and in that instant, Hira understood that Mrs. Culpepper had known they were there. "Dear girl," the housekeeper said. "I have missed you. We've all been so afraid of what had happened to you."

Hira moved cautiously toward her. "I'm not going to stay. I have a better place to live. My uncle planned to send me away to a poor school in the north."

Mrs. Culpepper's eyes dropped as shame stamped her features. She'd known this all along, too. "How can I help you, Hira?"

"You could take my uncle's keys. Tell him he left them by mistake."

"I'm so sorry, child. I've always wanted what was best for you, but Mr. Wickham, he's such a scoundrel of a man."

"Yes, he is," Hira replied, her voice gaining strength.

"I'll tell him he's left his keys," the housekeeper said. "I'll also tell him you took the letters before you left. Tell him I saw them in your drawer. I owe you that one kindness at least."

Hira moved toward the door and threw her arms around Mrs. Culpepper's middle. "Thank you."

"Oh, you poor darling," the woman said. "You poor, poor darling."

"I'm not poor anymore," Hira said, brushing at tears that had sprung to her eyes. "I don't need Uncle anymore."

"Not that you ever did, my child. Not that you ever did."

Hira gave the dear woman a last squeeze and made for the door. As she bounded quickly down the steps for the second and last time and melted into the crowded city streets, she smiled. She felt like a queen, with all that she now possessed! She didn't need her uncle anymore. He'd always shunned her, made certain she didn't rely much upon him. Now, she had what she needed, all on her own.

She skipped the last blocks, humming a merry tune and daydreaming about all that would come next, feeling for the first time in her life like the luckiest girl alive.

Epilogue

Alice chewed on her thumbnail, already raw from too many nights locked in the nick. She was going to have a visitor that day, or so she was told. Warned more like. She couldn't try any funny business, not that she'd be dumb enough to do that now, given her short sentence. Eighteen months in prison plus hard labor. It could have been worse—a lot worse. At least the coppers hadn't managed to nail the Forties with the warehouse robbery. Those spoils would be waiting for her when she finally broke out.

She grimaced as the jailer slipped handcuffs over her knuckles and fastened them around her wrists. He stank of sour laundry, and judging by the flecks of brown on his tie and meat on his breath, he'd had a three-day-old cold pasty from the lunch cart.

And they called her a criminal. At least she had taste.

"This way." He grasped her arm and dug his fingers into her flesh, yanking her forward.

"You sure have a way with women," she quipped.

"Not sure as I'd call you a real woman," he said.

"Not one you could handle anyway."

He blushed then, and Alice smirked at his stupidity.

At least prison didn't bother her all that much; she'd had scarier nights in the streets of Lambeth and Elephant and Castle. But that wasn't the point. The point was, she'd had plenty of time to stew over Ruth's death. The impotence she felt choked her at times. And worse, she'd temporarily been dethroned from her gang, and that meant things weren't running as smoothly as they should in the neighborhood. It also meant her queen status was ripe for the picking. Whoever tried to take her place...well, Alice would have to scare her off. A part of her worried it would be different this time. That she would have much more to regret than losing it over Marie's insolence.

Alice followed the jailer the short path to the holding room, the place where prisoners met with their barristers. But today, there were no barristers. It was the lady detective she'd done a good turn to that night in the alley, the one who had pushed her against the wall the night she was arrested. Inspector Wyles, the traitor. She could spit in the woman's face. But bad behavior would only make things worse in prison, so she'd pretend she was a lady for the time being.

Directly behind the copper another figure entered.

Hira.

Alice's stomach turned over. Had the kid ratted her out? Told the police everything? With Alice in prison, Hira had been on her own with no one to look after her or, more importantly, to *guide* her. Or so Alice had thought. Perhaps she was wrong. Hira was rounder in the face, clean, and pretty in her dress and ribbons—but happy. And how could Alice possibly begrudge the girl that?

"Hiya, kid," Alice said as she sat at the table in the middle of the room. "What are you doing here?"

Hira blushed deeply, giving her light-brown skin a lush rosy hue.

"I came to tell you I've found a home," Hira said.

Alice stared at her for a long pause, not saying anything. Was this her way of saying she wasn't a part of the Forties any longer? An unexpected twinge of sadness made Alice look away. She liked the kid, saw real potential in her. But she'd never belonged on the streets. Alice had always known that. At last she said, "Good on you. I suppose we won't be seeing you."

Hira shook her head. "I suppose not."

"That's too bad, kid."

After another pause, Hira said, voice soft, "Did you kill her? Marie."

"Of course not," Alice replied, though she knew why the kid was afraid. Hira had seen her lose her head that night with Mike. "Gave Marie a little roughing up is all. And you know why. In fact, you know a little too much."

Hira looked down at her hands and back at Alice. "I don't know anything."

Alice cracked a smile. She always knew Hira had a keen mind, and it was a crying shame to let her go, but let her go she would. As long as she kept her mouth shut. "That's my good girl."

"I came to say goodbye. And to say thank you."

"Thank me? For what?"

"Taking me in."

The lady detective interjected, "I think she's trying to say there's a good person in there somewhere. It's a shame you don't humor her more often."

Alice went rigid with anger. "And what would that bring me? In my neighborhood?" she snapped. "Well, goodbye then."

"It's time to go, Hira," Inspector Wyles said.

Hira stood and took a last lingering look at Alice. "Goodbye, Alice."

Alice fought the urge to call her back, to leave the door open for her, should she wish to return to the Forties. And oddly, she felt a little like embracing the kid. Instead, Alice said nothing. She watched Hira go, just as she'd watched others leave her in the past and would again in the future. No one stuck around for long when you were the queen of the London streets. Only her closest girls. Some would call it a less-than-savory lifestyle. It was, and it was a lonely one, but it was hers.

Head high, Alice let the jailer lead her away.

Author's Note

Queens of London was a real joy to research and to write. I could see the story almost instantly, like a movie reel playing behind my eyes. Whip-smart and resourceful little Hira, beautiful and artistic Dorothy, fastidious but passionate Lilian, and of course, Alice, diamond in the rough. She was a fierce and clever woman who looked after her own, who knew how to survive—and also how to have a good time while celebrating the moment. I admire all of these qualities in her, even if she was also unsavory at times and deeply flawed. I hope you find these characters as compelling as I did.

A few of my favorite resources include, *Alice Diamond and the Forty Elephants: Britain's First Female Crime Syndicate* by Brian McDonald, *The British Policewoman* by Joan Lock (my copy has the most beautiful inscription from a husband to his wife who worked as a female detective in the Met in the 1950s), *Forgotten London: A Picture of Life in the 1920s* by Elizabeth Drury and Philippa Lewis, and last but certainly not least, Lilian Wyles's memoir, *A Woman at Scotland Yard: Reflections on the Struggles and Achievements of Thirty Years in the Metropolitan Police.*

FACT VERSUS FICTION

As this wasn't a biographical novel, I thought I might share where the

lines between truth and invention converge. The Forty Elephants—
and all gangs mentioned in the novel—did exist. The Forty Elephants
dated at least as far back as the Victorian era for certain, with sev-
enty members accounted for through the years via newspapers and
police reports. Certainly many more members existed that couldn't
be traced due to lack of records.

Alice Diamond, also known under the aliases mentioned in the
novel, was the most ambitious and cunning leader the Forty Thieves/
Elephant gang ever had. She ultimately extended her dark "empire" from
London to Brighton, Liverpool, and Bristol. There's little known about
Alice's personal life outside of her brief romance with Bert McDonald.
As for Simon, I ran across a single mention of him in one of my research
books. The passage alluded to a potential romantic involvement with
Alice, though there was no evidence or any other mention of him after
it. The lack of details left me plenty of room for speculation, so I chose
to give him life and make him a part of Alice's tragic arc.

At the end of the novel, and in real life, Alice served eighteen months
of jail time at Holloway Prison. Once released, the Forty Elephants were
still operating but were considerably less organized, and their strength
had waned. She never managed to restore the gang's strength to what it
had been before she and her lieutenants went to prison, though there
was still some semblance of the gang that lasted into the 1960s with
Shirley Pitts deemed queen until her death of cancer in 1992. Alice and
Maggie went their separate ways only a few years after Alice's arrest
because of Maggie's intense alcoholism. Maggie was later arrested in
1928 for stealing five hundred dresses from a warehouse.

By World War II, Alice had started another of her own operations,
running scams from a brothel. Robbing department stores had become
too risky due to strengthening security and her notorious reputation.
Over time, Alice slowly became paralyzed and lost use of her limbs.

Her sister, Louisa, lived near her at the time and often stopped in to take care of her. She died in 1952 of what they believe was multiple sclerosis. Alice was buried in a common grave alongside strangers at Streatham Park Cemetery.

THE COMPLICATED HISTORY OF WOMEN POLICE

There are books written about this, so I couldn't possibly do it justice here in a couple of short paragraphs, but the most important aspect to understand is that there were women patrols composed of volunteers that assisted with police work, namely shepherding young women who were carousing at the makeshift soldiers' camps in the parks of London during World War I. They did perform other duties, but they had little to no power, or rights. Their existence was tied closely to the suffragette movement.

The Metropolitan Police began an official female squadron, separate from these volunteer patrols, which caused a lot of confusion among the citizens of London. Their uniforms also resembled each other for a time, making things worse. Eventually, between the confusion, lack of power, and lack of funding, the volunteer patrols were eliminated. Women hired and trained as official police for the Met remained, albeit in a very small group. Upon marriage, they were forced to resign. Over time, the female squadron did expand, but it was a long road before it became a permanent fixture, and as you might expect, a very difficult, sexist one.

Like in the novel, Lilian Wyles was, in fact, one of first female police in UK history, the very first to be admitted to the Criminal Investigations Department, and later became one of the first female chief inspectors. I enjoyed hunting down her memoir that has long-since been out of print (title mentioned above). Most of Lilian's time on the force was spent taking statements from and assisting sex workers, as well as other disadvantaged and victimized women. This probably began as early as 1922, but given that female police were incredibly short-staffed and carried out many duties at various times, it isn't unlikely that Lilian would fill in where needed, including the dreaded "women's work" of chasing orphans or going undercover in department stores.

OTHER NOTES

Selfridges is spelled with an apostrophe in the book, though in later years and today, the apostrophe has been dropped.

Beyond Alice Diamond and Lilian Wyles, there are other true-to-life characters in the book, including Lily Rose Kendall, the Bob-haired Bandit, Gertrude Scully, Maggie Baby-Face Hughes, Marie Britten and her cheating husband, Bertha Tappenden, Bert McDonald, head of the Elephant and Castle gang (after his brother, Wag McDonald, fled England and his police record for America to become Charlie Chaplin's bodyguard), Chief Inspector Frederick Porter Wensley, and Alice's brother, One-legged Tommy as mentioned, as well as her violent father.

Many of the events in the book, though imagined, were fashioned after situations that were probable or were on record in some form or other; department store robberies, warehouse heists, violence toward women, gang-controlled bookies at the horse races, knifing scenes where the Forties defended their own. These sorts of scenarios took place regularly in the underworld of London. The riot in Lambeth at the book's climax when Alice marches drunkenly to teach Marie a lesson, is a true-to-life event that did lead to her arrest and subsequent incarceration for eighteen months. She was not, however, officially arrested by Lilian Wyles. That was my own invention.

Dorothy and Hira—and scruffy little Biscuit—are a work of fiction.

READ ON FOR A LOOK AT ANOTHER
HISTORICAL FICTION NOVEL FROM
HEATHER WEBB, *THE NEXT SHIP HOME*.

⇛ 1 ⇚

C rossing the Atlantic in winter wasn't the best choice, but it was the only one. For days, the steamship had cowered beneath a glaring sky and tossed on rough seas as if the large vessel weighed little. Francesca gripped the railing to steady herself. Winds tore at her clothing and punished her bared cheeks, reminding her how small she was, how insignificant her life. It was worth it, to brave the elements for as long as she could stand them. Being out of doors meant clean, bright air to banish the disease from her lungs and scrub away the rank odors clinging to her clothes.

Too many of the six hundred passengers belowdecks had become sick. She tried not to focus on the desperate ones, clutching their meager belongings and praying Hail Marys in strained whispers. She wasn't like them, she told herself, even while her body betrayed her and she trembled more each day as they sailed farther from Napoli. Yet despite the unknown that lay ahead, she would rather die than turn back. As the ship slammed against wave after unruly wave, she thought she might die after all, drift to the bottom of a fathomless dark sea.

She couldn't believe she'd done it—left Sicilia, her home, and all she'd ever known. It had taken every ounce of her courage, but she and Maria had managed to break free. Dear, fragile Maria. Swallowing hard,

Francesca looked out at the vast tumult of water and pushed a terrible thought far from her mind. Maria would recover. She had to. Francesca refused to imagine life without her sister.

She tucked her hands under her arms for warmth. Everywhere she looked, her gaze met gray, a slippery color that shimmered silver and foamed with whitecaps or gathered into charcoal clouds. Already she longed for the wide expanse of sea surrounding her island home in a perfect blue-green embrace, the rainbow of purples and oranges that streaked the sunset sky, the craggy landscape, the scent of citrus and sunshine. She wrapped her arms around her middle, holding herself as if she might break apart. Reminiscing about what she once cherished was foolish. Somehow, she had to find things to like about New York.

Freedom from him, if nothing else.

She would never again meet the fists of her drunken papa. At the memory of his bulging eyes and the way his face flowered purple, she rubbed the bruise on her arm that had not quite healed. She would no longer spend her days stealing so he might buy another bottle of Amaro Averna or some other liquor. Paolo Ricci could do it himself. He could tumble from his fishing boat into the sea for all she cared.

A shiver ran over her skin and rattled her teeth. Like it or not, it was time to go belowdecks. As she weaved through the brave souls who paid no heed to the wind despite the cost to warmth, she wondered briefly if any first or second class passengers had defied the cold on the upper-class decks overhead. The ship was tiered and divided into three platforms; the two above her were smaller and set back so a curious lady or gentleman might lean over the railing and peer down at steerage. As if they were a circus of exotic animals.

Francesca descended the ladder into the bowels of the ship. The air thickened into a haze of stink and rot, and the clamor of hundreds of voices floated through the cramped corridors until she arrived at the large room designated for women only. She passed row upon row of metal cots stacked atop each other, filled with strangers. Some women lounged on the floor in their threadbare dresses and boots with heels worn to the quick. Their eyes were haunted, their wan figures gaunt with hunger. One woman scratched at an open sore; another smelled of urine and sweat and squatted against the wall of the ship with a rosary in hand, pausing briefly in her prayer to swipe at a rat with greasy fur, driven by hunger, the same as her. The same as they all were.

Francesca tried not to linger on their faces and moved through the room to her sister, who lay prostrate on her cot, and reached for her hand.

"You're so cold," Maria said through cracked lips, clutching her sister's hand. "You'll catch your death, Cesca. Promise me you'll be careful."

Heart in her throat, Francesca swept her sister's matted curls from her face. Death was not a word she wanted to entertain. The terror they'd harbored since they'd sneaked away from their home in the middle of the night, that overwhelmed her each time she considered the unknown before them, was bad enough. Death had no place here.

"Nothing can catch me now. We're too close."

Maria smiled and a glimpse of her cheerful nature shone in her dark eyes. "That hard head serves you at last."

Francesca forced a smile, desperate to hide the concern from her face. Maria had always been frail, easily ill and quickly bruised, yet still she glowed with some internal light. Often, Francesca imagined her as a fairy, an angelic creature not of this earth. She laid a hand on Maria's brow. Her skin burned with fever, and sweat soaked through her gown. Maria had fallen ill on the first leg of their voyage from Palermo to Napoli and had worsened each day since. Francesca had worried the captain wouldn't allow them to board, but she and Maria had passed the inspection rapidly—after Francesca paid an unspoken price in a back room on a narrow cot. But they were on their way and that was what mattered now.

"Another few days, Maria," she whispered. After five days at sea, New York Harbor must be close. Once they arrived, they would need to find a doctor to tend to the fever immediately.

Maria moaned and turned on her side, her shoulder nearly scraping the underside of the woman's cot suspended above hers. "I'm so thirsty."

Francesca was thirsty, too. Their water rations had scarcely been sufficient, or their food for that matter. What did the crew care about a pack of hungry, dirty foreigners? They saw so many, week after week. Desperation was nothing new to them.

Francesca turned over her water canister in her hands. No one would part with their rations; she'd asked passengers in steerage all day yesterday and had finally given up. Poverty didn't move them, or the story of her very ill sister. Each had their own story of woe. And it was out of the question to approach second or third class passengers. A guard stood at each of the doors connected to the upper levels to keep the wanderers out.

Unless…? An idea sparked suddenly in the back of her mind.

"I'm going to find more water." She pulled the blanket around Maria's shoulders. "Don't try to get up again. You need to rest."

Francesca rummaged through their small travel case for the only nice things she owned. She pulled on her mother's finest dress, fastened on a pair of earbobs, slipped a set of combs into her hair, and kissed the medallion of the Virgin Mary around her neck. The medallion she had stolen two years ago.

For months, she had admired the shiny golden trinket as it winked from the hollow at the base of Sister Alberta's neck. It was the first time Francesca had felt the sharp edge of envy. A rush of shame soon followed. She loved the nun like family, and Francesca knew it was a sin to want what wasn't hers. One day when Sister sent her to fetch a book, Francesca found the necklace gleaming in a bright ray of sunlight that streaked across Sister's dressing table. She'd held it a moment, stroking the outline of the Virgin Mother with her thumb, wishing she'd had the medallion's protection. She'd been unable to resist it, and slipped it inside the folds of her dress. It wasn't until the following day that she wondered why Sister had sent her to look for a book that wasn't there. Perhaps it had been a test—a test Francesca had failed.

Francesca's chest tightened as she thought of the nun. Sister Alberta was a Catholic in exile, though she'd never explained why, and had lived two lanes away from Francesca and Maria in their little village. The nun had befriended them when their mother disappeared, taught Francesca to cook and both sisters to read and even speak a little English. Sister had loved them.

"You putting on airs for someone?" said Adriana, an Italian woman from Roma. She wore thick rouge, and though she was traveling in steerage, her dress looked finer than those of the other women with its lace trim and shiny beading. It was also vivid purple. All the better to attract male attention.

"I need more water." Francesca's gaze flicked to her sister and back to the woman she was certain traded lire for sex. Not that Francesca minded. She wasn't bothered by other people's choices, especially when it came to survival. God must understand need when he saw it, if he was truly a benevolent God.

Adriana crossed her arms beneath her bosom. "Plan on flirting with the captain for it?"

Francesca snapped the compact closed. "I'm going to the upper decks, see if someone will spare some."

Or perhaps she would just take their water. She was good at that, taking things.

"Better work it harder, *amore*, if you want to fit in with that lot." A woman with no front teeth rose from her bed and dug through a handbag tucked beneath her pillow. "Here. Have some of this." She held out an elegant bottle of perfume.

Francesca felt a rush of gratitude. She reached for the bottle and dabbed her neck and wrists.

"I've got some rouge, too." Adriana produced a small tub. "You'll have better luck with the guards this way."

Another cabin mate watched them quietly, pushed up from her bunk, and took something out of a bag she'd been using as a pillow. "It was my *nonna's*." She clutched a cashmere shawl to her chest. It didn't look new, but it had been well cared for and could still pass for acceptable among the upper class, at least Francesca hoped. "The gray will be pretty with your eyes," the woman continued. "Please, be careful with it."

Francesca hardly knew them, yet they lent their most precious belongings to help her. An unspoken sense of unity hung in the air. Tired of suffering, they'd all left their homes behind and hoped for better times ahead.

"I...I don't know how to thank you all," she stammered as a swell of emotion clogged her throat.

"Show those *puttanas* they aren't better than us," Adriana said, winking.

At that, Francesca smiled.

She blew her cabin mates a kiss to whistles and cheers. Holding her head high, she threaded through the narrow hallway, wound through a room filled with barrels and clusters of steamer trunks, and passed a huddled group of passengers playing card games. She approached the ladder leading to the second-class deck quickly, before she could change her mind, and ascended it.

And there, at the end of the next passageway, a crewman stood guard.

When he spotted her, he stepped to the right and crossed his arms, blocking the entrance.

She clasped her hands together like a lady should, stretched her five-foot, three-inch frame to full height, and, ignoring the thundering in her ears, marched toward the guard.

He stood stiffly in a navy uniform, the name "Forrester" stitched across his breast pocket in yellow thread. "I can't let you through, miss. There's no steerage allowed here."

Her stomach tightened, but she forced a smile. "Excuse me, Mr. Forrester, I am second class. I have friend in steerage. I visit her but now I return."

The wiry seaman peered at her, his gaze traveling over her worn shoes and dress.

Nervously, she dug her thumbnail into the flesh of her index finger, willing herself to remain calm.

"Second class, you say?" His eyes rested on her rouged lips.

"Yes. Excuse me," she said, her tone clipped as if she were insulted.

He stared at her for a long, uncomfortable minute. At last, he angled his body away from her, leaving just enough room so her body would brush against his in an intimate way.

She pushed past him, ignoring his groping hands, his breath on her cheek. Too relieved to be annoyed by his behavior, Francesca darted quickly down the narrow corridor. At the first door, she peered through a small oval window. The room was crowded with luggage. She continued forward, pausing at each window, becoming more anxious as she went. When she came upon the dining saloon, she found the door locked and the room empty. Though the evening meal wouldn't be served for another couple of hours, she'd hoped the room might be open for late-afternoon tea or libations. It must be the first class who were offered such luxuries. She huffed out an irritated breath and continued down the narrow corridor.

Ahead, she saw a young woman wearing a pale-blue frock with a fashionable bustle and a wide-brimmed hat trimmed with ribbons. She was prettily dressed, her frock likely one of a series that she rotated every other week, something Francesca aspired to have one day soon. As she neared the woman, the scent of roses drifted around them and filled the cramped space. Francesca met the woman's eye briefly and nodded, even as she stared back at Francesca like she were diseased.

Ignoring the uncomfortable exchange, Francesca continued to the end of the corridor to the last room before the cabins began. It was a storage room filled with barrels and shelves of foodstuffs. It, too, was locked.

She leaned against the door. Of course it was locked. They wanted to prevent thieves from pilfering goods—thieves like her. Sister Alberta's lectures about letting God provide rang in her ears. Yet had Francesca let God provide, she would have starved to death on more than one occasion. Had she let Him provide shelter and comfort, she would have suffered broken bones at her father's hand for many more years. God gave her plenty of free will, and with it, she chose to provide for herself. Only she wasn't doing that so well either.

She fought back tears. Maria needed water desperately. Could Francesca risk it, try first class? It would probably turn out the same, but she had to try. Fists clenched, she pushed back from the door. She weaved around several male passengers and a woman in a striped dress, pausing to ask them for water, but they first looked annoyed and then ignored her. When she reached the first-class deck, another steward stood watch at the top of the landing.

"You there!" He pointed at her. "You aren't allowed here."

Reading Group Guide

1. What motivates Alice in the beginning of the novel? How does that change as the story goes on?

2. What does loyalty mean to the different characters in the book? What role does punishment play in their definitions? Who do you most agree with?

3. How does Lilian view criminals? Do you think her opinion is common among police officers? How does this view change the way our justice systems work?

4. Unlike the Forty Elephants, Hira comes from a well-to-do background. Why did she run away? Why did she gravitate toward the Forty Elephants?

5. Lilian, Alice, and Dorothy all have their work occupying their time and feel too busy to participate in women's suffrage demonstrations. Who has time to protest, and how does that affect which issues are prioritized?

6. How do the Forties operate? What is the key to their "shopping" successes?

7. How does Alice try to help Ruth? If you were Alice, how would you approach the situation? What resources would be most important to you?

8. Hira is always aware of Alice's hold on her and hesitates when she thinks about tying herself more closely to the Forty Elephants. Why does she push through those feelings? If you were in her position, how would you handle the request to steal from Dorothy?

9. How does Hira's character act as a catalyst for change for Lilian, Alice, and Dorothy? Does Hira change by the end as well? What does she learn about herself?

10. Describe each of the character's relationships with the men in their lives at the beginning of the book and then again at the end. What do they look like?

11. Most of the people around Dorothy look down on her. Why do we mistake beauty and/or kindness for stupidity?

12. At the end of the book, Alice doubles down on her ambitions. What do you think is next for her? Do you think she lives without regrets as she claims?

A Conversation with the Author

How did you first hear about the Forty Elephants? What drew you toward Diamond Annie as a character?

I first learned of the Forty Elephants, also known as the Forty Thieves in the earlier years of their existence, while reading an article about something else entirely. I don't even remember what it was, but there was a single phrase that referenced a Victorian all-female shoplifting ring, and I got goose bumps. Instantly fascinated, I wrote that single phrase onto a blank document and saved it in a folder of book ideas. When I was deciding on my next book and I looked at that document again, I grew so excited by the idea that I started researching. Diamond Annie is a tough character and a survivor. I'm always drawn to characters who broke the rules and are also less than perfect. They're interesting and nuanced and a challenge to write, which I really enjoy. I'm always trying to stretch my wings a bit and develop my craft.

The Forty Elephants have a wide array of strategies for pulling off their heists undetected. How did you learn about these

techniques? Were there any details that you found but didn't have space for in the book?

I discovered their techniques in my research. There's always so much great information that doesn't make it into the book, sadly, as I don't like to bog down the narrative. The story is the most important thing, after all. A few of the fascinating details I learned took place after Alice served jail time at the end of the book. When she was released, the Forty Elephants were still operating but were less organized, and their strength had waned considerably. She never did manage to corral everyone again, though there was still some semblance of a smaller gang. She and Maggie went their separate ways because of Maggie's intense alcoholism. By World War II, Alice had started another of her own operations, running scams from a brothel. Robbing department stores had become too risky because of their strengthening security and her notorious reputation. She died in the early 1950s of multiple sclerosis. She was living with her sister Louisa at the time.

Alice's idea of independence removes the possibility of romance entirely. How does that reflect the gender roles (or at least her impression of them) of her era?

1925 is a time when women are really starting to benefit from the women's rights movement and also from the societal changes that happened after the Great War. They are working, they can move about town freely, and some can vote. (That doesn't happen in full for everyone until 1928.) If women can work, they can rely upon themselves—they don't need a man to give them money and provide a home for them. The majority of men, however, haven't changed their traditional views in that era. Some have, certainly, but within a set of narrow parameters we'd find appalling today.

Given Alice's relationship with her father and the men who have come and gone and tried to force her into a submissive role, it's no wonder she wasn't interested in long-term romance, and luckily, she has the ability to provide for herself—even if it's illegal.

Ruth's demise is one of the biggest tragedies in the book. What did you most want readers to take away from her story? Do you think Alice and Lilian did enough to help her?

This is a difficult question to answer. How do you do more for someone who won't leave an abuser? The abused has to make the decision for themselves in the end. You can't force them to leave, short of kidnapping them, and even then, they might find their way back to the abuser until they've had proper counseling and received some sort of support. Thankfully there are support services for women today, but back then, especially if she was married, a woman had very little power in the male-female domestic space. I'd like for readers to understand that difficult dynamic of abused and abuser, of the power differential. Perhaps it might inspire someone to reach out and help a friend or neighbor find the support they need.

Why do people underestimate Dorothy so consistently? How does success count against women who enjoy and excel in traditionally feminine pursuits?

There's a persistent stereotype that if you're beautiful—especially a beautiful woman, but the same applies to men, too—you lack intelligence. I'm not really sure where this comes from historically. I do think it's partially rooted in jealousy. When someone has the gift of beauty and intelligence, they're a double threat and likely make others feel inferior in some way. You see this with

Dorothy. She's smart and capable but uses her strengths through her experiences as a woman and through her feminine sensibilities to advance in her career. Use what you know, right? And yet, traditional female pursuits have long been considered lacking in substance because women are viewed as the weaker sex. What a joke. Women have long had to strive harder to reach the same goals because of society prejudices that are centuries old. They're tenacious, tough, and clever. There's nothing weak about this. You can probably tell I have a few feelings on the subject.

Alice always argues that her life allows her to live without regrets, but by the end of the book, she must face the true sacrifices she has made. What do you think was most painful about that for her?

I think, when all is said and done, the most painful thing would be that the life Alice has chosen is lonely. Who can she truly trust? Who does she love? Who loves her? She has her inner circle of thieving friends, but should they be caught by the law, and it comes between their freedom and hers, they would choose themselves every time...as would she. She was somewhat close to her sister Louisa and her brother Tommy so there's that, at least. Blood is thicker than water, as they say, and this seems to be especially true in her life.

Acknowledgments

The Thank You Parade is always so much fun. I enjoy counting the many wonderful people who have lent their expertise in the making of my latest novel. First and foremost, I thank my agent, Michelle Brower, with whom I recently celebrated our twelfth anniversary over a fabulous Italian lunch. What can I say, M, you're the bomb. (I'm pretty sure that dated me.) To my wonderful editor, Shana Drehs, for all of her support and terrific insights to helping me bring the book to its fullest potential. Also a big thank-you to marketing expert and all-around cool person, Molly Waxman, and also Anna Venckus and the rest of the Sourcebooks team that works tirelessly in packaging and launching my books into the world. I'm lucky to share a corner of this zany business with you all.

I am forever grateful for the early reads from dear friends Kris Waldherr, Julianne Douglas, and Sonja Yoerg. My books would be so much lesser without your input. Thanks for not letting me get away with anything! A huge thank-you to my beloved "book wife," Hazel Gaynor, who is my forever cheerleader and shoulder. She was the first to say, "You must write this book, Heather." And to Eliza Knight, with whom I had a blast as we trekked all over London for research, followed by many excellent brainstorming sessions for our novels in a corner pub or two. I also owe a debt of gratitude to my dear friend Sonali Dev, an extraordinary Indian American author, who read the book and thoughtfully helped expand my knowledge of Indian culture. I love you all to the moon.

I couldn't do any of this without the love of my family and friends, who not only read my books but seem to actually like them! Sometimes I feel like the luckiest, richest person alive.

Finally, I'm grateful for my readers; for the incredible reviewers and bloggers (Andrea Katz and Suzy Approved—you are stars), who spend hours with my books and afterward, write reviews, make beautiful graphics, and spread the word. You are one of the very brightest spots in publishing, truly. Thank you.

About the Author

Heather Webb is a *USA Today* bestselling and award-winning author of historical fiction, including her latest, *The Next Ship Home* and *Strangers in the Night*. In 2015, *Rodin's Lover* was a Goodreads Top Pick, and in 2018, *Last Christmas in Paris* won the Women's Fiction Writers Association STAR Award. *Meet Me in Monaco* was selected as a finalist for the 2020 Goldsboro RNA Award in the UK, as well as the 2019 Digital Book World's Fiction Prize. To date, Heather's books have been translated into seventeen languages. Heather is a teacher at heart, so after obtaining her bachelor of arts degree in French and education and a master of science degree in cultural geography, she taught high school for nearly a decade. Currently, she is a freelance editor and also works as an adjunct for the MFA in Creative Writing program at Drexel University in Philadelphia. She lives in New England with her family, a mischievous kitten, and one feisty rabbit.